I0578455

ORPHAN DREAMER

AND

THE GLASS TATTOO

ORPHAN DREAMER SAGA
Episode Two

A Novel

J. NELL BROWN

Orphan Dreamer Saga: Episode Two
Orphan Dreamer and the Glass Tattoo (A Novel)

Copyright © 2019 by J. Nell Brown, LLC (Jeanelle Denise Brown)

All rights reserved. No part of this publication may be reproduced, distributed, or transmitted in any form or by any means, including photocopying, recording, or other electronic or mechanical methods, without the prior written permission of the publisher and author, except in the case of brief quotations embodied in critical reviews and certain other noncommercial uses permitted by copyright law. For permission requests, write to J. Nell Brown, LLC, using the "contact us" page on www.JNellBrown.com.

Scripture quotations are taken from the Holy Bible, New Living Translation, copyright ©1996, 2004, 2007, 2013, 2015 by Tyndale House Foundation. Used by permission of Tyndale House Publishers, Inc., Carol Stream, Illinois 60188. All rights reserved.

Scripture taken from the New King James Version®. Copyright © 1982 by Thomas Nelson. Used by permission. All rights reserved.

Scriptures taken from the Holy Bible, New International Version®, NIV®. Copyright © 1973, 1978, 1984, 2011 by Biblica, Inc. ™ Used by permission of Zondervan. All rights reserved worldwide. www.zondervan.com The "NIV" and "New International Version" are trademarks registered in the United States Patent and Trademark Office by Biblica, Inc. ™

"Stand by Me"
Words & Music by Jerry Leiber, Mike Stoller and Ben King
Copyright © 1961 Sony/ATV Music Publishing LLC
Copyright Renewed
All Rights Administered by Sony/ATV Music Publishing LLC, 424 Church Street, Suite 1200, Nashville, TN 37219
International Copyright Secured All Rights Reserved
Reprinted by Permission of Hal Leonard LLC

"The Word"
Words by Isaac Wimberley
Reprinted by Permission of Isaac Wimberley
Published by J. Nell Brown, LLC and Rogue Reads, LLC

For ordering information, contact the publisher via the author's website, www.JNellBrown.com.

Printed in the United States of America.

First Edition, 2019

Cover by: www.whiterabbitgraphix.com and FrinaArt.com

ROGUE READS
LLC

BOOKS BY
J. Nell Brown

NONFICTION

Shhh, My Father Is Speaking, and I Am Listening: A Bible Study on Hearing God's Voice

Blood Moon—God's Warning: Why Knowledge of Jewish Feasts Is Essential to Understand the Blood Moons of 2014 and 2015

FICTION

Orphan Dreamer Saga
Orphan Dreamer and the Missing Arrowhead

Orphan Dreamer and the Glass Tattoo

House Guest

A Generation of Lighted Evergreens

She Laughs Last

Collector's First Edition Paperback
The Omega Journey: Blood Moons Whisper

COMING SOON

Orphan Tree: Rooted in Eternal Love

Little Peach Lies

Orphan Falls: Wild and Free

If Love's a Fish

Everything
STARTS
with a
DREAM

Dear Reader,

I wrote the Orphan Dreamer Saga as a transcontinental, sweeping love story spiced heavily with thrills, comedy, and a pinch of that horror-trope element called dread. The saga reads as a contemporary epic that defies time, taking the reader from the pre-dawn of humanity's beginnings and then catapulting the reader into a future of what-ifs.

The saga is a work of fiction; however, a thread of truth weaves throughout the tapestry of words in the Orphan Dreamer Saga. The saga should be read in order, starting with episode one, *Orphan Dreamer and the Missing Arrowhead*, a story that answers the question, what makes the main protagonist tick?

The themes explored in the first novel of the series, *Orphan Dreamer and the Glass Tattoo*, hold true to my mission as a novelist: to write fiction that paints a human likeness upon the faceless and gifts a voice to the voiceless. As a result, *Orphan Dreamer and the Glass Tattoo* paints a picture of distressed children and will jolt—and possibly disturb—some readers, just as *Twelve Years a Slave* and *Uncle Tom's Cabin* challenge their readers. However, after I learned about certain atrocities that children experience, I kept my word to expose these children's stories in the Orphan Dreamer Saga.

If you want to skip the chapters that feature the most heart-wrenching parts of Cillian's journey, **do not read** Chapters Nine, Thirty-Eight, Forty-Nine, or Fifty-Six. You will miss some of the plot points. For those readers who choose to read his complete story—which I recommend for those sixteen and older—this experience will provide two options: pretend the social issue isn't real or do something about it. As the author, I hope for the latter response. Enjoy the first full-length novel of my series, the Orphan Dreamer Saga, previously known as the God Factor Saga!

With gratitude,
J. Nell Brown

Powerful mothers leave a legacy for their children to discover. Purposeful fathers gift their offspring with a will and a purpose to live. Mine did. Mom and Dad, thank you.

—J. Nell Brown

Strange is our situation here on Earth. Each of us comes for a short visit, not knowing why, yet sometimes seeming to divine a purpose. From the standpoint of daily life, however, there is one thing we do know: that man is here for the sake of other men—above all for those upon whose smile and well-being our own happiness depends.

—Albert Einstein

PROLOGUE—ADELAIDE: #MOM, IT'S GREEK TO ME

I'M CHEWING THE LAST OF my fingernails down to the nub as I sit at a reading carrel inside Phillips Exeter's Library, hunched over a closed calculus textbook, a three-ring binder, and Mother's weathered journal.

I stole the journal.

I needed to.

The last few bars of Steven Curtis Chapman's "I Will be Here"—one of my da's favorite ballads to chisel away at Mother's crumbling wall of nos before you know what—plays through my earbuds as I stare at the carrel's back panel, letting the bass notes vibrate the strings of my soul.

What can I say?

They are crazy about each other, but their craziness didn't conceive me, and for now, that's my secret. My bestie, Cordy Grey, doesn't even know. Thinking about my parents' tenacious love, I relish a quick smile, then glance over my shoulder.

No spies.

Gingerly, I open Mother's journal and stare at the first page.

Pages crinkle, eager to tell me their secrets.

As though an invisible force wants me to snoop on my own mother, a folded sheet of lilac-scented paper falls into my lap. I retrieve the insert and attempt to decipher her doctor's handwriting:

> Legend says Yeshua's last surviving apostle, John, penned a riddle before he died on the Isles of Patmos. The riddle's answer possesses the power to save humanity from annihilation by a future tyrant.
>
> Hode este sophia means "here is the riddle."
>
> "Here is the riddle. Let him that hath understanding count the number of the beast: for it is the number of a man; and his number is Six hundred threescore and six—Chi Xi Stigma" (Revelation 13:18).

I stare at the three random Greek letters, desperate for answers. "Chi Xi Stigma . . ." I repeat that several times before it clicks.

"In the language of mathematics," I whisper. "Chi Xi Stigma is a palindrome, like *racecar* or *taco cat*—spell it backwards and it says the same thing. But this is better than a typical palindrome since it's a number."

Mathematics is universal. *Sweet pickle juice!*

I find a blank page in my three-ring binder while trying to conjure up the fading details of my Greek language lessons.

Slowly, I jot down my answer: *Chi, Xi, and Stigma are Greek letters with the gematria of 600, 60, and 6.*

Chi=600. Xi=60. Stigma=6.

But do I add the numbers together—666—or interpret them separately? I continue reading her note.

> Adonai gave His prophet Daniel a vision, and Daniel penned these words: "But as for you, Daniel, conceal these words and seal up the scroll until the end of time" (Daniel 12:4).

Adelaide, the key to solving the mystery of the scroll and unlocking the riddle is wisdom.

What is wisdom?

Judea's wisest leader—King Solomon—wrote, "The fear of the Lord is the beginning of wisdom" (Proverbs 9:10). The Hebrew word for fear translates into the modern English word reverence—not terror. Adelaide, you must enter into a close relationship with Yahweh in order to learn His secrets and solve this final riddle.

With all my love,
Mommy

P.S. Hint: wisdom is not a "thing."

She is a person: "I, wisdom, was with Adonai when He began His work, long before He made anything else. I was created in the very beginning, even before the world began. I was born before there were oceans, or springs overflowing with water . . ." (Proverbs 8:22-24).

Take the time to meet her one day!

Footsteps thud on the carpet, nearing my desk. Quickly, I fold the letter and stuff it into my backpack alongside Mother's letter about Seurat paintings. The footsteps pass, leaving me to remember.

A soft-spoken North Carolina minister once said, "The sins of the fathers are visited upon their children's heads to the third and fourth generations." Mother, Father, and I were the only people in attendance that Sunday, so I kind of believe the message was for us.

But what if a kid's parents were perfect, like mine?

I smile—tight-lipped, knowing I'm blowing smoke. No parents are perfect, but let's say that mine are. Then, according to that North Carolina preacher, my seventeen-year-old, rich-girl life should flow smoother than Oregon's glacier-fed Crater Lake; or at least, this is my perception of the Guy Upstairs's rules.

No ripples.
Definitely no waves.
Right?
Wrong.
Because as of late, my day-to-day is akin to a Category 5 hurricane. Still, I must believe Mother's and Father's characters are beyond reproach.

When I lie, it's because I'm terrified. I've learned a few things about their pasts. Mother healed sick people. Father tortured and executed the ones she healed—or at least that's what my aunt told me. But I need to believe that my da's character rises above my aunt's accusations.

Because if that Southern preacher was right about a father's sins haunting his kids, I am beyond screwed.

Period.

A student in the library carrel across from me shuffles her papers, drawing me back to Mother's journal. Mouth dry and hands shaking, I open it and dare to read the first page.

Mother's serene, alto voice seems to replace mine.

> Leo Tolstoy said, "I sit on a man's back, choking him, and making him carry me, and yet assure myself and others that I am very sorry for him and wish to ease his lot by any means possible, except getting off his back."

> I never wanted to be that person, riding on top of another's misery.

> My name is Daniela Rose Cavanaugh.

> Daddy called me the Orphan Dreamer. I called him *rafiki*, "my friend" in Swahili, the language of my ancestors.

> Mom called me Daniela Rose Cavanaugh—on the rare occasions when she was mad at me—or Danny Rose for short. I'm her firstborn and her last. When I was a few minutes old, the doctor performed a hysterectomy on her, due to uncontrollable uterine bleeding. I learned about her surgery during one of

our girl talks. In addition to calling her Mom, I also called her a kindred soul—a more endearing title than Mother.

My Irish grandmother escaped the Irish famine.

My Cherokee forefathers walked the Trail of Tears.

My African ancestors crossed the Atlantic Ocean, packed like sardines into a slaver's wooden tomb.

My Mongolian relations descended from Genghis Khan.

My English ancestors traveled on the Mayflower, escaping the yoke of the British Crown while seeking religious freedom in the New World. On July 4, 1776, they signed the Declaration of Independence and cast their chains off forever.

Compassion gives more generously than any inanimate religious title can, so I rarely call myself a Christian. I am a follower of Yeshua—the One who said, "For God so loved the whole world that He gave" and then spread His arms wide, sparing not even His life after saying, "Father, forgive them for they do not know what they do." He is the essence of compassion and life, so He lives, gently giving this invitation to those with an open heart: "Follow Me."

To ask an American of Cherokee, African, Mongolian, Irish, and English descent to separate her faith from her story would be as sacrilegious as asking a WWII Jewish veteran to fly a Nazi flag in his front yard.

Or must I scour the DNA, stories, and faith of my ancestors from my soul and story and hide them to please you? Neither can be done without killing my spirit. Is the purpose of political correctness to silence a viewpoint until we bleach the spice of life from the

American spirit and resemble a track of nondescript
suburban homes?

My questions will not matter tomorrow.

Some say knowledge of one's joyful ending can make
the present misery tolerable. But who knows if one's
last act will be full of joy or sorrow? Maybe we all
sense our final act and don't realize it, or maybe we
deny the facts of our final curtain call. Inspired by the
One whose beginning and ending defies time—the
Alpha and Omega—an ancient prophet wrote, "And
as it is appointed unto men once to die, but after this
the judgment." I am no prophet; I am a woman and a
mother, but I am sure this saying applies to me as well.

Adelaide Rose, my love, if I had known my ending,
how would I have lived my beginning?

—Daniela Rose Cavanaugh

Mother's voice trails off into oblivion, and I sniffle and dab my
eyes. "You would have lived as you have—amazingly well, my kindred spirit."

Her thoughts invite me to a place of peaceful discovery, and I
continue to read my parents' stories.

I will not judge.

I am their darling daughter, and according to my mother, I am
breathtakingly beautiful, brave, and very sane. An Irishwoman's
fiery-red hair spills down my back in tumbles of ringlets. Father
gifted me his pale hue and winter blues, tinged with flecks of amber
and green. African and Sri Lankan blood courses through my veins,
splashing my cheeks with cocoa-colored freckles.

A bat cave, sun-deprived version of Meghan Markle, the Duchess
of Sussex, with red hair.

That's me.

Could Cordy Grey's memoir about my parents create a Simmie
Knox portrait out of their legacies? Ten pages through the journal,
I ache for Mom's embrace. Here is their story: an orphan, and the
girl who dreams of him—the Orphan Dreamer and her glass tattoo.

I share their secrets. They're about all I have left of my family—their memories, their stories hidden in the words of Mom's journals.

You judge.

Or don't.

But if my mother and my father had not lived, then I hope you'd be down with Pluto because Earth would've had different occupants, and because we would've needed a new home, that thimble-sized star sometimes known as a planet, a.k.a. Pluto, would've been our best option for a new address!

A voice seems to whisper, "Take me to the stars, oily boy . . ."

"Mummy, is that you?" I clench Mother's journal to my chest.

1—Lighted Evergreens

"MOMMA, I'M GOIN' TO WAR."

"Why, Son?" Austin's stepmother, Rosa Lee Cavanaugh, had steel in her voice.

"I'm goin' to fight Hitler and his bloodthirsty Nazis." Sitting on the porch of their quaint farmhouse, Austin Cavanaugh kept talking to Mother Rosa Lee, asking her questions about life and death, light and dark, and good versus evil.

"Preacher man," her voice sang more than spoke. "Some babies die during birthin' yet go on livin' in death. Death isn't the end for everyone. Make sure you're one of those."

"I ain't no preacher, Momma. Not even close."

"Not yet. But in time."

"There you go believin' in me again." He smiled.

"That's what a parent does." She gazed up at the starry sky. "One day, that's what you'll do. You'll believe in your own special child."

"Ain't nothin' ever come my way that was special or good. Except you and Daddy, and he's gone. Taken."

"By the good Lord."

"Maybe." Austin swallowed hard and cleared his throat. *Why does the good Lord need to take people? Ain't He got enough angels?* "What does a daddy or a momma do about good versus evil?"

"Before humans ever roamed the earth, the angels were created right alongside the devils. It just took a bit of time to tell who was who. You asked me what a parent does about good versus evil. They wait. They pray. Time and wisdom eventually tell everyone's secrets."

"Light and darkness. Why do they go on livin' together—coexistin'?"

"Coexistin'. That's a highfalutin word." She jutted her chin into the humid night air. "Takin' to your studies again?"

"Yes, ma'am."

"Ain't no child deservin' of just a sixth-grade level of schoolin'. Wish your daddy and I could've given you more."

"You gave me everything you had, and I love you both for it."

"Coexistin' is it, then? Well, a lonely star shimmers brightest against the darkest of night skies. Don't forget that," she said, her voice quieter, "while you're over there fightin' those Nazis, Italians, and Japs. You hear me?"

"Yes, ma'am." Austin held his mother's gnarled fingers. The peanut fields hadn't been gentle on her once delicate hands. That night, Rosa Lee Cavanaugh had trawled the deepest oceans of a mother's knowledge and gifted treasures of timeless wisdom to her sixteen-year-old stepson, Austin.

America was like a pretty girl with so many beaus on a string that she couldn't decide who she wanted to love or who was the most loyal to her. He shipped off the next morning and went to war to fight for America, a country who never loved him as much he loved her.

Some in America labeled him colored, as though God had forgotten to scrub him clean, and treated him like he was stained with something God-awful.

Over four decades later, some things had changed in America, and others . . . maybe in time.

★ ★ ★

WEDNESDAY, JULY 8, 1981
GAINESVILLE, FLORIDA

IN THE DARKNESS OF PREDAWN, the memories of his late mother, their little talk, and the war seemed an eternity ago.

Austin stood in the hospital room beside his wife and sponged a tear from his right cheek with his handkerchief. *Wish you were here, Mother Rosa Lee. You'd be right proud. I'm a husband now and getting ready to be a daddy.*

He gazed past the square window anchored in the eastern wall of the room. The sun hadn't cared to rise just yet; out of sight and out of mind, it left a swath of shadows and darkness for those eager to get on with their diabolical plans.

Beneath florescent lights, a battle raged inside the cold, sterile room.

Austin could feel it—evil fighting the good—and he had no intention of allowing his unborn baby to die at the hands of any devil, be it human or non-human.

He clenched his jaw and fist, allowing his thoughts to slip back into the comforting, familiar Southern dialect of his youth. *And ain't no sun settin' on my baby girl's birthday, plunging her brightest moment into the darkest sea. Demons, stay away. Don't even think about being born on the same morn as my angel. My baby girl.*

His Daniela Rose Cavanaugh, and in time, his Orphan Dreamer. She'd be an ordinary girl destined for the extraordinary—that is, if she survived. His precious daughter's survival was his utmost responsibility. He knew that Daniela's goodness would have to conquer some human devil's evil—a son of perdition, an antichrist.

But who was this evil one?

Would the monster be a boy or a girl?

Even though Austin had forbidden the birth of evil on the same day as the birth of his angel, he knew demons didn't listen to mere mortals. Like it or not, the beast was coming into the world on the same morn as his Daniela Rose. July 8, 1981—the birth date of a leviathan and a cherub.

Daniela would have to fight the sea monster and win. "For all of our sakes," he whispered, then reached for Jeanette's hand as another contraction pulsed through her rounded belly. "Come on out, Danny

Rose. Your daddy's here, and so is your momma. As long as I'm living, nothing and no one's going to hurt you."

★ ★ ★

Crickets chirped, gators bellowed, and in a chilled and otherwise quiet labor room inside the obstetrics ward of Alachua General Hospital, stifled moans wrapped in joyful anticipation echoed off gray walls.

Austin Cavanaugh held his wife's hand with a protective grip. With his handkerchief, he soaked up perspiration from her brow, then wiped sweat from his hairline—a low-cut Afro, speckled with tight gray curls—before he returned the starched white cloth to the front pocket of his red-checkered cabana shirt.

An EKG monitor beeped at regular intervals. Oxygen hissed into a face mask clamped onto Jeanette's face.

Nurse Judy—a petite woman with a seventies-style Afro—assisted Doctor Banks. Three pairs of eyes stared at the parts of a woman intended for modesty, unless a baby was pushing its way into the world.

Doctor Banks supported the crown of the baby's head between his skilled hands. "Push."

Jeanette panted while pushing. Her lips moved as she whispered a prayer for their unborn child. A woman of resolute faith but softer than a vat of cream. The expectant father smiled.

Minutes seemed to stretch into hours.

"She's here!"

A newborn's cries began where Jeanette's ended. *Hello, world.*

Doctor Banks cradled six pounds and five ounces of squalling mocha flesh in his arms and cut the umbilical cord, separating the newborn from her mother and releasing the little one into the world. "Momma and Daddy, what's her name going to be?" The doctor's diction was crisp but softened with an Afro-Southern accent.

"Daniela Rose Cavanaugh." A knot stuck in Mr. Cavanaugh's throat, and joy welled in his eyes. He massaged his wrists where shackles had once chained him. The One to whom his wife prayed had freed him from the chain gang.

"What's wrong, Austin?"

"So many years of praying and waiting, and it's finally happened. What if I'm not a good daddy?"

"You will be."

"One day, we'll have to surrender our little girl to her destiny."

"But not today." Jeanette placed her baby at her breast. "Mommy loves you, Danny Rose." Petite lips latched onto her nipple. Jeanette stroked her newborn's cheek and whispered her favorite poem, "'Here sleeps a girl with a head full of magical dreams, a heart full of wonder and hands that will shape the world.'"

"Beautiful." Austin kissed his wife.

After Daniela finished nursing, Austin lifted his daughter into the air. "She's yours. Give her a dream, Adonai—a mighty purpose for living. Don't put her in no cane fields. She's too good for that."

"Let her grow out of diapers before sending her on a swashbuckling adventure. She may want to grow up into a normal girl. Have you thought of that?"

Austin's heart raced. "But Tibet said—"

"Not to me and not to Daniela."

"I can't break my vow to the Almighty."

"We're her parents. We'll do what's right for her." A few minutes later, sleep drew Jeanette into a relaxing coma.

"Rest, Momma. I'll hold her for a while." He timidly touched his sleeping baby girl's skin. Calloused fingers, hardened in the fields of a sugarcane plantation, moved against smooth silk. Doctor Banks worked, his movements calm but purposeful. "She's still bleeding. Give her another dose of Pitocin followed by an IM injection of Methergine."

"I'll take Daniela to the nursery." The nurse placed Daniela into a bassinet and wheeled her away. The doctor shed his gloves. Blood dripped from them. "I'm taking Jeanette to the operating room."

"Doc, what's going on?"

"She's losing too much blood."

Adonai, don't let our child be motherless, Austin cried silently. "Don't lose her, Doc. She and Daniela are all I have."

"Stay calm. Whisper a prayer."

The obstetrics nurse wheeled Jeanette toward the operating suites. Austin followed as far as he was allowed, then another nurse led him to the nursery. He paced on the other side of the glass window, yearning to kiss Daniela's delicate cheeks and hug his wife.

Two men dressed as doctors stopped at the other end of the nursery window. Recognizing one of the men, Austin ducked into an alcove. What was he doing here?

2—THE ORPHAN

THE GAELIC TOWN'S NAME TRANSLATED into "town of a castle," and it hugged Ireland's northern border. Fog lay thick across the island. Beyond Ailsa Finn's window, a crow sang her praises to the One who dipped her wings in tar and said "Fly."

Sixteen-year-old Ailsa Finn didn't live in a castle.

Instead, for the last ten months, she had gotten by in a hovel of stones and mortar. Rolling hills and valleys in a palette of greens created a backdrop for her hovel, nestled in the coastal town of Ballycastle.

This morning, she lay on her back, her malnourished legs spread-eagle. The midwife sat in a chair beside the bed, smoking a fag.

Pinned to her filthy mattress by daggers of pain, she couldn't see through the cracked window above her bed, but she'd memorized every detail of the calming seaside when she had hiked its shores during her contemplative but fretful walks.

If she could walk, a short stroll from her cottage in a northern direction would lead her to the seashore of the Antrim coast, the second stop of her Ireland adventure turned nightmare.

Ailsa closed her eyes and inhaled the familiar scents of fish and salt, recalling the delicate touch of cool mist draped around her arms. Her heart slowed and her body relaxed. These memories had soothed her before, after the men had finished with her, leaving bruises across her thin body and tossing her less money than she'd hoped for.

Prostitution hadn't been her first career choice.

She had wanted to paint seascapes.

One of those pigs would eventually murder her in his drunken stupor, and then when he sobered up, he'd dump her body into the sea like a gutted, rotting fish. Cold clung to her skin as a shiver swarmed around her arms.

Ailsa nestled her swollen belly between her hands and waited for another contraction.

In her mind, Ailsa was strolling down the coast.

Sapphire waters of the Sea of Moyle licked the black basalt, and white limestone scattered along the shoreline. A royal blue boat accented with a red stripe bobbed about as winds stirred the waters.

A thick, cool mist rolled over the picturesque town, blanketing it in gray.

Nineteen miles across the North Channel would return Ailsa to where she'd started—the Mull of Kintyre—the place where she could see Rathlin West Light, the upside-down lighthouse, on a clear day. It was meant to guide ships through the North Channel, but she hadn't needed the lighthouse's guidance that day months ago.

John, a man she met in a local Scottish pub, had promised to take her to a better life. Men had been rare, especially one as handsome as John, and he had even said that he owned a retail store. He had been her guide on that cool morning, but she had never thought to ask him where he was taking her.

She wished she had.

It turned out that the merchandise in his retail company was young girls and boys.

John had never sold Ailsa for sex. She had sold herself for sex, but he hadn't. He had kept her to himself until nine months ago, when they had sailed the North Channel from the Mull of Kintyre in a floating tub of rust meant for fishermen and their catch. She sat in the back with a tattered blanket tied around her shoulders, dreaming of a better life.

Her dreams were cut short.

John stopped short of Ireland's mainland and docked his boat on the small, almost deserted Rathlin Island. It was picturesque, with more birds than people, and it maintained a population of about one hundred Irish citizens.

But instead of a dream, a nightmare ensued. This encounter would be the first time she had not given herself willingly.

Images of a muscled, stocky man pawing at her body in a dark and dank abandoned cottage in the middle of the island danced a shiver around her swollen belly. She hadn't known his name, only the memory of his cologne—much too floral of a scent for a man. Where had he come from? He hadn't been on the boat.

Why had the mysterious man paid John one million pounds to rape his girlfriend?

Some men would sell their souls for a few coins.

Judas Iscariot, Jesus's disciple, did, betraying his master to the Roman tormentors for thirty pieces of silver. Ailsa was no one special.

That left one person in this sordid equation who must be special—the child. But what good could come of a bastard conceived in such a vile manner?

The only facts she knew for sure: nine months ago, the mysterious man had been waiting for her inside the cottage when John threw her inside and locked the door. He wore a strange ring—a wide gold band etched with a blackened image, the head of a bull and outstretched arms that sloped toward a belly that resembled a fiery pit.

She still remembered the stranger's cold ring pressing into her flesh. She'd planned to steal it as he showered after his cruel deed. Ailsa should have been trying to escape, but instead she'd studied the ring that lay on the table outside of the bathroom.

Evil had pulsed from the gold.

Moans laced with anguish erupted from her mouth, then a scream. The man's seed was ready to come forth.

Ailsa shivered as a gust of cold wind from the Irish North Channel blew through the cracks of her shanty. Cigarette smoke melded with womanly secretions, forming a nauseating stench. The contraction abated. "He's not the Christ child," Ailsa said, "but he's being born in a filthy stable."

"The only things missing are the animals, shepherds and wise-men," the midwife added.

Ailsa gripped her thighs and pushed her twisted religious words to the corners of her mind.

"Don't throw a pity party just yet. That baby isn't going to come unless you push." Midwife Morna's retracted, pencil-thin lips pulled back into a jagged grin, and a lit fag dangled from her bony hand.

Ailsa looked away, stared at the empty icebox to her right, and pushed until her belly relaxed. A tear rolled down her cheek. A wee bairn was coming, and there was no food to feed it. She swept the tear away.

I'll find a way.

Her breaths hitched, her face contorted, and her skin glistened. Tendrils of red hair clung to her cheeks. She bore down and exhaled. The contraction eased. "I dinnae believe there's room for my bairn in this shack, just Master Freddy."

"Is there no room in your heart for the child?"

Room? Ailsa looked away. *How could a broken heart hold anything— much less a wee bairn?*

"You've abandoned your parents, and now you'll neglect a help-less infant—flesh of your flesh and blood of your blood?"

"I didna abandon anyone." Ailsa set her jaw. "Explorin', that's all."

"You sound no different than a Scottish wench. Speak properly, like an English lady. That'll push you into the finer circles, where the rich men are." The old hag crossed her arms and watched her charge suffer one contraction after another. A smirk crept into the edges of the woman's lips. As though the midwife's tongue would swell, choking the very life from her body if she didn't use it, she rebuked Ailsa once more. "Master Freddy, he's no master. Doesn't even have a job. Where is he, anyway? Doesn't he want to raise his own baby?"

How could a woman whose fag dangled from her lips con-struct a paragraph of accusations during one ragged, tobacco-laden exhalation?

That's talent.

Ailsa ignored the string of insults.

She knew the truth. For the last four weeks, Freddy, her new boy-friend, had familiarized himself with her in ways her parents would have been ashamed of, but unlike the others, he'd been gentle, almost loving.

But commitment hadn't been woven into the tapestry of his character any more than it had been in the others.

Stomach round and full with child, she hadn't been able to see the tips of her bare toes or rub them after he'd stepped on her foot while wearing his boots. She'd stifled a scream as he hoisted her onto the moldy cot, where she was now birthing her child, to do his business. If he'd minded the extra company of her unborn child, Freddy hadn't shown it. He eagerly took what she gave—and more.

The baby hadn't moved an inch during the ordeal. She'd smiled like a proud momma.

But would an infant remain quiet after birth?

Ailsa needed to make a living.

There would be consequences from the men if the child cried. She'd punish it herself and teach it to mind—every child needs discipline. Her guidance might save the baby from a beating by a cruel, impatient man.

The mystery man from the shack on Rathlin Island was probably the father. The timing was right, but she hadn't asked his name—only remembered his scent. And he'd not made the customary introductions before overpowering her.

Her bones still ached from John's last beating—five weeks ago, before Freddy arrived. He had changed his mind about his girlfriend birthing another man's baby. She hadn't known that a chair leg could be used with such violence. She'd tossed the chair into the ocean four days later, as soon as she could hobble.

Ailsa clamped down around the child, desperate to keep it inside.

Safe.

Innocent.

But another contraction defied her attempts, stealing breath from her lungs until a shudder crept down her back as her uterus relaxed.

She had hoped for a little girl, but her stomach hung low—a sure sign of a wee lad. What would she do with a lad after the men who eagerly took their fill without a thank-you? She might despise a male bairn.

Afraid, she grasped a fistful of bedsheets between her thin fingers.

Her cheek moistened, and Ailsa sponged her face, removing the evidence of any hint of the possible disappointment. Ailsa answered Morna. "Freddy's the only man under fifty on this island. Besides, it isn't his." She panted.

"What?" Morna propped her hands above her scrawny hips.

"As I said, it is not his." Her voice landed crisp, like any fine English lady. She'd been practicing.

3—Orphan Dreamer

BEHIND THE ALCOVE, AUSTIN LISTENED. "Is she the one?" the short man said.

"Nurse said so. Her father worked for me in the cane fields. Creepy old fella."

"Brown skin darkens the tips of her ears." The short man stared past the glass. "She can't be the one. The world hasn't progressed that far. Let's go. We'll come back when Nurse Sally says another one's been born."

Austin's heart raced until the men moved on. He ran to the nursery door and knocked.

"Yes, sir?" a nurse answered.

"When will I be able to take our baby back to my wife's room?"

"In a few minutes. She's almost cleaned and swaddled."

"I'll wait here." He patrolled the hallway for another twenty minutes. Jeanette survived, and Nurse Jackie moved the new family to Jeanette's post-op room.

Another nurse knocked and then swung open the door. "Chaplain Cavanaugh, your friend's here." A man with an Afro entered. Coal eyes and a milky white smile warmed his deep-ebony complexion.

"Pastor Jackson, thanks for coming." Austin pointed to the seat beside him. "Jeanette's sleeping. Can you blame her? She labored over thirty hours and lost gallons of blood, forcing the doc to cut out her uterus."

"No more children?" The pastor rested his hand on Austin's shoulder. He shook his head, fighting back emotion.

"She made it." Pastor Jackson sat down on the couch. "Your baby girl's a looker."

"As pretty as her momma."

"You've come a long way. A family man."

"I'm trying." Austin blushed. "Did you bring the frankincense? Would you bless her?"

"That's why I came." The pastor removed a vial from his pocket. "How's the chaplaincy at the state prison?"

"I offer spiritual freedom to men with no hope of physical freedom."

"You understand their story."

"I lived it." Austin shifted in his seat.

"Is your church pastor coming to bless your daughter?" Pastor Jackson asked.

"He's busy." Austin looked away from the pastor's gaze. How does one navigate such a tender issue? They'd been called African-Americans, but Austin had come to think of himself as a plain American.

"Why do you make your wife attend that church? They'll never accept a black family. Come to our church. We look like you. We'll accept you with open arms."

"It's difficult and sometimes lonely, but that's where the good Lord has placed us."

Pastor Jackson shook his head. "This is a happy day, my brother. Let's not argue. What's her name?"

"We named her Daniela Rose Cavanaugh—after Daniel in the Hebrew Scriptures."

"Why?"

"Her mother and I want her to become a woman of virtue, integrity, and purpose."

"She was born for this moment in history." The pastor stood over the bassinet. "Her face glows as though the Almighty has already touched her."

"Laboring in the cane fields, I begged the good Lord for her, and I made a deal with Him that I hope I don't regret."

"Keep your end of the bargain." Pastor Jackson dipped into Southern slang. "You ain't gotta worry about His. He can't lie 'bout nothin'." The pastor cradled the child's head. Her skin appeared white in contrast to the deep-ebony tone of Pastor Jackson's hand, but it would darken to a rich mahogany hue before long. He dabbed a drop of oil on her forehead, and a fragrance of woody spice filled the room.

After a long pause, the pastor lifted Daniela toward the heavens. "The Almighty speaks this over Daniela, 'Before I formed you in your mother's womb I knew you, and I destined you to proclaim truth to the nations.'"

"Did the Almighty give you those words just now?" Austin held his breath.

"He did. Daniela Rose will be one of His last blood moon prophets, warning humanity before some creep unleashes hell on Earth."

Austin's brow wrinkled.

"Don't fight Him. You won't defeat the Almighty."

Why had Austin promised Adonai that He could use his little Daniela for anything if Jeanette became pregnant? He wiped a lone tear from his cheek, and his expression released into a surrendered peace. "His will be done."

"Give her all the love you can spare. She'll be fighting hard, most times all by herself. She'll need to pull from any reservoir of compassion. Why not let it be yours?"

"We'll give her all we have." Austin choked up. "One snowflake falls from heaven to quench hell's thirst."

"One. That's all the Almighty needs. He uses the smallest and seemingly insignificant—a snowflake, each unique, yet as common as dirt during a winter storm. But you done gone and found favor with the One who spoke our solar systems into existence yet knows how many hairs are on your nappy head." Pastor Jackson released a full-bellied laugh. "Yes, sir. The One who sings over you with His love. He chose you!" He pointed his finger at Austin, reminding the new father of the Uncle Sam poster hanging on the wall in the colored section of the recruiter's office telling young men, "I want you."

Austin had answered Uncle Sam's call, fighting for his country in the United States Navy during World War Two.

"He chose my Daniela, in spite of me," Austin's tone dripped with awe. But will she choose to follow the Almighty's path for her?

Humanity's future depended upon her saying yes.

If she hesitated, how would he convince her?

A father's love.

4—The Orphan

"WELL, WHOSE IS IT, THEN?" The midwife insisted.

Suddenly realizing that she couldn't care for herself, much less a child, Ailsa cried, "Never you mind. Get this thing out of me. If I could've afforded it, I would have gone down to the butcher and asked him to take a carving knife to me months ago. I'm not afraid to die."

"And the child?"

She ground her teeth and clenched the sticky sheets. "This baby's ripping me apart. I don't want it to come. I don't want it at all."

Morna slapped Ailsa's thigh. Skin clapped skin, and Ailsa's pale flesh waggled. She gasped and stared at her leg. A red mark the size of Morna's hand remained. "Why did you do that? I'm already in pain. She fell back into the bed. Panting, she waited for another contraction. "I should've gone to a hospital."

"You said you didn't want to go because you're ashamed you're pregnant. Besides, you'll love the baby when he comes and he's sucking at your tit, so push."

Ailsa's face contorted. Guttural screams filled the room. Drops of sweat rolled from her temples.

"I see his head, and the gates of hell willna be stoppin' him now." The midwife pressed into Ailsa's belly, and in moments she held five pounds of writhing moon-pale flesh, darkened with a kiss of blue and a cap of black hair. The baby pushed a cry through his tiny mouth.

"He's hungry. You'll need to feed him." Morna raked a rough gray towel over the baby's body. "It's a boy."

A boy?

She wanted to cry. "Babies don't need to eat as soon as they're born. I'm sure of it." Ailsa's protests fell on deaf ears.

"Here, put him to your breast." Morna placed the squalling infant in front of Ailsa. "The sooner, the better. His tiny lips will drive the madness from your brain."

Ailsa cupped her breast and its small peach nipple. "He isn't sucking."

"What's wrong with you, Ailsa Finn? Are you going to let him starve?" The newborn's legs dangled in the air as Morna cradled his back and head, then wrapped the child in a tattered blanket.

A dark presence arrived in the form of gray clouds that rolled in from the sea, seeming to swallow the shack in one hazy gulp, seeping in around the cardboard cutout and filling in for a missing glass square.

Broken glass had sprinkled the whitewashed floorboards yesterday—the day John returned and lost his temper when he learned of Freddy, her new boyfriend, and she learned of the money John had received from the man who had raped her. She'd been having contractions regularly, and John couldn't take his fill. Besides, women in labor couldn't be leased out to perverted men.

If John returned and tried to enslave her like he had the others, she'd stab him to death.

But who would care for her bairn if she was imprisoned? How she longed for the Highlands of Scotland. Her mother and father would have taken this baby.

Something disengaged in Ailsa's mind, and her thoughts darkened into disorganized patterns. Her mama always said she'd have a nervous breakdown if she went out exploring on her own.

"You feed it." Ailsa narrowed her eyes.

"I don't have milk." Morna turned on her heels and marched to the rickety chair by the icebox with the squalling baby cradled under her arm.

Ailsa dabbed her forehead with a soiled towel. "Ye could've shown me a wee bit of mercy."

"Why? No one else will," the midwife said. "Pregnant with no husband. No job. No future." She mixed water and stale bread until it softened, then slid the mush between the baby's lips. "It isn't good, but you have to eat something." She hummed an old Scottish tune. "You're a pretty thing," Morna said to the baby. "Look at those sky-blue eyes. You have a mess full of raven hair too. You've got a little Spanish blood in you—one of those Black Irish. You're going to be a looker, wait and see."

The baby opened his mouth in a toothless yawn.

Morna tapped fingers against her thin lips. "Ailsa, what are you naming him?"

"He doesn't deserve a name."

"How can an innocent baby not deserve a name?" Morna scratched her thinning gray hair. "I'm going to name you Cillian, after my da," she said. "Da came from Northern Ireland, and my mum hails from the Scots. It's your mother who doesna deserve you."

Cillian yawned.

"Give me my baby!"

"Oh, now you want to mother him." The midwife marched to Ailsa's side.

The young mother reached for her child. "Cillian Joseph Finn." She lifted him in the air, and he cooed. "Egyptians enslaved wee Joseph, but he defied them all and became a prince." Heat flushed her face. "It's true, wee one, though I'm not the most learned or religious."

"You can be sayin' that again."

Ailsa rolled her eyes. "Learned that story in Catholic school." She pinched Cillian's button nose. "One day you'll go to school."

He tracked her feathery voice, knowing it belonged to his mother. She pulled the child close, and he attempted to suckle. "Sorry, wee one. I don't have a drop of milk to give." She kissed his forehead.

The midwife stroked the baby's scalp, then his mother's brow. Morna's gaze softened and found the inquisitive stare of Ailsa.

"Dinna worry, lassie. In the end, we women weel be stickin' together. Ye'll be alright and so weel the bairn. Big destinies quite often begin awkward and even insignificant."

"Mine or my lad's?"

"Didna you tell yer bairn the biblical story of Joseph—a slave becoming a prince? Ye'll be believin' it for wee Cillian, then."

"No mother knows if her child will grow up to be the next Reverend Billy Graham, Adolf Hitler, or even the dreaded antichrist. If Catholic school taught me how to pray and ask that my son wouldn't grow up and become a monster, I wasn't listening during that lesson." She paused.

"But . . . I think I will . . . believe." Ailsa lifted her chin. "He's a bastard. But he's my bastard, conceived with a man I never granted permission to." She blew her nose. "Maybe my wee Cillian will mean something to someone one day."

"One snowflake can quench a man's hell." Morna snuffed out her cigarette, then smiled. "He'll matter to someone. In time, he'll be the fire to the delicate icy crystals of his snowflake, melting her heart." She spoke in her native Irish Gaelic. *"Chuisle i chroí."*

The pulse of her heart. *"Is é sin mo Cillian,"* Ailsa said in quiet contemplation.

5—Orphan Dreamer

Tuesday, April 20, 1993
Gainesville, Florida

NOT EVEN A TEENAGER, BUT wishing she was twenty and done with middle school, Daniela stood on the edge of the playground and slipped her St. Jude Math-A-Thon workbook into her pocket.

"Danny Rose still sucking up oxygen. Totally grody to the max." Claire pushed past Daniela. "Bag your face then die, dweeb." The unkind words pierced Daniela's heart with more force than a crocodile's bite.

Even aliens belonged.

In outer space.

But they belonged, somewhere.

She drank another cup of her classmate's rejection.

It burned like vinegar.

"You're too white, your hair's too long, and you talk different." At fourteen years old, Tameka Jenkins, the ruling dictator over the girls at Milweekee Middle School, taunted eleven-year-old Daniela.

Tameka's skin was the same mahogany as Daniela's, but hatred was hatred, no matter who spewed its acidic barbs.

Charlie, a boy who Daniela thought must be full of worms, ate his boogers while he watched the squabbling girls.

"Just because you is eleven years old and read good don't mean nothin' to us." Tameka rolled her neck and eyes in sync. "You ain't no African-American. You's an Uncle Tom, and we don't even care you is gonna start high school with me next year." In Tameka's dictionary, *is* and *are* were interchangeable.

"But I'm a girl." Timidly, Daniela challenged Tameka's ignorance.

"So?"

"How could I be an uncle?"

"Don't know. Don't care." Charlotte, a kid who wore Coke-bottle glasses, pushed her spectacles up her nose as she chimed in, then shoved Daniela.

Mean girls ran in packs like hyenas.

"No pushing." Daniela pushed back. "What's an African-American?" She asked, knowing that the girls hadn't a clue as to the historical origins of the label. Her mother had educated Daniela about the history of labels in America, and Daniela's question was another kind of pushback.

Why couldn't a girl with brown skin acknowledge her *other* grandparents? She wasn't a nondescript brown girl with no heritage who had magically appeared on the North American continent. No American was.

"You is sooo stupid, girl." Tameka giggled, and the girls, like mindless robots, joined her taunting. "You ain't gonna be able to keep up in no high school."

Daniela would start high school two years early.

Tameka propped her hands on her hips. "You ain't black. Now do you understand, smarty-pants?" The cluster of girls laughed and smirked, soundly rejecting Daniela from their group of friends.

"I know I'm not black. How could I be?" Daniela studied her fingers—mahogany with a blush of red. "My great-granddaddy's Cherokee, and my grandma's part African and part English. Don't know where my daddy's from."

"There you go, tryin' to be white."

"I'm brown."

"Course you are, and in this here country that means you're black—African-American—don't you forget it."

"You said I wasn't African-American." Daniela laughed on the inside.

"Shut up." Tameka swatted a fly from her face. "Don't confuse me."

Didn't seem to be hard.

"You're the one with loose screws." Tameka said as she stood two inches from Daniela's face. "Talking to people nobody sees and making up stories about faraway places."

Daniela shouldn't have shared her dreams during show-and-tell. Keeping a secret from the wrong ears was as important as the content of a secret itself.

Next time, lips shut.

"Ethan would run away from you if he had two legs that worked—but he doesn't, does he?"

"You leave Ethan alone." Pure hatred iced Daniela's words. Tameka stepped back, fear in her eyes. Backing away from the mean girls, Daniela whisked a fresh trail of tears from her cheeks as her lower lip trembled.

Don't let them see you cry.

That doubles the pain.

The girls had not wanted to play with her today, or for that matter, on any other day she had approached them.

They looked like her—brown skin. Check.

Tameka and her friends lived in her neighborhood. Check. But long black pigtails dangled past Daniela's shoulders.

A brown girl with long hair. Epic fail. Daniela might just as well have been born with the bubonic plague.

And did Daniela's mother dare drill proper grammar into her child's speech pattern?

Daniela sounded too white—and that sin remained unforgivable.

Application to join Tameka's clan of friends—DENIED.

Not that the color of one's skin mattered.

She was different, so was Ethan, and at Milweekee Middle School, that was a crime punishable by solitary. Mom said the girls were ignorant and jealous, and these two mortal sins drove people madder than a nest full of hornets. The naming of the motive hadn't mattered to Daniela.

Rejection stung harder than a wasp.

The girls turned in sync and marched to the bus stop, leaving Daniela standing alone.

She ran in the opposite direction, bolting across the lawn, stopping amid stalks of cattails. Scents of fresh-cut grass filled her lungs.

"Yeshua, will you send me a friend who is also a girl, please?" She clasped her hands together, her prayer quickly becoming a plea, until a rustling beside her feet stopped her words. A wide red stripe was followed by a thin yellow stripe; the footless creature slithered toward her maroon jelly shoes.

A coral snake, deadly.

The snake slithered by.

She exhaled.

A few feet away, water splashed in the small creek. Daniela surveyed the murky brown water, noticing a frantic baby duck swimming toward her.

A water moccasin slithered behind it, closing in for the kill.

Legs shaking, Daniela pushed through cattails and stood at the edge of a creek. She hated water and snakes, couldn't swim, and had almost drowned a year ago after Harry pushed her into Newnan's Lake.

Save the duckling. You can do it.

The duckling's webbed feet propelled its body faster, but quickly it slowed, tiring from its futile escape. Daniela slid off her shoes and socks, then dipped her right toe into the pond. Cold. Water sucked unless she was drinking it.

Save the baby duck!

"Leave that duck alone, snake!" She balled her fists.

Animals didn't listen to humans. As expected, the snake ignored her command. In its wake, a lifeless mother duck floated in the brook. Daniela ached for her mother's touch. "I said, leave it." She tossed her St. Jude Math-A-Thon workbook onto dry ground then waded toward the duckling. The snake stopped, as if inviting Daniela into its lair. How would a snakebite feel?

"Be brave."

What about Daddy and Mom? If I die, they'd miss me. "Friends come in all shapes and colors." Murky water lapped against her knees. She reached out and grabbed the fatigued duckling.

"Daniela!" Her teacher called from the field behind her.

She turned and sloshed through the stream toward the shore, churning up water behind her to disorient the snake, but her foot slid over a smooth rock hidden in the creek bed. Losing her balance, she crashed into the water. The duckling flew from her grasp and tumbled into the cattails.

Had she killed her newest friend? It righted upon small legs and ran toward Daniela's teacher.

It's safe.

The snake floated inches from Daniela's head and rose above the water's surface, ready to strike. Someone splashed into the water after her. Hands gripped her arms, pulling her from the creek.

"What on earth are you doing?"

How had Ms. Bender arrived so fast?

"I-I-I'm sorry, Ms. Bender. I'm sad. I wanted—I mean, I needed a friend." Daniela fell into her teacher's embrace. "Is the duckling safe?"

"What duck?" The teacher walked Daniela to safety, knelt, and looked her pupil in the eyes. "You listen to me and listen real good. Your friend will come. Wait and see."

"She will?" Daniela smiled.

"She's reading the map of friendship and trying to find you."

"Really?" Hope flitted inside Daniela like a butterfly set free. "Anything I can do to help her?"

"Stay away from snakes." Ms. Bender muted her chuckle.

"But I was saving the baby duck." Daniela pointed behind her teacher, then picked up the duckling. "Her mother's dead—killed by the mean snake. It's an orphan now."

"But you rescued it?" Daniela nodded, and her teacher smiled. "You're a brave girl. How does it feel to save something that's helpless?" Ms. Bender's eye color lightened to violet. Daniela blinked twice, then rubbed her eyes.

"Splendid."

"I'm glad."

"Your eyes, Ms. Bender." Daniela squinted. "They're turning purple. Anything I can do to help?"

"Don't worry about my eyes. I never do." Her irises twinkled like diamonds, as though they were saying "Ms. Bender is special."

"The bus is here. Take this." The teacher slipped off her sweater. "Wrap it around your arms and hide your new friend inside the front pocket." Ms. Bender's knit sweater radiated heat. Had she just pulled it from the dryer?

Daniela nestled the trembling baby duck inside a deep pocket, then slipped past Tameka and the others, rounding the corner before the school bus stopped.

"She runs here and there like loose poop." Their mocking words pounded an ache deep into her chilled bones.

Daniela rushed up the steps and sat in the front row, knowing the others wouldn't pull her pigtails as long as Mrs. Johnson could see her from the driver's seat.

Riding the bus mimicked a faraway adventure. Daniela had packed her small bag light and tight, prepared to adapt to any after-school situation. She removed a Ziploc bag of sunflower seeds and dropped a few into the duckling's new home—her pocket.

With one arm, she hugged her tattered Bugs Bunny bag and stroked her motherless friend with her other hand.

Charlie sat beside her, knowing he'd be safe.

Mrs. Johnson, petite, with an easy smile and a perfect brown bun atop her head, was kind and protective. "Charlie, did you remember to bring your homework paper this time?" Her voice sounded like a scratched record, and she smelled like a chimney.

"Not on my life." He swung his legs back and forth.

"Where is it?" the bus driver asked.

"In my pencil."

"You're funny, Charlie," Daniela said.

"I know—and smart. I keep my pencil with me in case I forget something."

"I don't want to forget either." Daniela unzipped her tattered backpack and pulled out last year's birthday present, *Anne of Green Gables*. She opened her favorite book to read the magical line by Anne Shirley.

"Read it out loud." Charlie rested his chin on Daniela's shoulder.

She smiled and obliged. "'Kindred spirits are not as scarce as I used to think. It's splendid to find out there are so many of them in the world.'"

Daniela removed the duckling from her pocket and showed Charlie. "Shh. Don't tell. It's my new friend. I'm going to show Ethan."

"Sooo cool." Charlie hunched low and stroked the frightened bird. "Sorry Ethan's sick. He's nice. If he dies, you'll find another human friend."

"Ethan won't die. He can't . . . but boyfriends can't do everything girlfriends can. I'm figuring my kindred spirit must still be locked in my dreams, and just like Anne Shirley, she'll have spitfire red hair, love to read, and escape with me on amazing adventures."

"Not many redheads in the world. Just sayin'."

"But I believe there is one tucked away for me. Ms. Bender says, and I just have a feeling. Mom calls my feelings Yahweh's voice or my knowing. A Cherokee spiritual leader calls these kinds of feelings the wolf within."

"Rrrr . . . the wolf within—nice."

"I still can't figure everything out." She paused. "Charlie, you're smart. Do you think Ethan would leave me if he had two legs?"

Charlie jammed his pencil into his nose. "Downloading. Bummer answer, Danny Rose. One never knows." He removed his pencil. "Step into your dreams," he spoke with a robotic voice, "you'll find your redhead."

"Never thought of that."

"You said I'm a genius."

"You are . . . can I tell you a secret?"

"Ears open and receiving."

"My dreams are always nightmares—haunted by a dirty, stinky boy with oily black hair, no eyes, and bruises all over."

"He's an alien," he whispered. "Don't talk to him, or he'll abduct you—and who will I sit beside on the bus?"

"I won't—promise." She glanced over her shoulder. "Don't tell Tameka, okay?"

"Charlie's no snitch."

"Ditto. Thanks." Daniela slipped the duckling back into her pocket, closed the book, and gazed out the school-bus window.

"Danny Rose." Charlie elbowed her. "Maybe your new friend is sitting beside you." He grinned wide. "I don't have red hair, but I could dye my hair like my mom does."

"But you're not a girl, so you couldn't be Anne Shirley."

"Didn't think of that." He stuck his pencil in his left nostril.

"Why are you sticking your pencil up your nose again?"

"Downloading information . . . I'm not a girl, so Danny Rose refuses to let me be her bosom buddy."

She blushed. "I'm not allowed to be a bosom buddy with a boy—except Ethan, but that was by mistake. Daddy says—no bosom touching with boys."

"A fine mistake you made in Ethan," Charlie said as Daniela thought, *If only Anne's words resembled reality.* She clamped her hands over her mouth.

"Charlie, I've got it. I know how to find her!" The girls turned and stared. She overheard their whispers.

"She's talkin' to herself again."

"Told you she's crazy."

"No, she's talking to her only friends, an invisible friend and booger-eating Charlie." Each word gouged a hole in her heart, but she refused to cry. Babies cried. "Daddy said prayer changes everything."

Mrs. Johnson, the bus driver, glanced into her rearview mirror.

"Then pray," Charlie said. "Maybe your prayers will turn into a plunger, flushing the alien down the toilet. Or they could unlock a secret portal."

"Allowing oily boy to escape, roam Earth, and devour human flesh." A sly grin slipped across her face. "He'll come for you, Charlie."

Charlie screamed, "Don't do it! Don't pray. Don't release the Kraken—oily boy!"

Daniela laughed so hard a button popped off her shirt. "I won't. Promise." Her laughter ended abruptly. She had ignored Yahweh for weeks. He might not want to talk to her again. Friends don't ignore friends then ask for a favor.

The bus wove through two-lane roads, finally halting on a corner. The red stop sign on the bus extended.

"Bye, Mrs. Johnson." While running toward the steps, Daniela removed the duckling from her pocket with one hand and waved with the other.

"Keep on reading. Stay smart," Mrs. Johnson said. "Don't pay any attention to those fast girls; they'll be popping out babies, and you'll be accepting your degree. Don't be afraid to pray. No prayer is powerful enough to release a sea monster like the Kraken. You're safe."

"Okay, Mrs. Johnson," Daniela called over her shoulder.

"Get home before the bullies catch up." Charlie charged off the bus behind her, pumping his arms to keep up with her. "See you at school. Maybe we'll become friends."

"We are friends. Bye." Their journeys separated.

Daniela held the duckling to her chest and kept moving. Running to stay ahead of life's bullies was her reality. Grinning wide, her legs did what they did best—made her fly. She took a shortcut through Mrs. Juniper's backyard, then charged down her narrow driveway and across the neighborhood park; the wind blew past her face, carrying scents of spring: mowed grass, churned garden soil, and roses. Chirping birds overhead slowed their flight to watch her run.

On the other side of the park, a stone building came into view.

The stones matched the colors of the earth—gray, brown, and sand—and formed the exterior walls of Daniela's house. An arch framed the front door. White peonies bloomed right and left of four brick steps that led to the front porch. In the front yard, one protective maple jutted toward the sky with outstretched arms laden with leaves, blocking any street voyeurs' view past the Cavanaughs' living room windows.

Her house wasn't like the mansions on the other side of the small park, but the stone cottage remained her favorite place, one of safety and love. Out of breath, she weaved her way past her mother's car parked in the half-circle driveway that was shallow like a kiddie pool, according to her mother.

Thirty-foot Texas cottonwoods waved above the roof, providing the home's only source of air-conditioning. Their house sat in front of her grandfather's peanut farm—four acres of wide-open space behind a fence of Texas cottonwoods fifteen feet behind the house.

Daniela opened the front door, ran straight to the kitchen—a room anchored with buttercup-yellow terrazzo floors and a matching L-shaped counter top—and dropped her schoolwork on the table. "Hi, Mom."

"What's that?" Her mom pointed to the homeless duckling.

"Umm . . . my new friend."

"A duck?" Her mom rested a spatula beside the stove.

"A snake almost killed her. She's an orphan and needs a home."

"Snakes!" Her mom crossed her arms. "You weren't near any snakes?"

"Sort of—but Anne is safe now."

"You've named the duckling."

"Just now."

"Lordy mercy, child." Her mom untied her apron. "Fine. Put Anne in the pond by the garden."

"I was hoping—"

"Even hope demands propriety. In the pond, Daniela."

"Yes, ma'am."

"Are you going to play outside?" her mother asked, stepping away from the stove to straighten Daniela's pigtails.

"Yes, ma'am." Always be polite, even if mad—Mom's rule.

"Eat a snack before you go."

Daniela ate a slice of cheese and an apple and fed the duck a slice of cheese. Her mom kissed her forehead. "Be back before dusk, so you can finish your homework." She would sprint to her next-favorite place: the neighborhood playground across the street.

Her neighborhood was shaped like a ceiling fan. The motor in the middle of the ceiling fan was the playground encircled by a two-lane road. Houses sat around the park like fan blades.

Opposite Daniela's home, Claire's big redbrick house commanded two lots on the other side of the park, but Daniela's family owned the most land in the neighborhood. In five minutes, she could run across the park and arrive in Claire's front yard.

If Daniela had been invited.

Mom said times were tough, and Daniela had overheard enough conversations between her parents to know why. Her father had worked at the state penitentiary as an assistant chaplain, but he'd become ill and had to take an extended medical leave. Between medical bills and their home expenses, there was no money for fancy gadgets.

"We aren't victims—never victims. We adapt." Her mother had said. "Time to tighten our belt a notch."

The playground didn't cost anything except a little effort, and she enjoyed the short, oak-shaded journey.

Picnic tables scattered on carpets of grass.

Sunlight rained down on the heads of oaks, maples, and pines, spilling puddles of shade on the ground beneath. A wading pool anchored the middle of the park, and a sunken garden fifty steps north of the pool made for spooky adventures.

She peeked past the screen door. The bullies hadn't dispersed, so she cradled the duckling in her hand and made a stop at the mill-pond, a little slice of heaven nestled smack-dab in the middle of her grandfather's farm.

Grandpa Cavanaugh had died long ago, but she still felt close to him out here. He had taught her to shoot a bow and arrow in this field. His gravestone leaned crooked against the ancient bark of a moss-laden oak, and a canopy of trees hid the weathered wooden shack that sat on the other side of the pond, its mill winding clockwise within the wind's invisible hands, wood creaking upon rusted iron hinges.

"Time changes things," she said, repeating her mother's words. Time to set Anne free. "Sorry about your mom. I wonder what it feels like to be an orphan."

Weeping willows swept the surface of the pond, and sunken water lilies cast their emerald glow on the surface. A red bridge arched over the water like the curve of Danny's archery bow.

On the other side of the pond, several rusty blackhaw trees' petite white flowers contrasted against the canvas of green leaves. A tranquil west wind blew across the millpond's surface and rustled the waters. Scents of soil mixed with the fragrance of yellow roses tickled her nose.

A big brown bullfrog jumped and missed his landing, splattering into the water beside a water lily. The bright yellow duckling quacked, its baby voice sounding more like a chirp.

"Don't make fun, Anne. That's not nice." Anne dipped her orange beak as if she was apologizing. "Do you understand me?" A shiver rattled Daniela's body.

Anne nodded, and Daniela dropped the duckling. Anne landed in the pond, making a splash. "I'm sorry . . . I didn't mean to drop you, but you scared me." She dropped to her knees. "I-I-I didn't know you could understand me."

"Quack, quack—don't you want to be understood?"

Daniela glanced over her shoulder. No one watched or listened in. She whispered, "Of course. I just never thought a duck—"

"Could understand?"

"It's not normal."

"In your reality. But in the Torah, animals spoke to people. Didn't my Creator speak through a donkey to warn a prophet named Balaam that he was traveling in the wrong direction?"

"Yes."

"I think He can talk through a duck. I'm much cooler than a donkey."

"I agree. Do you need help, Anne or Mister Bullfrog?"

"Ribbit, ribbit—nope. We'll be fine."

"You can talk too, Mister Frog? Watermelon and ice cream cool!" Daniela chewed the corner of her lip and watched Anne paddle to the frog's side. They sloshed water on each other. Daniela laughed. "I'm glad you like each other. Mister Frog, please share some of your bugs with Anne."

"Ribbit—okay."

"Wow. You can both understand me. I'll tell Ethan. I should stay here with you. But . . . no, I can't stay."

"Ribbit—why?"

"Papa wants me to make more friends—human friends." The frog rumbled in a low tone. "Sorry. You're special too. I'll come back before supper."

"Ribbit—wanna swim?"

"I can't."

"Quack, quack—Stop saying 'I can't.' You can do anything with our Creator's help. You saved me from the snake, and you can hear Ernie and me. That makes you extraordinary."

Or weird. "Ernie. I never knew your name, Mister Frog. You're right, Anne. I can do a lot. Okay. I'll try harder. Gotta go."

Daniela left, and when she arrived at the playground, she knew she'd face a problem in the form of a pint-sized girl throwing a ball. Claire.

White tendrils of the girl's hair danced in the wind. The stick of a bright-green lollipop dangled from her lips, and drool dribbled from her mouth. Before Daniela could join the other kids, Claire exclaimed in her loud, congested voice, "You can't play with us."

Be brave and ask. "Why? We go to the same church and school." Daniela slid her hands into the pockets of her shorts. She had never been bold enough to ask *why* before.

"Because you're black and poor, and my daddy doesn't like poor, black people." Claire tossed the ball into the air again. Up and down, up and down.

Daniela wished she hadn't asked. Head down, she lifted her left arm. "What's wrong with the color of my skin?" Her voice quieted to a whisper. "Besides, my skin is brown, not black. You should learn your colors."

She felt it before she could see it and gulped hard, knowing what was coming.

No, not now.

Warm liquid rolled over her lip and chin, landing on her shirt and pooling into an unwanted crimson bloom.

Daniela brought her hand to her chest, hoping the other children hadn't seen the blood, but they had. Their glares seemed to follow each drop from her nose to the ground. Her gaze lowered, she began her retreat in slow motion, not wanting to aggravate the tiny disturbed blood vessels in her nose and end up releasing a geyser.

"You and your kind are full of disease." Claire laughed. "Daddy says so. 'Send 'em back to Africa,' he says."

"America's my home," Daniela whispered as she kept backing up. Her feet tangled in a tree root, and she plopped onto her behind. The impact reverberated through her ribs, deepening the ache within. The blood dripped faster.

She focused on a mother pushing her child in a swing. *She'll help.* The tall lady stopped the swing. *Good—she's going to help.*

Cautiously, the mother approached Daniela, whose eyes widened into saucers.

Daniela wiped her nose. Slick blood trailed across her hand and flowed freely down her chin. She dug her fingers into the sand, pushing herself away from the curious mother who had slung her toddler onto her wide hips.

"Are you supposed to be bleedin' like that, honey?"

Daniela shrugged. "Happens sometimes, ma'am."

"You ain't been to the jungles of Africa and picked up a deadly virus?" Claire said in her sweetest Southern accent.

Daniela remained quiet.

"Have ya', hon?" the woman asked.

A crowd of children gathered around Daniela, not to offer help but to observe and point. She shook her head.

"Good."

The woman seemed reasonable enough. *Ask. No, don't.* Daniela's broken heart formed the words before her mind agreed. "Miss?"

"Yes, child?"

"M-m-my mom's Cherokee, African, and English. Why does everyone ask me what's happening in Africa? Am I supposed to know? Because Mom and Dad have never taken me there."

The woman retracted her neck as though she was a king cobra, and Daniela leaned back, preparing for a poisonous strike of words. "I don't know. Just the way it is. Don't matter where you came from, but you shouldn't infect the rest of the kids, hear me? Don't want Ebola spreading in the states. Take this." The woman handed Daniela a tissue.

"Yes, ma'am." *No cobra's going to catch me.* Daniela squeezed her nose and ran past her favorite gnarly oak tree, past the slide and swings, and past the popcorn truck, not caring if she bled to death.

A while after applying pressure, the nosebleed stopped. A trail of dust flew behind her agile retreat as she darted down a street north of the park.

She had never taken this path before. The wind brushed past her face as she burst into a full sprint.

She stopped.

A stone pillar stained with green slime and black mold hid in the bushes.

She navigated past it, through the shrubs. Tiptoeing, she paused when she spotted a sprawling old house. Backing out, she traced the indentations in the aged stone, the letters *A.B.* and a funny-looking, scaly sea monster in the shape of a gigantic snake. Her neck hairs prickled. Someone was watching her. She looked around and saw a tiny camera anchored to the gate.

"Storm!"

Daniela bolted through lush green fields, over the little red bridge, and arrived at the far side of her granddaddy's peanut farm.

Her breath heavy, she climbed a sprawling oak tree, mistakenly destroying a cobweb before nestling inside her thinking place—a red treehouse built by her granddaddy.

Sticky silk coated her fingers, and a hairy brown spider scampered to the opposite side. Daniela held her breath and leaned into the wall behind her. *Even if you're afraid, apologize for mistakes.* "I'm sorry."

The spider started to rebuild its new home.

Winds blew across the field into the small home, and the spider struggled to make its web. "I wish I could help you, but if I tell you something, please don't laugh. I-I-I'm afraid of spiders." Daniela stood on the opposite side of the treehouse. "I'll block the wind while you stay over there," she pointed to the wall farthest from her position, "and weave your web again."

The spider continued its work as she stood in front of the treehouse's entryway. Watching the spider tack strings of silk from one corner to the next, Daniela asked, "Where does the silk come from? You're so small."

"From inside."

Daniela's eyes widened, and she stumbled backward, almost falling out of the treehouse. "You can talk too!"

"No, you can hear. Not everyone can."

"Holy smokes."

The spider jumped to the wall nearest Daniela. She screamed.

"Calm down. I'm not coming any closer. Don't wanna get squashed. Humans step on us bugs."

"I should tell Mom and Dad."

"Leave them out of this."

"Good idea. They'll think I'm making up stories again."

"Voices—the daily conversations the masses can't hear. You came back from the playground early. What's on your mind, little one?"

Daniela gasped. "Are you spying on me?"

"I get around, keep track of everyone and everything."

"I'm having a hard time making friends, particularly girlfriends. My only friend—a boy—is in the hospital. Daddy forbids me from befriending more boyfriends, and he's not happy Ethan's skin is paler than mine. Tells me to be careful, as though his skin will hurt me."

"Give Papa Bear time. Stay true to Ethan. You'll meet all the right kids." The spider went back to work. "Wouldn't hurt to talk to the Person who gave me all these legs. He's got all the answers."

"I'm scared to talk to Yahweh."

"Why?"

"He's probably mad at me. I've been ignoring him since the surgeon cut off Ethan's leg."

"He doesn't hold grudges. Tell Him you're sorry. He loves to forgive humans."

"But what if he releases oily boy from my dreams?"

"Who?"

"The stinky boy who scares me at night. He doesn't have eyes, and he probably ate them!"

"You do have a jungle-wild imagination. Calm down. Just pray."

"That's why Mom and Dad said." She blew a forceful breath from her nose. "I'll try." Daniela clasped her hands together. "Will you listen and make sure I get it right?"

"Okay, but prayers are meant to be whispered in secret."

"Next time." She paused. "Yahweh, my daddy likes to use your true name. He says it makes him feel closer to you. Sorry for being a snob and dissing you like Claire disses me." She paused. "Daddy's sick. Make him better, please. Those girls won't let me hang with them. I don't know what to do. My mom's tired. Give her a bit more energy and give me a friend—a girl just for me, please. And please make Ethan's leg grow back. Thanks, Yeshua. You rock!" Maybe Mister Spider would donate one of his legs to Ethan?

"He does rock—and by the way, I'm your friend."

"No way! I don't make friends with creatures who have eight furry legs." Unless he wanted to give Ethan one.

"You don't like me because of my hairy legs. Shucks! Everyone nurses an excuse not to like their neighbor."

She sat down, wrapped her arms around her knees, and exhaled a sharp breath. "I don't dislike you. I'm scared of you. Can't you understand?"

"Do your schoolmates like you?"

"No. Claire doesn't like me because my skin is brown. Tameka doesn't like me because of how I talk and my long pigtails."

"Claire is scared of you, doesn't know any better. She believes her papa, but she'll grow out of his misguided advice if you give her time. Tameka feels small when she's around you. You're supersmart and she struggles with her lessons. Help her."

"Thanks for the advice." Daniela stared at her toes. "Am I ugly because my skin is brown? My dad calls me Red. He says my skin has a red color because my bones are red. Red sounds silly to me, though."

"I'm color-blind."

"I won't tell anyone, but so is my dad! He patched a hole in his beige car seat with blue cloth." Muffled giggles escaped between her fingers. "But he understands colors enough to tell the difference between my skin and Ethan's. I think he's secretly mad about how pale people treated him in the past."

"The pain of rejection is like a weed: hard to kill. Don't let it suffocate your love, Danny Rose. You're a rose. Act like one."

"What about the thorns?"

"They keep predators away."

Like oily boy.

She smiled and waited with the spider until it finished spinning its web. From the new web, the small spider seemed to speak again. "My feelings aren't hurt because you're afraid of me—actually, I don't think I have feelings—but I won't harm you. Still friends."

"Thanks for giving me another chance."

"Give Claire and Tameka a second chance too—okay?"

"Promise."

"Mister Spider, you say that you get around. Have you visited the haunted house hidden behind the big iron gate?"

"Stay away from that house!" Mister Spider jumped from the wall, landed on the floor and scampered toward Daniela. She screamed. "Chill out, Daniela."

"I'm trying." Her teeth chattered. She partially closed her eyes.

"I've seen children wander behind those gates and never return. A guy by the name of Bushcroft owns it."

"Okay. Next time, I'll bring lunch. What do you like to eat?"

"Bugs. Bugs. Bugs—the bigger, the better."

"I don't like bugs."

"Why don't you introduce yourself to a few? That's the first step to liking someone different from yourself."

"I'll check out a book at the library and read about them."

"That's a start."

"Time to go." Ask him to donate a leg to Ethan? No. Super creepy.

"Thanks for protecting me while I built my web again."

"You're welcome. I usually come here after school if you wanna talk again."

"I get around—remember? See you again. Careful climbing down."

Daniela dangled one foot over the branch, launched herself, and landed in a patch of soft green grass. She strolled back to the abandoned park.

No one was there.

A soft breeze scooped leaves from the ground and rustled them around the legs of Claire's trampoline in her front yard, making the toy look like something that belonged in a ghost town in one of her dad's westerns.

Daniela picked one lavender bud, then walked across the park, kicking a rock until she stood in front of her home. She tapped the tattered screen door, and it rocked on its hinges. "Mom . . . Dad . . . I'm home."

"Shh. Your father is sleeping. The pain meds finally worked." Mrs. Cavanaugh lowered her fingers from her lips as she opened the door for her daughter.

"Sorry, Mom. I didn't mean to be noisy." She embraced her mother.

"Another nosebleed?" Jeanette sponged red stains from her daughter's shirt.

"Yes, ma'am."

"Don't worry. You hungry?" Her mother fingered Daniela's hair.

"Yes, ma'am. So is Mister . . . Never mind."

"Fill up your cup with tap water." Daniela's mother placed a mound of canned tuna fish on flatbread and spread it. A coffee pot percolated, spilling chestnut and vanilla spice into the kitchen.

"Why are we eating on flatbread again?"

"Remember, yesterday was Passover, today is the Feast of Unleavened Bread, and tomorrow will be the Feast of Firstfruits. You must remember the meanings of these spring feasts."

"Why?"

"It's important to Yahweh's purpose for your life—your calling. You must understand His timetable. His calendar."

"We already have a calendar: January, February . . ." She recited all twelve months.

"The Gregorian calendar isn't Yahweh's. He established the Jewish calendar."

"Who changed the calendar?"

"Pope Gregory."

"So we have the important dates all wrong?" Daniela asked.

Her mother laughed. "That's one way to look at it."

"What do the spring feasts mean?"

Her mother slipped into her storytelling voice, and Daniela leaned on her hands and listened. "In the Torah, when the Hebrew people were still captives in Egypt and longed for freedom, Moses— their deliverer—instructed the people to mark their doorframes with lamb's blood."

"Creepy."

"This mark showed the death angel which homes to pass over."

"Like a secret code."

"True. That night, the death angel killed the firstborn male of every household not protected by the mark, but each family who applied the blood of an unblemished lamb to their doorframe was protected from the death angel. We believe that was a foreshadowing of the coming unblemished Passover lamb—the Messiah."

"Why do we care now?"

"Today, Jewish people celebrate Passover to commemorate God setting them free from slavery in Egypt."

"Were we set free from Egyptian slavery?"

"No."

"Then why do we celebrate and eat flatbread?"

"We celebrate Passover to remember that Yeshua has passed over our house, forgiving our sins by dying on the cross and setting us free from death."

"Are these Jewish feasts like Christmas and Easter?"

"Absolutely not!" Her mother dropped the serving spoon on the countertop.

Daniela jumped. "Sorry. I didn't mean to make you angry."

"I'm not, just a little tired." She kissed Daniela's cheek. "The history of Christmas and Easter are pagan, and we're not pagans."

"I'm glad." Daniela chuckled. "I don't like the sound of being pagan."

"Nor do I. Finish eating, and you can read before you prepare for bed."

"Can we watch a movie? Ethan told me *Honey, I Shrunk the Kids* was hilarious, and I'm dying to watch it."

"*May* we watch a movie, and no—not tonight."

"May you finish telling me the story?"

"Yeshua was our Passover lamb. The bread used during the feast is flat because the leaven has been removed from the dough. We celebrate Passover to remember that Yeshua gave his life for our sins."

Daniela reached for her favorite book.

"Danny-girl, keep eating."

"Yes, ma'am."

"Leaven represents sin," her mother said. "During the Feast of Unleavened Bread, flatbread is prepared with no leaven—no sin—and hidden for three days. After Yeshua was offered as a sinless lamb, he was placed in a tomb for three days, and on the third day—the day Jewish people celebrate the Feast of First Fruits—Yeshua rose from the grave, overcoming death and becoming the first fruits of those who will live forever."

"That's complicated. Are we Jewish?"

"No, but our faith is built on the promises of the Hebrew Scriptures."

"Will we live forever?"

"Yes, because when Yeshua said to us, 'Follow me,' we did—and in Him, the Light of the World, there is no death, only eternal life."

"Living in the light." Daniela ate the rest of her sandwich in silence, gulped down her glass of water, and cleaned her place setting. In her room, she wrote in her journal.

Time to save Ethan!

Daniela snuck past her snoring mother and crept down the hallway.

She pressed her ear against the thin wood door of her parents' bedroom—quiet. The door creaked on its hinges, and Daniela tiptoed inside. She sat on the little chair beside her father's hospital bed. His bones poked through where his thin muscles sagged, but he was getting better. The doctor said his white blood cells were normalizing. Supposedly, his type of blood cancer would get better, worse, and better again.

"Daddy, are you awake?"

Sheets rustled, and Chaplain Cavanaugh's lids retracted. Black eyes nestled within yellowed sclera caressed his daughter's face. The doctor called them sclera, not the whites of your eyes. Something a doctor must know so she can take care of her patients.

"My rafiki, how are you?"

"I'm doing great now—since you are home."

"Speak softly." She lifted her forefinger to her lips. "Mom will be mad if she knows I woke you up."

"Talk and laugh all you like, little one." A sparkle lightened his eyes. "Tell me about your day." She told him everything, except about her talking to a duck, spider, and frog. "Daddy . . . my rafiki . . . are you going to die?"

"We're all going to die."

"But Mom said we could live forever."

"Our spirits. Not our bodies. Since I know Yeshua, He will give me a new body after I die, and I will live with the Almighty forever."

"Pinky swear?"

Austin interlinked his pinky with Daniela's. "I swear."

"How do you know He'll let you live with Him? Maybe His house is full, or He doesn't want people like you in His neighborhood."

"He's not prejudiced. Yeshua loves everyone. No one sacrifices their life for someone they dislike."

"He's not like Claire."

"He's not like any of us."

"Will He need Ms. Bender's friendship map to find you? There are so many headstones in Forrest Lawn Cemetery."

"Long ago, Yeshua planted his eternal bloodline deep in my bones. I know what it's like to sleep out in the cold with no blanket or family to call my own, and He won't turn me out. I'll live with him, alright."

"I'm sad." Daniela sighed. "I wish we could afford more treatments, and I didn't know you had to sleep outside."

"The leukemia's getting better. And sleeping outside was long ago. Now I share a home with the most beautiful ladies in the universe."

She became quiet, remembering that her mother had told her only brats demanded their way 100 percent of the time. "Daddy, if you're going to leave me and go heaven, may you ask Yeshua for a favor as soon as you arrive?"

"What's that?"

"Tameka and Claire didn't want to hang out with me because my hair is long and my skin is brown. Ask Him to send me another friend—pronto. I'm worried about Ethan too. He's been missing school."

"It breaks my heart the way those girls treat you and that Ethan's been so sick."

"I don't like breaking things." Daniela rested her hand over her father's heart, and he clenched his trembling jaw. "He'll hear our prayers?"

"Promise. Yahweh's preparing someone special for you now. She—or maybe he—will love you unconditionally."

"He? You mean Yahweh will send me another boy for a friend? Daddy, I thought you didn't want me to make friends with any more boys. I'm okay with that because most boys stink. Especially Harry . . . he pulls my hair on the playground, and Charlie picks his nose—but Ethan's different. He's perfect."

"Ethan, perfect?" Her dad's Adam's apple rose and fell. "Girls are safer."

"Why?"

"Trust me."

"You've never let me down." Daniela removed the crushed lilac from her pocket. "For you." Austin rested the bud against his nose and inhaled.

"Daddy, Zoya, a new classmate from Ghana, told Charlie, 'We're not like them.' What does that mean?"

"It's silly." He chuckled. "But some recent immigrants from Africa and the Caribbean think they are better than brown girls whose ancestry goes back hundreds of years in America."

"Huh?"

"I know. It's stupid. You tell Charlie, we're not like *them*."

"Isn't it just as mean to say those words?"

"Not every fact is kind."

"Daddy, you're spikey." Daniela glanced over her shoulder. Her mom hadn't come in to scold them.

"No, just sick of staying quiet. Your ancestors, burdened by oppression, helped build America, fighting in every war since the War of Independence. Every immigrant who steps foot on this soil after the 1800s owes your grandparents—African, Native, and English—a debt of gratitude because those new people walk on the graves and progress of your ancestors who sacrificed all. We didn't move to their countries. They moved to ours. Entitlement—rottenness to the bones of any society."

"Claire tells me to go back to Africa."

"This is our home. We're staying. Your native ancestors wouldn't have it any other way. Not everyone is blessed with a conscience or reason, so raise your chin, child. Dream big. Yahweh sees."

"I am dreaming big. I'm going to be a doctor." She stretched her arms wide. "And save the world." Then she planted her hands inside her bubblegum-pink shorts pockets. Her right foot seemed to tap out a beat. *Yahweh, hurry; Yahweh, hurry.*

"But now, time for bed, Doctor Cavanaugh. Sweet dreams."

"Easy for you to say."

"Maybe the boy is tired of haunting your dreams." Her father touched his lips against his daughter's cheek, and she squeezed his face, relishing his warmth. Her teacher had told her that dead people are cold, and her dad's cheeks were as warm as a cup of tea.

"I shouldn't be mad at Yahweh, but sometimes I am." Daniela's elbows dug into her father's chest as she cradled her chin in her palms. "Will I still go to heaven and live forever with you and Mom?"

He touched her cheek. "I guess you think me lying in this bed for so many weeks has been unfair."

"It is," she mumbled.

"You're His favorite little girl. He longs to embrace you."

"Will his hugs feel like yours—warm and safe?"

"Even more. Did you know that He said, 'Let there be light,' and the sun flew into space? Nothing's warmer than the sun."

"What about Claire, Zoya, and Tameka? Are they his favorite girls?"

"I haven't asked."

"Will you? They're mean. I don't want them to pick on me in heaven."

"He's kept me busy." He paused while stroking her face. "Daniela, I need to tell you something."

"A secret?"

"Sort of."

"I adore secrets."

"I know, darling. Long ago, I used to pick sugarcane in Belle Glade, Florida, and I met a man named Tibet who showed me a vision."

"A vision—like the dreams that make me wake up with nosebleeds?"

"Similar."

"I hate the nightmares and the nosebleeds."

"I know, darling, but I wonder if the Almighty is connecting your spirit to someone who needs you—stitching two hearts together."

"Heart surgery? No, thanks."

"You're too smart for your own good." Her father laughed, quickly clamping his side to stop a wave of pain.

"Sorry for making you laugh." While rubbing his side, she changed her voice, sounding like a schoolmarm. "From now on, I'll be serious."

"Oh, Danny Rose, make me laugh every day. You've been the answer to my dreams from so long ago."

"You dreamed when you were a boy?"

"I did, and the most precious dream came true—you."

She smiled, her eyes emanating a love that only a daughter has for her doting father. "Daddy . . ."

"Yes, my darling?"

"You'll get better. Yahweh-Yireh will heal you, like the people in the Bible. Mom says."

"I'm sorry you overheard your mom and me talking about my condition. The doctors have been very generous. I'll go back to work soon, and things will change. We'll go on a vacation."

"Let's go digging for treasures."

"It's a deal."

"I made ten dollars at the lemonade stand in front of the library."

"Did you save it for college?"

"I gave it to Mom for your treatments."

"I don't deserve you."

"I'm not as good as you think I am. I hate those girls, and if I wasn't afraid of fighting, I'd punch them all in the face."

"It takes more bravery to forgive than to fight."

"Then I'm the most afraid girl in the whole universe." She stretched out her arms for emphasis. Her T-shirt rose above her belly button, and Austin couldn't resist. He tickled her soft spot and she giggled, slapping her hand across her mouth so she wouldn't awaken her mother.

"On your thirteenth birthday, I have a special gift for you."

"We'll have balloons and cake?"

"We will." He hugged his only child. "Every dreamer needs her rest. Go to sleep, my Orphan Dreamer."

"I don't like it when you call me an orphan. I'm scared you and Mom will leave me."

"We could never leave you."

"What about the secret?"

"It'll wait."

"Daddy, can I still go to Ethan's this Saturday if he's feeling better?"

"A promise is a promise, but tonight is a school night. Seven o'clock. Bedtime."

"Good night." Daniela tiptoed down the hall past her sleeping mother. She put on her favorite cotton-candy-pink pajamas. Her knees indented the green shag carpet, and her steeple-shaped hands pressed her button nose flat. "Yahweh, please protect my friend wherever she—"

Silence.

"Or he—is. Can you ask your really fast angels—especially the big ones with strong muscles—to protect my friend? And Yahweh, heal Daddy and Ethan. They'll want to meet my new friend. In Yeshua's name. Amen."

Daniela climbed into her bed and pulled her grandmother's patchwork quilt under her chin. Dreamers needed their rest.

After closing her eyes, she tasted the seaside—salt, fish, and the grit of sand—before she saw the boy and smelled his fear, week-old sweat mixed with stale breath. She heard the rejection, a frustrating and humiliating stutter, but then she tasted and smelled compassion: Southern-fried chicken, collard greens, and yellow roses.

Why had her prayers seemed to help oily boy instead of Ethan or her future Anne Shirley? "He's no kindred spirit. Not today—not ever."

6—THE ORPHAN

TUESDAY, AUGUST 24, 1993
BALLYCASTLE, IRELAND

FOG DIMMED THE GREEN, LUSH pastures of Ballycastle, a small sea village on the coast of Ireland.

A misty chill migrated past Cillian Finn's thin, twelve-year-old frame and deep into his bones. He bent over and nursed each numb, bare foot until warmth returned, then willed his feet and growling belly toward Mama Kelley's dinner table.

Little feet scratched the mulch and dried grass as a red squirrel scampered beside him.

"F-f-following me to the dinner table again?" He fought to move words past his nervous mind and subsequently twisted tongue. "M-m-mama Kelley d-d-dinna like you eatin' her food last time."

The squirrel chirped for a while as if saying, "If you tell her you're my friend, she won't mind."

Cillian's mum had another man over, and the child hated the noises—chairs hitting the wall, screams filling the room, and moans rising with the squeaking of the old metal bed in their one-room shanty. His eyes watered, and his lower lip quivered.

"R-r-rory, d'ye like the home th-th-that I built for you?" He had named his friend in honor of his reddish fur.

The squirrel chirped.

"I-I-I know i-i-it's a wee thing, but it'll keep ye safe and warm."

"The runaways at Mama Kelley's house ha' been callin' me the Orphan, but isna an orphan's mum dead? Mine's still livin'. She doesna want me, that's all. I dinnae like the name. Makes me feel like a monster. Something twisted."

Rory whined.

"Dinna be worryin' a bit. Almost there. Mama Kelley always listens."

Rory stood up on his hind legs and dashed ahead.

"Aye. Smellin' her food from a mile away, then." One foot of belt spanked his thigh as he walked. "A growing boy should be letting his belt out, not pulling it tighter," Mama Kelley had said.

His mouth watered, and his mind raced with images of a hot meal waiting for him in her modest cottage—fried chicken, apple pie, and macaroni and cheese. Mama Kelley was a brown-skinned woman from America, stuck in Ireland after her Irish husband of eighteen years had died. He had been an adventurous fisherman who had convinced himself that he would fare better in Ireland than in America.

Cillian thought she talked funny, even funnier than his own mix of Scottish burr and Irish brogue or his stuttering attempt at the Queen's English.

Thinking of how the ancient Gaelic language affected his English, Cillian rubbed his backside—still sore from his mum's discipline with a willow switch.

Speak like a proper English lad.

Ye'll get further. Ye ken.

D'ye want to live like a wretched beggar for eternity, Cillian?

I'll not have it.

Ironically, last night during the beating, her English rolled with a burr. Afterward, nursing her son's bloodied wounds and downing a glass of Scotch, she whispered in the guttural language of her ancestors—Gaelic.

"I-I-I wouldna want to live in England verra much if I'm to get a thrashin' for not forcin' my tongue to speak like a proper wee lad."

Rory squawked as though he agreed.

"I-I-I'll go to America. Mamma Kelley speaks verra funny, and she's not thrashed or picked on for the way she talks."

His furry friend bounced up and down on his hind legs.

The stone cottage appeared in the distance. A wide smile pushed dimples into the corners of his mouth, and then he ran. The cottage's dilapidated red door was the last remaining obstacle between Cillian and Mama Kelley. *She's always excited to see me.*

As he banged on the splintered door, his knuckles smarted. Her hearing wasn't as good as it used to be. "Rory, hide in the bushes."

"I'm coming," called a voice from within the cottage.

A smile crossed Cillian's face as he imagined her running to the door.

"Cillian!" she said. "My favorite little boy. Are you coming to visit Mama Kelley? You're getting more handsome every time I see you." A smile lit up her face, and her eyes danced. She pinched the thin layer of skin above his cheekbones between her fingers. He bit his lower lip, but a smile broke through as he looked at the ground.

"I'm gonna pack some meat on your bones if it's the last thing I do." She balanced her hands on her ample hips. "You're wasting away, suga', and I don't like it."

"Y-y-yes, ma'am." He smiled, loving her nickname for him—sugar without the *r*.

"Take your time." She waited, and a rubber band seemed to release his tongue.

"Thanks. Umm . . ."

"Speak up, Cil."

"Rory would like to join us."

"You've brought that little mouse with you again?"

"It's a squirrel. I wouldna be disrespectin' your table with the company of a mouse."

She peeked out the door. "Everyone needs a friend. He can stay in the little crate I made for him yesterday." She winked. "Come on in. I'll fix him a bowl of food too."

"Thanks." Cillian waved Rory in, then hurried behind Mama Kelley, brushing a pleat of her soft paisley skirt with his hand. *Aye, she doesna mind me touchin' her a wee bit, then.*

Rory jumped into his crate and waited for dinner. Mama Kelley stopped, looked down, then turned and searched Cillian's face. "Does my favorite boy need some hugs and kisses?"

Cillian lifted his chin and then sharply pulled it down. *She reads my mind too.*

She embraced him in motherly love. He relaxed as she pulled him close and put his ear to her chest and listened. *Dub . . . dub . . . dub . . .* His heart rate slowed to match hers. Calm. He looked up. "Mama Kelley, can you tell me what love is, then?"

"Love's patient. Oh yes, she is. Kind and a bit gentle. Why'd you ask?" She leaned back and looked down through her spectacles at him.

"This morning, my mum said she doesna love me, and she wished she could've afforded the butcher to slice me from her belly before I was ready to come out." He gripped Mama Kelley's arms tighter.

She winced. "She isn't makin' any sense—just talkin'. No woman who has a grain of sense in her head wants a butcher to slice open her belly with a knife, hear me? Sit down. Want me to tell you a story while you eat?"

"Could ye be tellin' me two if we ha' time?"

"I'll talk fast. Mister Kelley thought I always did." From the stove, she brought a plate filled with fried chicken, collards, and macaroni and cheese to Cillian—and a little bowl of the same to Rory's place.

"Smells good." Cillian reached for the food.

"Wait a minute. Are we forgetting something and someone?"

Cillian bowed his head.

"That's more like it. Lord, thank you for bringing my friend Cillian to the house. Bless this food, in Jesus' name. Amen." Her story began. "Joseph had a coat of many colors . . ."

Minutes passed as Mama Kelley told the story from Genesis of a young man who was hated by his brothers, but through God's guidance, overcame his obstacles to become second only to the Egyptian pharaoh.

Mesmerized by her story, Cillian swallowed his last bite of chicken, lifted the plate, and licked it until he could see his reflection. "I want to be like Joseph one day—powerful, handsome, and smart."

"You and every other red-blooded boy. But most never get there, and those who do don't have the character to make any bit of difference."

"I'll be makin' a difference. Promise. But for now, I'll be runnin' home, then. Can I take a wee bit of food for Mum? It'll smooth things over for me, and I willna have a punishment before bed."

"What's she whippin' you for now?"

"Sometimes for the way I talk and other times . . ." He shrugged. "I canna be sure."

"Mm-hmm. I'm happiest when you smile and when you speak with the tongue of your Highlander ancestors."

"I canna speak like this at home." Mama Kelley leaned down and held Cillian's small hands in her own. "She says I speak with the tongue of losers, and if I'm to become an English gentleman, I should learn to talk like one." His tone returned to an English accent—uncouth around the edges.

"Listen to your mommy now, but when you become an adult, be your own person." A rim of moisture pooled around her eyes. "Do you want me to tend to your back again, suga'?"

"If it needs tendin'." Cillian turned and slid his shirt off, and Mama Kelley gasped.

"Mama, what's wrong?"

"Nothing—almost plain forgot to tell you that second story." As she dabbed his back with a cool, wet cloth and then applied an antibiotic salve, she told him the story of a Hebrew boy, David, who killed a lion and a bear while he cared for his sheep in the field. "When he became a mighty man, David became king of all Israel. Some start small, but they don't allow their beginning to determine their ending. Hear me?"

"Aye." His voice quivered as pain shot deep into his muscles each time she touched him, but he stood rigid. He had learned how to take agony like a man.

She returned to the stove and picked up a brown sack as he slid his shirt back on. "I packed your mom's dinner. Clean your teeth. Remember, a little baking soda on a washrag will keep your teeth nice and milky white. You don't need fancy toothpaste."

"I should hurry. It's late, Mama." He wet a rag, dumped baking soda on it, and scrubbed his teeth. "May Rory stay here? He'll freeze outside."

The squirrel's ears perked up upon hearing his name.

"I'll look after him. Come here, son. I'm gonna say a prayer over you. Let me get my anointing oil." Mama Kelley dipped a finger into a clear vial and whisked it across his forehead. He touched the oily substance and waved his finger in front of his nose. "Smells like apple spice and roses."

"For the most beautiful rose I know." She closed her eyes.

"Almighty . . ." Her voice broke. She waited until strength returned to her vocal cords. "I'm anointing my little suga' pie, Cillian Joseph Finn. Make him into a mighty man of Yours—a man with the courage of David when he killed Goliath, a man with the virtue and purpose of Joseph. If I should never see Cillian again, let him know I love him, and You love him. He will always be my son. He's in Your hands. You're the potter, and he's the clay. Shape his character to fulfill Your purpose, in Jesus' name. Amen."

"Bye, Mama, I'll be seein' you next time." Cillian waved, clutching his mother's dinner in his left hand.

"There won't be a next time, honey," Mama Kelley said under her breath. Rory hopped to his feet, protesting her premonition with his chirps.

Cillian turned. "D'ye say something?"

"I love you, and Godspeed on your journey." Mama Kelley picked up the pint-sized mammal. "He'll be alright. We'll whisper a prayer or two." Rory tilted his head downward and quieted. "Run on home before it gets dark."

Cillian pushed open the cottage door. A mournful squeal erupted from the hinges.

"And here I go feelin' the same way as this old door."

"I'll oil the hinges when I come back in a couple of days." He waved. "Rory, I'll take you for a walk."

"You're mama's little man." She dabbed her face.

She's crying. A knot spiraled his stomach into a million circles. "Are ye angry with me, then?" Cillian dared a glance at Mama Kelley's face. A trail of tears meandered down her cheeks.

"Don't pay any mind to me. How could I be mad at you? You're the son the Almighty only saw fit to allow me to dream of."

"Last night, I dreamed of a girl with long black pigtails and brown skin like yours."

"I've not been a girl for a long time. Maybe she's someone waiting for you in your future, thinking of you and praying that life will be kind to you."

"The whisper of *mo chridhe.* I'd like that."

"So would I. Run on home before dark." She waved the boy away, toward whatever life held for him.

Cillian dashed across soft heather.

The sun dipped behind the rolling western hills, and black shadows shifted to push any remaining light from the horizon. The one-bedroom shack—his mum's house—loomed in the distance. He tiptoed the last few feet to the wooden shack, pushed open the door, and stopped, straining his neck and cupping his ear with his hand.

No strange sounds.

He tiptoed further inside and looked around. Everything was packed. Why? Had she left? He shouldn't have gone to Mama Kelley's, but she liked Mama Kelley's cooking. He swallowed hard, not knowing what to do.

"Cillian, have ye decided to be comin' back from the grave?" The door slammed shut after she entered. He hadn't been at the graveyard. Surely she knew that, so he planted his feet on the tattered area rug and stared at the ground, waiting.

"Well, what are ye standing there for?" his mother shrieked.

He looked from his mother's feet to her knees to her waist cinched with a red belt, and finally, to her scolding green eyes. She craned her neck, balled her fists, and propped them above her hips.

"I-I-I brought you some dinner." He crept closer to her.

She snatched Mama Kelley's dinner bag, jerking him forward. He nursed his pained shoulder.

"We're leaving for England first thing in the morning."

"W-w-why?"

"Don't you talk back to me."

"I-I-I'm sorry."

"I've taken a strap to you before, and I'll do it again." She rubbed her right shoulder. "I'm a right bit sore from yesterday, though." Ailsa Finn held her open hand above Cillian's head. "I don't like your eyes. There's mischief in them. I'll mix the ammonia with Clorox and lock you in the bathroom again."

He crouched and lifted his arm to shield his face. "Puh-puh-please don't." He coughed, remembering the blood coming from his throat after being locked in the bathroom with toxic gases. "I-I-I didna say goodbye to Mama Kelley." His tone slipped into the burr of his Scottish ancestors.

"I told you to speak properly, didn't I?" Ailsa scurried around the room, flipping over the clothes and pillows that covered the floor.

A tear slipped from Cillian's eye.

He knew what she was looking for—a switch.

She'd thoroughly used it yesterday morning, bruising his backside until the switch splintered and then returning an hour later to finish up her task with the nub of the stick across his bare legs, back, and arms. "M-m-mummy, I'm sorry. I won't speak like that again. I-I-I promise," he said in his best English accent.

Ailsa whipped her gaze back to her offspring. "She doesn't care about you. You're a nuisance to her, like you are around here." She opened the dinner bag. After removing the food, she tossed the bag toward her son. "Use that to pack. In England, I'll teach you to become a proper lad if it kills me."

He lunged forward to grab it, but his palms collided with the splintered floorboards. He clenched his abdomen, the wave of nausea growing.

She doesn't care anything about me. An ache rose in his throat. *I guess she willna miss me.*

"Put your stuff in the bag and stop crying. Ye whine now more than ye did as a wee babe." Ailsa turned on her heels and walked to the kitchen. She had found the treasure, Mama Kelley's cooking, and the whipping could wait until before bedtime.

He'd be prepared. Cillian wouldn't pack his second pair of pants. He would use them for extra padding. She wouldn't notice. His mother drank a few tumblers of whiskey before bed.

I'll be okay. He packed.

7—ORPHAN DREAMER

RELENTLESS ABUSE SHREDDED THE CHILD'S spirit and will to live. Refusing to stay in Daniela's nightmares, oily boy's fear compounded her own this morning.

"Fight! Fight! Fight!" the other kids chanted. Daniela's tongue stuck to the roof of her mouth. Harry reached to the ground, scooped up a handful of sand, and threw it at Daniela. She blinked. Grit scraped her eyes, and tears formed. Temporarily blinded, she crawled toward where she thought she'd left the book. *Don't leave me, Anne.*

"Looking for your only friend—a girl in a book?" Daniela recognized Claire's nasally voice.

"Thank you." She reached up without opening her eyes.

"Pysch! Take it to the dumpster, Harry," Claire said. "Danny's trash, and that's where her imaginary friends belong. You're never joining the Untouchables, ape-face!"

"No," Daniela protested. "The book belongs to the library."

"No more books for you, four-eyes." Harry spat his insults.

"Break it up!" Ms. Bender's voice rang throughout the playground. "Motor!" Harry screamed; voices faded into the distance as feet thumped across the ground. "Daniela, why are you crawling in the dirt . . . why are your eyes closed?"

"They took my book." Daniela kept her eyes shut. "And Harry threw sand in my eyes."

"Harry, come here at once!" Daniela could hear the chubby boy's feet pounding the ground.

"Ma'am?"

"Return the book to Daniela at once!"

He obeyed, tossing the book at Daniela.

"Why would you do such a thing?" the teacher asked.

"We were joking."

"No one's laughing. Listen to me. This is a school. Not a dungeon. Not a prison. That means you're a student, sent here by your parents to learn. You are not an inquisitor, and Danny Rose isn't your heretic, so stop being a bully. Put on your thinking cap, Harry! Find a different way to deal with your insecurities."

"Yes, ma'am."

"One day, Danny Rose may save your hiney."

"I doubt it."

"Go sit in the classroom." Ms. Bender held Daniela's hand. "Let's wash the sand out of your eyes." The teacher led Daniela to the bathroom sink. The stench of urine clung to the insides of her nostrils as the teacher splashed water into her student's eyes, but they still burned.

"I'd prefer not to go blind."

"You won't." Ms. Bender turned off the water. "Open your eyes."

Daniela lifted her eyelids, but everything was blurry. "They hurt."

"I'll call your parents, so they can take you to the doctor."

Daniela's shoulders slumped.

"What's wrong?" her teacher asked, and Daniela shook her head.

"Nothing."

"Sure?"

"Daddy's wasn't feeling well, so he had to take a few days off, and we're a little short on money."

"I'm sorry." The teacher rested her hand on Daniela's shoulder. "You're smart—special. Don't let the likes of Harry kill your spirit or your destiny."

"If only he'd stop teasing me, I could think clearer." She wiped her face with a paper towel, and they left the bathroom.

"Has he told you why?"

"He said his uncle doesn't like people like me. He wishes we'd all go back to Africa."

"Stupid is as stupid does. Like the rest of us, your heritage is as varied as the flowers of the field."

"My vision is too blurry to look at any flowers." Specks of dirt scratched Daniela's eyes. "They still hurt."

"Let's visit the school nurse then I'll call your parents."

"I hate being left out." The ache in Daniela's heart was so intense that she ground her teeth.

"No friends?"

"A frog, a duck, and a spider. They're not exactly the friends I expected to meet. They all eat bugs, and I'm afraid of bugs. But then, there's Ethan—my dearest Ethan."

"Poor Ethan. Always in the hospital."

"We're supposed to have a sleepover this weekend."

"At a boy's house?"

"He's a big exception, according to my dad."

"We all need exceptions." She winked. Her brown eyes lightened to violet. *She's no ordinary teacher.*

"Ms. Bender, can I tell you a secret?" The teacher crossed her heart and hoped to die. "Daddy said to pray for a friend. Here comes an insect, a reptile, a duck, and oily boy—my nightmare. The animals . . . they all talk to me, and so does the eyeless boy," Daniela whispered.

"You sure?" The teacher's brows turned down toward her nose.

"You don't believe me—do you?"

"Doesn't matter what I believe. What do you believe?"

"They can talk. I can hear them. I never expected to make friends with a hairy-legged spider." A wide grin pushed dimples into Daniela's cheeks. "Am I weird?"

Ms. Bender tapped her chin and didn't answer for a full ten seconds. A smile creased her lips. Teacher and student burst into laughter.

"Well, that settles it," Ms. Bender said. "More legs to get away from Harry."

"I like you, Ms. Bender. You're nice."

"I like you too." They walked hand in hand into the school nurse's office. "You remind me of me when I was a little girl."

"But you're so pretty."

8—The Orphan

Monday, November 8, 1993
Fallowfield, Manchester, England

CILLIAN NO LONGER LIVED BY Ireland's Antrim Coast. He and his mother had moved to Manchester. Three days ago, he went missing. No one would file a missing person's report. At least Cillian prayed that no one would.

"Out!" The petrol station worker seized Cillian by his ripped T-shirt and threw him across the room. His body slammed into a brick wall. Dazed, Cillian tried to get onto his feet and take flight, but the man was on him again, kicking him repeatedly in the gut.

"Puh-puh-please! Please!" Cillian cried between labored breaths. "I'll leave, but will ye not let me rise?"

"You're a Scot." The man stopped kicking.

"I-I-Irish-Scot, Mister."

"I like Scotland."

"So do I." Cillian crawled toward the door. He blinked, trying to forget the nightmare of his existence.

"Scottish, English, or Irish, there are no freeloaders in my shop. Don't come back. Next time, I'll douse you with petrol and set you on fire."

"Yes, sir. I-I-I promise . . ." Cillian crawled from the warm room and into the cold Manchester evening.

Burned to death.

How would that feel?

Icy wind barreled past his threadbare clothes and shoved an ice pick of dread into his body. He gripped the window ledge and pulled himself to his feet, stumbling along until he found a new home behind a dumpster.

If the Irish-Scots boy could remember how Mama Kelley had prayed, he would have begged her God to let him fall asleep and never wake up.

He hoped her God didn't hate him as much as most adults did.

His stomach rolled and pitched, then threatened to launch more green liquid from between his cracked lips. He dug his bony fingers into his abdomen, feeling the ache of the beating and the sickness that brewed beneath. Sickness had driven him to the petrol station, and he'd only been inside to use the toilet.

Even a filthy public toilet was too good for him.

Too tired to cry, he laid his head directly on the asphalt, remembering the morsel of meat he had found in the trash can earlier that day. The brown meat hadn't stunk or crawled with maggots, but some mysterious bug punished his gut for stealing it from the refuse pile.

Toilet, again.

He pushed himself onto his elbows and tried to crawl but collapsed. His abdomen cramped, sending a stabbing wave down to his bottom. His forehead dripped with a cold sweat. His bottom contracted, moistened, and then burned with a foul-smelling substance.

Hopeless.

He was dehydrated, but a lone tear trickled down his cheek as his body convulsed on its own. He pulled his blanket, which consisted of more holes than cloth over his thin body.

How would his frozen body be discovered?

Would a stray dog chew at his parts until it had its fill, or would a merciful stranger like the Good Samaritan in Mama Kelley's Bible story bandage him up and pay for a stay at a posh hotel? The orphan closed his eyes, yielding to the darkness that rolled over Manchester's slums.

In the distance, brakes squealed.

Cillian peered through a crack between an apartment building and the dumpster. A long car with black windows stopped, then a door opened. Fine shoes planted themselves onto the street. Brown slacks draped around the beige shoes. Then the owner of the fine pants and shoes stepped around the car door, closing it.

The man lumbered like someone Cillian knew—Joe Sanders—and soon towered above him. Broad shoulders ended in bear-paw hands and sausage fingers. A beer-fed belly cast a shadow over oak-tree-sized legs.

Cillian gulped hard and prayed to Mama Kelley's God. *Would ye be lettin' me become invisible?*

Instead, pain knifed into the back of his neck as hands yanked his shaggy hair. "Stupid boy." Joe pummeled Cillian's backside with a razor strap. "For the last three days, your mum made me scour this dreadful neighborhood looking for her whelp. You'll pay."

Cillian knew what "you'll pay" meant. The strap had been a beginning, and it wouldn't matter that he was sicker than death. No one answered the orphan's prayer, and Joe dragged Cillian to his car.

No need to whisper another prayer.

Devils shout louder than orphans.

9—THE ORPHAN (PG-13)

HEAVY GRAY CLOUDS SUFFOCATED THE English town.

Cillian looked out the first-floor window of his mother's rented flat. Trash littered the sidewalk and smells of sewage burned his nose, reminding him of the petrol station. He had arrived home from the littered park, which was his school, thirty minutes ago.

Mummy will be furious if she comes home and I'm not here.

He had completed his usual routine of gingerly walking into their apartment, checking the refrigerator for any scraps of food, and locking himself in the only bedroom, which was divided into two by a sheet for privacy.

The precaution of locking the bedroom door was not a real barrier to Joe Sander's rage. He had kicked the door down on many occasions. Cillian locked the door only as a delay tactic.

Would Joe come today?

He opened a math book and laid it on his mattress. An hour passed. The front door creaked on its hinges.

"Cillian," Joe hollered through clogged nostrils.

Fear exploded in the child's gut, and his body seized with tremors. He wrapped his arms around his chest, hoping the shakes would stop. Staring at the closed door, he backed away from it until his posterior reached the dividing curtain. "Do not enter," she had instructed him, and he dared not disobey her.

"Cillian!" His name again penetrated the walls of the apartment. He could hear Joe clanking bottles in the kitchen. Cillian pulled thicker jeans from under his mattress, yanked them up around his bony hips, and cinched the frayed belt tight.

He waited, facing his miserable reality alone.

The day after their arrival in England, Joe Sanders had applied at a local pub to be Ailsa's newest lover. Why would a finely dressed man want to come to his mother's apartment? In spite of all Ailsa's flaws, beauty still radiated from her face, and it wasn't hard for her to get along with men. He had never known his father, and none of his mother's visitors had ever taken an interest in him until now.

Joe Sanders was different.

He was rich, and he had a special purpose for visiting Cillian. These visits dealt a devastating blow to Cillian's health.

Joe owned a toy store on Manchester's posh side. Any toy a child could dream of could be purchased from his shop.

Cillian had seen Joe's store once. A taxicab had arrived in front of their apartment, and Ailsa had pulled Cillian in; they'd gone to Joe's store. Cillian had waited outside, cupping his hands around his eyes and peering through the window while Ailsa talked to Joe.

Later that evening, Joe had walked from behind the sheet that separated Ailsa's bedroom from Cillian's and tossed a brand-new truck at Cillian—calling it charity—before he exited. Cillian had vowed that he would buy a toy for himself one day.

Not today, though—today, he needed to survive.

Joe Sanders's appearance was menacing—a barrel chest, a ruddy complexion, sandy blond hair, a bulbous red nose, tobacco-stained teeth, and stale-beer breath. Bushy brows shaded his eyes, which Cillian thought of as Christmas-tree eyes: bloodshot whites surrounding green irises.

"Cillian!" Joe brayed again.

Where could he hide?

Joe banged on the bedroom door, and Cillian's skin tingled with dread. The sagging, splintered door rattled on its hinges. Ten icicles dangled from his frail arms. His heart raced. He clamped his palms to his ears, fearing Joe could hear his heartbeat over the loud claps of the thunder outside.

"You little rascal, open this door at once!"

What could he have done this time?

"Aye, sir," Cillian weakly replied and limped across the room. His bare feet left footprints in the damp, moldy carpet. Joe had gifted the limp to Cillian only two days ago when beating him with a wooden paddle. The reason for the beating remained a mystery.

Cillian wrapped his hands around the door handle, but his grip slipped. He wiped the sweat off his hand and twisted the handle. The door squeaked on its hinges as it swung open. Joe exploded through and Cillian stumbled back, the door barely missing him.

"You kept me waiting, boy."

"I-I-I'm sorry, mister." He stuttered while backing away from his abuser. The words barely left his lips before the first crushing blow found Cillian's face. He lifted his arm to protect himself.

"Undress—now!" Joe ordered.

"Puh-puh-puh-please don't," Cillian petitioned. "I didna do anything wrong, and if I did, I'll be makin' it right."

"You'll take what I give like a man," Joe barked.

Cillian slipped off his threadbare shirt, uncovering his bruised back, now vulnerable to Joe's vicious actions. Joe beat him where no one could see. Didn't want nosy people who don't understand asking questions about Joe's making the boy into a man.

"You know how this goes. Jeans off."

His mouth opened in protest, but no brave words came. All plans to protect his backside failed. The secondhand jeans, two sizes too big, fell to the floor as soon as he unbuckled his belt.

Cillian covered his backside as Joe flicked his instrument of punishment through the air.

The long, green switch made a high-pitched whistling sound.

Ailsa would not arrive home for a few minutes. Her job at the local launderette kept her occupied for now, and the housing complex teemed with more desperate people than roaches, people too destitute to care about the cries of an illegitimate child.

Joe poked Cillian's back with the tip of the rod, lifted it, and sliced the air. Cillian's lungs emptied. Blows fell. He lost count. Joe's ears seemed deaf to the boy's cries. "I'm going to follow the voice and kill you this time."

The voice? What voice?

"You're a threat to my master's plans. Today, you'll die." Joe took a swig of his drink. Then he lifted the rod again, bringing it down right in the middle of Cillian's back. The boy's screams gutted the apartment.

Every blow struck his skin with a purposeful slice, attempting to shred his spirit and his will to live, if the beating itself did not kill him. He curled into the fetal position, protecting his head. Cillian screamed, "He's killing me! Help, please, someone!" His hair clung to his skin as sweat and tears mingled down his face. "What did I do wrong?"

"You were born. Then you dared to take a breath through your illegitimate lips, choosing to live." The words echoed through Cillian's soul.

The door to the bedroom squeaked open. Cillian raised his head slightly, and his gaze met his mother's.

"Mum, please . . . I didna do anything wrong." Mama Kelley had taught Cillian to say *please* and *thank you.*

The indifference in Ailsa's eyes told her son everything he needed to know.

She navigated past Cillian's mattress, stood on her tiptoes, kissed Joe, then pulled the sheet back and disappeared into her side of the room. "Come to me when you're done, Joe."

Though mother and father forsake you, I will never leave you, Cillian. A calming voice spoke to him. He had never heard it before, so he peeked between his fingers, trying to find the source of it. No one occupied the room except Joe.

Cillian turned his face to the man.

The beast's blond hair danced to the devilish rhythms of the frenzied, vicious beating, only pausing to toss an empty beer bottle onto the mattress. Cillian's cries quieted to muffled moans, and then everything went black.

★ ★ ★

Joe didn't stop, even after Cillian's body was limp and drenched in sweat. His skin, marked with old and new scars, welts, and bruises, adequately reflected Joe's hatred for the boy.

Finish him off.

A sneer possessed Joe's face, and he raised the willow rod to hammer the unconscious boy's back once more.

10—Orphan Dreamer

SLEEPOVER AT ETHAN'S!

The school day ended, and Danny Rose climbed up the stairs of the school bus. Her body throbbed as if a man o' war had lashed her with its stingers. Her throat begged to scream, but what would her classmates think if she unleashed a seemingly random shriek? Her mother called her ability to feel another's pain *supernatural empathy*.

But whose pain was she feeling—Ethan's or Anne's?

She paused and closed her eyes. The pale, eyeless face of oily boy flashed into view. Her eyelids ripped open. "Not him."

"Who are you talking to, bozo?" Tameka asked. *None of your beeswax.* Daniela licked her moist lips. Anemic blood. The taste of a life rapidly slipping away. Thick, warm, heavy blood mingled with the previous taste. Blood pooled inside her nose. She pinched a handkerchief around her nostrils, staunching her nosebleed.

Two seats remained on the last two rows of the school bus. Freckle-faced Harry sat in the last row and glared at her.

"Find a seat." Mrs. Johnson closed the bus door.

Here goes nothing. Daniela slid into the patent-leather bench in front of her nemesis, nursing her nosebleed and wishing for a pain reliever to numb the pain oily boy had inflicted on her body. She stared at her toes and braced herself for the first blow.

"Are you real?" she asked oily boy. "If not, please stop hurting me."

"Who are you talking to, ghetto rat?"

"Shut your face." Ornery from the pain, the words spilled out. Daniela slapped her hand over her mouth; Harry's mouth opened wider than a sinkhole.

I just stood up for myself.

Anne, the duckling, had been right—with Yeshua's help, she could do anything.

"Ugly rat." For the next twenty minutes, Harry spat insults at Daniela and flicked the back of her head until brakes squealed and the bus lurched forward. A thud on the back of her seat—followed by *ouch!*—told her Harry's face had collided into the back of her seat.

Glancing over her shoulder, she smiled—a nosebleed. Harry's turn. "Sweet!"

Fist balled and ready to teach Daniela a lesson, Harry jumped up. She bolted from the bus, and warm liquid filled her right nostril again.

Two heavy feet pounded behind her.

She kept running.

Minutes later, Daniela clamped another one of her father's handkerchiefs to her nose. She'd already soaked the first with blood, and now her legs threatened to buckle. She mustered the rest of her energy and dashed behind an oak tree. Sharks smelled blood. Quickly, she stuffed the cloth into her lunch box.

"You're disgusting." Harry approached her hiding place, but he hadn't found her. There was a reason he'd been held back two grades. With a round face and curly brown hair, he looked like an evil clown let loose from the circus. He searched behind a shrub.

"What's wrong? Crack fryin' your nose again?"

She hunched lower and held her arm above her head as though his words were a raised wooden paddle. Hateful words opened old scars, inflicting wounds that would fester for years.

Harry waddled closer. Only a few feet away. Daniela closed her eyes. "Make me invisible," she whispered.

I am with you, a gentle voice said. *Do not be afraid.*

"Found you." Harry lunged toward Daniela but stopped mid-stride. Jumping backward, he slapped his right shoulder. "Ouch! Get off me!" He ran around in circles, swiping at his body. What was happening? She hadn't touched him. Daniela froze.

"Get it off me!" He slapped his cheek, and that's when she saw it—a big, hairy tarantula spread across the middle of his face.

Mister Spider spit a piece of silk and flew from Harry's face to the oak's trunk then back to Harry, landing across his nose, eyes, and mouth. "Get out of here, Danny."

"Mister Spider, I won't abandon you."

"Off you go."

"Meet up at the treehouse?"

"Pronto." The spider spat silk, and Daniela ran.

A few seconds later, Harry hollered, "That's what you deserve."

Daniela stopped cold. Mister Spider was in trouble.

She ran back; Harry was stomping the ground. *Please let Mister Spider be okay.* Her eight-legged friend could shoot silk faster than Spiderman. When she arrived, Harry was sliding his shoe back and forth over a patch of grass.

"Stop it." Daniela elbowed Harry. He threw a punch and punished her shoulder, planting Daniela on the ground.

He lifted his foot. "Is that what you're looking for?" Body crushed, blood and guts smeared across Harry's shoe, Mister Spider was dead.

"You killed my friend."

"You are some stupid crazy." Harry balled his fists. "Imma gonna bury you if it's the last thing I do, girl."

Daniela sliced her leg beneath Harry and knocked his standing leg from under him. He face-planted. She jumped up and ran until her legs burned. "See you in heaven, Mister Spider."

She ran faster than the wind, and the fat boy couldn't keep up.

Sometimes Yahweh answered prayers a little differently than his children requested; the answer to her childhood prayers had been a sprinter's legs and a lithe body. She ran until the sounds of Harry breathing hard faded into a cool, crisp winter wind.

Someone needs you, little one.

"I'm too weak. Feels like I'm dying slowly." The air seemed to carry laughter. Was Yahweh laughing? None of this was funny.

Exhausted, she crawled into the empty park and hid in the sunken garden.

I'm with you.

Sitting on a swing, she whispered into the wind. "If it's You speaking, I'm sorry Mister Spider died." Had she been worth his sacrifice?

Earn this, Danny Rose.

"How?"

Sacrifice. The ingredient true friends willingly give, the calm voice said. She remembered her mother's biblical instruction, "This is real love: not that we loved God, but that he loved us and sent His Son as a sacrifice to take away our sins." Dead leaves danced within wind currents, dodging between the legs of Claire's empty trampoline in her front yard. She walked to the trampoline and sat down in the middle of Claire's favorite toy. The leaves stilled as though an invisible fan had lost power.

Across the street, the playground quieted along with her heart. Yahweh had answered her prayer. No more blood dripped from her nose.

"Please make me stop bleeding—forever."

The nosebleeds are not meant to torment you, but to remind you to pray for him.

"I won't lie. It feels splendid to be needed, but can't I be needed by someone pretty and popular like Claire?"

You're misplacing value. It's not outside appearance, but character that counts.

"Winners win—and losers lose."

A person can finish in a very different place than where they begin, especially if a friend prays for them. You asked for a bosom friend. I'm giving you one. Oily boy needs you—now!

"Dad forbids male bosom friends. Didn't you know that? You know everything." She sat ridgepole straight, determined to not restart the nosebleed.

Leave your dad to me.

Her mother's words echoed in her spirit, "The insistent prayer of a righteous person is powerfully effective."

"Okay . . . if that's all you want me to do for him, I can pray for him . . . if he's real." Daniela bowed her head, and for the first time, she followed her father's advice and prayed for the boy who haunted her dreams, "Because he may be real, give him a day of happiness. Make him brave. If he's lonely like me, give him a friend . . . if there is only one friend to spare, give him one first. I can wait. I still have Ethan, Mom, Dad, the frog, and my pet duck. If he's not had a hug for a while, hug him." She glanced at her Bugs Bunny watch. "Gotta go, Yeshua."

She ran home, glad to have done something to help the boy trapped in her dreams—even if he was a figment of her imagination.

II—THE ORPHAN

JOE SCRATCHED HIS SCALP AND threw the splintered willow rod beside Cillian's mattress, taking pleasure in knowing the fear it would cause the boy when he regained consciousness and saw the switch.

"Don't you dare wake up, boy. Or else." Joe kicked the mattress, missing the boy's abdomen entirely. He grabbed his back. "Damn it."

"What's wrong?" Ailsa peeked around the dividing curtain.

"Threw a muscle out." Joe lumbered to Ailsa's side of the room.

"Will that interfere with . . ." She twirled a red silk scarf between her fingers. "Us?"

"I've earned my keep. The boy's quiet." A shadow crossed in front of Ailsa's mirror. Joe's heart thumped harder. He grabbed his chest and doubled over. "What was that?"

"What?" She ran to her lover's aid.

"Something walked in front of the mirror." Joe turned left, then right. "That boy of yours is possessed. I can feel it."

"Don't keep me waiting. I need comforting." Ailsa's neck glistened with the dampness of a hot shower. The heavy aroma of expensive candles overwhelmed the small space. The finest silk sheets Joe Sanders's money could buy draped the metal bed. Quieted, Cillian would not interfere with Ailsa and Joe's pleasure.

They satisfied their lustful, selfish passions over and over.

"Danny Rose, you called for me just in time." Legna lies beside Cillian. "A few more minutes, he'd have been dead. Next time, don't freeze."

The boy is unconscious, unaware. Hearing sensual human noises, Legna looks up and stares through the black sheet that separates Cillian's section from Ailsa's. *If humans knew that we watched as they engaged in their folly, would it make a difference?*

Cillian stirs.

Legna rests his hand on the child's head, knowing his touch will feel like a loving mother's womb—safe and warm. A fretful snore escapes Cillian's bruised and bleeding lips.

As Legna glares at the lovers, his lips curl into a sneer, and his eyes fill with disdain. If Legna's master, Yahweh, had not defended Joe, Legna would have gladly ended the sadist's life. *Give me a reason to kill you, human.* Legna reaches for his sword, then wraps his other arm around Cillian. The boy settles into a sweet sleep.

Joe grunts, crying out in ecstasy.

Legna sneers. *That's humans for you. Adonai, I don't understand why You give them all so many chances.*

"Finish him off, Legna. I dare you." The voice isn't Legna's master.

"Nomed," Legna whispers.

"Bingo!" Nomed replies. "Joe failed. Finish him off."

"Death is your master's friend—not mine."

"Fine. I'll do it." Nomed escapes the world of the mortals, appearing as a black shadow above Ailsa's bed. He reaches inside Joe's chest, then yanks his heart out. Joe goes limp. In the morning,

Ailsa will believe her lover suffered a heart attack. Too many fish and chips and beers.

It's done. One tormentor dead. In the darkness, Legna holds Cillian tight.

12—The Orphan

Friday, November 12, 1993
Fallowfield, Manchester, England

NIGHT SURROUNDED AILSA FINN'S APARTMENT while a drizzle of rain created an eerie mist. Cillian opened his swollen, tender eyes and dug his elbows into the dingy mattress, his breathing labored. The room stunk of sweat and stale flesh.

Cillian . . .

Looking all around, Cillian didn't see anyone.

Cillian . . . Cillian . . .

He swallowed hard, and a whimper escaped from his mouth. "Is someone there?" His voice sounded more like sandpaper scratching wood than anything human. "Please! Dinna hurt me." His elbows slid out from under him, and his body crashed into the mattress. "I'll be a good boy." A lightning bolt of pain ignited in his legs and back. He grimaced, and sobs wracked his skeletal frame.

Do not be afraid. The voice, a gentle breeze, brushed past his ears. "Who are you?"

Name's Adonai. Someone asked me to be with you.

"Mama Kelley?"

No. Another friend. May I come in?

"No. I d-d-dinna talk to strangers, much less let them come in for a visit."

I love you.

The three words sounded foreign to Cillian. "Only Mama Kelley said she loved me. We moved. She stayed in Ireland. Nobody's been lovin' me since then."

I gave My life so you may be free.

"Freedom? Joe thrashes me, and Mother barely feeds me."

All humans possess free will. A person must decide to follow My commandments.

"Ye should be changin' your commandments to include sharing food and not beating wee lads tryin' their best."

My commandments are simple: Love Me with all your heart, soul, and mind. Love your neighbor as yourself. Evil results when humans disobey My commandments. For their disobedience, Joe and your mother will suffer consequences. Hurry! Empty your knapsack. Fill it with your blanket, water, and the yellow apple you hid in your closet.

The gentle voice knew about the yellow apple!

Dress warm.

"Mister, my shoes have holes in the bottoms."

Trust me, Cillian.

"You know my name?"

Look in your closet.

Cillian opened the door and looked down. A wry smile indented his puffy face. "A new pair of trainers?" He pressed a scabbed forefinger against the red-and-blue shoes. "I've never worn anything out of the box. Thanks!" He dressed, laced his new trainers, and swung his tattered knapsack around his shoulders.

Then, one foot over another, he climbed out of his bedroom window and walked into the unknown. He waved a hand through the mist; it clung to his fingers like the fresh silk of a spider's web. A chill shook his waiflike body, and pain pulsed down his shredded back. Determination for a better future encouraged him to walk. He had run before, and Joe had caught him, but this time something invisible and strong seemed to carry him.

"Thank you for the help. I'll be makin' a better future for myself.

13—THE ORPHAN

PEWTER RAYS OF DAWN PEEKED through nighttime darkness, and shadows danced like ghosts behind tree trunks.

"I'm scared." Cillian's muscles tightened as he scanned his surroundings. "Where am I?"

As though on command, the fields illuminated.

Apricot streamers of sunlight burst through the darkness, playing in patterns across green grass. An owl's hoot faded into the waxing dawn. Rolling hills dotted with grazing sheep were a welcome sight. Flowers as yellow as Mama Kelley's Bundt cakes stood at attention along the path, the fragrance as sweet as her roses.

Wherever he was radiated a calming peace. He inhaled. A wave of warmth relaxed his muscles.

Had he traveled back to Ireland's countryside? Would Mama Kelley's cottage pop up on the horizon? Had he arrived at the heaven she'd told him about? A rolling river bubbled across the field. Scents of grass and country air soothed him. He strolled through the field, the tall grass tickling his hands.

He stopped.

But that would mean I'm dead.

Fear crept into his chest, making his heart pound. *Wait. Death isna so bad. Joe and Mum aren't here.*

He sprawled atop soft green grass, no more stiff springs digging into his back. His stomach growled, and he removed the apple from his knapsack.

No worm. Okay to eat.

The brook bubbled with clear, cold water, so he filled his bottle and drank. "Anything that moves can be a friend—the wind, the stream, a flower, or the sun. Bubbling waters, my name is Cillian Finn. Would ye be wantin' a friend?" He smiled through his pain.

Gurgles erupted from the brook.

It talks.

"We'll be makin' our acquaintance." He threw a rock into the water, watching as the ripples grew bigger and bigger.

★ ★ ★

Did Daniela's dad have to know everything about oily boy, especially his skin color? She craved her father's approval. There would be no friendship between her and oily boy unless her dad approved of him.

Her dad was most comfortable near his dad's grave.

"Introduce him slowly," she whispered as she stood in the middle of her grandfather's peanut farm, pulled the bow tight, and released an arrow into a waterfall of gray Spanish moss that hung from a massive oak tree.

"Bull's-eye," Her dad said. "My daddy taught you well. Boy, this place brings back some memories."

"Good ones?"

"Simple times, but make no mistake about it, times were hard—real hard."

"You had to deal with bullies?"

"Well, a few of those too. When we weren't growing peanuts, we were dipping turpentine, and that was some hard, backbreaking work. Never wanted you to have to labor in the fields like I had to."

"I don't mind helping you and Mom with chores."

"Show me your hands."

Daniela slung her bow over her shoulder and held up her hands. Her father cupped them in his own. "Yes, ma'am. The hands of a skilled archer—soft, but strong. Keep on practicing, but remember what your grandpappy told you before he went on to glory: 'Don't be pointin' that there arrow at no human.'"

"That's bad English."

"We won't tell." Staring off into the distance, her dad smiled as though reliving his youth. "You should be proud of your grand-pappy—good English or not. He was a good man, a part of the Underground Railroad."

"I'm proud of you both." Daniela loaded another arrow, pulled her bow, and aimed at the base of the oak tree. "I hate reading about what mean people did to some of my ancestors."

"We don't have to love them, just live with them." She thought of Ethan and oily boy. And the color of their skin. Daniela reached for her rafiki's hand and squeezed. "What if my Anne has ivory skin and freckled cheeks? Would you be angry?"

Silence.

"We'll cross that bridge when we come to it." He interlinked his arm with hers, and they crossed the red bridge over the millpond. "I couldn't imagine you being ashamed of me."

"What do you mean? You're the most amazing dad." She faced her hero.

"You're someone special. Don't give all of yourself to *them*. Give your specialness to our people—people who look like us."

Definitely not the time to bring up oily boy. "I was eavesdropping at school today."

"Danny Rose!"

"Don't worry. I asked for forgiveness."

Her dad glanced left, then right. "Wanna share?"

"Claire's dad hit her mom so many times they had to move in with her grandparents. You wouldn't ever hit Mom, would you?"

"A man shouldn't hit a woman, and when you become older and marry, if any man hits you, that'll be the last thing he does."

"You'll beat him up with your cane?"

"Yes, ma'am." He struck the wooden bridge with his cane as Daniela giggled.

"I overheard my teacher say that Claire's dad gets away with beating her mom because his brother's a senator."

"Politicians seem to live by another set of rules. Let's grab some snacks for your weekend with Ethan."

"I can't wait to tell Ethan about the class trip to the Smithsonian next summer. Can I go?"

"If Ethan goes, you go."

A flock of yellow butterflies took flight from the knee-high grass, surrounding the pair in a yellow haze. She ran through the cluster of insects. "Where did they come from? They're all around me!"

"You must have done something good, baby girl."

"I did. I prayed for the boy in my dreams." *Tell him. No, don't ruin the moment.* The butterflies dissipated, and Daniela returned to her father's side. He opened the car door, and she climbed in. "Dad?"

"Yes?"

"Do you think the butterflies are for oily boy? Yesterday, I prayed that God would give him a friend if he needed one."

"Then the butterflies are for him."

"If he's real, I hope he loves butterflies as much as I do." Daniela smiled. "I think butterflies are quivering in my tummy."

"Are you sick?"

"No—I'm happy for him. I'll pray he finds love." She buckled her seatbelt. "How did you and Mom fall in love?"

"Big questions for a twelve-year-old."

"I'll be in high school next year."

"True. I'll tell you what I know: If love's a fish, she must be a pink salmon, swimmin' up a cold-water creek—troubled, tryin' somethin' mighty to find her intended."

"Mysterious."

"Good." They both laughed.

★ ★ ★

Cillian lay beside the brook, eyelids flickering closed. A bright yellow butterfly landed on his nose, waking him up. He fanned his face, and the butterfly flew away. "Not so fast." He ran after it, but it escaped.

"I'd be runnin' from me too. My luck isna so good. Next time, I'll be bringing ye a wee bit of food. Then, ye'll be stayin'."

The insect disappeared into the haze of the sky. "Visit me again, wherever yer from."

Freedom pushed time faster in Cillian's mind, but in reality, only half a day had passed since he had fallen asleep. The midday sun beat down on his neck, baking his pale skin tomato red. "Will I be findin' a place to sleep or food to eat?"

He glanced behind him.

Would his mother come for him?

Don't worry about what you will eat, where you will sleep, or what you will wear. He heard the voice speaking to him again. *The lilies of the field and birds of the air don't worry about these things, still I clothe them with splendor. Are you not more important than them?*

Cillian curved his hands around his eyes. "Is it a shed?" He walked, then ran.

He glanced around. No people were watching, so he inched closer and peered into the window of the little building. "It's vacant." He buried his hands in his pockets and stared at the cabin.

Would he be punished if someone came in and found him?

A howl in the distance encouraged him forward. He shouldered the splintered door, and it creaked upon its hinges. Gingerly, he tiptoed across the threshold and pushed his posterior against the door until it closed tightly, shutting the world out.

Bigger than his old bedroom, a cot was pushed against one wall, and against another wall stood an old wooden desk, decorated with a tattered book and a red vase holding a fresh yellow rose. Mama Kelley loved yellow roses. He relaxed. An oil lamp sat on the other end of the desk. He remembered how Mama Kelley would hold her Bible under the glow of her oil lamp and read him stories.

He picked up the paperback. "Anne of Green Gables," he whispered. *In my new home, I'll be readin' a book by the fireplace.*

He found a box of matches tucked beside the lamp and used one of them to light the wick. A warm glow bathed the walls, and Cillian spied a large, creased brown bag on the countertop beside the stove.

He peeked inside the bag. His mouth watered. Fresh fruit and vegetables—including a one-pound bag of potatoes and turnips—as well as a glass bottle of water and several flip-top cans of food were neatly arranged in the bag.

A yellowed paper stuck to the bottom of the bag.

He pulled it out.

Cursive writing scrawled in smudged black ink read:

Eat and drink. I will help you. You are not alone.

—Legna, Servant of the Most High

The letter bore the date 8 July 1981. "My birthday?" He frowned. *Why is there an old note at the bottom of a bag of fresh food?* His stomach growled. "Aye, patience." He rubbed his abdomen. "Food's comin' to ye, then."

No one was present to degrade his usage of his forefathers' language.

He limped in the direction of the stove, turned up the blue flame, and layered potatoes and cabbage in a cast iron skillet. Mama Kelley had let him cook with her on many occasions. She had teased, "No respectable woman wants to marry a man who can't cook. So you, God help me, will learn how to do more than boil water."

The vegetables tantalized his nostrils while fatigue crept into his bones. Gazing at the steam rising from his anticipated meal, he sank into the cot, a forty-year-old soul clothed in a twelve-year-old body.

Last Easter, he had attended church at Mama Kelley's house, and the pastor had said a prayer of thanksgiving. Cillian knelt on the bare floor, trying to remember the feeling of that prayer.

He bowed his head and talked to the calm voice.

"Are you there?" A whisper of breath tickled his lips. "Only Mama Kelley wanted me; dinna leave me. I may need yer help again verra soon. If you dinna want me, will ye be tellin' me? You dinnae have to live with me if you dinnae want to." He looked up, focusing on the wooden rafters. "I'm not the smartest, but I could love if given a chance."

Dinner bubbled in the background, and he licked his lips. His imagination blossomed. "Finn Family, yer dinner's ready. No—clean yer hands before goin' to the table." An imaginary mom, dad, and siblings ate dinner with him that night.

He chewed each piece of food until it was mush in his mouth, every drop of flavor sucked out before he licked his plate. *No reflection like in Mama Kelley's plates.*

His eyelids drooped. Time for bed.

He climbed beneath the bedding of the cot, inhaling the fresh scent of crisp sheets. The fragrance triggered a memory of flowers at the base of Mama Kelley's stone cottage. Tonight would be a night of big dreams: a plentiful table of food and a large family to share his newfound prosperity.

Finally, a safe place—home.

He yawned, and sleep enveloped his mind. But fulfilled dreams were for dreamers, not orphans.

14—Orphan Dreamer

"HURRY UP, ROSEBUD. THE *MACGYVER* rerun has almost started."

"I'm hurrying." Missing *MacGyver* embodied in the handsome form of Richard Dean Anderson was a mortal sin in Daniela's eyes. Inside Ethan's palatial home, Daniela pushed her friend's wheelchair into the elevator car and pressed the button for the basement.

"What's happening at school?"

"So much to tell. Where do I start?"

"The beginning. Don't leave out any details." They exited the elevator. A soft blue light cast the room in night shadows. Daniela gazed at the ceiling. A million stars twinkled. "Major cool!"

"It's a fiber-optic star ceiling. Parents had it installed."

"Sleeping beneath the stars."

"With my Rosebud," Ethan said. *Romantic.* Daniela's face flushed hot. "No mosquitoes. Dad already pitched our tent, and Mom loaded it with snacks." He reached for her hand. "Shall we?" His eyes twinkled. "To the stars, Rosebud."

She held his hand as a reluctant grin spread across her face. He had lost some of his grip. Chemo was a brat.

"Claire and Harry still dimmer than dead flashlights?" Ethan asked, forcing Daniela to shrug off her shyness.

"Batteries-rusted-and-leaking-acid dumb." Daniela explored their tent. "I can't believe their brains remember to tell their lungs how to breathe."

"Don't put up with their stupidity."

"It's easier to fight back when I have an ally." Daniela helped Ethan stand. "Trust me. I'm trying to bounce back." He wrapped his arm around her shoulder and sat on his air mattress. Two battery-operated lanterns cast a glow inside the tent. Ethan turned on a small television.

"I wish we had cable at my house."

"If you come to here every night, you can watch cable anytime you like."

"Not possible." *MacGyver's* theme music played, and Daniela hummed along. "Harry crushed a helpless spider."

"You hate spiders."

"I know, but not this one."

"Joan-of-Arc brave."

"Don't pick on me." She emptied the contents of her knapsack onto the tent floor. "Dad took me shopping."

"He did." Graham crackers, marshmallows, chips, and M&M's—Ethan's favorite—lay on top of a bright orange flyer.

"Almost forgot." She handed the flyer to Ethan. "Summer trip to the Smithsonian." She sat cross-legged. "If you go, I get to go."

"Count me in."

"Awesomeness."

"We'll get lost in the basement, discover ancient secrets, then make out." Ethan's face lit up.

"Ethan!"

"Rosebud."

"If we can steer clear of Claire and Harry . . . then I'm in." She opened a water bottle and gulped down half. If she kissed her best friend, would her nose bleed? A possible 'yes' to her question made her feel smaller than a speck of sand. "No kissing, though."

"You're breaking my heart." Ethan placed the flyer back inside Daniela's bag. "It's the closest I'll come to an archeological dig." He rubbed his amputated stump, and she slid her air mattress next to Ethan's.

"After I become a doctor, I'll figure out a way to regrow your legs, but for now, I'll dig, and you give the orders."

"I could get used to that. Tell me about the spider."

"He spoke; I understood." Daniela shrugged. Ethan gazed at her, his face registering no expression. "Say something. Don't leave me hanging."

He traced the lines in her palms with his finger. "You're special, Rosebud. I've always known that." His face turned red.

"Short-bus special."

"Stop putting yourself down."

"You sound like my parents."

"Maybe they're right."

"Not about everything." She thought about her dad's racist ideas but didn't want to tell Ethan and hurt his feelings. "There's more . . . weirdness."

"Spill it."

"That boy I told you about—oily boy—he not only still haunts my dreams, but now I can see him, feel him, and smell him when I'm awake."

"You're in love with him?"

"It's not like that. Dad wouldn't let me date a . . . boy anyways."

"Your dad wants you to be a lesbian?"

"No! Stop being difficult." Ethan was her bestie. If she couldn't talk honestly with him, who could she be honest with? "My dad's a racist." Her voice dropped to a whisper. "He doesn't like people with pale skin. I never told Dad that oily boy is umm . . . white." Ethan laughed.

"You promised not to laugh."

"Sorry. It's the way you're telling me. This isn't the secret of the century, Rosebud. We're not discussing Roswell, New Mexico, government conspiracies, and aliens. Besides, your dad can't be a racist. Newsflash—my skin is paler than yours."

"Not as pale as oily boy's. Think Casper, the ghost."

"Ghosts aren't real. Forget about him."

"Trust me. I've tried." She paused and grinned. "You're so jealous."

"So?" A sheepish grin tucked in between dimples.

The elevator bell chimed. Someone was entering their lair. "Who's that?" Daniela grabbed Ethan's arm.

"Oily boy coming to kill off his competition—me?" Ethan said, and Daniela slid into the crux of her friend's embrace. He pulled the blanket over them. "Stay close to me forever, Rosebud."

"Forever." Daniela closed her eyes and whispered, "You live. I live. You die. I die."

"So Romeo and Juliet." He kissed her cheek. Honeyed-warmth embraced her body, making her forget about the intruder. Prayers accomplish their purpose even when the person who utters them becomes distracted.

Tonight, Ethan Mohammed Solomon equaled a major distraction.

15—THE ORPHAN

COLD AIR PENETRATED CILLIAN'S DEEPEST parts, waking him.

He curled his toes, drew up his legs, and wrapped the cotton sheet around his frame. Beneath a full moon radiating a bright glow into his one-room home, his shivers wilted and then sprung up again, like a dandelion cast off by the wind. As he yawned, his breath formed a fine mist. He pursed his lips and blew again.

What makes hot breath turn to mist in a cold room?

Magic?

No. Magic didn't exist. Only cold reality.

He scanned the shed for firewood, crawled out of bed, and walked toward a stack of kindling in the corner. *Mama Kelley never liked coal.* Cillian lit a match and cast it onto the hearth as Mama Kelley had taught him. He stoked the tinder with an iron poker until a hearty fire danced between the iron gratings. Fragrances of burning maple and oak wafted through the shed. A new scent. A happy scent. A hopeful scent.

My mansion will be havin' grand fireplaces fit fer an English king. His smile burst into a full-blown laugh, and he forgot about the pain that wracked his little body. Jumping, he pumped his fists in the air.

Joe Sanders will never beat me again.

Never!

He filled a pot with water. Soon, scents of a scrumptious breakfast filled the shed. A soothing fire cast warmth over his body as he ate.

What should I do after breakfast?

* * *

Seven days of feasting and sleeping passed, with Cillian living happily as his body healed.

On the seventh day, he peered over the edge of the grocery bag. One yellow apple, one potato, and a can of green beans remained.

I shouldna have eaten so much. He brushed his clammy hands across frayed jeans. "I canna go home." The whisper seemed to remain on his lips instead of lifting heavenward.

Think.

Cillian swallowed hard, his eyes burning. "Where are Ye, gentle voice? I dinna want to starve."

A gentle voice: *Take a trip, explore the countryside, and look for a farm.*

"Got it. I'll be sleepin' in a stable, feedin' the animals, and eatin' the farmer's leftovers. Leftovers wouldna be as tasty as warm potatoes and cabbage."

He shrugged. He had eaten worse.

A mouse had perished in his hands after he had not eaten for seven days while living in Manchester. The mouse hadn't deserved to die. With a steady source of food, England's mice would live.

School. A calm whisper warmed his ear.

"Aye, then. I'll be findin' a school, then study and become the smartest lad, and I'll not have an empty grocery bag again." Cillian tiptoed to the lone frosty window and blew a mouthful of air, fogging the glass.

"I'm free." Freedom felt airy, prickling with possibilities. He climbed back into the warm cot; an explorer needed his rest. Soft snores bounced off the shed's walls.

★ ★ ★

In a cottage, on the other side of town, a woman named Martha Barry opened a letter.

The next child is coming.

She smiled, pocketed the note, and climbed the stairs, excited to prepare the spare bedroom. The blessed anticipation of the wait!

16—Orphan Dreamer

THE INTRUDER EXITED THE ELEVATOR, invading Ethan and Daniela's campsite. Daniela squeezed Ethan's hand until his fingers blanched. Footsteps thudded across the carpet. A tall, square-jawed man appeared in front of the tent, dropped to his knees and sat in the doorway of their tent.

Who was the stranger--a burglar, a murderer, or both? Tension laced up Daniela's spine as she held her breath.

"Uncle Jakob!" Ethan would have run into his uncle's arms if he could. Daniela exhaled, and her muscles relaxed.

"There's my troublemaker. Who's the beautiful girl, Casanova?"

"Rosebud." Ethan grinned wide, and Daniela looked at her feet as she shook Uncle Jakob's hand. Ethan explained that his uncle was his mother's brother, a professor and a director of the Israel Antiquities Authority. He had studied archeology and was an expert on the Torah, Bible, and Quran. Daniela asked the professor more questions than a lawyer cross-examining a witness.

"What are blood moons?" she asked.

"They are simply lunar eclipses," Professor Jakob said. "A lunar eclipse occurs when a full moon passes in the earth's shadow. The moon appears red because the light from the sun is bent due to the earth's atmosphere. This is why sunsets appear in hues of red or orange."

"I love sunsets."

"They're romantic." He glanced at Ethan. "A tetrad of blood moons that falls on certain Jewish holidays is a type of time stamp."

"For what?"

"'*The sun will turn into darkness and the moon into blood before the great and terrible day of the Lord.*' The Hebrew prophet Joel wrote those words."

"Creepy." Ethan shivered. Daniela rolled onto her belly and kicked her legs up. "My mom already told me about Jewish feasts."

"Are you Jewish?"

"No—but we're definitely not pagans." The trio laughed. "Mom believes understanding Jewish holidays is important for my calling."

"A special girl." Uncle Jakob nudged Ethan and winked.

"Stop! Rosebud and I aren't like that."

She wished they were.

"Too bad." His uncle ate a handful of Doritos.

"I'm not special." Daniela ate a handful of M&M's. "Mom's trying to make me relevant because the kids at school live to hate me."

"Claire and Harry define misery, though," Ethan said.

"Taking up for your girl . . . adorable." Uncle Jakob winked. "Rosebud, maybe your parents know something they're not willing to tell you. Don't despise your journey before it begins. In the end, you may like it. What's this?" Ethan's uncle pulled the flyer from Daniela's bag and read it. "A trip to the Smithsonian. Ethan, take your girl on this trip."

"Ethan's dying to go on an archeological dig," Daniela said. "When he recovers, may we join you one day?"

"Anytime. Anyplace. Anywhere. Bedtime for me." The professor got up. "Nice to meet you, Rosebud. And Ethan . . ." He rubbed Ethan's bald head. "Let the girl sleep."

"Uncle Jakob!"

"Casanova. Don't let my nephew fool you, Rosebud. Boys don't camp with girls they don't like." Daniela had never heard of that rule. Maybe her dad was right—girls were safer. Ethan's supercool uncle entered the elevator and disappeared.

17—The Orphan

FRIGID DARKNESS LAUGHED AT A few stubborn coals flickering upon the hearth.

The cover of night would block prying eyes. Time for an adventure. Cillian swung his legs over the side of his cot.

He stuffed a glass bottle of water and a flashlight into his tattered knapsack. A blue jumper fit snugly around his neck. He slipped on his trainers, laced them tightly, and exited the cottage. His flashlight illuminated his steps, and the algid English fall evening chilled him.

"Gentle voice, can ye be helpin' me find a farm like we agreed?"

The moon cast a cloak of shifting shadows. The crickets' chorus ceased and quiet reigned. The mist lifted. He rubbed his eyes.

A stone cottage?

A haze seemed to hug the rocky walls. He shuffled toward it. Ten minutes later, he crouched near a bush. He inhaled, and his mouth watered as the scent of fresh onions, carrots, tomatoes, and greens filled his nostrils. "I cannaa take the vegetables."

Bleating sheep and a mooing cow agreed.

He tiptoed closer.

A vision of happiness moved behind glass panes. A family of five—father, mother, and three smiling children—bowed their heads. The father's lips moved while steam clouded their faces. He rested his hands and chin on the windowsill, drinking in every detail. No screaming or beatings. Everyone ate: potatoes, cabbage, and roasted chicken.

The family finished dinner, and the father brought in dessert, apple pie with ice cream. Cillian licked his lips. Mama Kelley had often baked wonderful apple pies, and he had stuffed his cheeks so full that he'd almost choked. He covered his mouth, stifling a laugh as he watched the smallest child stealthily feed the rest of his cabbage to the family dog.

To be a family dog! His stomach rumbled.

"I'll be comin' back in the morn, tryin' to blend in with the family somehow." Cillian buried his cold hands in his pockets and skedaddled back to his shed.

He stopped at his launderette—the bubbling stream—and scrubbed his tattered clothes in the brisk water, then washed his body. Now shivering in his wet clothes, he ran back to the shed and pushed open the wooden door. His trainers squeaked as he slopped water along the wooden floor. With his skin now numb and bluish, he threw tinder on the hearth.

A fire roared to life.

He disrobed, wrung out his clothes and trainers, and hung them beside the fireplace.

Cillian slept until the morning sun peeked through frosted windowpanes. He rolled from the bed and shuffled to the fireplace. Fog puffed from his mouth as he pulled his hardened clothes from the fireplace mantle and stepped into his jeans.

Time to go and face life.

He sauntered along the grassy path back to the cozy cottage and ducked behind a lone weeping willow, watching.

Every face seemed to glow, almost unnaturally.

The flowers were redder and pinker than any Cillian had ever seen at Mama Kelley's house, the scents sweeter. The scene before him seemed otherworldly, like a dream. He pinched his arm. It hurt. *Not a dream.*

Three children played and laughed outside. Each carried a small backpack across their shoulders. The happy lady planted a long kiss on the lips of a man in overalls, with a tool belt draped at his hips.

Cillian wiped his scabbed lips. Drops of blood salted his mouth, so he pursed his lips together until the taste subsided.

The children ran down a cobblestone path, past weeping willow trees and flower beds, and the happy mother followed her brood as the father walked in the opposite direction. *One day, I'll be takin' care of my family like the happy father.*

"I hope Mrs. Barry has snacks," one of them said.

Cillian followed from a distance, his head down.

After ten minutes, the happy family strolled into a town square and stopped. Quaint cottages circled a park with swings and a tall slide.

The orphan stared at the red sign above green doors. The word *Schoolhouse* was painted in big red letters. "Dinna be afraid." He set his jaw into a stubborn smile and started forward. *Be brave.*

He stood in the doorway of the one-room school and looked around. Again, colors seemed brighter. Voices seemed softer and sweeter.

Was this heaven?

Students turned in their chairs and stared at him.

Not likely. He swallowed, hard. The temptation to run burned in his leg muscles, but his growling stomach glued his feet to the white-washed wooden floor.

A smiling woman with a black-and-gray bun atop her head strode toward him. The corners of her eyes creased in fine lines, and her soft gray-blue eyes lit up. She sat on a stool and studied his face. He smiled and then creased his brow to mirror the teacher's expression. *She's cryin'. What ha' I done now?*

He shifted his gaze to the floor, and she swept the bangs from his eyes. "My name is Mrs. Barry." She cleared her throat. "What's your name?"

"Cillian Finn."

"Let's find you a special seat." She placed her hand on his back, guiding him to his seat. A whimper escaped his lips, and he arched reflexively. The teacher retracted her hand. She grasped his hand and led him to the one empty desk. Paper and pencil lay on the desk. "Class, we have a special new student. His name is Cillian. Everyone, welcome him."

"Hi Cillian, welcome to our classroom," the students stated in unison. Their faces seemed to glow.

Were they real?

A smile punctuated all of Mrs. Barry's sentences. *I love her.* Cillian twirled his new pencil between his fingers. *School will be fun.*

He sat in an empty desk next to one of the children from the happy house. "Hello," she said. "My name's Suzanne, but my friend's call me Sponge."

"Hi, Sponge." Cillian pulled one of her braids.

"That hurt." *She's real.*

"Sorry."

After class, he dawdled by his desk. His gaze trained on Mrs. Barry's desk, where a red apple sat. His stomach growled. No food for lunch and no food at home. The apple was just sitting there. *I canna be beggin' her fer food. She may ask me where my parents live, sendin' me back to my mum. Should I take the apple? No. I dinna want to get in trouble.*

"Cillian, did you enjoy class?"

"Yes, ma'am." He stuffed his hands in his pockets and stared at Mrs. Barry. Kindness seemed to reach out and hug him. "Gather your things."

Dinna ask for food today. No need to be disgustin' her yet. A growl erupted from his stomach; he held his belly until the sound ceased. He picked up his pencil and notebook, then shuffled toward the classroom door, pausing to dare another glance at the bright red apple.

"Cillian," Mrs. Barry called.

"Ma'am?"

"Where are you from?"

"Ireland."

"I thought I heard an Irish accent."

"I'm sorry," he said with an English accent.

"Why?"

He shrugged.

"Where are your parents?"

"Gone."

"Did someone take them?"

"I dinna believe so."

"Hmmm . . ." She hesitated. "I'll need to call the authorities."

"Please don't." Cillian dashed to her and gripped Mrs. Barry's arm. "Please." His brave resolve melted, and tears ran down his cheeks. "Let me be stayin' here for a wee bit. It's like paradise, and I've been a good boy. Will ye be lettin' me stay?"

She smiled. "I'm making chicken dumplings and cherry pie. Come for dinner. Do you like cherry pie?"

"How does it taste?"

"Tart and sweet all at the same time."

"I'm thinkin' I will." He licked his lips.

"You'll stay for a while."

"Can I stay—I mean, thanks."

Mrs. Barry held her pupil's hand. Her shoes clacked along the mosaic cobblestone street as they walked to her cozy flat.

He catalogued each detail.

Beige and brownstone homes lined the narrow street, and lime-green glass lamps illuminated the walkways, casting halos around the heads of passersby. Dwarf-sized evergreens grew from window boxes, and bird feeders dangled from doorposts. Children played, mothers cooked, and fathers walked home from work. Paradise indeed.

"The village is beautiful, like a picture. Where are we, Mrs. Barry?"

"Bibury, England."

"I'll be wantin' to live here forever."

After a short walk, Cillian entered Mrs. Barry's home. Inside the flat, a man cleared his throat. Goosebumps surfaced on Cillian's arm. *How could I be so careless? Why did I trust anyone? No man has ever treated me kindly.* He backed toward the doorway and covered his buttocks.

"Come on," Mrs. Barry said in a cheery voice. He willed himself to trust again, but fear paralyzed him. A man with curly white hair, a large belly, and a warm smile strolled around the corner. He wore a red flannel shirt and overalls.

"Father Christmas." Cillian gasped.

"Martha, who do we have here?" the man's baritone voice boomed. He bent down. His blue eyes radiated warmth.

"Cillian's a new student of mine, and I invited him to eat dinner and stay with us."

"Wonderful! Come on in and make yourself at home." The man extended his hand. "Grandpa Barry's the name. The rest of the children call me that."

Cillian looked down, then forced himself to hold out his own hand. Grandpa Barry shook it. "Pleased to make your acquaintance, my boy. Let's eat."

The orphan bit the edge of his lip, quarantining a full-blown smile. He dared to look into the man's eyes, where he saw an unfamiliar expression.

Kindness?

"Don't be shy. I've never gobbled up a lad." He patted his belly. "Grandma keeps me well fed."

"Yes, sir."

"My first priority is to give you a proper bath," Mrs. Barry said.

"I used to take a wash off at Mama Kelley's house."

"You're in practice." Mrs. Barry climbed the stairs; Cillian followed. "Let's get you clean and ready for the Almighty's big plans."

"I dinnae ken anyone had plans for me."

"It's a lang road, Cillian, that's no goat a turnin'." She spoke in a thick Scottish burr. He knew she had said in a Highlander's English, "Don't lose heart in dark times, things can't keep going in the same direction forever."

"Are ye Scottish too?"

"I've known a few Scots in my time." She entered a room upstairs. Blue walls, a bedspread decorated with cars, and a small wooden desk anchored beneath a lone window welcomed him. "How could a wonderful boy like you not have a family?"

"Butterflies come from cocoons. Could I be comin' from one of those?"

"Being afraid doesn't give you permission to lie."

"My mum lives in Manchester. I dinnae ken where my da is."

"I already knew, Cillian." He looked up. Her face radiated warmth. "Mortals wounded you. You'll stay with us until Yahweh decides differently."

"I'd like that."

In her eyes, a bright flash softened to a glow. "This room will be yours."

"My own room!" He embraced his teacher, then pushed back. "Yahweh? You know Mama Kelley's friend?"

"I've been knowin' Him a great while." She laid out some clothes, including a blue sweatshirt and matching sweatpants. "Wear this outfit for school tomorrow. The weather will be chilly."

"And warm pajamas?" Cillian caressed the soft blue-green flannel. "Thanks."

"I'll draw a hot bath." She opened one closet door and then another. "Soap. Shampoo. Bathe and scrub your hair while Mr. Barry and I cook dinner. How about that?"

He followed the kind woman into the bathroom. A large white box sat on bronze, clawlike feet. "I'll be drownin' in that thing!"

"It's not deep." Mrs. Barry turned off the faucet. "Undress."

"Did I do something wrong? Ar-r-re ye goin' to thrash me?"

"Whatever made you think such a thing?"

"Ye told me to undress."

"You must undress to take a bath . . . like when you take a wash off." Mrs. Barry stepped out of the bathroom and called downstairs, "Grandpa, please start dinner."

Slowly, he unbuttoned his shirt.

"Yes, dear." The deep voice echoed in Cillian's ears, and for the first time, a man's voice made him feel protected.

Mrs. Barry reentered the bathroom. "Cillian . . ." She stumbled, slapping her hand across her lips. Moisture rimmed her eyelids.

He stood by the tub. "Are ye okay, Mrs. Barry? If something's wrong, I'll fix it. Just give me a chance."

She looked away, avoiding Cillian's eyes. "Climb into the tub."

He stepped in, the water lapping his skin. "Water's warm. I think I love baths."

She's cryin', but why?

"Finish bathing, we'll see you downstairs."

He washed his skin gently, then scrubbed his scalp. After rinsing his black locks with warm water, years of grime floated in the bathtub. Skin blemished with scabs and scars now shone.

A soft knock. "I have a towel for you." The door opened, and Mrs. Barry entered.

"Are ye an angel, Mrs. Barry?"

Silence, then she smiled. "The human or the heavenly kind?"

"There's a difference?"

"Quite."

After his bath, he stood behind a privacy screen and dressed. The warm flannel pajamas hung loosely about his shoulders. "My head doesna itch anymore." He walked from behind the dressing screen.

"Hair like a raven's, clean, lighter than a feather."

"Should I be takin' a bath every day?"

"I insist." Mrs. Barry laughed. She hugged him, and he melted into her arms. "Yahweh has loved you always, Cillian."

"I dinna feel loved . . . until now."

"The fact is, you are loved." A smile concluded her chiding as the pair climbed down the stairs. The cozy fragrances of chicken and baked cherries made his mouth water. While Cillian lost himself in his plate of chicken and dumplings, followed by a huge slice of cherry pie, Mr. and Mrs. Barry placed their forks on the table. The couple watched the famished child devour three plates of food.

His meal finally finished, Cillian's eyelids sagged as he struggled to hold the fork. Sleep won. Grandpa Barry guided him to his bed, and Mrs. Barry read a story about Daniel in the lions' den.

"Can you read me a Bible story every night? Mama Kelley did."

"I will." Mrs. Barry tucked Cillian under an old patchwork quilt. "Sleep. If you're going to bother dreaming, dream big."

They both kissed Cillian's cheeks and then retreated to the family room, holding hands in front of the fireplace. Mrs. Barry's old rocking chair creaked in rhythm with the dancing flames.

"His backside is riddled with scars and bruises. He thought I was going to beat him when I asked him to undress for his bath."

"We'll help him heal, like every other child Yahweh has sent to us." Grandpa Barry dabbed a lone tear from his wife's cheek. "Every child is a seed packed full of promises and potential, and we must be careful what soil we plant these little seeds in.

"I was starting to think He wasn't sending another." Mrs. Barry's blue-gray eyes caressed her husband's face.

He responded, leaning in for a kiss. "I'd like to hope parents have grown kinder toward their children."

18—Orphan Dreamer

DANIELA'S RECORD OF UNANSWERED PRAYERS extended longer than her Pocahontas ponytail.

Or so she believed.

Less than forty-eight hours after their weekend sleepover, Ethan couldn't move his non-amputated leg. His oncologist performed an MRI of Ethan's back and diagnosed cancer metastasis to the spine.

Really?

What had Ethan done to deserve Yahweh's wrath? If Yahweh planned on killing Ethan, why torture him first? How could He be trusted to not do the same to her? Gone too soon. Killed off by a *loving* God before he reached his prime and his dreams. Wasn't the Great I AM supposed to love humans?

Rejection from rude humans like Claire and Harry was intolerable.

But when Yahweh rejected a kid—His kid—and said no for no good reason—that was unforgivable—a hypoxic reality with no chance for survival. Powerful currents of negative thoughts swirled inside Daniela's mind, sucking her into riptides of depression before spitting her out in deep waters.

Still, in public, Daniela fought to tread water, painting a brave smile across her face until her facial muscles ached.

In private, she drowned in a sea of depression. Her belly concave, she hadn't eaten for a day. Sitting cross-legged on the floor of the Alachua County Library, her eyes tracked the words on the page, searching for hope.

Alternate realities could be found in a book.

But in her world, she was erecting a wall brick by brick between her and Yahweh, shutting out His voice.

Forget praying for oily boy! Daniela screamed inside as she gripped the edges of her favorite novel. As she read, she imagined that she was Diana Barry meeting Anne at Green Gables's annual ice cream party. In Anne's world, bosom friendships could begin over lemonade and ice cream. Friendships that lasted a lifetime, not a few fretful months.

Hope in the form of warmth settled deep inside Daniela. Was this Yahweh extending another life raft—an olive branch?

Should she trust Him and reach for it?

Or was this another mirage?

Daniela hugged herself, attempting to keep the feeling inside. But she refused to lean fully on this burst of hope. Charlie might be right: Ethan might die, and if he did, would Daniela meet her Anne before Ethan said goodbye for the last time?

"Daniela, time to go." Her father walked around the corner. A slight limp slowed his gait, but he was strong and working again. "Kiddo, what're you reading?"

"*Anne of Green Gables*." Daniela raised the book.

"You're almost in high school. How many times are you going to read that book? Aren't there any nice girls at your school?"

"I'm looking. Promise."

"Don't limit yourself. Your kindred spirit may not be a carbon copy of your imaginary friend."

"You forbid me to make friends with boys, especially pale-skinned boys, and then pick on my version of Anne. Maybe I'm a tomboy, and pretty girls will never want to be my friend."

"I'm trying to protect your heart. That's all."

"Maybe you're suffocating it," she whispered.

"What did you say?"

"Nothing."

"It's a Southern thing. I've never known a pale-skinned boy to respect a brown-skinned girl's virtue and not treat her like a—"

"Prostitute. Dad, I'm not that kind of girl."

"Who did you learn that word from?" He frowned.

"From Mom."

"Why in the world—"

"You should be happy I'm not a hooker."

"Watch your language!"

"Changing the subject. Two new girls, Prissy and Ruby sat next to me at lunch yesterday. Prissy cheers for the football team, and Ruby dates Jeremy, the middle-school hunk. I'm not sure if they'll like me. I'm not a cheerleader, and I'm definitely not datable. Nosebleeds."

"You're not datable because you're only twelve." He shook his head. "That girl is growing up way too fast, and for the record, you only named two girls, Danny Rose. Two girls I'm not keen on you spending much time with."

"I'm trying, Dad." She tossed the book back onto the library cart.

"Attitude check."

"Check." She flashed a grin.

"What's got your goat?"

"Sometimes my feelings about my self-worth agree with Claire and Harry: I'm not good enough. Ethan would run away from me if he wasn't an amputee. I am fighting back. The best way I know how—keeping hope alive by reading about what could be my own Anne Shirley friend while I sit in the peanut stands and watch my classmates enjoy their friendships." She shrugged. "Finding a true-blue girlfriend isn't easy for me. I'm different, so it's a treasure hunt for the rarest jewel. You did call me Indiana Jones, remember?"

"I do." Her dad wiped his eyes with the back of his hand. "Keep reading your map and searching for clues. You'll find your Anne."

"Thanks for believing in me."

"We've got church tonight, so let's get going."

"Can I wait in the car and read while you go inside?"

"Hiding in the car with your nose in a book?"

"It's safe there."

"Don't pull away from Yahweh."

"It's not Him. It's the kids at church. They don't include me. It's getting old—purposefully asking to be rejected by hanging with those jerks."

"The religious rulers never included Yeshua either."

"But I'm not Jesus."

"Don't remind me . . . prostitutes. Hookers." He laughed. "You'll find a way. You have to, Orphan Dreamer. For our sake."

Could he please stop with the Orphan-Dreamer-save-the-world tripe?

After checking out two books for a book report, Daniela stuffed them into her backpack, and she and her father climbed into the car. Once seated, she laid her head on her father's shoulder, and he laid his cane over his knee. For the next fifteen minutes, they meandered along neighborhood roads to a church with a tall, white steeple.

Bong . . . bong . . . bong. Daniela looked upward until her eyes found the church bells swinging in the white steeple.

She loved those bells, but they were about the only thing she liked about that place. She inhaled deeply, clenched her fists, and prepared for battle.

"Your mom and I won't live forever."

"I know."

"It's time for you to secure a friend—somewhere, somehow." What was her father not telling her?

Was he dying as well?

Daniela's heart raced, and her father's shoes scraped along the concrete sidewalk as his cane tapped out a hurried rhythm. "Don't be late to youth group."

"Let's make a deal: I'll go with you to the adult church."

"No. Learn about Yeshua with children your own age." Austin took a book from her grip. "Get your nose out of these pages and talk to people. Many of the neighborhood boys ignored me before Chuck and I became the best of friends." A parent's angry words have a way of ripping a kid's bruised heart into pieces, but she was a quiet fighter.

It was the friend part that kept giving her trouble.

Her father planted a kiss on her nose. "Sometimes, I don't know how to help you."

"Don't keep secrets."

"You're not old enough to know everything."

"Okay. So here's my secret: Indiana Jones—I don't want to be like him," she said flippantly. Stubbornness was coded into Cavanaugh DNA.

"You may not have a choice."

"You shouldn't have made that promise to Yahweh without asking me, Dad."

"I didn't feel as though I had a choice." He lifted his chin. "But it's done, and a vow cannot be broken between man and God." He walked away in silence. Stopping, he looked back. "I'm scared for you."

"Don't be. I've survived this long."

"Existing isn't living. Maybe your friend's no spitfire redhead, but don't reject the love of a loyal friend, whoever she is."

"No matter how that friend looks?"

"No matter."

Yeah right. He'd already excluded 70 percent of America's population—white people. Daniela quietly chuckled. "Come get me as soon as church lets out. Don't leave me in here one extra moment, and I'll forgive you—agreed?" Daniela bit her lower lip, then smiled.

"Pinky swear."

"Forgiven." Daniela walked to her classroom, and as soon as she entered, pale-skinned classmates stared at the brown intruder. She looked down at the carpet, trying to find a pit to jump into.

You can do it. Keep walking.

"Come on in, Daniela." Mrs. Madison's words rolled off her tongue in a slow drawl.

"Thanks," she whispered, scanning the room. At one table, children played games. Don't interrupt. That's rude.

Daniela walked up to a group of girls who had gathered around a box of books, but they retreated to another area of the room, leaving her alone. By now, she should be immune to rejection, but did an abscess feel better the second time around? She sat by a plastic bin with two Barbie dolls, toys left behind from the younger kids' Sunday school class.

Dolls make me feel like a baby. She sighed, keeping the dolls company until free time ended.

"Class, time for the lesson. Clean up the games."

Daniela jumped to her feet, abandoning her plastic companions and feeling thankful that everyone would be forced to sit together so she wouldn't stick out.

She waited until everyone sat down, then chose a chair closest to the group. Last time, she had taken a seat first, only to have all the other kids sit on the opposite side of the room.

Mrs. Madison's story enraptured Daniela as the teacher read about Prince Jonathan saving his friend's life from the prince's angry father.

Daniela closed her eyes, imagining that she and Ethan were traveling back in time to 1018 BC to meet the prince and his friend. If she could time travel, maybe she could save Ethan's life too, proving Charlie wrong. A smile grew across Daniela's face. The story ended. "I'd like to time travel to Prince Jonathan's world," she blurted out.

"Lame-boy could join you, weirdo." Harry sucked on a lollipop.

"Don't talk like that in Sunday school, Harry. It's not Christian," Mrs. Madison said as Daniela's face flushed, and her eyes begged to cry. *Don't show emotion.* She blinked back her tears and stuffed her despair into a vault.

Do it.

Take up for yourself.

"Takes one to know one," Daniela said.

"Don't you dare, girl," Harry said. "I'll smash you like a pancake."

"You're fat enough."

"Prince Jonathan's dead." Harry stood up. "If you run into him, it means you're dead. Like your spider friend . . . Not a bad idea: Daniela Rose Cavanaugh dead. Let's annihilate her!"

"You better hope I live, or you're toast."

"Huh?"

"Time travel's a fairy tale, dummy," Claire said. *But not your father smashing your mother's face.* Daniela rolled her eyes.

"Settle down. We're not in a gladiator arena," the Sunday school teacher said, preventing Daniela from verbalizing her retort.

Daniela stiffened as she realized Claire was right—traveling with Ethan on an adventure to a faraway land was impossible. Hope escaped her soul like a butterfly, and dark thoughts filled the void, sinking her dreams inside an underwater coffin of negative thoughts.

Harry assassinated Mister Spider.

Ethan's sicker than death and couldn't travel.

Maybe Yahweh only answered the prayers of pretty girls like Claire, or maybe Daniela's requests were Goliath-sized miracles found only in the pages of the Bible.

"Don't worry, Danny Rose." Mrs. Madison rested her hand on her pupil's shoulder. "It's okay to dream." *But it was best to stop a runaway train.*

"I don't like nightmares," Daniela replied.

After the story, the kids completed their assignments before eating sandwiches. No one spoke a word to Daniela. They didn't even look at her.

She must be invisible.

Daniela pinched her arm to make sure she was still real. Better to be invisible than ridiculed. What was real?

Daniela blinked her eyes, wondering if the scene before her would evaporate like a mirage. It didn't.

Too bad.

Finally, her father arrived. As they left, he asked, "How was youth church?"

"Great. I sat beside my two favorite friends during game time." Daddy was getting better; there was no need to upset him again.

"I knew you would make friends. Invite them to your birthday party—okay?"

"If you want." Daniela reached over and found her father's protective hand. After they arrived home, she changed into her favorite pink pajamas, knelt, and prayed. "Yahweh"—she paused, climbing over a mountain of doubt—"I'm trying to trust You. Honest I am. Don't take Ethan. Please don't."

Silence.

She slipped beneath her covers and faded into sleep. Her eyes tracked right to left, faster than the ceiling fan that rotated above. A girl's heart possesses enough space to truly adore only one boy.

Daniela loved Ethan.

19—Orphan Dreamer

Thursday, November 18, 1993
Gainesville, Florida

"MOM!" THE NIGHT-LIGHT ILLUMINATED DANIELA'S sheets. Pools of blood coated white linens. Stains drenched the front of her pink silk pajamas. Blood gushed like a waterfall from her nose. "Mom, come here! I'm dying!"

"Danny?" Her mother's footsteps pounded the floor toward Daniela's bedroom. "I'm coming, baby!" She clicked on the wall light. "Oh, Lord Jesus!" Mrs. Cavanaugh dropped to her knees. "Austin! Austin!"

It would take some time for Daniela's father to hobble down the hallway, so Jeanette ran to the bathroom, returned with moist towels, and sopped up as much blood as she could. "You're going to be okay, Danny Rose."

"Mom, I'm frightened."

"The bleeding will stop. I promise."

"It's not that. I'm scared because of why I'm bleeding."

"What do you mean?"

"Something evil's been born. It wants to kill me and everyone."

"How do you know?"

"I never had a dream like this." Blood sprayed from Daniela's nose and splattered her mother's nightgown.

"Shh, don't talk. We're going to the hospital."

"But we can't afford it."

"Don't worry."

Her father hobbled into the room. "What happened?"

"A nosebleed, Dad, nothing to worry about." Danny clamped a moist rag to her nose.

Jeanette yanked her daughter's sheets back, revealing pools of blood. "Nothing to worry about! My little girl is bleeding to death. The dreams about that boy have to stop." Her mother's hands formed into fists. "Stop encouraging her, Austin!"

"But, I didn't—" Austin's shoulders rounded.

"Mom, it wasn't the boy." Daniela had never seen her mother take an angry posture like that before. "Besides, he's helpless."

"It's her *calling*, Jeanette."

Daniela's mother whipped her head around and stared at her husband, seething. "Her calling?"

"What are you guys talking about?"

"Stay out of it, Daniela Rose." Jeanette anchored her fists above her hips. "Do you want her to bleed to death like I almost did after she was born?"

"Of course not—"

"What are you, a father or vampirish slave driver?"

Austin clutched his chest. "I made a promise." He knelt beside his only child's bed. "It's God's will—not mine. Can't you understand?"

"No—I cannot." Jeanette's voice dropped to a whisper. "Is God a bloodthirsty vampire who does nothing to stop my daughter's pain?"

"What of her nightmares, the boy—the Glass Tattoo?" he said.

"I don't care about the boy." Her mom threw a bloody towel across the room. "He's not even real, and why did you have to take the diamond from Tibet?"

"Without the vow, Daniela never would have been. That was the deal."

"You're delusional. Selfish." She threw the soiled sheets at her husband. "Put those in the washing machine!"

Austin recoiled from her words.

"Who's Tibet, and what diamond? Diamonds are worth lots of money. Let's sell it, and then I can go the hospital." Daniela leaned forward. Her world spun. She was losing blood fast. Light-headed, she crashed back into her bed.

"And sell your birthright?" Her dad shook his head.

"This isn't a Bible story," her mother seethed. "It's our only little girl."

"Jeanette, don't upset the child."

"The child? She's your daughter!"

"Jeanette, please. I'm trying my best." He hugged the stained sheets to his chest.

"Try harder! Call 911. We're taking her to the hospital. Enough is enough!"

"I'll call, then warm the car and follow." Head down, Austin shuffled out of Daniela's room.

Fifteen minutes later, the Cavanaugh family arrived at the same hospital where she'd been born, Alachua General. Another three washcloths had been soaked with blood, and Daniela's world rotated.

"Sit down, honey." A woman with kind eyes helped Daniela's mother into a chair while her daughter was moved to a hospital stretcher.

In the distance, Daniela heard a *tap . . . shuffle . . . tap . . . shuffle . . . Daddy's coming.* She smiled and then frowned. "Mom, don't scream at Dad, okay?"

"Your dad will be fine. I'm worried about you."

"Mrs. Cavanaugh," the kind nurse said, "we'll take good care of your daughter."

"Thank you."

"Ma'am, what's your name?" Daniela asked the nurse.

"Anne with an *e*."

"You see, Mom?"

The nurse smiled, wrapped a blood pressure cuff around Daniela's arm, slipped a pulse oximeter on her finger, then glanced over her shoulder as a man dressed in a white coat entered. "Her blood pressure is low, doc."

"Let's place an intravenous line and give her some fluids," the doctor said.

"Will it hurt?" Daniela asked.

"Just a little," the doctor said. "We'll check her hemoglobin level and give blood, if necessary. When did the bleeding start?" He turned to Mrs. Cavanaugh.

"I'm not sure. Danny Rose woke me with her screams. I ran into her bedroom, and there was blood splattered across her sheets."

"Has she had a nosebleed before?"

"Yes." Her mother hesitated and cleared her throat. "Nothing like this one."

"And you're just now bringing her in to be seen?"

"They've never been this bad. We've spoken to her pediatrician."

"Were you going to wait until she bled out to bring her in?"

"Please don't talk to my mom that way." Daniela tried to sit up but collapsed onto the stretcher. "She's trying," she said in a quiet voice.

"Let's get you into a hospital gown and take off these filthy clothes." The nurse slipped Daniela's shirt over her head. "What's this, now?" Anne glared at Daniela's father as he shuffled into the room and leaned over his daughter.

"She's black-and-blue on her back, buttocks, and thighs." The doctor stopped writing his report. "How did this happen?"

"I don't know." Austin leaned in and studied the marks.

"We've heard that before." Nurse Anne rolled her eyes.

I wish Nurse Anne's name wasn't spelled with an e. My friend Anne wouldn't talk like that to my rafiki.

It had been the dream; something had beaten her up, but how could the doctor and nurse be convinced of that?

Think hard, Danny Rose.

Austin looked pitiful—vulnerable, really—bent over his cane. His knuckles blanched as he gripped the stick. "We don't beat our Daniela, if that's what you're suggesting."

"Are your parents hurting you?" the doctor asked.

"No," Daniela said. "My dad's fighting cancer and Mom's doing all she can. It's my dreams—my nightmares. I got bruises before, but I didn't tell my parents."

"You should've told us, Daniela Rose Cavanaugh." Even though her voice was stern, Jeanette interlaced her fingers with Daniela's.

"I'll tell the truth from now on. I don't want you and Dad getting into trouble."

"The truth is always best," her mother said.

"Whatever hurts the boy in my dreams hurts me too. My body aches in that same place for days. Sometimes I bruise, but the pain goes away when I pray for him. I guess the pain is a reminder, like your timer on the stove." She looked at her mother for approval. "There's more. I can talk to spiders, frogs, and ducklings, and they talk back."

"Sounds odd to me," the doctor said. "Are y'all part of a cult?"

"No," Austin said. "We're followers of Yeshua."

"You mean Jesus?" the doctor asked, and Austin nodded. "Jesus freaks—same thing," the doctor said beneath his breath.

"'They will hate you for My name's sake,'" Austin whispered.

"Are you preaching at me, boy?"

"No, sir." Austin crossed his arms.

"I'm a regular girl with a weird problem." Daniela turned toward the wall. "I'm a freak—so what?"

Jeanette knelt beside Daniela's hospital bed. "You're the bravest girl I know, but next time, tell your father and me. We'll help."

"I don't know if you can, Mom."

"How come?"

"I think something weird is happening to me—something my science teacher wouldn't be able to explain either, something no parent can fix."

"Maybe it's your hormones," the nurse interjected. "You're almost a young lady."

"Mothers can fix anything, Danny Rose." Jeanette caressed Daniela's cheek. "Even hormones."

"Not this, Mom. I can't explain it. I just know."

"Your knowing—Yeshua's voice," Jeanette said. "I understand."

The doctor walked to the doorway. "Anne, hang a unit of blood if her hemoglobin is less than six."

"Yes, Doctor," Anne replied.

"Danny Rose." Her father coddled her hand. "Next birthday, we'll tell you about something special—a secret."

"Next time," the doctor paused. "Bring the girl in. Don't worry about your little secrets."

Anne started the normal saline infusion and exited the room, returning later to start a blood transfusion. As the blood dripped, Daniela's father held her hand. "Sacrifice runs through a hero's veins. It's almost time."

"For what, Daddy?"

"War." He smiled weakly.

THE CRUCIBLE

He sent a man before them, even Joseph, who was
sold for a servant: Whose feet they hurt with fetters:
he was laid in iron: Until the time that his word came:
the word of the LORD tried him. The king sent and
loosed him; even the ruler of the people, and let him
go free. He made him lord of his house, and ruler of
all his substance.

—Psalms 105:17-21

20—THE ORPHAN

A FIRE CRACKLED IN THE hearth as a blueberry cobbler cooled on the windowsill above the kitchen sink. Molten pools of berry lava bubbled atop the crust as steam escaped, sharing a summertime's fruity aroma.

Chin resting on his hands, Cillian sat at the kitchen table and watched the dessert settle.

"Happy birthday!" Grandpa Barry said, startling Cillian as he struck a match and lit thirteen candles atop a skillet of jalapeño corn bread that sat on the kitchen table. "What's your wish?"

"To live with you forever." Cillian tugged at the silver-blue wrapping paper of his gift, revealing a shiny, mint-condition 1994 silver dollar. "American money?"

"In case your journey leads you across the Atlantic."

"But I dinna want to be leavin' you and Grandma Barry."

"We'll be with you wherever you go—in your memories." Grandpa Barry kneeled beside his son.

"I dinna like the sound of that. Are ye tryin' to give me away gently, then?" Cillian tucked the gift in his pants pocket and fell into the old man's embrace.

"Are angels not ministering spirits to the chosen?"

"Aye?" Cillian held his breath.

"Grandma Barry and I have never initiated giving away any child. You'll understand when the time's right." Grandpa Barry's eyes twinkled. "My Einstein blended with Mozart—you're a genius and a musical prodigy."

Cillian ran over and kissed Grandma Barry as his heart beat to rhythms of joy, peace, and hope. "Thanks for the present." A cheerful tune escaped his throat as he stored the happy memories on top of the bad ones. "Grandpa, I want to live here forever and be a farmer when I grow up." He scooped a spoonful of blueberry cobbler and ate it. "I'll help ye wi' the garden. Yer my new family, at least I can be imaginin' it."

"Imaginations, like stray dogs," Grandpa Barry said, "require leashing and taming before they can deal with reality."

"Don't be a grump." Grandma Barry laughed as she rocked in her chair.

After eating, Cillian sat on the worn piano bench. Warm toes hovered over the damper pedal; he lifted his hands above the keys, allowing his fingers to relax into their natural curved state, and played Claude Debussy's "Clair de lune." He played on, the notes spilling from his soul—as memories filled his heart of Mama Kelley sitting by her tape player, listening to that same tune. One day, he would play it for her on a grand piano inside a concert hall.

Grandma Barry rocked back and forth to the peaks and ebbs of the enchanting tune. "Do you hear the notes in your head?"

"On the inside." He pointed to his heart.

"You're a prodigy. You've practiced diligently for the last year, and the Almighty rewards diligence." Grandma Barry walked to Cillian's side and massaged his shoulders. "He refines, then uses your talents."

"Mama Kelley played this song on the recordplayer in her house."

"She must have been a special woman. Now, off to bed, my love. Tomorrow will be very different."

"Why?"

"Because life moves on." She pulled Cillian into her embrace. "Off to bed." He climbed the steps to his bedroom. "We'll rise early tomorrow. Rest well."

"Grace, he'll need his rest. Let him sleep late in the morning."

"He's wrapped your heart around his little finger, like all the rest of the children we've cared for." She sat in the rocker besides Grandpa Barry. "Most important, he needs his education. Imaginations, stray dogs—remember?"

21—Orphan Dreamer

TODAY WAS HER THIRTEENTH BIRTHDAY, and Thursday she'd received her first present: a gate of braces that would slowly squeeze Daniela's gapped upper teeth together. Several days ago, she had overheard the conversation between her parents.

"Jeanette, she's a girl."

"I have eyes, Austin."

"I don't want her covering her smile with her hand any longer. We'll have to cut back, but she's suffered enough rejection for reasons she can't and shouldn't change." Chaplain Cavanaugh tapped out the numbers in the calculator once more. "If we use the bus and my Plymouth, then sell your car, we'll have the thousand dollars to pay for her braces."

"I bought that Ford LTD when I worked at the Extension Service. It was my first brand-new car." Daniela's mother had stood at the front window, gazing at the bright yellow car. "But if you think it's worth it—"

"Let's sell mine instead. I'll work a few extra shifts to make up the difference."

"Last time you took an extra call, you ended up being the prison chaplain giving Ted Bundy hope before the executioner fried him." Jeanette turned, a wry smile upturning the edges of her lips. "That girl has you wrapped around her pinky finger."

"And who are you to judge?" He walked to his wife's side, slid his arm around her waist, and they kissed. "Even a serial killer staring Old Sparky in the face craves forgiveness and redemption."

"Point taken on both accounts. I'm pleased the nosebleeds have stopped."

Electric chairs. Serial killers. Daniela had stifled a gasp.

This morning, standing in the hallway while her parents sat in the living room, Daniela had eavesdropped again. "Did she share her last dream with you?" Austin asked.

"She's still having the nightmares?"

"Since November 15, no more nightmares," he said. "Just dreams."

"How is it that the mother is the last to find out?"

"She wants to talk about the details right after the dream, and you're usually sleeping. I don't blame you. You've been a nurse for both of us, and I'm healthy, so it's my turn to wake up in the middle of the night and calm her fears."

"The dreams are different?" her mother asked.

"Recently, they've been happy dreams—fields of flowers, peaceful lakes, sunrises, and sunsets."

"No boy?"

"Nada," Austin said.

"Should we still give her the gift?"

"Tibet told me to give it to her on her thirteenth birthday."

"I still don't like it." Jeanette crossed her arms. "Ethan's on life support. Seeing him last week almost destroyed her. That doctor wanted her committed to an asylum. She's all we have."

"They don't put kids in asylums. You've been reading too many mysteries before bed, Jeanette."

"Well, they wanted to take her away from us. She doesn't need any more erratic changes in her life. That's all."

"Every mother is afraid of her child approaching independence." He laughed. "If we'd followed your plan, she wouldn't be starting as a freshman in high school one month after her thirteenth birthday with the opportunity to earn community college credits."

"Oh, so I'm the bad guy, keeping Doogie Howser's sister in her diapers?"

"I didn't say that."

"Why do you want her to grow up so fast? An innocent little girl should marinate in her childhood."

"You must be hungry. I'll put the hamburgers on the grill in a bit."

"Not funny." Jeanette waved her husband away. Daniela held her breath while digging her toes into the green shag carpet, afraid her parents would catch her eavesdropping. The purr of the window air conditioner filled the empty space.

"I never had anything. Let's not hold her back. Why not let her soar to the stars if she wants?"

"If she falls?" Jeanette asked.

"We'll catch her."

"And what if we aren't there when she falls?"

"I'm afraid too." He sighed, and his voice lowered.

"Then don't do it. Don't give her that cursed diamond. She's happy now—safe."

"I'll think about it, but I love her too much to keep her from her destiny, even if it kills me."

"Waiting is the right choice." Jeanette retrieved her keys from a hook by the front door. "I'll drive her to the coed softball game. It keeps her busy."

"Busyness isn't an accomplishment."

"And idleness is the devil's playground."

He kissed his wife, and Daniela vanished, running to her bedroom. Questions ran through her mind faster than her legs moved: What was this gift? What did it do? Maybe the gift would lead her to her kindred friend. If so, that would be awesome. But her dad had said that one day, she would be the next Indiana Jones. *Raiders of the Lost Ark*. Monkey brains. Bleeding Nazis. Snake pits. Sadistic religious rituals that included removing a living man's heart.

A bloodcurdling nightmare.

22—Orphan Dreamer

SIX WEEKS AGO, DANIELA HAD started classes during the summer to prepare her for her first year of high school. Now, four hours until her birthday party, her guest list looked anemic.

One invited: Ethan.

Zero RSVP'd.

Status of guest: admitted to the intensive care unit, on life support.

She sighed. With a rattle, a rattlesnake at least warns victims that its fangs are loaded with venom and its coiled body is ready to strike, but a black mamba—the world's deadliest snake—gives no such courtesy. It strikes, lightning speed with no warning.

Daniela felt more like a black mamba.

She knew it was her hormones. The inevitable truth that her best friend was dying. Becoming a teenager. All three explained why

Daniela's fangs were loaded, prepared to bite into and annihilate anyone who annoyed her.

"Metal mouth, metal mouth, metal mouth is coming!" Running out of the dugout, Claire covered her mouth as she laughed.

"I don't care what you say," Daniela shot back. For the first time, she really *didn't* care what Claire thought. The bully was cursed with absolutely no imagination.

Besides, Daniela had turned thirteen years old. She *was* special, just like Grandma Gertrude had said, or her parents wouldn't be hiding her birthday present. Chew on that. "Once my smile's perfect, you won't laugh anymore."

"I'll still be laughing, turd breath." Claire ogled Tommy, a sixteen-year-old image of masculine beauty. "Don't wig out. Some of us were born perfect." She slinked to Danny Rose's side. "Slender. Perky." Claire bolstered her breasts with her hands. "Tall, blonde, and a killer bod." She touched her forefinger to her hip and made a sizzling noise.

"Talk to the hand." She held her hand up in front of Claire's face. "Anyone want steaks?" Daniela rolled her eyes. "They're burning on the grill and stinking up the place." Someone had to fight ignorance. Ethan couldn't. "You're so shady, ferns refuse to grow."

"Sweet." Tommy laughed.

Heat flashed into Daniela's cheeks. She was a teenager now; time to grow up and kick enemy butt. "Tall?" She propped her hands on her hips. "If I wore four-inch wedge heels to softball practice, I'd be a lumbering giant too."

"All sauce and spice." Claire fought back. "You're awful mouthy."

"Blonde—comes in a bottle, doesn't it? Anyone with five bucks could buy it."

"You couldn't afford it."

"So what? Lemonade stands. Car washes. Small potatoes. Besides, I'm going to be a freshman in high school after the summer. Teasing is so middle school. And why do girls dye their hair yellow anyways?"

"Don't worry about it. Wouldn't look good on you anyways." Claire jutted her chin, slicing humid air. "You're not the only one. I'll be in high school next year, and I won't be a nerdy, immature thirteen-year-old like you."

"You're fourteen. I'm thirteen. Guess it took a whole 365 days for your brain to catch up to mine. Hope my little 411 just now will save you some embarrassment." The black mamba kept striking.

"Whatever."

"Vocabulary run out?"

"I'll sic Harry on you."

"Opens a can of worms but can't eat them." Who cared what Claire thought; Daniela's smile wasn't for her. Besides, Claire's teeth had been locked behind braces last year. She must've had a stroke since then and become an amnesiac. Sweat poured from Daniela's pores as the unforgiving Florida sun baked her face, but she smiled, loving the big words that had flowed through her brain since joining the Future Scientists after-school program.

"Danny Rose." Tommy smiled at her. "The real O.G."

"The what?" Daniela tilted her chin.

"You're next, Daniela," Coach Rogers, the softball coach, called.

"I'll explain later." Tommy walked back to the dugout.

"Here comes gap-toothed Smalls." Claire huddled with a group of bored girls. They taunted Daniela as they scurried behind the chain-link fence. To hide—maybe? Daniela held the bat over her right shoulder, eyes focused on the softball.

"Come on, Danny," Tommy said. "Hit a homer."

She pulled back and threw her slight frame forward. The bat cut the air with a *whoosh,* and the ball rolled behind her feet.

"Oh snap! Metal mouth can't even hit the ball." Claire roared in laughter.

"At least I'm playing. What are you here for?"

Claire didn't answer.

"That's what I thought." Daniela gripped the bat harder, imagining the ball was her tormentor's neck. But she wasn't a killer. After three strikes, she trudged to the dugout and sat on a vacant bench while the whispering girls snickered and pointed at her.

Tommy sauntered into the girls' dugout. His father was born in Cuba, and his father's family had left Cuba in the seventies. His mother defined a North Carolina Southern belle. With bronzed skin, muscular arms, deep-set black eyes, and chocolate hair with flecks of auburn to match, Tommy looked like a dream dressed in a baseball cap, jeans, and cleats.

Danny Rose's face flushed. Dreams don't belong to gap-toothed losers—at least not Tommy dreams. She'd struck out. Best settle on oily boy dreams. Anemic pale. Starving. Ugly. *Worms to butterflies,* her mother's words chastised her criticisms.

"Hey, Danny Rose," Tommy strutted into the dugout, stopping in front of her. Why was he talking to her? Daniela averted her gaze, bracing herself for a round of teasing.

Say something. Break the ice. Be brave.

"Hi, Tommy?" That was it? Her voice upticked with a question mark as she swung her legs back and forth.

"You'll do better next time, and FYI, O.G. means the original gangsta."

"Th-th-thanks. I think?"

He chuckled. "Want me to teach you? That is, how to hit the ball?" Even though he had lived in the city for most of his life, Tommy possessed country-boy manners. He had been nice to Daniela after they had been assigned to a Future Scientist summer project together. While Tommy suffered from a bout of viral meningitis for a week, she had pulled up the slack, and their project won first place.

"It's hopeless."

"Only if you give up."

Claire swaggered toward Tommy and planted a long kiss right on his lips. "Little miss never-been-kissed . . . I bet you can't do that. Oh, I forgot—the nosebleeds. Goodness knows what kind of diseases you'd pass along."

"Maybe you should ask before you kiss someone." Tommy spit on the ground. "There's a word for that. Taking. Not asking."

"You're so gay."

He's cool. Daniela smiled big. She studied the red dirt beneath her feet before looking up. "I'm thirteen. What's the big rush to kiss a boy?"

"Rewrite: you mean you can't get a boy to kiss you." Red-faced, Claire laughed, and the other girls joined her.

Tommy strolled toward Daniela. "May I?"

"No." Her breath caught in her throat. "My parents wouldn't understand." *We don't have to love them, just live with them.* By *them* her father meant white people. Her father's prejudiced words replayed in her mind. "I'm sorry."

"See. Such a dork." Claire marched out of the dugout.

She hoped Ethan's life was going a bit smoother than hers. But how could it be? He was hooked up to fifty million lines while Daniela attempted to play softball.

Harry, Claire's cousin, lumbered into the dugout, and even the ants scattered as the dirt shook beneath the Goliath-boy's feet. Daniela had left him behind in middle school, but during summer softball camp, his age decided what classes he attended—hers. His presence was like a trigger. Warm liquid slid down the back of her throat.

Not now.

Tommy's here!

"Snorting crack again," Harry ridiculed. "Why do you live on planet Earth?"

"To save your butt. He speaks again—another alien species heard from." She searched through her bag until she found a handkerchief and slapped it to her nose as she bolted from the dugout and stopped a few feet away.

"Good one, Danny." Tommy strolled after her. "Hey, Harry, go run a few laps and drop the baby flab."

"Go back to Cuba, Castro boy."

"Very original." Tommy glared at Harry, then gazed at Daniela. "Want some water?"

She nodded. Tommy filled up his water bottle as Harry waddled toward the catcher's mound. Tommy returned to her side. "Piece of work."

"Thanks." She drank. "Mom says, 'You shouldn't expect people diseased with a bad case of backwoods, inbred ignorance to be delivered from their ailments during one healing service.'"

"Your mom's cool, but you do sound nerdy quoting your parents, just a 411." He brushed her arm with his, and electricity pulsed though her entire body. "I'm happy you spoke up. Pudge boy needs some training."

"The words fell out."

"Let 'em keep falling." Tommy laughed.

"You think so?"

"For sure."

"Soon enough, I'll become a doctor, and maybe I'll invent a powerful antibiotic and ram it down Harry's throat."

"What will it do—make him pretty?"

"No. It'll rip the insides of his colon out, and he'll puke into eternity." She grinned, and mischief settled behind her eyes.

"I'd like to be there." Tommy placed his hand in the middle of her back. "I like your dark side. It's edgy. Cool."

I like your dark side.

Everything inside her warmed, and she smiled, proud of her quiet bravery and her admirer. The words triggered thoughts of her mother's response to her daughter acting vengeful. "Daniela, according to the Bible, vengeance is God's prerogative. Not yours. 'Vengeance is mine. I will repay, says the Lord.' Let Him handle correcting people's wrongs." Daniela had answered, "He's molasses slow."

Today, she slinked away from Tommy's touch. She should not have said that about Harry.

"I don't eat pretty girls. Promise."

"Cute boys can't be trusted, especially by girls who look like me. Dad says."

"There you go quoting your parents again." He furrowed his brow.

"I don't want to explain myself, if that's what that look means."

"Okay. Don't. But I think you're judging me unfairly because you're afraid to fall for me. You don't deserve a toad."

"Humble—I see. I might like frogs?" She thought of Ernie, the talking frog in the pond behind her house. A hungry snake had finished Ernie off a couple months ago. Another friend dead.

"Ribbit." He laughed. "So, you're going to med school?"

"In her dreams," Claire butted in. Tommy ignored her.

"If my dual-enrollment credits transfer to University of Florida, I'll apply to the Junior's Honors Program at U of F and shave a year off undergrad."

Tommy counted on his fingers. "You'd only be sixteen when you start med school."

"Sweet sixteen as they say—whoever *they* are. No. I'll be seventeen. Skipped kindergarten and another grade in middle school, and I'll have a year's worth of college credits at the end of my freshman high school year."

"Never was good at math."

She laughed—full, free, tossing her head back.

"You're pretty when you laugh."

She blushed. "Smart girls don't have to be pretty. I want to become a physician and help people." She looked down. "I guess inventing a bug juice to harm someone—even Harry—isn't being a real doctor. I'm not the prettiest on the inside."

"No—just proactive, thinning the herd of morons."

"I don't want to murder people, if that's what you mean."

"Too busy being smart." He lifted her chin with his thumb. "But Harry's not people. He's an alien. Remember. Assassins don't mind killing people."

"I'm no assassin." A swarm of butterflies seemed to take flight inside her tummy all at once. She rested her hand on her abdomen.

"What was all that talk about Jewish Feasts for your English paper? Are you Jewish?"

"No, but my mom says that I need to understand them for my *calling*." Daniela used air quotes.

"You've got nothing else to do." Claire's eyes gleamed.

"Put a sock in it," Tommy said.

"Why do you want to talk to *her*?" Claire asked.

"She's interesting."

"Your eyes not working? You color-blind?"

"Are you?" Tommy glared at Claire.

"Go ahead—ruin your life. Don't say I didn't try to help." She crossed her arms. "Can't wait till Harry's uncle passes legislation to send all those monkeys back to Africa."

"You'll be the first to go," Tommy said.

"One day, you'll find something better to do than pick on me. If I were you, I'd be so bored with it by now." Daniela rolled her eyes. Tommy winked at her, and before she could think, she asked, "D-d-do you wanna come to my birthday party in an hour?"

"For sure." He licked his lips. *Totally kissable!* Her heart pounded beneath her sweaty jersey. "Where do you live?" he asked.

Fudge! She hadn't thought of that—she lived on the wrong side of the tracks, and he'd be the only one attending. "Umm . . . not too far away."

"So am I invited or not?"

Time for the outfield. Daniela ran to her position, happy to avoid answering his question. After the game, Tommy walked with Daniela to the parking lot.

"Wanna give me directions?

"Umm. Actually, Dad said no boys. Sorry."

"Plenty of boys attend high school, and I'm not a monster."

"I know. It's just . . . Maybe I'm the monster, and you're sixteen. I just turned thirteen today, and that's a problem with my parents." Seeing their Ford LTD, she ran toward the pickup area.

"When will you be old enough to date?" Tommy chased after her.

"Never." She disappeared into a trail of dust that led to her mother's car and jumped in.

"What about your birthday party?"

"Changed my mind. It's a private party."

"Why was that . . . white boy running after you?" Her mother glared at her.

"We were talking. That's all."

"Your father wouldn't understand, Danny Rose." Her mother floored the accelerator, and the banana boat lurched forward.

"Could you understand?" Daniela asked.

"I could—I do—but I'm married to your father, and I cannot disrespect his wishes."

"I'm sorry, but I don't agree."

"Danny Rose!"

She dared a glance at Tommy. He waved. *That* was not going to happen. She looked away, tucking her lower lip between her teeth. How would it feel to kiss a boy on the lips? If her father had his way—and if the boy who wanted to kiss her looked like Ethan or Tommy—she would never know.

But Daniela wasn't a racist. Racist people were lazier than dried snot. Who was she to pass judgment about a person's character based upon a thin layer of epidermis? Explore the real person.

For starters, all humans pooped brown.

Peed yellow.

Spit white.

And bled red.

"And it shall come to pass in the last days, says God,
That I will pour out of My Spirit on all flesh; Your sons
and your daughters shall prophesy, Your young men
shall see visions, Your old men shall dream dreams."

—The Book of Acts 2:17

23—ORPHAN DREAMER

THAT NIGHT, PROVIDENCE MANDATED THAT time move out of Daniela's way. She would be entrusted with defining Earth's reality. Father, thy will be done on Earth as it is in heaven.

"Happy Birthday, Danny Rose." In their kitchen, her mother removed a chocolate cake from the oven and placed it on the counter. After it cooled, she would slather a layer of chocolate frosting across the top.

"Thirteen years old," her father said. "You're a teenager now."

"Med school, here I come."

"Still a few years to go," her mother chuckled as her father squeezed fresh lemons, then dumped chilled water and a scoop of sugar into a glass pitcher, making his favorite summertime drink. "Lemonade's been like your life, Danny Rose," her dad said.

"How?" She chewed the inside of her lip, wondering about Tommy.

"The sour, you've lived it. Now, your mother and I will make sure you live the sweet."

As long as that sweetness didn't include Tommy or anyone who looked like him. But why challenge her parents during this happy moment? They loved her.

Her father poured the lemonade into three glasses, and they toasted. "Here's to making Danny Rose's life sweeter than Southern tea." Even though it was evening, without air conditioning their stone and cinderblock house was roasting, so the three of them escaped the heat and sat in their backyard beneath the enormous Texas cottonwoods. They laughed, reminisced, ate cake, and guzzled their lemony drinks.

Suddenly, the atmosphere changed.

July's hot summer breath blew ice cold.

Birds stopped their chirping, and where a bright blue sky had been, dark clouds turned somersaults, blacking out the sun.

A fat raindrop thumped Daniela on the forehead. "Ouch." She scrunched her nose. Moments later, a deluge descended. "The heavens are crying. Come on, guys." Daniela jumped to her feet. "We'll melt."

Her mother grabbed the cake and dashed into the house behind her daughter. Austin grabbed the pitcher, his stiff leg slowing him. "Must be tears of joy, because today's a happy day."

"Dad, hurry." She waved her father toward her. "You'll drown."

"That water's coming faster than Noah's flood." Her father laughed as he walked to the house, the water up to his ankles.

Daniela stole another look at the sky. "What's happening?" Within the blackness, a circle of light formed—a vortex; a window into heaven. Amazing! Slipping back inside, she towel-dried her face and then passed the towel to her parents.

"The cake's not too soggy." Her mother ate another bite.

Daniela's father kissed his daughter on the forehead. "Rain spoiled my little Orphan Dreamer's birthday."

"Don't call me that, Daddy. Not today, on my birthday." She closed her eyes and relished his gentle touch, then ran into the small living room, her family in tow.

Stuck in the 1970s, green shag carpet covered the terrazzo floor beneath. Puke mustard-gold wall paint to match what her dad thought was brown carpet. "Let him be creative. He's involved, and that's what counts," her mother had said when Daniela complained.

They cuddled together on a plaid couch while looking through an old picture album.

"Look at that Afro." Her mother held up Daniela's baby picture.

"Came out with a head of hair," her father added. "Boy! you had some lungs. You didn't want your momma to wander too far. 'A prophet's lungs.'" They laughed, joked, and ate more sweets.

A whistling wind snaked through the living room, followed by a thud. "Dad, did you hear that?" Shivering and still damp, Daniela glared at the front door.

Austin stood and forged ahead, determined to find out what was shaking the front door. Was it the wind?

"It's as though someone is knocking," her mother said. "I thought you didn't invite anyone for your birthday?"

"Tommy . . . ?"

"A boy?" her father asked, his voice concerned.

"Yes, Dad—a boy. The same species as Ethan, but you'll be happy to know that I didn't tell the male alien where we live."

"Good."

"She's a teenager," her mom teased. "One day our Danny's life could be made sweeter with a young man."

"After she finishes medical school. Turns forty. Learns how to shoot a gun and grows armored plates."

"I thought you were going to answer the door," Jeanette added.

"Dark-roasted coffee, absolutely no cream. Understood?"

"Stop, Dad. I don't even like coffee."

"Milk?" Her dad stopped at the door.

"Lactose intolerant—remember?"

"Exactly."

"Maybe the boy in her dreams is her kindred spirit." Her mother winked at her daughter while twisting the screw into her father's heart again. "And maybe her kindred spirit—the one who will love her as she is—is all cream—absolutely no coffee."

"If that's the case, there's a reason she calls them nightmares."

The doorbell chimed.

"Answer the door, Austin." Jeanette hugged her daughter. "Don't worry. We'll wear him down. Is this Tommy a nice boy?"

"He is." Daniela watched the tennis match of words. They hadn't fought in front of her for as long as she could remember. Austin reached for the door handle.

"Be careful, Austin." Jeanette toyed with the string of fake pearls around her neck.

"Oh, now you're concerned. I'll be fine." He yanked the door open, but no one was there. "Where'd they go?"

Daniela peeked around her father. "Should I check the gate?"

"No, I'll go." Austin left the protection of the house.

Water sloshed around his calves, and dogwood trees bowed in a stiff wind. He rattled the lock that hung from the fence; it remained intact. He shook his head and returned to the house. "It's secure. Maybe it was the wind."

"That was a human knock—regular, urgent. And the wind can't ring the doorbell. Everyone, come inside," her mother urged. "We'll be safer inside."

The storm strengthened.

Black clouds rotated above as though a tornado with an appetite to consume their small house was forming.

"Mom, look." Daniela pulled away from her mother and pointed at a package wrapped in a black garbage bag sitting on the porch.

"Leave it alone." Jeanette stormed past Daniela. "It may be a bomb."

"Jeanette, come on now," Austin said. "We're not that important. No one wants to blow us up." He leaned over the package and inspected it.

"Danny Rose is my only child."

"If this is a bomb, Danny won't be the only one splattered to smithereens."

"Maybe Tommy left me a birthday present." Daniela inched closer to the package, careful her mother didn't hear her approach.

"Who leaves a gift in a deluge and then disappears?" her father asked. "If that's his style, leave him alone. He's psycho."

Jeanette scanned the bag as though she possessed x-ray vision. Daniela leaned forward and grabbed the bag before her mother could interfere.

"Daniela Rose Cavanaugh! How dare you!"

"It has my name on it. See." She pointed at the letters— D-A-N-I-E-L-A.

"You directly disobeyed me."

"Not directly, Mother. You never told me not to pick it up and open it." Daniela cradled the package. "It's heavy. Must be important."

"Should we open it on the porch?" Austin asked.

"*If* we open it at all," her mother said, glaring at her daughter. "But I'm not sayin' a word."

"Who's there?" Daniela glanced over her shoulder. Potted African violets sat on the porch ledge behind her, but no one was present.

"Are you playing around? If so, stop it." Her mother surveyed the porch.

"Something or someone brushed my arm."

"I was right." Jeanette pulled Daniela close. "Throw it away; even the paper is cursed."

"Let her open it. It's addressed to her."

"We had an agreement." Jeanette gripped her husband's arm, communicating something unspoken.

"It's impossible to override God's will," Austin protested. Daniela faced her mother, allowing her facial expression to beg with the skill that only an only child could muster. "We could use a bit of good news, Mom."

"If something bad happens, I'll never—"

"It won't, Mom."

"Don't interrupt your mother, Danny-girl."

"Yes, sir." She pulled the package to her chest.

Jeanette's eyes scanned the neighborhood. "Let's open it inside. There are bound to be prying eyes behind every window."

Austin gaffed. "Way too suspicious for your own good. I thought you were concerned about a bomb."

"Be sensible, Austin. Someone may be watching. All these houses clustered around a park. The whole world doesn't have to know about our girl's gift."

"Eventually, they will. It's their butts she's saving."

"What are you two going on about?"

"You're getting ready to find out." After her family entered the living room, her mother bolted every lock in the house. "Close the curtains, Austin."

"Closing the curtains," he said, then chuckled.

In the living room, Daniela opened her gift. The edges of a bronze-and-brown wooden box peeked through. Ivory covered the top. "It's a bronze box."

A knowing smile spread across her father's face. "Well, open it." She did. The jewel sparkled even beneath the dim yellow lights.

"A snowflake?" Daniela asked as her father removed the mysterious object and held it to the light.

"Ah, ole Tibet was right—it takes your breath away."

"Tibet didn't trust us to give it to her." Jeanette fingered her pearls again.

"His Master intervened." Austin sighed. "That was probably old man Tibet brushing past you earlier. He's a complex old fella."

"If this is a diamond, we're rich. Now we can afford any doctor we want. Mom, you can buy a new car."

"It's not just any diamond," her father said. "It's an ancient stone with special powers. Tibet called it the Glass Tattoo."

"What does it do—magic?" Daniela asked.

"No," Austin said. "Tibet told me the stone is more like a security blanket, but there is no real power intrinsic to the stone. It signals that Yahweh is entrusting you to become the next Orphan Dreamer, the keeper of the God factor."

"What's the God factor?"

"When humans refuse to correct their wrongs and repent, Yahweh corrects them, keeping Earth balanced. The Glass Tattoo is useless without the power of the one who created it—Yahweh."

"Daniela, do you remember," her mother asked, "the day you gave your heart to the Master?"

"I do. I was four years old."

"Since then, his power has rested dormant inside of you.

"'The Kingdom of God is within you.'" Austin studied the ancient stone. "Time to awaken it. Use the power for good."

"Did you believe Tibet?" Daniela asked.

"I did. I do."

She palmed the snowflake. Translucent white turned a deep royal blue. "Look! It's changing colors."

"Don't touch that!" Her mother grabbed the stone, and it paled to a translucent white again.

"According to old man Tibet, few possess the characteristics necessary to activate the jewel," her father said. "Fewer still are willing to be used by Yahweh."

"What traits are those, exactly?" The razor-edged tone of her mother's voice made Daniela cringe.

"Honesty, loyalty, and humility toward the One who controls the jewel's power," he answered.

Didn't Dad have a clue that he was insulting Mom? Wasn't she honest, loyal, and humble? Daniela rolled her eyes. *Get a clue, Rafiki.*

"Goodness, Daddy. You're digging a grave deeper than the Marina Trench."

"The Marina Trench?" Austin raised his right eyebrow, and Jeanette raised her chin.

"The deepest part of the Indian Ocean. Over thirty-six thousand feet deep."

"Deeper than Mount Everest is tall." Her dad paused. "You know what I mean, Jeanette. I don't want to quarrel. Today, we celebrate Danny's birthday. Release her to her purpose." He leaned toward her mother and kissed her. Holding her cheeks, he said, "Never accuse me of not protecting my daughter, but are we to go back on our promise?"

Jeanette shook her head and tears slipped from her eyes. She held her husband's hand. "Here, Danny Rose." She dropped the jewel back into her daughter's palm. "Take it and accomplish your purpose." Transparent white darkened to blue, and a swirl formed in the middle.

She poked her finger into the center. "Feels funny, like a wet, jelly vacuum."

"I never wanted this for my little girl," Jeanette said.

"Mom, I'm not little anymore. I'm thirteen—remember?"

"You'll always be my little girl."

"You'll be fine. Yahweh will guide you." Austin swiped stray hairs from his daughter's eyes. "Did you forget, Jeanette? We never would have conceived her otherwise. Let her fly. It's time for our butterfly to leave our cocoon."

"Our daughter isn't an insect."

Austin's smile flattened into a thin line. "You never belonged to us, my Orphan Dreamer." Her father paused. "You always belonged to the Great One—I AM."

"Who was Tibet?"

"One of Yahweh's agents. He told me to give you the stone. I had planned to do so, but the nosebleeds stopped, and you were finally happy. I decided to wait."

"He didn't agree." Daniela eyes her parents. "He sent the storm and dropped off the package from heaven. What's the stone supposed to do?"

"Allow you to bend time."

"What?

"If time doesn't limit you, then you can travel anywhere you like—into the past or future.

"How?"

"I don't know."

"Why would I ever want to leave you and Mom and travel to other worlds by myself?"

"A dark force seeks to eradicate humanity and inhabit Earth, and you will be the one to stop it."

"You're kidding—right?" She laughed. "I can't even stop my nosebleeds. I thought the night you left me in the dark after telling me Earth was doomed was an April Fool's joke. Besides, Claire taunts me and oily boy crashes my dreams and ruins my world. I can't control those people, so exactly how am I supposed to single-handedly stop a dark force that I don't even know how to find?" *Crazy.* "And what if I don't want to stop this dark force?"

"Then your mother and I will die."

"Happy Birthday to me! So not cool." The gelatinous ink formed a tattoo.

"What's that?" Her mother stared at her hand. "A tattoo. I despise tattoos!"

"I know." Daniela hid a cheeky grin and rubbed her finger across the midnight-blue tattoo on the inside of her right palm. "But you weren't going to give it to me. You would have let yourselves die? Just to protect me?"

"What parent doesn't want their child to be happy?" Her mother attempted a smile, but her lips spoke of surrender more than joy. "The nightmares had stopped."

"Gosh, Mom." Moisture rimmed Daniela's eyelashes.

"I just want you to be happy," her mother's voice broke.

"I don't deserve either of you, and I'm sorry for all the times I've disappointed you."

"You've been our joy, and we have prayed that the Almighty would gift you a friend during your journeys." Her mother hugged herself.

Careful to avoid the Glass Tattoo, her dad rested his hand on Daniela's knee. "It's terrible to think of you going about saving the world alone, but you must make the final decision: are you willing, Danny Rose?"

"I-I-I don't know. I don't want to start something I can't finish. I may be awkward, but I'm not a quitter."

"Yahweh will help you." Her mother assured.

But would He? Hadn't Daniela's God all but abandoned Ethan, leaving him attached to ventilators and drips? "I'm exhausted. I need to sleep. Can we talk about all this in the morning?"

"Of course," her father said.

"Dad or Mom, can you take me to see Ethan in the morning? I want to tell him about the Glass Tattoo . . . see what he thinks . . . if he wakes."

"I'll take you," her dad volunteered.

"I have a bad feeling."

"About?" her mom asked.

"Ethan." She stood. "If Yahweh can't save Ethan, then how could He save me if I travel to these mysterious worlds to fight whatever this dark force is?"

"It's Lucifer," her dad said calmly. "The dark force is Lucifer."

"Satan! The devil! I have to face the old dragon? I don't think so. Not going to happen. Storm!" Daniela marched out of the living room.

24—The Orphan

Monday, July 11, 1994
Bibury, England

IT WAS A LOVELY MORNING to take a stroll.

Gentle sunlight spilled through a crack between banks of gray clouds, bathing the pond in the middle of town a golden hue. A hot wind rustled the tops of trees. Wearing a navy-and-red silk pleated skirt and a red cardigan, Mrs. Barry strolled to the schoolhouse while sipping her favorite cup of brew, purchased from the William Morris Tea Shop.

A light mist threatened to evolve into an English thunderstorm. Rain or shine, there was no reason to hurry toward what lay ahead.

Thirteen-year-old Cillian walked behind her, eating an apple, just as the children from the cozy farmhouse had done almost one year ago; but the setting had changed.

Gray skies had replaced blue.

The hum of cars had replaced the songs of birds.

A stench—a mix of petrol, body odor, and a sulfur scent like the smell that had pressed around his mother's flat—had replaced the usual sweet fragrance of summer flowers. Still full of hope and love, he intended to burst through the schoolhouse door, eager to claim his seat in summer school, but he hesitated on the steps.

Something was wrong.

"Go inside, Cillian. Class is waiting." Mrs. Barry nudged him from the back.

"Yes, ma'am." He pushed opened the door, which led into a quaint foyer, finding two police officers sitting on a weathered pew donated by the parishioners of the local church. Hands resting on their guns, the pair approached Cillian and Mrs. Barry.

Were they waiting for him?

Was he a criminal? Desiring love and being willing to run away from his mother's home to find it—was that a crime?

The larger one said, "Mrs. Barry and Cillian, please come with us."

Cillian froze. They were after him.

The lights in the small school dimmed.

Sounds merged into chaos, and the stench of sulfur sullied the previously cinnamon-candle- scented room.

They followed the officers, and five people stuffed themselves into Mrs. Barry's office: an authoritative man, Cillian, Mrs. Barry, and two police officers. Too many pounds of sweaty flesh and not enough oxygen.

"The name's Sergeant John James," the chief officer introduced himself, and that's where his politeness ended. He bombarded Mrs. Barry with questions.

Cillian held onto the silver dollar in his pocket. *This canna be happening.* It was. A monster was eating his courage, one bite at a time.

"The whelp's mother, Ailsa Finn, recently reported the boy missing," Sergeant James explained. Cillian frowned. *Why now?* He dared not verbalize his questions. The officers were not talking to him, but about him.

"He's only thirteen years old. Surely, you're not going to return this child to his mother's house," Mrs. Barry said, "after the details that I have given you in regard to her prior treatment of him. It's a miracle he's alive." *Grandma Barry knows a lot about me.* His heart swelled as she desperately attempted to convince the officer to leave Cillian in her care.

The sergeant hesitated. "Be pleased I'm not arresting you."

"Freedom fighters quite often spend a bit of time in a jailhouse before their jailors realize their folly."

"Mrs. Barry, we have no interest in making you into a martyr, but to answer your question—his mother doesn't want him back."

"What? Then, why are you here?"

"She stated her wishes clearly: send him to a care home for orphans and rehabilitate him as a troubled runaway."

"Cillian requires no rehabilitation, only love." Mrs. Barry fingered Cillian's raven locks as Sergeant James stared at the boy, guilt masking his plain face.

"We aren't all mean," the officer said to the boy.

"Please. We're travelers from a faraway land." She sputtered through her next words as her power seemed to slip away. "We take in children when they are lost and hurting." Her voice took on a plaintive tone. She was losing. Tears burned Cillian's eyes.

"I don't care what faraway land you lived in, but this is England, the queen's country, and we have laws."

"But the care home . . ." She shifted her weight, trying desperately to find the right words. "Let the boy stay here!"

"No, no, and no."

"He's thriving."

Cillian tilted his head toward Mrs. Barry's face, and for the first time since he had come to live with her, anger overshadowed her soothing, kind voice, but her facial expression registered despair.

She was fighting for him; he was grateful.

Sergeant James's eyes appeared to turn bright green and then brown again as he rotated a gold ring on his right forefinger. Cillian inhaled a noseful of the man's cologne—much too floral a scent for a man, but what did he know about cologne?

"Ailsa Finn is Cillian's mother," the officer replied. "She has the right to make this decision."

"Donating an egg doesn't give one the right to bury a child in the social welfare system when capable adults are willing to care for him."

"In England it does."

"I don't—"

"The child welfare system has already heard her case and ruled in her favor. We've been barmy, so it took us a while to come get him."

Sergeant John tapped Cillian on the head. "You're grateful for your little vacation, aren't you?"

Cillian flipped the coin from heads to tails and back again in his pocket.

"I'm speaking to you, my boy."

"Yes, sir. I'm grateful."

"Time to rejoin the real world and keep on living with the rest of us." Darkness loomed behind the man's eyes. He lowered his voice so only Cillian could hear him. "We knew where you were all along, but you were protected."

"Don't taunt him," Mrs. Barry said.

"Mrs. Barry, your hearing's exceptional—it's as though you aren't human. But you're powerless now. He's in our hands."

Cillian watched as the officer stamped a document. *9 July 1994.* The midnight-blue ink sealed his fate. Loneliness and hopelessness weighed down his heart, sinking his spirit into the deepest ocean. Drowning in despair, for the first time he begged to hate Ailsa Finn, but what son could hate his mother?

His body shook.

The intensity of his lust to birth hatred for his mother frightened him.

"May we at least gather Cillian's belongings from the cottage?" Mrs. Barry blotted her moistened eyes with a pink lace handkerchief. "Grandpa Barry will want to give his farewell."

"Anything of value?"

"They're his things. A child requires the familiar."

"Certainly, madam. I could do with stretching my legs." Constable Collier—the quiet one—squatted for emphasis.

Cillian turned to take one last look at the schoolhouse. Cobwebs reached their spidery fingers across the blackboard. The red apple on Mrs. Barry's desk turned brown and blackened into mush. The children faded into ghosts. The lights went black. He narrowed his eyes and rubbed them.

Constable Collier followed Mrs. Barry and the newly proclaimed orphan. The officer with the gold ring stayed behind and walked through the empty room before following them. The pair extended their usual five-minute walk to ten minutes. Cillian savored every detail of his home.

Grandpa Barry greeted them at the door with tears filling his gray eyes. "Cil, the officers searched our home first."

"Am I a criminal?"

"Never." He squeezed the child's hand and released. "You couldn't hurt a bug."

Mrs. Barry slowly gathered her boy's things. She neatly folded five sets of clothing and tucked two pairs of shoes into a small satchel, then Grandpa Barry set the satchel by the door. Cillian stood with his head down, refusing to cry. "Do I ha' to be goin'?"

"We'll always fight for you," Grandma Barry said as Grandpa Barry stood beside her. "I love you, Cillian Finn. You're a Barry in our hearts."

"Adonai, protect your little boy." She gave Cillian the travel bag.

When emotion stifled her words, Grandpa Barry finished the prayer, "Adonai, keep our boy safe, no matter what path he must travel." His meaty finger lifted the young orphan's chin. "Wherever life takes you, my son, remember—you will always be ours."

"Ten seconds," Sergeant James said, "and we leave."

The orphan threw his arms around his adopted grandpa's neck. Cillian's bruises had healed, leaving red and blanched marks. "One. Two. Three . . ."

"Why are you counting?" Grandpa Barry asked.

"For ten more seconds, I'll be belongin' to ye, then."

"You'll belong to us for a lifetime." Grandma Barry hugged both of her boys.

"Come on, lad." Sergeant James pulled the tearful orphan boy out of the Barrys' arms. Cillian didn't fight.

He crawled into the back of the copper's car and rode in silent anguish, his dreams evaporating with every mile traveled.

Sheets of rain slapped the pavement and welcomed Cillian to the foreboding, gothic-looking care home. Tears tumbled down his face, washing his soul clean of hope. He clung to his travel bag, inhaling the familiar scent of Grandpa and Grandma.

Was this all he could expect from life—rejection and loss? His stomach turned with a lurch and he swallowed, willing his breakfast down.

Is there anyone who could be lovin' me as much as the Barrys?

A raindrop fell onto his nose.

A melted snowflake. He forced a smile.

25—The Orphan

CONSTABLE COLLIER OPENED THE CAR door. "Come on, lad. Let's get you where you belong." The constable sighed, sounding as if he cared. He placed his meaty hand on Cillian's shoulder.

Where did an orphan belong?

Cillian stumbled along in silence. *I dinna belong to anyone.*

Truly, he was an orphan—abused, abandoned, and unloved by his mother. His heart and mind attempted to convince him to run. Run where? Bibury? He remembered watching the schoolhouse age in seconds. Had Bibury been real? Glancing over his shoulder, he realized he didn't know the way back to the Barrys; he'd have better luck trying to find his way to heaven without help. He hadn't contemplated living without them.

He hadn't planned to be unloved. Again.

Chilled rainwater sloshed under his feet and numbed his toes. Hopelessness weighed down his waterlogged body as he scanned the two-story care home. Towering gray stone walls, a rusted iron gate, and a large brass door handle shaped into the form of a sea dragon locked the pathway to Cillian's future.

The constable opened the creaky metal door, and Cillian timidly crossed the threshold. "Sir, it looks like a prison."

"It was, housed a bunch of schizophrenics."

"What's a schizophrenic?"

"Someone too stupid to tell the difference between what's real and what's not."

"Maybe they're not stupid, but we dinna understand what they see and hear."

"Not bloody likely. The matron of the care home follows her own rules. Don't whine; don't get punished."

Cillian stepped back outside. A fat raindrop fell onto his lips. A raindrop—a melted snowflake, the first touch of spring's embrace. He jogged to keep up with Constable Thomas Collier's long strides. The large wrought-iron doors slammed shut behind them, sounding like a heavy, stone tomb door closing.

Cillian stopped.

"You're fine. Come on. I gotta get home to my own sons."

"Could ye be takin' me with you?" he asked. "I'll be no trouble; I can be doin' a fair bit of farm work."

"We've got more mouths than money, son, and we live in the city, not a farm."

Still voice, are you there? Cillian buried his hand in his pants pocket and touched the silver dollar. His breathing slowed.

He smelled her before he saw her—vinegar, unbrushed dentures, and mothballs. A sullen woman with a taut, yellowish-white updo and sickly gray complexion crawled around the corner, interrupting Cillian's thoughts. As though on a diet of lemons, she puckered her lips into a scowling pout; her brows creased into a frown.

"Scraggly little fellow. What is your name, child?" the prison warden pronounced each syllable in a high-pitched, scratchy voice as she bent down to study Cillian's face. Groups of children marched from room to room, not saying a word.

"M-m-my name is Cillian Finn, ma'am."

"Speak out, boy!"

He cleared his throat. "My na-a-ame is Cillian."

"Well, you look more like a drenched rat than anything else. I'm Miss Grey. That's what you call me. Understood?" She turned to a cupboard, pulled out a musty towel, and threw it in his direction. "Dry off."

He stumbled and fell as he reached for it. She yanked him up by the arm, her spindly fingers leaving indentations. "You're sloppy too," she added, rounding out her criticism. Then she turned to the constable. "Come with me. You have paperwork to sign."

They all trudged into her stark office where the constable signed the papers. "He's all yours, Miss Grey. Hopefully he won't be any trouble for you."

"One more unwanted mouth to feed. If he's any trouble, I'll get him in line." Cillian pulled his sweater closer. He hated the sound of "get him in line."

Miss Grey growled, "Come on, child!"

He ran to keep up with the crabby old woman, peeking over his shoulder toward the iron door closing behind Constable Collier.

Finality.

What lay ahead? The fear of punishment jolted his legs forward.

"This orphanage has rules." Miss Grey spoke in a nasally, matter-of-fact voice. "You must follow all of them, or you'll pay with your skin." She whirled around to face him. "Do you understand me?" She creased her brow as she studied his expression.

"Yes, ma'am," Cillian weakly replied, then hung his head in total surrender, returning to a loveless but familiar place. One day at a time. Survive. The matron marched on, and her little soldier jogged to keep up.

"This is your dormitory." Row after row of metal bunk beds filled the large room. "Put your bag under this bed." His mind wandered back to Bibury. A gurgle erupted in his abdomen at the memory of Grandma Barry's warm school lunch of hot soup, a sandwich, and love.

"Come on, stop dawdling!" Miss Grey's harsh voice brought him back to reality.

He hurried past the bed's shaky legs and tripped, causing the upper bed to come crashing down. He jumped back, but Miss Grey was quick upon him. She commenced to teach Cillian what she meant when she said that he would pay with his skin. After unleashing a leather strap from her belt, she lashed the orphan with such ferocity that he crouched beside the broken bed, his hands above his head.

"I-I-I'm sorry, madam." The strap stung him all over, as though he'd irritated a hive of bees. Fresh welts erupted on his skin.

"Fix the bed, you ungrateful whelp. Your mother probably didn't want you because you are a destructive child." Miss Grey emphasized the tongue-lashing with her leather beast. Cillian struggled to move the top bunk, but his muscles were fatigued from weeping and having little breakfast. He grunted, then whispered, "Someone, please help me."

Legna, hidden in the world of the immortals, lifts the upper bunk back into place. With Daniela's prayers, the imposing angel grows ever more powerful.

★ ★ ★

Cillian stumbled back from the repaired bed, amazed at his strength.

What had he done to deserve his life? Joe Sanders's words haunted him—*you were born, Cillian.*

As though nothing had happened, Miss Grey turned and marched to their next destination, her whip in hand, her heels clicking and clacking through the long hallway. She readjusted the strap at her waist. He struggled to keep up.

She stalked into the lunchroom, a cavernous space with lantern-topped wagon wheel chandeliers dangling from the ceiling and concrete floors lined with dark wood tables and benches on each side.

The chatter died to a deafening silence after she entered.

"Go." Eager to pawn Cillian off on a willing subordinate—*Miss Bailey*, her name tag read—Miss Grey pointed toward an enormously fat woman in a purple dress with a much-too-tight, bright yellow belt cinched around her elephant waist.

Miss Bailey prodded him to his seat with her pendulous stomach. "Sit there." She slammed her hand down on the table. Silverware rattled, and water rode up the sides of amber water glasses.

He sat across from a young, wispy blond boy who slurped his soup.

The little boy peeked over his bowl, then quickly continued slurping but never took his apple-green eyes from the newest orphan's face.

Hmm. Scents of stewed beef and vegetables tantalized his taste buds. Cillian smiled and spooned a mouthful of soup. It tasted amazing.

The boy's eyes twinkled with a hint of childish innocence and mischief. "Did Grey Thunder strike your face with her strap?" he asked, as the children resumed their whispering. "She never misses."

Cillian's face warmed as he nodded an affirmative. "Aye," his words rolled with a Scottish burr. "She thrashed me verra good." Best to be honest, even though he was ashamed that the curious boy knew he'd been punished. A private beating was one thing, and his mother had doled out her fair share of those, but a public one—absolute humiliation.

"You sound like a pirate." The boy chuckled. "Arr. The name's Black Jack, and weel be searchin' the seas for booty."

Thank goodness the boy hadn't dwelt on the thrashing. Pirates he could deal with. "Name's Captain Finnegan Prometheus." Cillian reached across the divide and offered his hand, and they shook.

"What kind of name is that? My name's duller than Miss Grey's teeth." They both laughed before Cillian answered.

"Dinno." Cillian shrugged, and the sting of the beating subsided. "Made it up."

"Don't talk, whine, or dawdle, and the strap stays on her belt." *Great, he's talking about it again.* The nosy boy leaned over the table. "Usually she flogs your backside though, unless you destroy care home property. Did you destroy it on purpose?"

Cillian shook his head. "What's yer name?" he asked, hoping for a distraction.

"Paul Ambrose Cole Hansen, and by the way," he positioned his hand into the shape of a gun. "Pow. She's never beaten me."

"Lucky one, Paul Ambrose Cole Hansen. Maybe I'll be doin' the honors myself."

"You wouldn't."

"No—I couldna do it. I'm not much for fightin'." Cillian scooped a spoonful of soup into his mouth. "Ye have a lot of parts to yer name. How old are you, then?"

"Eleven." He glanced at the teacher's table. "Shh. We'll talk later," he whispered, looking around at the other boys at the table. They were quiet.

"Why?"

"Don't have much time before drop time."

"Drop time?"

"Drop your spoons and stop eating."

Cillian took the hint and shoveled his soup into his mouth, then lifted the bowl and drank the rest. The beefy broth and dry piece of bread warmed his stomach. It was a big improvement from his mum's home, but not as good as Mama Kelley's or Grandma Barry's home cooking. Love was the missing ingredient.

Finished, he belched. They laughed.

While Paul finished his soup, Cillian swatted a stray tear from his cheek, then glanced at Paul. Had he noticed?

"Are you cryin' like a baby?"

Bloody crap.

Paul scanned the faces of the boys next to them. Focusing on the face of a thin boy with a giraffe neck, long nose, and wire-framed glasses, he shivered. "Aggie, the class bully, will beat you up. He's skinnier than a beanstalk, but he's tall and mean."

"It's the raw onions."

"You must've gotten the good part." Paul sopped the remainder of his soup with his last bite of bread. "There weren't any onions in mine." Paul paused. "Hey, wait a minute. Miss Grey hates onions." Paul gave Cillian his napkin. "Don't worry. We all cry when we first arrive. I did, and I wet my bed."

"Something to look forward to—pissed pants." Cillian's face creased with a grin. The bell rang. Miss Grey shrieked, "Drop time! Spoons down. Everyone stand. Go outside for a break." She rang a cowbell for emphasis.

"Does she think we're deaf?" Cillian dropped his spoon inside his bowl.

"Come with me!" Paul ran around the table, grabbed his new friend's hand, and jerked Cillian forward. He stumbled after the younger boy, sprinting into the tepid English air.

"Let's play catch," Paul suggested, then grabbed a baseball from the cardboard toy box.

As they played and chased each other, Cillian realized he could survive whatever this new home had in store for him—as long as he had Paul. Out of breath and alone, they sat on gray steps by a courtyard fountain. The sound of cascading water drowned out their worries, and Paul shared an apple he had stolen from the cafeteria.

A bellowing voice—"Recess over!"—followed by a whistle ended their play. The boys lined up with military precision. Cillian followed Paul.

"What's your name, really?" Paul asked.

"Cillian Joseph Finn."

"Your name is just as boring as mine, but let's be friends, Cil. Okay?"

"Done." Cillian thrust his chest out, standing taller, and marched close behind Paul. *Dinna lose him, whatever ye do.* The seedlings of his family of love were sprouting. He buried his hands in his pockets and caressed the special coin. He was the lucky one, not Paul—or was it luck at all?

Maybe Paul was a gift from the gentle voice?

26—Orphan Dreamer

Monday, July 11, 1994
Gainesville, Florida

DANIELA CREPT INSIDE ETHAN'S COLD, sterile hospital room, carrying her patinated box.

He slept, a plastic pipe jutting from between his lips.

Would he survive?

He must.

The world's fate was riding on his survival.

If he died, his death would shatter Daniela's faith into a million pieces. Without faith it was impossible to please God. Would God listen to a kid he was displeased with? Could she listen to a God she was displeased with?

Not likely on either count.

She trudged forward, shoulders slumped, and stopped at his bedside.

"We're going for dinner." Ethan's parents left Daniela alone with their son. "See you later." She wasn't hungry, hadn't eaten for a week.

Caw, caw, caw. A lonely raven cried beyond Ethan's window. Daniela watched as it tightened its talons around a skinny, gnarled limb of a Florida oak.

The raven stared at her.

She glared back.

The raven turned its beak toward the pastel-blue sky, called again, then spread its wings and soared to the heavens. Daniela returned her gaze to Ethan's face—pale, a deathly gray. Alarms chimed. "Ethan," her voice broke, "don't leave me."

The alarm peaked, then ebbed as the ventilator struggled against Ethan's coughing fit. Daniela sat on the edge of a plastic recliner, waiting for him to open his eyes.

Hours passed. A fatigued sun began to set, bruising the sky with deep reds, purples, and blues. Bald and emaciated, Ethan woke, choking on the endotracheal tube. Daniela rushed to his side and held his hand. "You okay?" He had not been awake for four days.

He sluggishly blinked his eyes twice. Their code for *I'm okay— are you?*

She blinked twice and grinned.

Deep inside her soul, springs of hope sprung up from a barren dry land.

Was Yahweh going to perform a last-minute miracle?

She hooked her pinky finger into his. "I won't leave you. Promise." Tears welled up in the corners of her eyes. She swiped them away. "Be strong. When you're tired of being strong, be strong again," her mother had said. Clenching her jaw, she braved a glance toward his legs, or what was left of them. The doctor had amputated the right one a few months ago, and the left leg lay limp.

Lonely, awkward, and in need of a friend, she had shown up in his history class last summer. Would he still be healthy and happy, with a sun-kissed tan, big smile, and hypnotic, amber-brown eyes if she hadn't shown up?

Ethan closed his eyes.

Open them again.

Please.

The alarms quieted, and she retreated back to the uncomfortable plastic chair. The day after he'd been diagnosed with cancer, they had made a pact to live, and armed with wicked senses of humor, had enjoyed the summer of their lives. Both of their parents had replaced their middle names with "trouble."

Ethan often started it, but his being sick usually helped them avoid punishment.

"We reap what we sow," the preacher had said on the television. One month later, when summer ended, Mr. Osteosarcoma yanked out all the stops and began pounding Ethan Mohammed Solomon six feet under. Was this all God's doing? Had Yahweh made Ethan sick because of a wrong action?

A *yes* would be a major problem with Daniela. The possibility sucked the breath from her lungs. She gasped, coughed, and choked. Ethan opened his eyes and blinked twice—*you okay?*

"I am." She lied.

"Yahweh answers prayers in mysterious ways," her mother's words replayed. "Whatever you do, Danny Rose, don't lose hope—believe."

But if a person had never found hope, how could they lose it?

Ethan's mother had never read the Torah but claimed to be a Jew; his father claimed to practice Islam but had never read the Quran. So one day after Ethan and Daniela attended a Christian youth camp, Ethan had decided to follow Yeshua, the Light of the World.

Daniela embraced herself as she recalled that rainy, humid day standing around a dying campfire at youth camp. It was as if Yeshua had stepped down, beckoned to Ethan, and said, "Follow Me." In a manner consistent with Ethan's approach to life, he'd as good as said, "Sure, dude. Where are we going?"

Daniela laughed at the memory, then fought back tears. That journey had led him here, lying in the intensive care unit, moments from death.

She opened the patinated box, removed the Glass Tattoo, and laid the relic inside her right palm. The edges of the diamond darkened. Blue ink spilled into the center. Warm energy burst into her palm, pulsing throughout her entire being. What was happening? The jewel disappeared into her palm, leaving a beautiful, blue snowflake tattoo. "It's beautiful."

Ethan opened his eyes, rescuing her from an episode of self-pity.

"You're awake." She ignored the weird feeling pulsing through her body and walked to her best friend's bedside.

He gave her a thumbs-up. His eyes sparkled.

He's laughing.

She retrieved a notepad. Scrawled across college-ruled pages were Ethan's and Danny's dreams. "We're both thirteen. Wanna go somewhere amazing? What about the Smithsonian? Dusty basements, secret alcoves, and hidden treasure. Our class leaves in two days." She held the notepad so he could write.

Take me to the stars, Rosebud . . .

Ethan started another coughing fit. Seconds seemed like hours. Weak, his arms fell to the mattress. He was losing ground. He gazed up at Daniela, his eyes longing to say something. Desperately, he pawed at the sheets, searching for Daniela's hand. He found her clump of sweaty fingers. She interlocked her fingers with his, closed her eyes, and whispered. "To the stars."

A languid voice spoke, "Come up here." Warmed honey poured over her body, embracing her and pulling her into a long, dark tunnel. The corners of the room fell into oblivion.

Ethan and Daniela disappeared.

"I knew such a man—whether in the body or out of
the body I do not know, God knows—how he was
caught up into Paradise and heard unspeakable words,
which it is not lawful for a man to utter."

—Apostle Paul's second letter to the Corinthians

27—Orphan Dreamer

ON A MOONLESS, STARRY NIGHT, Ethan and Daniela were taken.

They arrived in Gibeah, nameless.

A midnight-blue tattoo stained Shiloh's hand, and Ezra possessed two legs. Shiloh chased Ezra, cutting left and then right, but Ezra evaded him. Worn out after an hour of fun, the kids walked side by side. "You won't be mad at me if I want to stay in Gibeah?" Ezra asked.

"You're down with slavery?"

"Doesn't seem so bad. The prince lets us play chase."

"For now. And for now, he thinks I'm a boy—which I'm not."

"Harry wouldn't let you live that one down."

"Nor Claire." Shiloh shook his head. "Our parents will be worried. We should go home. It's the responsible thing to do."

"But we're kids. Not adults, and if we go back, I'm not sure how long I'll be around."

"I know." Shiloh gulped hard. Don't cry. Don't you dare. "We'll find a compromise."

"You sound like an adult. Ugh."

Shiloh laughed, but questions gnawed at him for the rest of the day and into the night as the slave boys journeyed through the deserts of Gibeah with their master's caravan, eating stale bread while their master ate dried meat and fruits.

Shiloh made up his mind.

Freedom was the most precious treasure. Their parents' happiness depended upon their children's return. When they returned home, he'd find a cure for Ethan's disease. As for Earth's impending apocalypse . . .

No thirteen-year-old kid could ever stop that, except in fairy tales. Shiloh adjusted his turban. Secrets were kept safest behind plain faces and closed lips. The face of a slave would be the perfect mask for Shiloh.

First task: Find a map that shows the way home.

Shiloh clutched his tattered bag and trudged behind his new master.

The desert sun began to set. Shiloh thought about General Jehu's instruction about loving Adonai and thus loving oneself. "When you're lost, face your fears. He'll guide you." Shiloh's mother's words popped into his thoughts.

> God is our refuge and strength . . . we will not fear, though the mountains fall into the heart of the sea, though its waters roar and foam . . . God is within her, she will not fall . . . Be still, and know that I am God . . . I will be exalted in the earth."

His mother enjoyed mixing her thoughts with scriptures.

"Face my fears," he whispered. If facing his biggest fear was Shiloh's key back home, what was his biggest fear? Nosebleeds in public? Loneliness—an agonizing fear, indeed, but Ezra was here. "Why in the heck are we in Gibeah?"

"Freedom. Bravery." Ezra snuck up behind Shiloh and grabbed his shoulders. Shiloh jumped. "Ezra!" His heart rate fought to find a steady pace.

"I can run, and you can learn how to swim." Ezra said. "Face our fears. Conquer them."

"But that's it."

"What are you going on about?"

"My biggest fear: deep water. The pathway back home is most likely hidden underneath water—a lake, an ocean, or a river!" Shiloh slapped his hands across his mouth, hoping his master hadn't heard his plan to escape.

"We're in a desert, genius." Ezra winked. "Not much water."

"You're right . . ."

"Chin up. Every desert has an oasis."

"You're the best friend ever. Find the oasis. Face my fear. Take a dive. Return home." Shiloh grabbed Ezra's face and kissed his cheek.

"Hey! Watch it. They're watching us. We're both boys—remember?" Ezra wiped the kiss from his cheek, but Shiloh giggled. "Will you help?"

"As long as you promise me that we can visit Gibeah again."

"Deal."

For the next two days, they asked everyone where they could find an oasis in the desert before Shiloh had to leave to serve his master and his master's guest the usual midday meal inside the prince's luxurious desert tent.

Don't eavesdrop—or at least fake not listening.

Hold the tray steady.

Keep the wine goblets filled.

For the love of all things loveless, don't drop anything!

Mephibosheth, Prince Jonathan's son, sat on a rug near his father, his feet and legs contorted at odd angles, rendering the young boy's legs into useless sticks. His father's tunic clung to muscular legs. Despite all Prince Jonathan's supposed power, royalty could never change his son's deformities.

"My lord." General Jehu, a massive man and the prince's lunch guest, chewed a bite of his favorite dish: goat's cream spread across hot bread, topped with leeks and tomatoes. "As you know, my daughter desires to attend warrior school."

A hush swallowed the room as the prince studied his plate of meats and cakes, his lips greased with olive oil. Shiloh gripped both edges of the silver platter, anticipating the prince's disapproving response and the kind general's heartbreak.

"Why?" Laughing, Prince Jonathan's voice dripped with disdain. "She's a girl!"

The general's face darkened, and Shiloh cringed. "Miriam's my only child. My legacy." Methodically, the general dipped the corner of a linen cloth in a dish of water and dabbed the corners of his mouth while he waited for his master's answer.

"General, come now." The prince placed his wine goblet on a colorful Arabian carpet beneath his couch and stopped chewing. "If my father had relied upon a girl to save the kingdom from the Philistines' giant, we would have perished."

The general took another bite while Shiloh served a second platter of dates, nuts, and raisin cakes to his master and then his guest.

The slave's belly rumbled. Resting his hand over his thin abdomen, he quieted his hunger pains. Slaves ate after their masters, not before, and definitely not during. He eyed a raisin cake, inhaled, and imagined the buttery-sweet taste while the prince grabbed two and stuffed his mouth full of them, chewed, and swallowed.

Slavery still sucks!

"Tell me, General. Could your Miriam have defeated Goliath?" The prince didn't give the general a moment to answer. "No—never. A woman has her work," the prince continued. "In the home, under the guidance of her father and then her husband."

Shiloh's mother had told him that people saw what they wanted to see and believed what was convenient.

Prince Jonathan was no different.

"A young shepherd boy—your friend—killed Goliath, not a seasoned warrior." Leaning back on a sofa stacked with soft linen pillows, the general rested his wine goblet on Shiloh's platter, then shifted in his seat. "But if that is how you feel, my lord, I will keep her home."

"It is how I feel, and it is what I know."

A faint quiver trembling in the general's square jawline told Shiloh a different story. The general believed his Miriam deserved a chance to learn how to fight, just like any boy born into an aristocratic family, and he would give her that chance—somewhere, somehow, even if it meant betraying his master to the Philistines, Prince Jonathan's enemy.

Prince Jonathan glanced at his crippled son, his gaze filled with a mix of sorrow and the pride of a father's dreams. "Miriam is breathtaking. The lads will fight to the death to take her hand in marriage.

Maybe even my Mephibosheth . . ." Shifting in his seat, the prince swallowed his far-fetched paternal dreams whole. His son would never fight for anything or anyone. "More wine, slave." The prince clapped his hands.

Shiloh poured, and the prince drank a gobletful and then another.

Lost in drunken joviality, Prince Jonathan stood up from his sofa, wiped his mouth, and tossed a linen napkin toward Shiloh's platter, which missed the silver dish altogether and landed near the young servant boy's feet.

Good thing the prince hadn't wanted to be an NBA player.

Another time and another place.

The hungry slave smiled on the inside, having quickly learned to hide any truth about himself. He straightened his shoulders, leaned down, and picked up the napkin while keeping his gaze focused on his feet.

Shiloh knew how to endure social humiliation.

Stay invisible.

He inhaled, taking in the musk of warriors and cripples along with the delicate scents of wildflowers.

The prince tugged on his slave's ear. "You can eat the leftovers."

Shiloh bowed. "Thank you, my lord." He would eat one raisin cake and give the other one to Ezra.

"Dreaming about lads as handsome as Shiloh is what a girl's dreams are designed for. Nothing more. Definitely not swords, shields, and battlefields." Prince Jonathan turned to face the general.

The general's lips curled into a sneer. "Shiloh's a slave and a foreigner." His eyes narrowed, and Shiloh wilted into the shadows. The general's fists were the size of the boy's head. He didn't want to be near the general if he lost his temper, even though they shared a secret.

"Forgive me." Prince Jonathan reached for a third pitcher of wine and served Jehu, attempting to pacify the powerful, brawny soldier. "The comparison wasn't meant to insult your dear Miriam, only to refocus her purpose—as a girl soon to become a woman, a mother, and a wife. I want the best for her."

"Understood." Without taking a sip of the new wine, the general stood and placed his cup on Shiloh's platter and winked. The general had kept her secret. Indeed, Shiloh was a girl, and she was starting to realize just how brave she could be. "If you will excuse me, my lord, I will return to the camp and inspect the troops."

"Is that a question or a statement?" The prince cocked his head to the side and studied the general's face.

"However, you wish it to be, my lord."

"I'm sorry your Hannah died in childbirth. If I was younger, I would marry Miriam myself." The prince licked his lips and then glanced at his son. "Miriam should marry a royal. No matter what."

"Shalom." Jehu bowed and exited the tent.

The next evening, Prince Jonathan's mocking words lingered with Shiloh, and no matter how hard he rode his filly, Storm, through the desert night, the words clung to his slight frame, soaking through his deeply bronzed skin into his very bones and poisoning his tender soul.

It was true. In Gibeah, Shiloh was a slave and a foreigner, but it was the prince who had made a terrible mistake, underestimating the abilities of the general's daughter and others like her. Forty-year-old princes made mistakes all the time.

Their subjects and peers called them miscalculations.

Again, Shiloh laughed on the inside. Mastering mathematics wasn't required at How to Become a Royal in Gibeah School, but heaven forbid if a slave or a girl made a mistake in ancient Gibeah. Either one would be judged a criminal, then punished.

The world worked in strange ways: right became wrong and wrong became right, depending on the social status of the person committing the deed.

28—Orphan Dreamer

AGAIN, NIGHT FELL ON THE desert land. Yet within Shiloh's internal clock, time seemed to stand still.

Today, Yahweh mandates time to move out of your way. Shiloh remembered the odd words that had settled inside his spirit the morning of his thirteenth birthday. Time stood still, yet in a strange way it elapsed, falling away into the future.

Tonight was the first occasion that Shiloh had traveled alone with Prince Jonathan, a mentor more than a cruel slave owner, but a master nonetheless—one who played god and decided on a whim whether his subjects lived or died.

Questions pushed the young servant's thoughts of doomed warrior girls from his mind: What would become of Ezra's legs after they escaped from the palace?

Would he lose them again?

How could a thirteen-year-old misfit abort Earth's apocalypse when he couldn't save his friend's legs? And though they must escape, he didn't know what they would escape to. More torment, most likely, but the flavor of persecution would be different, and at least bullies couldn't flog Shiloh's back at will.

A crescent moon squeezed light down on Shiloh and Prince Jonathan's treacherous path, a steep, narrow, stony road with a sloped ravine to the left. Shadows shifted, promising death by a Philistine's hand at every turn. Down in the valley, lights sparkled. The palace was near, home even closer.

One more night.

Shiloh would join Ezra in King Saul's palace.

King Saul, Prince Jonathan's father, was a madman. Jealous. Murderous. The palace was not safe for Ezra. Shiloh must return quickly. The crack of a whip across the rump of a camel jarred Shiloh from his thoughts of friendship and home.

Don't anger the prince and risk a flogging.

Keep up.

"Giddy-up, Storm."

A slave with fresh lacerations may not survive the night, much less an escape. Digging his heels into horseflesh, Shiloh felt sweat pour from his hands.

The path flattened to a slight incline, and Shiloh finally took a deep breath. Ten horse strides ahead, Prince Jonathan's ivory tunic clung to his bronzed, powerful physique. A purple silk robe floated behind him, riding trails of stiff wind above the Arabian's rump as the beautiful midnight-black beast's hooves bit into the dry terrain, kicking up sand into Shiloh's face.

The prince glanced over his left shoulder. "Stay near," he commanded over the thud of the horses' hooves. "The Philistines lurk in the shadows."

"Yes, my lord." He crouched low, grasped a clump of his filly's mane, and tugged on the reins. "Into the wind, Storm."

The filly neighed, tossed her head against the pull of the bit, and charged downhill, past sage thickets and boulders, kicking up her own trail of dust. He pressed knobby knees into the horse's sides, and the chestnut lunged into a full gallop, pulling alongside the master's Arabian.

Night air whisked past his face, washing him with hints of spice.

Shiloh thought of Ezra running through the palace barn, past the gardens, and diving into a wadi, hidden deep inside a cave filled with warm, pastel-blue water—their quiet, safe place. Shiloh would stand on a boulder above the pool and watch his friend swim; he couldn't even tread water, much less swim.

Ezra had tested the water and hadn't found a portal to escape home.

Shiloh and his prince raced through the night, and as night yielded to dawn, the path widened. He pulled his turban below his dark eyes and tucked it behind his left ear, across the lower half of his face. Rough wool scratched his youthful skin. If he could remove the headpiece and cool his head, he would have, but secrets must be hidden.

Shiloh released the filly's mane; Storm galloped at full stride.

Bravely, the young boy dared a glance at the heavens.

The stars were aligning. Aryeh—the lion of the Hebrews—roamed between clusters of constellations, sparkling against an onyx sky. Shiloh's parents had told him that the fierce cat devoured sheep unless the Shepherd protected His flock. Surely, the lion's presence spoke of a dark omen, but one day, the lion would lie down beside the lamb.

Tonight was not that night!

Shiloh rode harder, the two riders' horses neck and neck.

"Why does your father want to kill your friend—David?" Shiloh's mind idled and grew familiar. His mouth followed. "I would never allow my best friend to be murdered by my father. Wouldn't matter if he was king." The moment he finished his free-spirited question, he realized his mistake.

He was not at home, and Prince Jonathan was not his father or his friend.

"Does a slave boy dare to commit treason?" Darkness crossed the prince's otherwise handsome face.

"I didn't mean to challenge you—or your father, my lord."

"Your king!"

"Please forgive me." Shiloh's eyes burned, but he refused to cry.

"Pay attention to the road or you'll fall off your horse, and I'll be short a slave." Prince Jonathan tugged his stallion's reigns. Shiloh jerked the reigns of his own horse, pulling away.

"Ride steady." The prince threw a casual look in Shiloh's direction. "I'm exhausted. I'll not punish you tonight, but there's always the morning when I'll be renewed of strength. Though the morning may offer you forgiveness—if you accomplish an important task tonight."

"Yes, my lord?" Shiloh diverted his gaze. His thin shoulders shook, but he held his tongue, redirecting further questions into his thoughts. *What did the master have in mind? More importantly, would the plan interfere with his and Ezra's imminent escape?*

"After we arrive at the palace, you'll deliver a letter to David, telling him to meet with me tomorrow."

"But your father hates your friend." Shiloh cowered. He had done it again—speaking his unfiltered thoughts into royal ears.

"You're begging for it, aren't you?"

"No, my lord." Shiloh gulped hard. *Secrets are more easily kept behind closed lips.* He dared a glance up at the prince. When he did, a broad smile spread across the prince's regal face, and he slowed the pace of his stallion.

Shiloh followed his lead.

"You're young and foolish." The royal words hung in the air for minutes. "But you'll make something of yourself. Because in the end, boys grow up into men." Prince Jonathan patted the top of Shiloh's turban. It slid down over his eyes.

The slave adjusted it so he could see the road.

"In the desert, a woman's destiny is nothing but death mingled with shame at the hands of those filthy Philistines, but there's hope for you, Shiloh. Pay attention. Serve me well. I'll train you with a bow and arrow, so one day, you may fight my enemies."

"Yes, my lord." *Don't ask about Miriam.* Shiloh tucked his chin to his chest and stared at the dusty terrain rushing past him. Despite his best effort, the question pounding on the inside of his head poured out through his lips faster than vomit. "Is there hope for you, my lord?"

"Ah, you overheard Samuel, Adonai's prophet." The prince bit into a pomegranate. "Were you listening?"

Shiloh's mouth salivated as he watched the blood-red juice drip onto the prince's hand. "I served the midday meal, and I couldn't help but hear what he said."

"The kingdom belongs not to me but to another—what do you think of that?" He took another bite, and Shiloh stayed quiet. "It's true. I am a prince destined to be defeated before I even start my reign as king."

"It's a shame."

"Being a king isn't all sunshine." Maybe kingship resembled nightfall?

Treacherous.

The city gate towered in the distance, and tonight, at least, Jonathan still reigned as prince, no matter what the seer had prophesied. The prince yanked his stallion's mane, stopping the Arabian midstride.

Shiloh's heartbeat upticked.

Had his master changed his mind? Was a whipping in his future? He stared at the braided leather attached to the prince's riding pack, praying for it to remain at the horse's side.

It did. Shiloh released a breath. The prince spoke in low, even tones. "Listen carefully, Shiloh."

"My lord?"

"David is my friend. As Adonai wills, he will become king, not me." Prince Jonathan reached into his leather satchel and removed a small scroll. "Deliver this message to David—tonight."

"What does it say? I mean, yes, my lord."

"Fail, and I'll unleash my wrath. You will die as a boy. Then, I'll feed you to my dogs." The prince's serene expression never wavered, as though he'd grown accustomed to threatening and then punishing wayward slaves. "Succeed, and my father may discover your treachery. If he does, you will die as a man, and I will bury you as a man." Prince Jonathan rested his hand on Shiloh's thigh. "You must not implicate me. Understood?"

Shiloh didn't want to die as a boy or a man. He was neither. Why not deliver his own letter? Because Jonathan was a prince, and Shiloh was his slave. "Yes, my lord."

"Hold your tongue at court, or Father will find out."

"I-I-If only you knew how much I wanted to say and didn't." Shiloh pinned his gaze to the ground.

"I'm sure. Accomplish the mission, and I'll forget about your indiscretions this night." The prince clicked his tongue, and his Arabian cantered toward the palace. "The thoughts of a child—all foolish innocence," he mused.

The thoughts of a prince: selfish cowardice.

Past the city gates, flatlands yielded to a city and then a stone palace awash in the sepia hues of a sleeping sun. Six gold buttresses supported a terra-cotta roof hanging over five porches. "Rosh Chodesh! Rosh Chodesh is sanctified," a voice cried into the night.

"We are still celebrating the new moon," the prince said, "the start of the month, Tishri."

Shiloh remembered his mother's words about the Feast of Trumpets, and his father's words about his destiny. He'd said time traveling would help Shiloh solve the puzzles. Puzzle one: When would the pandemic occur?

You can do this.

You're smart—chosen.

Shiloh inhaled deeply and tried to remember but couldn't make sense of his thoughts. "My lord, may you tell me about your country's feast days, particularly the feast that you're celebrating tonight?"

"It'll pass the time." The prince paused. "We call this feast Yom Teruah. It means the day of the awakening."

"In my homeland, we call it Rosh Hashanah or the Feast of Trumpets."

"Odd names." His voice deepened. "'Speak unto the children of Israel, saying, in the seventh month, in the first day of the month, shall you have a Sabbath, a memorial of blowing of trumpets, a holy convocation'."

"Leviticus?"

"What?"

"From Moses—"

"You mean the third and fourth books."

"Yes, my lord."

"Ahhh. The third book of the Tohrah is named Vayikra—He called. I'll eventually make a fine lad out of you." The prince laughed. "Our seventh month is called Tishri, a fall month. A time when the shofar's blasts sound the alarm for us to go before the Lord with offerings, crown Him king of all, and remember that we must go before Him in judgment."

Shiloh remembered that each Hebrew feast spoken of in Leviticus is a foreshadowing of our Messiah's visit to our world. The spring feasts are a foreshadowing of His first coming and what He will accomplish during his visit. The fall feasts are a foreshadowing of His second coming and His plans for that visit.

Shiloh also recalled his mother's words about the differences between the Hebrew calendar and the Gregorian calendar.

The Hebrew sacred (religious) calendar started with the Gregorian calendar month of March and ended twelve to thirteen months later.

All Jewish feasts were calculated from the first day of the month of Nisan (March-April), except for the Feast of Trumpets, the feast the prince and his people were celebrating this month—Tishri, Shiloh's September or October.

"Within the essence of Yom Teruah—your Feast of Trumpets— there may be hidden meanings. It's thought to be the month Moses went back up to Mount Sinai for the second set of tablets, the marriage contract with Israel."

"In my land, it is said that the Feast of Trumpets hides themes of surprise and marriage, a groom coming for his bride after he has prepared his home."

Shiloh whispered the words of the Apostle John, "'In my Father's house are many mansions: if it were not so, I would have told you. I go to prepare a place for you.'" The thump of horses' hooves drowned out his words.

"Well, it is a season of beginnings on many levels. And Tishri begins our civil calendar."

"My lord, I heard in my land where some believe that Elohim created the world during this month. If it is a time of beginnings, and He did create the world during Tishri, would it make sense for Him to allow the world to end during the same month?"

"It's up to Him, but no one can predict the exact day or hour when the month of Tishri begins."

"Day or hour . . ."

"In other words, you could not predict the exact day or hour of Elohim's final redemption or your apocalypse, but if your theory is correct, you could predict the month and maybe even the year. Why are you asking all of these questions?"

"I need to solve a puzzle."

"A riddle?"

"Yes, my lord."

"Well, the best stargazer could predict the start of the new moon within a day or so, but he relies upon seeing the first sliver of a new moon—the twinkling of an eye—before declaring 'Rosh Chodesh. Rosh Chodesh—the new moon is sanctified.' Then, the month of Tishri starts as well as our first fall feast, Yom Teruah, your Feast of Trumpets."

"Twinkling of an eye. The general's instruction? No. The Apostle Paul's mystery," Shiloh whispered.

> "Let me reveal to you a wonderful secret. We will not all die, but we will all be transformed! It will happen in a moment, in the blink (twinkling) of an eye . . ." (The Apostle Paul's first letter to the Corinthian church 15:51).

"Stick the fork in the chicken because I'm done!" Shiloh grinned, making the connection from an ancient Jewish celebration, the Feast of Trumpets, to a prophecy documented in the Apostle John's Isle of Patmos revelations—Yeshua's second coming, his future return to Earth as the King of all Kings: No one knew the exact day or the hour when Yeshua would return for His bride, His followers. Only His Father in heaven knew.

"Are you hungry?" The prince furrowed his brow.

"No, my lord. I'm excited."

"Why?"

"No one knows the *day* or the *hour*—those words should be taken literally, not loosely."

"Explain."

"Prophets in my homeland interpret this sentence to mean that no one can even determine the season or even the year of God's greatest redemption—His Messiah's second coming called the rapture," Shiloh says.

"A messiah? No. We need a king—a conqueror to defeat the Philistines. Your conclusion doesn't make sense. We know that the start of Tishri—your Feast of Trumpets—always begins on the new moon and in the fall."

"So my parents could figure out the decade, year, or even week of what we believe as God's redemption, the Messiah's coming?"

"Probably. Again, it makes sense if your theory holds true . . . it makes sense that it could happen during this fall feast, but you wouldn't know the exact day or hour."

"Makes sense: The element of surprise—not knowing the exact day or hour—and the themes celebrated during the feast." Shiloh gripped Storm's reigns. "The twinkling of an eye occurs at the beginning of a lunar month—every lunar month, but the month of Tishri—September—relies upon the new moon, the twinkling of an eye, to signal the month's beginning."

Beginnings and endings.

Didn't the Apostle Paul give the Corinthian church a huge clue—the twinkling of an eye, the sign most important to the month of Tishri? What feast was celebrated when the month of Tishri began? Feast of Trumpets—Rosh Hashanah, the most likely time for the Messiah to return to Earth.

Feast of Trumpets—Rosh Hashanah is the *when!*"

But what year?

And if Rosh Hashanah was the *when*, what was the pandemic that would occur during or after the Feast of Trumpets that would annihilate all humans from Earth?

Don't know.

Shiloh's heart sank. "Do I need to know?" Shiloh whispered.

"Talking to yourself again?"

"No, my lord."

Would the pandemic look like disease, famine, death? His heart kept sinking. How could the Orphan Dreamer save Earth if he didn't know the year of the pandemic or what started it?

"At the last trump," someone seemed to whisper. Was it the prince? Shiloh glanced at Prince Jonathan. "What's a last trump?"

"Tekiah Gedolah," the prince answered. "The last trump symbolizes our hope for redemption. At the end of the Feast of Trumpets, a ram's horn is blown for a long, final note, symbolizing the end of our celebration."

"Thank you." Shiloh remembered his mother's instruction.

> . . . at the last trumpet. For the trumpet will sound, and the dead will be raised imperishable, and we shall be changed. . . . When the mortal puts on immortality, then shall come to pass the saying that is written: "Death is swallowed up in victory. O death, where is your victory? O death, where is your sting?" (Apostle Paul's first letter to the Corinthians 15:52–55).

"What followed the Feast of Trumpets?" he thought out loud.

"The season of teshuvah."

"Big word. But my mom calls the next fall feast Yom Kippur."

"The word *teshuvah* means to repent. What does Yom Kippur mean?"

"Repentance." This season begins on the first day of the month of Elul, August-September, and continues for forty days until the beginning of Yom Kippur on the tenth day of Tishri. "Tell me more about the season of teshuvah—Yom Kippur, in my homeland."

"Thirty days into this season of repenting, Rosh Hashanah begins—the tenth day of Tishri," the prince said. "Every morning during this thirty-day period, the priest blows a ram's horn."

"What is the purpose for the priest blowing the ram's horn?" Shiloh asked.

"The purpose is to remind the people the King is in the field, to reflect on their ways and repent before the end of the Days of Awe."

"Days of Awe." Shiloh paused and let his voice drop to a whisper. "The tribulation period written about in the Apostle John's revelation." Shiloh's heart raced.

Bad news!

"You're giving me a headache, child."

"I'm sorry. Just a few more questions." Shiloh remembered his mother's words. After Rosh Hashanah begins, ten days remain until Yom Kippur. These ten days are known as the High Holy Days or Awesome Days. "Is the Sabbath that falls within those first ten days important?"

"The Sabbath that falls during these ten days is known as Shabbat Shuvah, or the Sabbath of the Return."

"The Feast of Tabernacles in my land," Shiloh whispered.

General Jehu's story about the Prophet Jonah recirculated in Shiloh's mind.

> "But of the times and the seasons, brethren, ye have no need that I write unto you. For yourselves know perfectly that the day of the Lord so cometh as a thief in the night. For when they shall say, Peace and safety; then sudden destruction cometh upon them, as travail upon a woman with child, and they shall not escape. But ye, brethren, are not in darkness, that that day should overtake you as a thief." (1 Thessalonians 5:1-4).

The astute watcher will know when!

No different than a completed circle, if Earth were to be destroyed, its expiration day would occur during the same season of its birth. Tishri was the seventh month of the Hebrew calendar, and the number seven in the Torah meant complete. Earth's cycle of life would be complete during the month of Tishri.

Armageddon will be in the seventh month. Tishri.

But what year?

A soft voice seemed to say *Later on, I'll tell you.*

Pope Gregory really screwed humans when he pushed the Catholic Christians to ignore the Hebrew calendar and focus on the Gregorian calendar. No wonder humanity was confused—lost, really.

After they arrived at the stables, Shiloh slid off his filly's back, glad to not have the horse's back pressing into his thighs.

At the barn, stable boys secured the horses and poured buckets of spring water into troughs. He darted past the stable, then navigated a tangle of flowering thorn bushes before entering the palace gardens.

Crimson buds yielded a sweet aroma, reminding him of home and his mother's roses. If the task of delivering the scroll to David took all night, how would he find Ezra so they could plan their escape? The general had told Shiloh how to find the eastern oasis.

Walking ten paces behind the prince, he stared at the floor, cataloging details from his peripheral vision and searching for Ezra.

A harp's soft melodies danced among lilies, jasmine, and cinnamon, contrasting against the stench and ugly face of the burly soldier standing guard at the court's entryway.

His smell would keep any assassin at bay. Shiloh fought back an impending giggle. The guard bowed. "My lord."

The guard gazed straight ahead, carriage-ramrod straight, as the prince strolled by.

Shiloh straightened his stance and followed, then—for a moment—yearned to be more than a mere servant boy. Maybe being chosen to be the Orphan Dreamer wouldn't be so bad. One day, would people bow to him?

No. Shiloh wasn't a god. Entering the palace behind his master, he rounded his shoulders again.

Inside the palace, torches blazed, as they had during the last seven days.

Shiloh entered the public court. Frankincense smoldered inside a bronze pot, releasing a heady scent of pine and lemon mixed with a woody aroma. The Egyptians claimed that the spice stimulated emotions—like Prince Jonathan's father needed to stoke his worsening insanity—but King Saul had insisted that the spice be burned, and who was Shiloh to judge anyone insane?

He was no inquisitor.

Against the eastern wall, the king lounged on a golden couch covered with silk pillows. Purple cloth draped across his aging yet muscular body.

"Master?" Shiloh picked up his pace. Prince Jonathan turned and furrowed his brow. Shiloh shrank back, realizing his mistake.

"Speak quickly, child."

"Your friend." Shiloh dipped his forehead toward David, a tall, handsome young man who stood beneath an arched ivory alcove tucked into the southern wall of the palace court. The prince's friend strummed his harp.

A quick smile flashed across Jonathan's face, and he nodded, his Adam's apple rising and falling as his hand went to clutch a leather satchel that hung from his girdle. Beads of sweat dotted his forehead.

What's in the satchel?

The prince was hiding something.

"Stay with the others and find an opportunity to deliver the letter to David." By *the others*, the prince meant the other slaves.

"Yes, my lord." The agile slave eased past a group of soldiers and lengthened the gap between them. As the prince crossed the court and strolled toward his father, Shiloh disappeared into a cluster of servants, his eyes fixed upon his prince.

What were the prince's plans?

Shiloh scanned the court, searching for Ezra.

Ironically, even though David had killed King Saul's enemy, Goliath, he still played his harp to calm the king's anxiety. But the people believed that David was a great warrior now—not just a shepherd or harpist. As the prince neared his father, the women started their chant, "Saul killed his thousands, but David slew his tens of thousands." Their shrill voices echoed through the dense smoke of burning incense.

Shiloh had heard the foolish song before, but why would the women sing it in front of the king? Beneath the amber glow of torches, darkness settled on King Saul's face, and his nostrils flared. He glared at David and licked his lips. Trouble. Shiloh's heart pounded beneath his tunic.

Deliver the message, find Ezra, then storm. Shiloh quickened his pace.

The prince stumbled. A guard grasped Prince Jonathan's arm. The court quieted. "Are you well, my lord?"

"I am." Prince Jonathan righted himself, pulled his arm from the guard's grip, and charged ahead, diverting his path from his father to his friend. On the other side of the court, dressed in a pale-blue turban, as promised, Ezra waited. Shiloh placed his hand over his heart—their signal of loyalty. Ezra nodded, then skirted the perimeter of the court, sneaking behind gasping adults who watched the prince.

Shiloh's gut cramped when he looked at David's face. Was the prince planning to murder his own friend to secure the crown for himself?

The shepherd turned warrior might not escape the palace tonight.

Nervously, David strummed faster, making more noise than music as the women's chants—as raucous and clanging as cymbals—drowned out his harp.

"I am the king of Judah!" King Saul screamed through the palace, but he wouldn't be for long. The entire kingdom knew that Elohim's spirit had left King Saul. David still strummed his harp, but their God had anointed David as Israel's next king. Silence invaded the palace faster than any enemy army at King Saul's words.

David stopped playing his harp.

The women ceased their song.

Prince Jonathan halted and rested his hand on the hilt of his sword.

Something hard and wet tapped Shiloh's face. He removed a spitball. "Ezra," he hissed. Heart pounding, Shiloh pushed through the noisy, restless crowd. "Ezra, really?" he cried above the hum of whispers and shuffling feet. "Where are you?"

The stupid women started singing again, louder, intentionally prodding the lion. "Saul killed his thousands, but David slew his tens of thousands." Elohim's spirit had left King Saul; why should they respect the soon-to-be dethroned monarch?

Because he still sat on the throne.

King Saul jumped up from his couch, brandished a spear, arched back, and hurled it at David's chest, screaming as the weapon flew, "Greedy boy, stay with your sheep!"

Prince Jonathan raced across the court, clutching the hilt of his sword at his back. If nothing else, the prince was a loyal friend.

David abandoned his harp and bolted toward the entryway.

Shiloh knew what he must do. "Ezra!"

"Shiloh!" The call was but a whisper above the chaotic shouts of an impending human stampede.

"Wait for me!" Shiloh screamed.

"Jonathan—my son!" The king screamed as Prince Jonathan stood trembling before him. "Do you run to kill my enemy or to save him?"

"No, Father. I meant to protect you." He sheathed his sword. A coward, but still a friend—maybe.

"Prove yourself." The king sat on his couch. "Kill David. Bring me his head and foreskin."

His foreskin? Shiloh stopped in his tracks. *Barbaric. Thank God I don't have one.*

Prince Jonathan bowed while backing away from the throne, then approached his general, Jehu.

Shiloh wanted to watch, but he had his own problems.

Deliver the message or face the prince's wrath. After being humiliated by his father, Prince Jonathan would show his slave no mercy if Shiloh failed to deliver the message. He removed the crumpled piece of parchment from his satchel and looked down the hallway. The fleeing warrior had disappeared and would soon be followed by an army of bloodthirsty soldiers.

You can do it. Save David like you saved Anne—the baby duckling— from the mean snake. Shiloh ran.

Footsteps pounded the marble behind him. *Keep running.* Swords screeched along shields, creating an eerie sound.

Shiloh saw David dart into an alcove.

Soldiers marched past the alcove, eager to slice him into pieces. The whole army would be upon the warrior-turned-traitor. He needed at least one ally. Had the prince really betrayed his friend to his father?

Hilda, a lanky female servant, scampered in the wake of sweaty men, their shields, and their swords. Her garment was sloppily draped off her right shoulder, and a fresh bruise encircled her neck.

"Hilda—" Shiloh grabbed at her.

"Don't say anything." She pulled back from Shiloh's touch. A feral cat's eyes would look less wild.

"I'm sorry." Shiloh reached to rest his hand on her shoulder.

"No, don't touch me. I'm unclean." She refused to look into Shiloh's eyes. "What do you want from me?"

"Making sure you're okay. That's all."

"I am." A tear mixed with dirt slipped down Hilda's pale face. "What do you really want, Shiloh? You men—boys—are all the same."

"I don't want anything. I understand. Truly, I do."

"And?"

"I need to tell Ezra to meet me past the stables."

"Why?"

"I have to deliver something to David, or I'll be punished."

"They're good at punishing." Hilda smirked.

Should he invite her to escape with them? Could she fit in, speak the language, and attend school? Would the kids in their village accept an immigrant like her if they wouldn't even accept Shiloh and Ezra?

Who cares what Harry and all the others would think? "Do you want to come with us?" Shiloh whispered.

"No. I'm exhausted—spent." She shook her head. "Thanks for inviting me. I drew a map that leads to the oasis and gave it to Ezra. Happy travels."

"Thanks for keeping our planned escape a secret."

"I'll tell Ezra you're looking for him, but then I'm off to bed."

"Wait." Shiloh reached for Hilda. Shiloh whispered, "I'm not a boy . . . I'm a girl." Hilda smiled wide, then tucked her lip between her teeth. "Don't tell anyone. Promise me."

"Promise."

"May the wind be at your back, Shiloh—a girl, the bravest girl I know." Hilda hobbled toward the opposite side of the palace, and that's when Shiloh saw the trail of bright red blood running down the inside of her leg.

What happened?

You men—boys—are all the same.

Shiloh gasped. He must tell Simon, her master. The letter would have to wait. Who cared if Prince Jonathan punished him? Hilda must be avenged. As if divinity agreed with the slave's plan, a portly man dodged and wove between bodies up ahead. Shiloh followed him, closing the gap. "Master Simon."

The man stopped and turned. Shiloh took in the crumpled shirt, loose belt, and untucked tunic. "Speak, child. I must witness the happenings outside."

"Uh—your tunic's untucked, my lord."

Wickedness flashed deep within the man's eyes. *They're good at punishing us.* "Hilda," Shiloh whispered. "Your—"

Simon lunged for Shiloh, but the slave was faster. He dropped to his knees and crawled between one soldier's legs, then another, until he saw feet sticking out from under the silk curtains hanging in a palace alcove.

Dirty sandals.

David?

Panting, Shiloh rolled beneath the curtain, then stood up beside the warrior. "A letter, from the prince. I hope you don't mind, but I read it."

"Dead men aren't picky." David read the letter. "'In the field when the sun rises, the crown waits for you. I'll shoot three arrows into the sand. If it's safe, I'll have my slave retrieve the first two arrows. If it is not safe, I will tell my slave to not retrieve any.'" He looked at Shiloh. "What does it mean?"

"We're to meet the prince in the desert—near the oasis, three miles east of the palace. The arrows will tell you if it is safe to come out of hiding." Shiloh gulped. General Jehu could write Hebrew and had rewritten the letter as a favor to Shiloh, adding the part about the oasis and removing the part about meeting near the caves.

Time to return home. Shiloh refused to stay one day longer in this crazy country. The oasis was their ticket out.

"Until tomorrow."

"Be safe." Head down, Shiloh strolled around the curtain, past a stone bench and marble fountain. He walked a few paces from David's hiding place.

"What are you doing, slave?" A soldier grabbed him. Shiloh slipped his grip, ducked and rolled away, then sped out of the palace. He glanced back, looking for Hilda. He found her. She lay dead, her bloodied corpse trampled by the king's soldiers.

Shiloh's fists clenched as he drew in a deep breath, moving to Hilda's side. He dragged her to a quiet place inside the stable. The cows mooed but kept their tails down and their poop inside their colons out of respect for the dead. There was no time to bury her, so Shiloh covered her body with hay, then whispered a quick prayer.

If Hilda had been trampled, what had happened to Ezra? Fear snaked down Shiloh's back, and a cold chill gripped his small body. How could he face Ezra's mother and tell her he had lost her only son?

Shiloh had delivered the message to David—a slightly altered message by kindred spirit General Jehu, but it was delivered. Time to find Ezra. Shiloh cupped his mouth between his hands and prepared to shout Ezra's name at the top of his lungs.

"Looking for me?" Ezra tapped Shiloh on the shoulder.

"How did you—"

Ezra tucked a grin into the corners of his lips, leaned down, and tapped his legs. "I'm fast. Faster than lightning! I saw you bolting out of the palace, but then you disappeared. Glad I caught up." Proud of his legs, he stood tall, his chest jutted forward. It would be Shiloh's fault when he lost them, again. Shiloh hugged Ezra. "I'm glad you're safe." He released his friend. "The oasis—tomorrow?"

"I don't want to go back home, Shiloh. Please. Let's stay. It's exciting here."

"No way. I already lied to Prince Jonathan. He may kill me. Besides, we're slaves, Ezra, and these people are crazy."

He laughed. "But when we swim at the cave pool, we're free."

"When *you* swim. If we never return home, our parents will die of worry. Don't you care about their feelings?"

"Maybe they don't know we're gone." Ezra shrugged.

Shiloh hadn't thought of that, but he hoped it wasn't true. "Our mothers? You can't be serious."

"My legs, Shiloh. I'm fast here."

"I know—and I'm sorry." Shiloh squeezed Ezra's shoulder.

"You're fast at home, Shiloh, but I want to run too."

"It's not right, disappearing and not telling our parents," Shiloh protested. Ezra stared at him with pleading eyes that said, *how could you ask this of me, Shiloh?* "Hilda's dead," Shiloh blurted out, and the news had the intended effect: shocking Ezra out of his daze. He'd crushed on Hilda. She was his type—or so Shiloh believed: straight, long blonde hair, pale skin, and thin lips.

"How?"

"Trampled by the king's soldiers." Should he tell Ezra about the blood on the inside of her leg? No. She was dead now. Let him treasure his beautiful memory of her. "I buried her—the best I could." Shiloh shifted so he was in front of the mound of hay, hoping Ezra wouldn't notice the hump in the middle.

"It's impossible." Ezra wiped a tear from his eye, and Shiloh rested a hand on his friend's shoulder.

"But it's true."

"You're right," Ezra said. "After tonight, it's too dangerous here. I don't want to lose you too."

"Really?" Shiloh's face warmed. "You care for me as much as you cared for Hilda? So much that you're willing to lose your legs?"

"Uncle Jakob was right. I like you . . . I have since the day I met you, but you've always been too busy beating yourself up to see it."

"I was scared." *How would it feel to be loved by a boy? Would he kiss her? Would her nose bleed?*

"Let's just go." Ezra reached for Shiloh's hand and led the way. "Promise me we'll come back if Harry and Claire wear on our nerves."

"Promise, hope to die." Shiloh interlinked his pinky finger with Ezra's.

"You're the only thirteen-year-old I know who *wants* to die." He shook his head. "I'm trying to avoid death."

"You'll get better. I didn't tell you, but I sent 'seed money' to one of those preachers on television before we left."

"Those guys who promise God will give you a blessing in exchange for money? They're cons, Shiloh. You could've taken me out to dinner."

"I think I will—on a date."

"No, Rosebud. You won't. I'll be seeing you again many years after the end." *What did Ethan mean? Had he surrendered to death?*

"You're going to live."

"True. But in death. 'O death where is your sting . . . where is your victory? For the last trumpet will sound, the dead in Yeshua will be raised imperishable, and we will be changed. For the mortals will be clothed with immortality.' Immortal clothes—right on." Shiloh knew that Ezra was quoting a part of the Apostle Paul's first letter to the Corinthians.

Ezra was going to die.

Because Shiloh didn't want to stay a slave, he was forcing his best friend to return to their homeland . . . to die.

What kind of friend was Shiloh? Definitely not a kindred spirit.

He was no different than Prince Jonathan: a selfish coward.

As they neared the palace gardens, soldiers shouted, "Give us the killer of ten thousands!" But David had vanished like a ghost, hidden in plain sight—inside the palace. Someone was protecting the future king so he could fulfill his destiny. Maybe that someone would protect Ezra when they returned home.

At that thought, Shiloh grinned ear to ear. That *someone* was Elohim. "Protect Ethan, Yahweh."

"Maybe the purpose of this trip is to teach you to trust Adonai, even with your friend." General Jehu's words mocked Shiloh's prayer.

"I-I-I can't," Shiloh whispered into the night.

Standing in the gardens with a scowl etched across his face that would scare the devil away, Prince Jonathan waited for his slaves. "Where have you two been?"

"Following your—" Shiloh said.

"You're lying." The prince pointed toward the barns. "Fetch my whip."

"My lord." Ezra gripped his friend's arm. "Shiloh was trying to save a girl—Hilda." He sputtered more than spoke. "Sh-sh-she's dead. Trampled." He looked down at the prince's dusty sandals, and Shiloh copied his submissive gesture.

"Is this true?"

"It is, my lord." Shiloh counted his toes, waiting for pain.

"Did you deliver the letter?"

"Yes, my lord . . . but David will meet us at the oasis in the east."

"Why?"

"Who doesn't enjoy an oasis?"

"David wouldn't make a unilateral decision like that."

"I-I-I made a little adjustment to our meeting place with David." Shiloh confessed. "I had to. I—" Ezra squeezed Shiloh's arm, causing brown flesh to rise like the crust of fresh bread between his fingers.

"I was afraid," Ezra interrupted, "that the letter had been compromised. I wanted to protect your friend David." It was true that the soldier who grabbed Shiloh may have overheard the location of their meeting place.

"I don't need a slave boy deciding my destiny." The prince paced. "It's too late to change again. David is probably hiding in the caves." He stopped pacing. "We will meet David at the eastern oasis. Ezra, you'll be flogged at the end of the Sabbath."

Shiloh gasped. The prince continued. "Before sunrise tomorrow, fetch the horses and bring my quiver and bow to the palace's east entrance—both of you! Understood?"

They nodded.

"Go sleep." The prince commanded, and they hurried to the slave quarters.

"Thanks for taking up for me," Shiloh whispered before they neared the common sleeping quarters. "Still want to stay in Gibeah?"

"Absolutely not. You can run for both of us."

"He'll never beat you. We'll be gone, or I'll die trying. Period."

Ezra kissed Shiloh's cheek. "My Joan of Arc." Past the gardens and the stables, they entered a small tent and unrolled their beds side by side. "What will you dream about tonight, Shiloh?"

"Hilda running through grain fields, and you chasing after her."

"Your impossible dreams–she's dead."

"Not in my dreams."

"Maybe I want to chase you through the fields."

"You'd never catch up." Shiloh cracked a smile, and Ezra lay down beside his friend. "No matter what, after we return home, don't leave me to die alone."

"You won't die. The offering to the preacher man will work—just wait." She wasn't good at lying to herself.

"Not holding my breath."

"Good. You need the oxygen." Shiloh giggled. "I'll push you around in your wheelchair and take you everywhere." He pulled a scratchy blanket over both of them and cuddled in the crease of Ezra's arm.

In the morning, the sun stood high above a barren land as Shiloh and Ezra followed Prince Jonathan over the seventh hill east of the palace.

"The oasis, my lord." Throat parched, Shiloh pointed toward a pool surrounded by a lush oasis. Would the pool feel like an anaconda to Shiloh, squeezing her to death? She gulped down a mouthful of parched air.

"Shall we swim later?" The prince shielded his eyes with his hands and scanned the horizon. For Shiloh, swimming equaled one big gulp of water, followed by another, until the thirsty victim drowned.

"Shiloh doesn't know how to swim," Ezra shouldered a quiver of arrows, and Shiloh clutched two of the prince's arrows between trembling hands.

"Zip it," Shiloh hissed.

"I'll teach you one day." The prince laughed, then strode ahead. After twenty paces, he took one of Shiloh's arrows, slipped the arrow into his bow, pulled the bracer taut, and released. "Fetch the arrow, lad."

Shiloh ran through the sand, retrieved the projectile, and returned to Jonathan's side. He repeated the exercise, but on the third shot, the arrow pierced a sand dune in the distance and stood erect.

"I'll run for that one." Ezra laid his quiver at Shiloh's feet and bolted toward the wayward projectile.

Jonathan cried, "Lad, is the arrow too far?"

Ezra stopped. "Should I not retrieve it, my lord?"

In the distance, a man peeked from behind a boulder, then disappeared. "Retrieve it, then come back." The prince waved Ezra to his side. After Ezra returned, Jonathan squeezed the child's shoulder. "Both of you, go home and eat. I'll return to the palace tonight."

"Shall I take your weapons?" Shiloh asked. He and Ezra might need them while they explored the oasis pool for their escape route back home.

"Take my bow and arrow; I'll keep my sword."

Shiloh nodded, relieved. He knew how to use a bow and arrow. He and Ezra disappeared into the haze of the horizon and traveled toward the oasis.

"Shiloh, wait a minute." Ezra sat at the edge of the oasis and kissed both of his legs.

"What are you doing?

"Saying goodbye."

Even if the prince's arrow had pierced Shiloh's heart, the pain wouldn't have been as strong. He gripped the arrow so hard that he thought he might snap it in two. "I'm sorry."

"Don't be. We made the decision together. Let's find the way out of this place." They trudged to the edge of the pool.

"Remember, I can't swim."

"I and the whole country remember."

"I wish our escape route wasn't an oversized bathtub."

"Face your fears, remember?"

Shiloh grimaced, and Ezra slipped off his sandals.

"I'll go in first and search for a portal."

"Don't leave me."

"Sit pretty and wait. Girls are good at that."

"Ha, ha, very funny! Watch out for my uppercut." Shiloh wiped sweat from his forehead, knelt, and ran his hand through the shallows.

"You mean your girl slap?" Ezra's eyes twinkled with mischief.

"How deep is it?"

"Deep enough." Ezra tossed a rock into the middle of the

pond. It sank. Without pausing, he splashed into the water and disappeared.

Behind Shiloh, palm fronds rustled. His heartbeat quickened. Were King Saul's spies nearby? He ducked behind a palm tree, cupped his hands around his eyes, and scanned the horizon.

About fifty paces north of Prince Jonathan, Shiloh saw David slip from behind a boulder and approach the prince. Jonathan looked over his shoulder just before Shiloh ducked behind a clump of bushes.

He could hear the wind rustling through the twisted branches of the desert shrub. A red-tailed hawk screeched as it soared high above Shiloh's head. It was as though the stones had amplified every desert sound. He watched and listened through the tangle of branches as David embraced the prince.

"Is the news bad?"

"My father asked me to kill you, proving my loyalty to him."

"When no one would face Goliath, I killed the giant with a smooth stone and a sling. Is death my reward?"

"Your bravery has become your executioner."

The shepherd turned warrior, who had slain a lion and a bear with his bare hands when he was just a boy, dropped to his knees and wept. Jonathan knelt beside his friend and hid his face in the crook of David's neck. "Nothing will come between us, not even death."

"And the crown?" David gazed into Jonathan's eyes.

"One day . . . you will be king." The prince's deep baritone broke. "Adonai's prophet Samuel anointed you, not me. We shall not fight about that." Jonathan pushed away from his friend's embrace. "Remember our friendship when my son is no longer your master but your servant. Keep my servant boys—Shiloh and Ezra—safe. They have no family."

"As Adonai lives, I will remember them."

Jonathan opened the leather pouch that dangled from his belt and retrieved a jewel—a thin diamond three times the width of a man's thumb that hung from a leather string. "For you." He held the stone in the air, waiting for David to take it.

David took the jewel. "A diamond snowflake frozen in time? It is priceless."

Wait a minute. That's the Glass Tattoo. Then what's inside my palm? Shiloh glanced at the dark-blue tattoo that stained his right palm.

"It is more than a diamond. It opens a portal to a timeless place, where answers beyond man's knowledge are found and the past, present, or future can be relived. A place where the constraint of time does not exist—another dimension. Elohim's place."

Mom and Dad were right about the Glass Tattoo. Cool.

"But only a king may enter the home of the King of all Kings."

"Hardly. Kings lack humility, but humility is the dreamer's strength; pain, her blood." *Pain. Blood. Ugh.*

"A girl?"

Stop underestimating us!

"Doesn't make sense to me either, but the seer told me, 'Men make war, and women are left to pray for peace and tend to the wounded, so it is the woman who wishes to fight on her knees. Thus, it is a woman who will lead the world to victory.'"

On the southern horizon, a dust cloud formed, growing within minutes into a towering black storm cloud—one whose rain was soldiers and whose glints of light were shields and swords.

"Go. My father's men are coming." The prince compelled his friend to retreat.

"I'll fight with you." David stood and unsheathed his sword; metal screamed against metal.

"Am I not a warrior?" The prince stood and paused. "Keep the stone away from my father and the Philistines. My fate will not change, no matter how many tears I spill upon my bed. But you—a shepherd-warrior—will reign in my place, so lead my sheep."

David was an Orphan Dreamer too?

"This is it, my friend," David said.

"It is."

"Be well." David embraced the defeated prince—his best friend— and retreated, leaving Prince Jonathan alone to face the doom, riding down the spine of the horizon.

The dust cloud spread out for a mile.

Horses whinnied and shields glimmered as warriors rode their beasts into the valley. As though shock had suddenly worn off, the prince turned and ran toward the oasis. His fear pulsated on blasts of hot air.

Friends don't leave their friends to die alone. The young servant boy shouldered his master's bow, loaded an arrow, and released it.

One soldier fell.

Stopping his retreat, the prince studied the oasis. "Shiloh?"

"Here, my lord." Shiloh waved, revealing his hiding place. "You'll not fight King Saul's army alone."

Jonathan ran to Shiloh's hiding place. "Those shields are not Judean shields. They are Philistine."

"But you told David—"

"He has enough enemies to fight."

"Storm—let's get out of here!" Shiloh's throat dried as he scooted from under a cover of foliage.

"Foolish child, you should have obeyed me. When will you listen to me? Now it's too late."

What about Ezra? Shiloh would die before leaving his best friend inside a watery grave. He loaded another arrow into his bow and fired. A hundred yards away, the arrow penetrated the neck of a Philistine, who fell from his horse.

"Where did you learn how to shoot a bow and arrow?" Prince Jonathan grabbed his sword.

"My father's father taught me." Shiloh grinned. "Shall we fight together, my lord?"

"A servant boy protecting a prince?" Jonathan released a pained laugh. "You should be at home—safe."

"Slavery isn't exactly safe."

"Where did Ezra go?"

"To find an escape. We wanted to protect you, to help you fight." The last statement was sort of true. "Besides, I'm not weak or—"

Uh oh.

Blue skies darkened to pewter as a shower of arrows rained down.

White-hot pain ignited in Shiloh's right thigh.

The culprit lay to the boy's side—an archer's arrow. Blood ran down his leg. "I can't die here. My mother will kill me! Was it poisoned, my lord?"

"Your mother? I thought you were an orphan." As the prince rubbed his finger across the wound, Shiloh diverted his eyes, keeping his lips closed for a change.

"You'll live. Foolish, youthful imagination, thinking you can fight seasoned warriors!" The prince yanked on Shiloh's arm and dragged his servant behind a cluster of shrubs. Thorns stabbed Shiloh's backside, and rocks scraped his skin raw.

"Please, my lord. Let me fight." Shiloh struggled to wiggle out of his powerful grip. The prince's grasp tightened before suddenly loosening as Jonathan gasped and collapsed.

"Master!" Mouth agape, Shiloh stared at the arrow jutting out of Prince Jonathan's chest.

"Leave me." The prince gasped, choking on his blood as he climbed to his knees. "The Philistines are cruel enemies. They'll make sport of you, enslave you, and you'll beg for death."

"But you're my friend. I mean, you're a prince, but . . ."

"Save yourself. The world's problems are not meant for you to solve."

"You gave Ezra and me a home when I thought we would die in the desert."

"I gave you slavery, not a home. There is a difference, but you're too naïve to understand, my boy."

"My mother said, 'The greatest among you must be a servant first.'"

"Then your mother is a fool and so is her son for believing her. Kings and princes rule the world, not slaves." The thundering of the horses' hooves came closer.

Shiloh's voice dropped to a whisper. "My lord, I *am* free."

"Not in Gibeah." Jonathan held the boy's hand. "Poison is eating away my flesh. Find David. Tell him his friend is dead, and that I thought of him in death. Protect my son."

"You'll tell him yourself, my lord. You can't die now! Trust me, you die in battle with your father, the king."

"Are you a witch?"

"Not on your life."

"Whatever you say—"

Shiloh slipped his wispy arms under his master's armpits and tried to drag the muscular man beneath a canopy of date palms. Fading quickly, the prince didn't resist. A spine jutting out from a desert bush caught hold of Shiloh's turban and ripped the covering from his head. Long black tresses cascaded down slight shoulders, covering Shiloh's deep brown eyes and accenting her soft, girlish features.

"Are you—a girl?" Jonathan grimaced, and Shiloh giggled.

"It's not a disease, my lord."

"Why did you lie to me?"

"You wanted boy slaves and warriors, not Miriam—and definitely not me."

"So I am the fool."

"I couldn't be separated from my best friend, my only friend, Ezra. Besides, it's scary being a girl in unfamiliar places. No one listens to us." Shiloh continued to drag her master to safety. "Master Simon forced himself upon Hilda, then the king's soldiers trampled her."

"And the Philistines will do the same to you." A smile spread across Prince Jonathan's handsome face. "The irony of it all. A girl." With the last bit of his strength, he yanked the arrow from his chest, broke off the thin reed with one motion, and presented the blood-drenched obsidian arrowhead to Shiloh. "Remember me, an old fool who underestimated a slave girl."

"I will remember you as a friend who gave refuge to homeless travelers."

"You and your imagination." His body seized and his face contorted, as though confronted by a demon. Moments later, the skies parted. Sunlight spilled down upon the young prince's face, and he relaxed. "Remember me as you wish, Shiloh. A girl."

"Then remember the real me. My name's Daniela Rose, but my friends—" her voice fell to a whisper, "my friend calls me Rosebud."

"Rosebud . . . the girl destined to fight on her knees—the Orphan Dreamer." His lips softened. His body grew limp. A life spent.

What just happened?

In the Old Testament, Prince Jonathan died years later in battle on Mount Gilboa alongside his father and two brothers.

Shiloh gulped hard, and a trail of snot that slid down the back of her throat may just as well have been a porcupine.

The pain ripped.

Not only had she messed up her parents' dreams for her by being taken away to a faraway land and forced into slavery, but she had also messed up the Bible, distorting its timeline and erasing life only to replace it with death, loss, and destruction.

Prince Jonathan wasn't supposed to die—not yet.

She glared at the midnight-blue tattoo that stained her right palm. How would it feel to cut off one's own hand? Blasted good, probably. Her hand brought death. Death brought loneliness.

Alone again.

Horses pounded across the arid terrain into the valley, surrounding the oasis. Where could she hide? Shiloh eyed the pool. Had Ezra already returned home, abandoning her to the enemy's whims? She deserved it, making him give up his legs.

Smelling the barbaric Philistine before seeing him, she began inching into the pool. *Kick and move your arms. That's all.*

Grinning, the Philistine left the cover of the trees and crept toward her. Tall, he had a wide face; a hairy mole dominated the whole of his right cheek. "The gods shine upon me. The sweet, succulent fruit of youth lies within my reach. I will possess you before killing you." He grunted and scratched his right thigh. "Would you like that?"

She balled her tiny hands into fists. "I don't belong to you! I belong to the prince." *Or I did.*

"He's dead. If you haven't noticed."

"But I'm not." She continued inching into the water and sighed in relief as warm water and sand flooded around her toes. She could hold her breath, fall to the bottom of the pool, and wait for Ezra— but for how long?

"Come here, little one." Closer now, he reached for her. "It won't hurt."

She sloshed backward into the water to avoid his grasp. *If you're going to dive, dive deep. Shallow won't do.*

The greedy soldier lunged for her, his rough hand gripping her waist before sliding down onto her thigh, making the wound throb.

Face your fear or die.

She half-treaded water and stumbled toward the middle of the pool, into dark-blue waters. "Though I walk through the valley of the shadow of death, I will fear no evil: for thou art with me; thy rod and thy staff they comfort me," she recalled her mother's biblical words.

"Walk with me—swim with me—Yeshua, please," she said as the water toyed with her like an anaconda playing with its prey.

The soldier charged toward her, hungry for sensual pleasure, even if he would die acquiring it. His rough fingers pawed at her backside.

Never!

The lake would possess her innocence first. She kicked at him. Water splashed into his face. He blinked, and she slithered away from his lustful grasp. An arm's reach from her position, the surface of the water broke. "Rosebud, in here!" Ezra cried, then disappeared below.

She grinned. *Friends don't leave friends behind.*

"I thought you'd enjoy it, slave girl," the Philistine dove beneath the surface and resurfaced behind her, circling her like a shark.

"Ethan!" Swallowing more water than air, Daniela rotated onto her back and splashed water into the Philistine's face. Dark waters swirled around her, creating a funnel in the middle of the pond. She dove toward the shifting, sandy bottom. The cold, dark maw of deep waters swallowed her whole.

For the first time, drowning felt safe.

29—Orphan Dreamer

COLD AND WET, DANIELA KISSED Ethan on the cheek. His skin was clammy and cold, but he grinned wide, tonguing the plastic endotracheal tube.

"We're back."

Ethan blinked twice. *Yes.*

"Now that we've kissed properly." She fidgeted with the button on her sweater. "You have to marry me, so no matter how loud the angels call your name, you can't leave now." She slipped a green-and-blue friendship bracelet over his hand.

Ethan's eyes blinked three times. *Thanks.*

She gave him the notepad, and he wrote,

I'm yours.

Then he pointed to a plastic Publix grocery bag sitting on the windowsill. She retrieved it and removed a tattered lavender envelope.

To: Daniela Rose Cavanaugh

From: Ethan Mohammed Solomon

She kissed the envelope. Lilac. Her favorite. Outside, the sun finished its final descent, and blackness claimed the sky. Nightfall. Tears streamed down her cheeks.

With one last burst of energy, the sky combusted, igniting clouds with tangerine, fuchsia, and violet. In the hospital room, a cacophony of deafening alarms blasted, echoing off the stark walls.

Irregular.

Emergent.

Morbid.

Daniela's heart sank to her feet. Life receded from Ethan's cheeks, leaving pasty gray flesh. Daniela pushed the emergency call button above his bed.

Footsteps pounded toward Ethan's room. *Run—no.* She had promised him she wouldn't leave him. *Hide.* Daniela ducked behind the plastic recliner and pulled it close to the wall. Peeking around the back of the chair, she watched.

A nurse charged into the room. Wild-eyed, another nurse ran in behind the first. "What's going on, Arlene?"

"Call a Code Blue. He's in V-fib," Arlene said. The second nurse pressed a blue button above Ethan's bed. Nurse One slid the roller clamp down the intravenous tubing until a tiny stream of fluid gushed into Ethan's veins.

Nurses, doctors, and other staff poured into the room as a voice over the loudspeakers called out "Code Blue, room twenty-three, nineteen. Code Blue, room twenty-three, nineteen . . ." The repetitive cadence of the call added to the eerie finality of the situation.

I can't watch, I can't—

In that moment, she realized what Ethan had prayed for: not to die alone as he followed the Messiah wherever He led. She would stay with him on this side until Yeshua arrived to escort her best friend through the valley of the shadow of death. Shadows were never permanent. They appeared and disappeared depending on the angle of the sun. Yeshua had answered Ethan's prayer. Not Daniela's. She stood up, refusing to hide from reality any longer.

"So long, Ethan."

A member of the medical team squirted multiple syringes of drugs into his veins.

The doctor placed a set of metal paddles onto Ethan's chest. "I'm clear. You're clear. Everyone's clear." The doctor pushed two red buttons and Ethan's body launched into the air as though he had rammed his fingers into an electrical outlet.

A burly guy started chest compressions again. The process of watching Ethan die felt as though an alien was sucking Daniela's insides out through her nose. With wobbly knees, she sat in the plastic recliner and curled her lanky frame into a ball.

His lips darkened to ocean blue. His skin blackened over his mutilated legs.

Ethan wasn't there.

He was free.

The Master carried her kindred spirit to his new home, and tonight, there would be only one set of footprints in the sand leading down the shores of the River Jordan. Who would fill the empty spot inside her heart?

Silently crying, she slipped past the medical team with Ethan's card tucked beneath her arm. Even a doctor couldn't save everyone. She called her parents. Her dad picked up. "I'm ready to come home, Rafiki. Ethan's dead."

"I'm sorry, Danny Rose. We'll be right there."

In the hospital's atrium, Daniela opened Ethan's card and read the note, which was scrawled in the worst possible handwriting.

> Swim out into the deep blue sea. Live for me.
> Adoring my Rosebud for an eternity,
> Your kindred spirit, Ethan

The mind plays games, forcing a person into a dark and claustrophobic space where they didn't want to go. Psychiatrists called this process depression.

"Daniela." Her dad's voice lured her from her depressed trance. She hadn't noticed the bright yellow Ford LTD in the circular driveway, nor the smiles of her mother and father. "Want to stop at McDonalds and eat a caramel sundae—your favorite?"

"What's the point of eating?" The idea of looking at food made her want to puke.

"You sure?" her mother asked.

"Positive." Daniela cradled *Anne of Green Gables* in her lap. No time to eat ice cream. She could feel herself slipping into the dark abyss, and she struggled to breathe. Paying the money to the television preacher hadn't accomplished anything.

Ethan was right. Those prosperity preachers were scam artists, giving false hope to desperate, gullible people.

Her body ached as though she had come down with the most voracious strain of the flu.

After they arrived home, she trudged through the front door. "I'm tired. I think I'll go to sleep."

"It's only nine o'clock." Daniela's mother stroked her daughter's face. "I made your favorite—fried chicken, mac and cheese, and collards."

"I'm not hungry."

"You have to eat, Daniela." Her dad's voice came off a bit scolding.

"I will—in the morning."

"No. You'll have something before you lie down." Her mother rested her hands on her hips. "You've hardly eaten all week. You're a stick."

"I'll drink a glass of orange juice." Daniela needed to retrieve something from the kitchen anyway. So after she poured a glass, she found what she needed beneath the kitchen sink, before locking herself in her bedroom and climbing into bed fully dressed. Her eyes focused on the spot on her dresser—the place for friendship bracelets.

A special place . . . and an empty one.

50—Orphan Dreamer

ON THE FIRST DAY OF high school, Daniela's eyelids peeled open, sticking at the corners; a layer of crust ran in lines down her face.

An image of a pale face framed by scraggly locks of raven hair exploded into millions of specks of sand.

"Ethan!" Daniela reached out, but the boy vanished, and she realized it couldn't have been Ethan; Ethan had nut-brown, curly hair, and he was dead.

She glanced at the red digital numbers on her alarm clock. *Five o'clock!*

It was almost too late.

She bolted up. Warm liquid flowed down her chin, dripping onto her sheets. She reached for a handkerchief and squeezed her nose. Blood soaked the cloth, and after three soaked handkerchiefs, the bleeding stopped, making her even later for her task.

Her impending task was necessary in the art of making friends.

Become invisible, one of the majority, and her options would become easier and more varied. The process might be painful, but it had to be done. Rubbing her eyes, she climbed out of bed, grabbed the object she had stolen from under the kitchen cupboard, and tip-toed to the bathroom.

Will it come off?

If so, how fast could she make another friend?

Only one way to find out.

She stood next to the bathtub while reciting her grandfather's words. *We colored folks, we are not victims. Victims look to their oppressors to fix their problems. Your ancestors built this country, so if it's broken, Danny Rose, fix it.* He had spoken slowly with meticulous diction, showing his grandchild that he could fit in if he had to. *We are survivors.* Her grandfather's words played again and again in her thirteen-year-old mind. *Survivors adapt.*

She turned the tub faucet on half-flow, hoping to keep the noise down.

After the tub filled, she climbed in. Tepid water soaked her body, and she shivered while unwrapping the object hidden inside the threadbare washcloth—a Brillo pad. Her mother had removed all sorts of stains from soiled pots and pans.

Daniela Rose would remove her stains.

She inhaled a deep breath, clenched her jaw, and then began scrubbing her right forearm. Brown skin gave way to blood and pale dermis. White-hot pain ignited each nerve, shooting agony into her body as the thirteen-year-old flayed herself alive.

Don't be a victim. Solve the problem. It'll be easier this way. The white girls don't have to try to make friends. They just do.

The water darkened from pink lemonade to cherry Kool-Aid.

She continued.

It's your fault Ethan died. You insisted on returning through the portal. He was healthy in Prince Jonathan's Gibeah. He ran with both legs. You told him that his parents and yours would miss you both. You just didn't want to be a slave. You're selfish—not a kindred spirit.

The dark thoughts kept coming as though an evil force was feeding them into her mind, and Daniela scrubbed harder, punishing herself.

"Daniela," her mother called from outside the bathroom. "Daniela, hurry. You'll be late for school."

The edges of the bathroom started becoming fuzzy. The room

spun. *Fumbling follies all imagined!* She had lost too much time and blood with the nosebleed. Would she die?

Her mother couldn't know. *She'd kill me if I died!*

Not ever.

"I'm almost done." Daniela placed her right arm beneath running water. Blood still flowed. It refused to stop. A knock at the door sent shivers down Daniela's body.

The click of the door handle told her that her mother was entering. "Wait, Mom!" Daniela hovered near the back of the tub. Cold, bloody water sloshed across her thighs. She clasped her small hands over her forearm, but the bleeding wouldn't stop.

Her mother's voice sounded closer. "Are you okay?"

"Y-y-yes, ma'am."

"Sweetheart, you're late, and you've been in the tub forever. That's not like you." Her mother's footsteps sounded across the tiles.

"I'm trying to be clean—like Claire with blonde hair, white skin— perfect . . ." Daniela's voice fell to a mumble. "Please. Don't come in."

"This is my house. Of course I'm coming in." The shower curtain moved along its rod, screeching like nails sliding across a chalkboard. "What on earth?" Her mother stepped back. Pain ripped into her face. Her lips quivered. "My God, Daniela! Why?"

Daniela looked away from her mother, the pain settling into a pulsating throb. "Pastor Donald said we should want to be whiter than snow. I don't want to look brown like sin anymore, Mom."

Stumbling backward, her hands across her mouth, tears gushed from her mother's eyes.

"Why didn't Yeshua make me whiter than snow, like Claire? Even Tameka doesn't pick on Claire, Sara, or Kim at school."

"Oh, my dear Jesus." Her mother fell to her knees. "The Bible doesn't say anything about sin being the color brown. It says, 'Though your sins be as scarlet, they shall be as white as snow; though they be red like crimson, they shall be as wool.' Sin is red. How else could Yeshua's blood cover the foul human stuff?"

"But—"

"There's nothing wrong with your skin, sweetheart."

"Ethan's gone, Mom, and I don't know if I'm strong enough to be without a kindred spirit. I don't know if I deserve another, but it's harder to find another in my skin."

"If friendship was based on color, would Ethan, a boy from the

Middle East whose mother is Jewish and whose father is Muslim, have befriended you? True friends love you for what's inside. One day you'll understand—until then, trust me."

"I'm trying." Daniela refused to sob. She deserved the pain and shame.

"When I was your age, I remember people picking on me because God painted me a beautiful shade of brown." Jeanette drained the bloody water from the tub, then ran a warm bath. "We marched across that bridge in Alabama, and those officers—men who were supposed to protect us—sicced dogs on us while calling us every name except for child of God." She gently washed her daughter's body.

"That was mean."

"And their actions made me sad and afraid, but I believed what Doctor Martin Luther King, Jr. told us." Jeanette looked up at the ceiling as though an angel would come down, but none did because an angel—Yahweh's messenger—already sat on the edge of the tub, washing her daughter's broken body. Her gaze, a mother's kind eyes, rested on her daughter's face as she rinsed Daniela's body, then washed it again with an oatmeal cream.

"What did the doctor say?"

"Doctor King said, 'We refuse to believe that the bank of justice is bankrupt. Now is a time to make justice a reality for all God's children.' Sounding like a preacher sent down from heaven, he proclaimed, 'I have a dream that one day on the red hills of Georgia, the sons of former slaves and the sons of former slave owners will be able to sit down together at the table of brotherhood. I have a dream that my four little children will one day live in a nation where they will not be judged by the color of their skin but by the content of their character.'"

Daniela ignored the pain as her mother washed her, her thoughts enraptured with Doctor King's words and the idea of dreaming a dream that wasn't a nightmare.

"'I have a dream that one day every valley shall be exalted, and every hill and mountain shall be made low. The rough places will be made plain, and the crooked places will be made straight. And the glory of the Lord shall be revealed, and all flesh shall see it together.'"

"The prophet Isaiah said that too."

"He did." Jeanette smiled—wide, proud.

"What else did the doctor say?"

"'This is our hope. This is the faith I go back to the South with. With this faith, we will be able to hew out of the mountain of despair a stone of hope.'"

"I'm in a mountain of despair, Mom. Maybe I can carve out a stone of hope like Anne did when Marilla threatened to send her back to the orphanage?"

"You can, and you will." Jeanette drained the water out of the bathtub and wrapped a clean towel around her daughter's trembling frame. "Let's dry you off."

"Mom, did the preacher-doctor say anything else?"

A wide smile spread across her face. "He did. He said, 'This will be the day when all of God's children will be able to sing with a new meaning *My country, 'tis of thee, sweet land of liberty, of thee I sing. Land where my fathers died, land of the pilgrim's pride, from every mountainside, let freedom ring.'"

"I love that song, especially mixed with July fourth fireworks and hamburgers."

"And if America is to be a great nation, this must become true. Free at last! Free at last! Thank God Almighty, we are free at last! Don't you be ashamed of who you are. Yahweh created you. Don't you forget."

"Free at last. Free at last," Daniela whispered. "Thank God Almighty, we're free at last. I want to be a doctor like Doctor King, healing people so they can run free."

"Fight for what's right. Don't give up and remember: roses are red, white, and pink, and they are all still roses."

"Roses aren't brown."

"The stems are—where all of the nutrition, strength, and life resides."

"I didn't think about that."

"Let's clean up your arm a little more before you get infected." Jeanette retrieved a bottle of hydrogen peroxide from the bathroom vanity. "If your dad finds out what you've done, he will pitch a fit."

"Don't tell him. He'd be ashamed of me."

"It'll be our secret, for now, but if you ever do this again—"

"I won't. Pinky swear." Daniela linked her fifth finger with her mother's and they both nodded.

"After school, I'll take you to the pediatrician's office." Jeanette nursed the wounds, picking out stray fragments of steel wool before pouring hydrogen peroxide over Daniela's raw skin. Afraid to wake her dad, she stifled her screams. After the torture of cleaning her hamburger-meat arm was over, Jeanette dabbed Daniela's eyes. "You're beautiful."

"I'm trying to believe you. Honest, I am." Daniela gritted her teeth as her mother applied a topical antibiotic to her forearm, then sprinkled the gauze with clean warm water before wrapping it.

"I'll be back." Jeanette reentered the tiny bathroom with a stack of clothes. "You'll wear a black long-sleeved shirt." Her mother handed her the shirt. "This way, if the wound bleeds, no one will see the blood. The bandages will dry by lunchtime."

"It's ninety degrees outside."

"Don't be disagreeable. It's late. Finish dressing. I'll give you a Tylenol for pain."

Daniela dressed. Late for the bus, they drove to school in silence. "I'll ask Dr. Dell for antibiotics. I placed two more Tylenol pills in your bag. Take one at lunch and the other at the end of the school day. Study hard."

"Promise. Thanks for not telling Dad."

"I have a theory about self-destructive behavior like this—one your father and I don't agree on."

"What is it?"

"Imagine a Jewish person living in post-Nazi Germany or a Christian living in a jihadist camp."

"That's scary."

"Well, I think Americans with African ancestry are quietly suffering from PTSD while surrounded by people with no understanding or empathy for their American journey. The same could be said for your Cherokee ancestors, and if a child grows up in a culture that whispers *you're not as important*, eventually that child may agree with the culture and start participating in self-destructive behavior."

"Granddaddy said we shouldn't be victims."

"Your daddy agrees with his daddy, and he accuses me of making excuses for those Americans with African blood."

"Daddy hates excuses."

"He's too scared to face his demons and agree with me. Asking questions and looking for answers don't make us victims. We're survivors with feelings and intelligent curiosity."

"What's PTSD?"

"Something you'll learn about in medical school. As soon as I pull up to the curb, run to class so you won't be late."

"Did Anne of Green Gables have PTSD?"

"For God's sake child, pull your head out of the clouds. Give me that book!" Daniela's mother yanked the book from her daughter's hand, rolled down the window, and prepared to throw the book out.

"Please, mom, don't! The words on the page are the map to my new kindred spirit."

Ms. Bender passed by the car, stopped, and then turned around. Slowly, she approached the car, a frown etched across her forehead. "Is everything alright?"

"It is, Ms. Bender." Jeanette flashed a quick smile.

"You're teaching at the high school now?" Daniela asked.

The teacher nodded and cast a suspicious look at her mom. "Your daughter's a genius, Mrs. Cavanaugh. Few of us regular folk can understand a genius's mind. Albert Einstein's teachers never did. Then he taught us all the theory of relativity." She nodded curtly. "Good day."

Jeanette tipped her chin down. "Don't read it during school." Her mother relented.

"I won't." Daniela opened the car door and paused. "If I'm smart, maybe I don't have to be pretty?"

"Can't you be both?"

"Claire is."

"Pretty is as pretty does. It takes special eyes to tell the difference between a piece of cut glass and a priceless diamond. Don't let a pair of dim eyes tell you who you are."

Daniela sprinted to the classroom. She opened the door just in time for Claire to give her the high school welcome—a sneer, a point, and a giggle. She walked to her seat, her arm aching with pain.

Class seemed to last for days. She asked to be excused to the restroom. In the bathroom stall, Daniela slid the sleeves of her shirt up over her arms and cringed. The bandage was soaked with blood. As she exited the stall, she made a beeline to the sink.

"Gross!" a familiar voice said. Daniela looked up and locked eyes with Claire's.

"What did you do to yourself, freak?"

"Nothing."

"It's because of Ethan—right? You're cutting. I've seen it before, and I'm telling the teacher."

"No. Don't!"

Claire ran out of the bathroom. Daniela stood at the sink, knowing the whole high school would learn about her secret, that she'd flayed herself, attempting to remove her mahogany skin so she could make a friend.

First day of high school.

Poster child of crazy.

Could life get any worse?

Finally, the school day ended. Ms. Tyler, her history teacher, stopped Daniela before she could leave. "Daniela, the principal needs to see you in the office."

"Ooooh," Claire mocked. "Daniela's in trouble—been cutting herself. Told you I'd tell."

Head down, Daniela followed her teacher, not knowing she was walking into a waking nightmare.

When you are a mother, you are never really alone in your thoughts. A mother always has to think twice, once for herself and once for her child.

—Sophia Loren

31—A Mother's Love

BLIND SINCE BIRTH, IT WAS separated from the others.

If you're ever lost, stay near the lake's edge and call for me.
I will come.

The newborn clothed in canary-yellow down obeyed its mother's instructions. Gingerly inching forward, it cried louder. One misstep and the baby duckling would fall into the murky, deep pond and be lost forever.

A red-tail hawk circled overhead.

Hearing the predator's wings cut the air, the baby duck called to its mother over and over, but no rescue came. The hungry hawk dove in for the kill. Foolishly, it forgot to investigate a clump of lavender muhly grass at the edge of the lake.

A cacophony of quacks sounding more like a banshee's shriek was the only warning the hawk had before the duckling's mother attacked.

It is a truth that reveals itself in nature: nothing in the world rivals the power of a mother's love. It's so powerful that it overwhelms everything. Every day, otherwise sane women ignore their offspring's flaws. Instead, they redefine their child's present and nurture outlandish dreams for their future.

But someone has to do it—believe in the children.

32—A Mother's Love

A TIMELESS, ETHEREAL BEAUTY EAGERLY kissed by the sun, Jeanette Cavanaugh strolled past the pond, watching the dead hawk float, beak up, in the water.

The mother duck preened her blind duckling as the fifty-three-year-old mother scurried past two automatic sliding glass doors and entered a simple redbrick building with rectangular windows.

She followed plastic signs to a bank of elevators, entered, then pushed the button for the third floor.

After exiting the elevator, she navigated a labyrinth of hallways before arriving at the secretary's desk of the Alachua General Hospital's Children's Mental Health Unit. "Good morning, Ms. Jane. I'm here to see my daughter, Daniela Rose Cavanaugh."

"Password?" The unit secretary asked.

"Apricot sulfur." Decided upon in honor of Daniela's favorite butterfly.

"Date of birth?"

"The eighth of July, nineteen seventy-seven."

"Just turned thirteen? Birthday party?"

Jeanette averted her gaze and flashed a pained smile—lips quickly sliding across her teeth, then brought back together faster than an incoming tsunami. "Balloons and chocolate cake."

"Isn't she the lucky girl? Lots of friends?"

A flush rose from the center of her chest and settled in her cheeks. "Umm. I don't . . . I mean. Daniela's has had a hard time of making friends—it's not her fault—really it isn't." A layer of sweat slicked her palms. "She's the sweetest and most imaginative girl, but the kids at her school and at church see her as—different. Maybe she is, and maybe it's my fault. I wanted a child so badly."

"Wanting a child isn't a sin. No need for purgatory. A lack of sleep when the newborn arrives is punishment enough." The secretary chuckled, typed into her computer, then paused. "Daniela's never had one friend? Is that possible?"

"She had one," Jeanette said, her tone tauter than a piano wire. Had she sounded too defensive? *Lower your voice.* "She met him last school term, but her father wasn't keen on her becoming friends with a boy."

"I'd be more concerned if her friend was an alien, but that's just me."

They laughed together.

"The two of them had such great fun. I was sad when they couldn't go on the trip to the Smithsonian with their classmates. Daniela would have pushed that boy into every nook and cranny of the National Air and Space Museum, and he would have educated her on the specs of every mode of air travel."

"This is her second admission, after that one?"

"It is." Jeanette cleared her throat.

"Don't worry. She'll get better."

"I hope so." Hugging herself, Jeanette imagined that she was holding her little girl. "Daniela adored dusty libraries and dimly lit museums. *History trapped in ink* is what she called the ancient books and paintings . . ." Jeanette's cheeks sagged from mountaintops of pure elation to valleys of depression, her smile fading. "That was her first time *traveling*—we think. Now we're here again."

"First time traveling out of state, you mean?"

"It doesn't make sense. She missed the trip to DC, and we had just given her the birthday gift the day before."

"Gifted what?"

"I'm rambling." Jeanette abruptly stopped, then straightened her bearing. "I'm sorry."

"Thanks for sharing." The secretary smiled, wide and full of hope. "I'm praying for your Daniela."

"Thank you."

"Has her friend visited her while she's been an inpatient?"

"He can't."

"I don't believe the doctors discourage any friend from visiting."

"You misunderstand. Ethan would visit her if he could."

"His parents forbid him from coming?"

"No. He died . . . a few weeks ago." Jeanette shifted her weight. "Because of bone cancer, he lost his legs soon after he started school with my Daniela. The other kids shied away from him, but she didn't mind the chair. Ethan's friendship resurrected my Daniela Rose from the grave, and for that I'm eternally grateful. She'll want to be discharged so she can visit him at his gravesite and say goodbye again, so I'm hoping the doctor gives me good news today."

"I'm cheering for her." The secretary pushed a clipboard toward the grieving mother. "Please sign in here. She'll be happy to see you today."

Jeanette scrawled her signature along the line.

"Visiting hours won't start for another fifteen minutes. Would you like to go to the cafeteria?"

"No, thank you; I'll wait here." Jeanette adjusted her purse on her shoulder and straightened her wool skirt and ivory blouse. "Thanks for listening."

"It's my gift."

Jeanette approached the locked double doors. Would she feel any different if the doors led into a tomb? How did Ethan's mother feel? She had no right to complain. Daniela lived.

Holding a bouquet of spring flowers, another mother walked up and stood behind Jeanette.

She hadn't remembered to bring flowers.

A pit of guilt exploded inside her gut. The thought of crying lingered in the shadows, but society demanded her strength, so she stood tall, raised her chin, and had a good cry inside, hating herself for forgetting to bring flowers.

33—A Mother's Love

Wednesday, September 7, 1994
Gainesville, Florida

LEAVING 1989 AND ENTERING THE 1990's wasn't just a time of scrunchies, whale-spout ponytails, fried bangs, glittering lime-green jelly shoes—a.k.a. jellies—and electric-blue eye shadow.

In 1989, *Driving Miss Daisy* won Best Picture; Bette Midler sang "Wind Beneath my Wings"; and *60 Minutes*, *The Cosby Show*, and *America's Funniest Home Videos* were all the rage. On a non-entertainment note, the Exxon Valdez tanker ran aground in Prince William Sound, spilling hundreds of thousands of barrels of crude oil into Alaska's waters.

US troops invaded Panama.

Berliners listened to Reagan and tore down the Berlin Wall, choosing to see neighbors as people instead of political enemies and savages.

In America, Doctor Christopher Broelsch quietly performed the world's first living-donor liver transplant at the University of Chicago Hospitals, removing a section of liver from a mother and then transplanting it into her twenty-one-month-old daughter. Back in Gainesville, Florida, home of the Florida Gators, another mother would give a part of herself to her child—not her liver, but her heart.

Unlike other mothers, who eagerly awaited their child's arrival at the bus stop, Jeanette was in Daniela's hospital room in the Alachua General Hospital's Children's Mental Health Unit.

Adrenaline tore through her veins, and her heart seemed to sprout legs, recklessly pounding blood through her arteries. The doctor would arrive in fourteen minutes to decide Jeanette's only child's fate: discharge or commit.

Her diagnosis: schizoaffective disorder, depressive type.

Jeanette paced the room with the restless angst of a wild lioness.

The hospital room felt as comfortable as the colored-section of a 1960s bus station and was blessed with the same bland, forgettable personality—slate gray walls, cream linoleum floors, and plastic-covered furniture. A Styrofoam cup of water sat half-empty on a cart, its bent straw dangling from the lip. Apricot nylon curtains sagged over the locked window.

Her mother knew Daniela wasn't a jumper.

The food on the breakfast tray had not been eaten, and Daniela's bones seemed ready to poke through her skin. When a child perceives the world as dark and hopeless, eating becomes a chore.

Jeanette kept pacing, planning.

The cold hospital air smelled of antiseptics and alcohol wipes, void of any of the familiar scents of home. After sliding her wrists across her neck, Jeanette inhaled—lilacs and orchids. Smiling, she massaged the fragrance into the threads of her sleeping child's brightly colored hospital gown; first her shoulders, followed by her chest, then her abdomen. She proceeded to the child's bandaged right arm.

A hard object beneath Daniela's thin arm stopped her descent.

Jeanette uncurled the child's fingers. Even in this grim place, her dreamer still dreamed of finding what mattered to her most: another kindred spirit—another Ethan. A bookmark revealed Daniela's simple message and wish.

To my dearest Yeshua,

Forgive me for killing Ethan.
    Please don't let him be the only friend destined for me. I can

design another friendship bracelet anytime, just need to know my new friend's favorite colors. I'm very fast at making them and creative too, so don't let my lack of friendship bracelets stop you from sending me another friend just like Ethan, but please allow my new friend to keep his legs. It's much easier to follow you on two legs.

Don't you think?

Why does Daniela believe she killed Ethan? Emotion choked Jeanette's breath. "I'm sorry for letting you down, Daniela." She clutched the child's tattered book—*Anne of Green Gables*—to her chest and whispered a promise. "When least expected, you'll meet your Anne-girl. But for now, let's make you well."

Maybe helping Daniela find that kindred spirit would keep her from having another delusional break.

The perfume forgotten, she shifted her weight for the hundredth time, left foot to the right, her stockings rustling in sync with her nervous tic. A pair of lightly scuffed, brown alligator kitten heels— her dress shoes and a treasured Goodwill find—tapped the linoleum floor in a chaotic rhythm.

The worried mother secured the classic novel inside her purse.

She reviewed her notes written on a folded piece of paper, assuring herself that she had followed all of the doctor's instructions. Her child's discharge from this prison would not be delayed because of her neglect.

Fighting the weight of sedatives, Daniela's eyelids lifted north of half-mast.

"Daniela, are you waking?" Jeanette rushed to her daughter's side and caressed her forehead.

"Mom, stay," her speech slurred.

"I'm here, my cinnamon-spiced bumblebee." Flashing a quick smile, she prayed that her facial expression conveyed more hope than fear.

Daniela fell back asleep. "Danny Rose, come back to me." Seconds later, her child stirred again. Jeanette almost leapt onto the bed.

"Ezra." Daniela's speech slurred again as her head lolled to the right and drool slid from her uncoordinated lips.

"What did you say?" Jeanette reached for a tissue and sopped up the saliva.

"Ezra."

Jeanette leaned down, placing her ear next to Daniela's mouth. "Do you mean Ethan? You don't know anyone named Ezra."

"No—Ezra. Arrow. Lost."

Jeanette's heart thumped against her ribs. She tapped her foot and glanced up at the clock: 12:48 p.m. The doctor would arrive in twelve minutes, and he could *not* hear his half-drugged patient saying crazy things, like talk of strange men and lost arrows.

"Just rest. Don't speak for now. Not until the doctor leaves."

"Ezra—dead." Daniela tried to emerge past the chemical fog.

"Please stop, Danny Rose." Jeanette kissed her daughter's forehead. "Please don't say these things. They'll take you away from me, and what would I do?"

"David. New moon. The pandemic. The end."

"The doctor can't misjudge what you don't tell him; rest for now—please, for your mother's sake."

The child disobeyed.

She couldn't help herself. The sedatives dictated her behavior.

34—A Mother's Love

THE DOCTOR WOULD ARRIVE IN five minutes, so Jeanette had four minutes and fifty-nine seconds to make her child appear normal.

"Ezra," Daniela slurred the name again.

Change the subject. "I can't wait! Can you?" She added a shrill soprano tone to her usual alto voice. "One day, you're going to attend college and then medical school. Are you thrilled?"

"The arrow."

"Earning a degree in history from Spellman College," Jeanette frantically spoke over her daughter, defying her own rules against rudeness, "taught me something besides how to become a teacher. Aren't you curious?"

"Ezra, Mom."

"The longer I studied history, the more I understood that facts can be created. History is nothing more than His story."

"I-I-I need to tell—"

"It's me who needs to tell you something very, very important." Jeanette placed her hand on her anxious child's shoulder and her finger across Daniela's lips. "Unlike facts, truth is absolute. It never changes, but truth can only be discovered by those who are patient. Like a treasure at the end of a treasure hunt."

The second hand on the clock ticked onward: 12:54 p.m.

"The doctor will arrive soon. One o'clock sharp, and we'll be ready." *Keep the voice light and airy.* She twisted one of Daniela's pigtails around her finger and unwound it again. "He may share a few facts that we don't like." She rubbed her palms down her plaid wool skirt, stripping the sweat from her trembling hands before reaching for the only child she would ever have.

This child had to last—forever.

"Here sleeps a girl with a head full of magical dreams, a heart full of wonder, and hands that will shape the world." She held Daniela's hands. "One day, my darling, your hands will perform something great. That's truth—not fact—but you must remember the doctor isn't your mother, and he doesn't know of your potential. You're ordinary, yet special."

"Oily boy."

"Forget about him for now."

"Ezra. Dead."

"I'm your mother. Obey me."

"The boy."

"Unlike the doctor, I've got all the time in the world, so let the doctor gather his facts, and don't challenge him while he does. Then, we'll go home, your father will be home from work, and we'll discover the truth together. Can you do that for me, my cinnamon-spiced bumblebee?" Jeanette traced the curve of her daughter's hairline; soft baby hairs flattened beneath her touch.

Society expected her to be strong, as unfeeling as a leper, and she had obliged, fighting hard not to cry; but in the vernacular of Sojourner Truth, she cried inside, "Ain't I a woman?"

Yes, she was a woman.

But as Eleanor Roosevelt had said, "A woman is like a tea bag; you never know how strong it is until it's in hot water."

Tears pooled across Jeanette's long black lashes, threatening to fall on Daniela's cheek. In America—in *this* world—the blacker the tea, the stronger it must be. "No exceptions, Danny Rose."

She thought of oily boy's pale skin.

Could he understand her Daniela? Could he tenderly protect Jeanette's beloved daughter's heart from a cruel world? Dr. King's words answered Jeanette's silent pleas: "I have a dream that my four little children will one day live in a nation where they will not be judged by the color of their skin but by the content of their character."

Did oily boy possess solid character?

Had she prepared her Daniela for *this* world and not a place of dreams? The mother blinked back tears, blurring her view of the dreamer, a face enraptured within innocence, framed by pigtails, and blanketed with velvet mahogany skin.

Jeanette brushed her fingers across the blood-tinged gauze bandages that wrapped Daniela's forearm, slowly pulling Daniela's hand into her lap as though she had caressed an open fire. She sniffled hard. "If I could understand why you want an *Anne-of-Green-Gables* kind of friend so badly, I could help you."

Had she ever asked?

No.

"Ezra. The arrow," Daniela said, her speech still slurred.

"Yahweh, if you care for us at all, make her stop talking about that strange man and his arrow before the doctor arrives!" The barren mother's voice oscillated from a flat note to a sharp one, skipping the natural notes altogether. "I want . . . no! I *need* to take her home with me today." She clasped her hands into steeples and knelt beside the bed. "I'm not a rich woman, and in this world, I'm not highly regarded. My cinnamon-spiced bumblebee is all you've given me besides her father." She stifled a sob. "I need to be her mother."

Nurse Paula waltzed into the room, syringe in hand.

"Please don't drug her again." Jeanette jumped to her feet and thought about ripping the syringe filled with liquid out of the nurse's hand.

Instinctively, she covered Daniela's bandaged arm.

If she yanked the intravenous line out of her child's hand, would that stop the caretaker from pushing more sedative into her veins?

No, she couldn't do such a thing.

Daniela's forearm was already tender, and the emergency room nurse had thought nothing of placing the intravenous needle so close to the raw hamburger meat. *This little needle won't add to the unsightly scarring. That's for sure.*

Mothers don't inflict pain on their children. Leave the intravenous line alone but fight for Daniela. "Ms. Paula."

"Yes, Mrs. Cavanaugh?"

"Daniela's all her father and I have."

"One child can be a handful." Paula slipped on a pair of gloves.

"We dream of our little girl becoming a physician and caring for others, and I thank you for caring for our Daniela."

"It's good to have goals for our children, even if they never reach them."

"I'm telling you because we don't want her to become a drug addict. Please don't give her any more medicine. I'd like to take her home today. I-I-I'm begging you."

"Doctor's orders." The nurse sighed heavily. "Mrs. Cavanaugh, if you cannot tolerate the treatments for your *sick* daughter, you'll have to go to the waiting room."

"But I'm her mother. I can't leave her."

"Then don't interfere." The nurse attached the syringe and pushed forward all of the liquid inside the clear tubing, then left as quickly as she came. Jeanette watched a trapped air bubble travel ahead of the medication and then disappear into Daniela's vein. The child's eyelids closed, and her head lolled to the left. Saliva ran down her face.

Why wouldn't they listen?

Her face flushed volcanic hot as she sopped up the drool once more. Daniela was too young to drool like an invalid. Jeanette lay down beside her sleeping child. "Emmanuel, God with us, if you help me get her out of here, she's yours. I won't stand in your way any longer. Please allow us to be her mommy and daddy at home, not here."

The hand of the clock struck one. A man cursed with more gut than height and dressed in a long white coat charged into the room, approached the bed, and stood beside Jeanette and her daughter.

Jeanette sat up, her blood still boiling. *Why couldn't he knock?* Her dark thoughts harkened back to her doctor visits in North Carolina in the 1930s, when she and her mother waited in the broom closet to be seen by the doctor in town because they weren't allowed in the waiting room. At least those days were over.

She gulped down a mouthful of indignation, averted her gaze, and stood. Hoping to rein in her pounding heart, she cinched her mustard-yellow sweater tight around her chest.

"No need to coddle you folks," the doctor stared at his clipboard, glanced up at Jeanette, then flashed a quick smile.

Don't you count my Danny Rose out—don't you dare!

"Daniela's got childhood schizophrenia. She had another break. That's why she did what she did to her arm. My boy, Harry, tells me that he's in the same class as Daniela."

That nasty boy who torments my Danny Rose. "Yes, sir."

"Says she thinks that she can talk to people who she doesn't see and sees places that are long gone or haven't even arrived yet. Lord of Mercy. It's weird—I know, but . . ." he tapped his pen to the clipboard. The sound rubbed Jeanette's nerves raw, as though a craggy old woman was dragging her nails down a chalkboard.

Don't leave me hanging. "Yes, Doctor?"

"Fortunately, the medicine's making her sleep, and that'll be her ticket on the express train out of here." He handed a half-sheet of paper to Jeanette. "I'm sending her home today. Here's a prescription. Don't skip a dose. See me back in the office in three weeks. I'm excusing her from school for a week. Take her somewhere nice and calm—away from this God-awful hurricane bearing down on us. When she sees me in three weeks, I'll decide if a special home is better for her."

"Thank you, sir, but my Daniela will be just fine living with her father and me. No need for a home."

"If she was fine, she wouldn't be here." He nodded curtly. "See to it, because she's scaring the other children. My Harry's having nightmares and wettin' his bed because of this girl. No tellin' what she's doing to the other children."

He's too mean to pee in the toilet. Keep your mouth closed. Jeanette clamped down on her lower lip and took a deep breath in. The doctor walked out.

Paula, the sedative, and the subsequent sleep had been a strange answer to her prayer; Daniela had remained quiet. Had the sun burst through the hospital's pale green walls and started its sunrise all over again?

Jeanette tilted her chin upward, feeling as though sunrays bathed her face. "Blessed Jesus!" she cried. "My baby's going home."

No longer willing to hold her emotions behind a false wall of strength, she lifted the floodgates, and rivers of tears burst forth, cleansing her fears in their currents.

She had earned this moment.

Besides, she wasn't crying because of pain.

The stubborn mother was laughing with her tears. A guffaw would have been too shallow. She remembered Augustine of Hippo's wisdom: Hope has two beautiful daughters; their names are Anger and Courage. Anger at the way things are—and Courage to see that they do not remain as they are.

"After you wake, my darling, shall we discover the truth together . . . just you, me, and your Papa?" Jeanette cradled the face of her child in a tender embrace.

Daniela opened her eyes and grinned. "Ezra and the arrowhead's real, Mom, and so is the boy. I wouldn't lie to you. Promise I wouldn't."

"Danny Rose!" Jeanette slapped her hand across her mouth. "You didn't?"

"I did. Nurse Paula stopped giving me drugs yesterday. We had a talk. Was I believable?"

"Treacherously deceitful."

"Good." Her eyes sparkled. "Nurse Paula's my friend. She believes me, and the syringe of medicine . . . sometimes it works more like water."

"That's it. I'm taking you away from this place to your grandma's farm. You'll be safe there."

"Can I run and play?"

"Once you complete your class assignments."

"You, Dad, and I will start our treasure hunt for truth at Grandma's farm. That'll be super cool."

"Super cool is right, but patience. Your dad has to work, and someone has to feed him. I'll stay in Gainesville. It'll be just you and Grandma for a week."

"Don't worry, Mom. We've got all the time in the world."

Nurse Paula peeked into the room, "Everything sweeter than a bag of Georgia peaches?"

"It's as though Earth has started spinning again. Thank you."

I had reasoned this out in my mind; there was one of two things I had a right to, liberty or death; if I could not have one, I would have the other; for no man should take me alive.

—Harriet Tubman

35—Adelaide: #Cordelia

I STOP READING MOTHER'S JOURNAL and cup my face between my hands. Harry, Claire, and the inquisitor had tormented her.

So did my da, oily boy.

But mother had come through in the end. "Thanks, Grandma."

"Addy Rose!" I jump, pulling away from cold, clammy fingers wrapped around my neck. Those hands and the light soprano voice could only belong to one person—Cordelia Grey, my best friend and dormmate. Even when she's angry, the tone of her voice fools the listener into thinking she's smiling while talking. She often wonders aloud to me why no one takes her chiding seriously, but she could sing—Mariah Carey, "One Sweet Day" sing. "Finals are in a week. Stop daydreaming!"

"Sorry." I push back from my desk, stand, and stretch until the edges of the room come back into focus. Around me, fluorescent lights cast long shadows across orange carpets, concrete pillars, and books. Exeter's library.

Fake logs crackle in a fireplace. "How long was I lost in Neverland?"

"Too fuc—"

"Don't say it." I plug my ears. "Da will commence to beatin' the Irish blood from my arse if I go home using that word."

Cordy Grey pulls my fingers from my ears. "I meant to say, too long if you want an *A* in calculus." She shakes her head, then a mischievous smile quirks the corners of her full, pink lips. "If your dad wasn't hotter than minus-the-tats David Beckham in a Calvin Klein ad . . ." she licks her lips, confirming her salacious thoughts about my da. *Gross.* "I'd think he was a twerp."

"They say beautiful people get away with everything. Including murder."

"Maybe he did."

"My da's no killer, Cordy Grey."

"Whatever. Wanna take a short break and gossip about boys?"

"No need to ask me twice, but let's leave off the talking-about-boys part." Gage, my on-again-off-again boyfriend, has been annoying me lately. Carrie Underwood's duet with Randy Travis, "I Told You So," could be the anthem to our relationship.

"No prob. In my book, Gage Barrington equals a non-habit-forming sleep aid."

"Pure cruelty."

She laughs, and I abandon my calculus text on the table, follow Cordy to an empty couch, and plop down onto the plush leather beside her. She pulls her knees to her chest, cocks her head to the right, and studies me. "Is it Gage?"

"It's not." Like a hungry dog, she refuses to release her bone.

"Gage Barrington." She slides down the armrest of the sofa, slips off her flats, and props her feet on my lap. "Webster's definition of boring, unless he's brandishing a high-powered rifle and keeping himself relevant by blowing holes into the heads of helpless lionesses innocently suckling their newborn cubs."

"Please, Cordy. I already have a headache." I rub my temples for emphasis.

"Why do you date that loser?" She crosses her arms. "Chugging a gallon of melatonin couldn't put me to sleep faster than listening to

Gage Barrington talk about himself, his guns, and his family's South African estate. What a douche."

"Leave it! It's not Gage. He's too stupid to be a career big-game hunter anyways. It was a mistake."

"Dating him or shooting the lioness?"

"Maybe both. Time will tell."

"And now two young lions are orphans. What goes around comes around, I'm telling you."

"Fine! I kissed his Armageddon lips on steroids. And the world fell apart."

Cordelia laughs so hard her face turns red.

I roll my eyes. "Glad to bring the circus." An ice pick getting hammered into my chest would be less painful. I recall the contents of the letter from Mother that arrived in the mail yesterday. Soon I'm to be an orphan, and my da knew that while we sloshed through luminescent blue water in the Maldives. But that story comes later. "I'm probably going to break up with Gage."

"Do it already. He's a bad omen."

But I don't want to be alone. Who does?

I remove Mother's letter from my jacket pocket and hold it close to my chest, hiding the tremor in my hands. "It's this—among other things."

Cordy reaches for the crinkled paper, eager to read my secrets or anything that could fuel the story lines of her unfinished novel.

I sigh, then relinquish the goods. "Can you make any sense of it? My brain's fried. I'm so worried, can't study."

She reads the letter.

My Dearest Adelaide Rose,

My life is a Georges-Pierre Seurat painting—and I'm mortified.

For two years, Seurat tapped his fine-tip brush onto a stretched canvas like a Morse coder, leaving a trail of minuscule yet distinct dots of oil paint that shared his story of an 1884 Parisian *Sunday Afternoon on the Island of La Grande Jatte*. I am that painting, half-done: a mosaic of colorful dots, insignificant on its own and not yet organized enough to count as a masterpiece.

Not at all what I had imagined for my life.

As an awkward and lonely girl, I studied art history and dreamed my autobiography would resemble a Simmie Knox portrait, layered with fluid and purposeful strokes of color meant to capture the character, spirit, and personality of the subject in a dignified manner.

Instead, my story became Seurat-like, scattered into a million fragments. Even so, I attempted to assemble the details of my life into a logical story line and create my own Simmie Knox portrait of my journey before I died. I failed, leaving you to pick up the pieces.

Truly, I am sorry.

Pity is a road I've refused to travel, even though, according to some, I have every right to pick up a map and find my way onto its path. But I knew that would lead to a dead-end and an even deader soul. So, my dearest Adelaide, do not pity yourself, even though you will soon become an orphan. Celebrate life!

Sail the world with Cordelia.

But before you leave, open your gifts. Your father purchased a gift for me before he disappeared. I gift it to you. Inside the wooden case, hidden beneath layers of shipping paper, you'll find the original study of Seurat's *Sunday Afternoon on the Island of La Grande Jatte*. Initially, I was angry with your father for spending so much money for the masterpiece. I don't mind so much anymore since it's now yours. If destiny is to take a mother and a father from you, then maybe this priceless masterpiece will soothe your heart, reminding you of us.

Your second gift is a quilt, made by my great-grandmother. There was a time when fabric squares hid mysteries, telling an escaped slave how to find a train that would escort them underground to freedom.

Escape before it's too late.

Keep your last gift inside its special case. It is the original score of "Blessed Assurance," my mother's favorite hymn. Harriet Tubman, a conductor on the train of bravery and freedom, understood that a song wasn't all notes, words, and tempo.

A riddle: follow the lead in a rich, soulfully syncopated rhythm in C major. CeCe Winans sang the hymn best when your father and I attended the Cicely Tyson Kennedy Center Honors, where we said hello to the First Family for the last time.

I was never brave enough to tell you, but when I was thirteen, a psychiatrist diagnosed me with depression and childhood schizophrenia. Hence, the flight of ideas. Mother and I refused to believe him. Maybe he was right and we were wrong. But in order to fulfill my destiny—which didn't include collecting friendship bracelets—I needed to believe his diagnosis was more appropriately translated as "You're different, and I don't understand different."

Was I crazy?

Was I a bad mother?

You be my judge, my darling daughter, my Adelaide Rose. You are breathtakingly beautiful, brave, and very sane, so I give you permission to venture into the melancholic chaos of my muddled legacy. Maybe you can create a Simmie Knox portrait out of it after all.

Most of all, finish school, be your own woman, and make a difference.

With all my love,
Mommy, Daniela Rose Cavanaugh

"Your dad left your mom? That sucks paint! He's so hot. Good grief! That man gives me fever."

I pinch her toes.

"Ouch!" She retracts her stinky feet. "Was he cheating?" She attempts to whisper, but a jet engine doesn't really purr. It roars, and so does Cordy.

"How would I know?"

"Were they fighting?"

"Not in front of me."

"Were they having . . . you know what?"

"Gross. How would I know?" I snatch the letter out of her hands. "I don't need a shrink or a sex therapist."

"Okay. Fine." She reaches into her bag and rips a sheet of paper from her notebook. Sitting beside me, she says, "What you need is a detective. Let's organize the facts."

"Oh great, Detective Cordy Grey Anderson kicks Sherlock Holmes to the curb."

"I like the sound of it." She chews on the eraser end of her pencil. *Poor pencil.* "I'm good at weeding out the bull. Always have been, and you know it." She verbalizes her bullet points as she writes them. "Your mom's a depressive schizophrenic."

"Wrong! Some crazy shrink said she was sad and her thoughts weren't organized. That describes most of the girls in our dorm. My mother's *not* crazy. Trust me. If she's insane, we're all toast."

"Fine." She smirks and keeps writing. "Your dad abandoned your mom after he bought her a multimillion-dollar painting. Reason—unknown."

"He disappeared. That's not the same as abandoning us." *Why did I give her the letter?*

"Like a technical foul?"

"Don't be annoying."

"I'm trying to help." She slams her pencil onto the sheet of paper, breaking the point.

"Calm down! It's not like you're going to be an orphan."

"Going to be? I already am."

"I'm sorry. I forgot."

"You forgot—really?" She shakes her head. "Forget it. We won't focus on the personal stuff. You're not ready for that now. Why does your mother talk about Harriet Tubman, the underground railroad, and your grandmother's favorite hymn?"

"I don't know, but I think there must be a common thread."

"Obviously—okay, so Harriet Tubman was a conductor of the Underground Railroad. She was a slave. A freedom fighter. An amazingly brave person. She was a woman—"

"You're wrong." I slide to the edge of the sofa. "I mean you're right, but not about what's important. Harriet Tubman was a spy for the Union Army." I roll my shoulders back, proud I remember the historical fact taught to me not by classroom texts but by my mother, who believed all American's histories should be championed.

"Read the part about Tubman again," Cordy says.

"'There was a time when fabric squares hid mysteries, and a train would escort you underground to freedom . . . Harriet Tubman, a conductor on the train of bravery and freedom, understood that a song wasn't all notes, words, and tempo. Follow the lead in a rich, soulfully syncopated rhythm in C major. CeCe Winans sang the hymn best when your father and I attended the Cicely Tyson

Kennedy Center Honors, where we said hello to the First Family for the last time.'"

"It's a code—a key that unlocks a mystery." Cordy leans back.

"So it's a key, but what does it unlock?"

"Heck if I know. You're the one with the odd parents."

"They're unique, not odd."

"More technical fouls." Cordy Grey grins. "But I adore you for them."

Behind us, a row of books slides over the shelf's lip and crashes onto my head. "Ouch!" I jump to my feet. A pair of black, beady eyes peers over the empty shelf space. I recognize the quiet guy with weird tattoos who sits across from me during calculus. "Levi?"

"Sorry." He shrinks back into dusty-book oblivion.

After he disappears, I sit down and lean toward Cordy. "Do you think he was eavesdropping?"

"Why would he be?"

"I don't know." I shrug. "He's such a creep."

"Creep. Loser. The common denominator of most guys in our classes."

"Cruelty is the blood that ices through your veins."

"And a monster wades into still waters."

"Let's stop with the artistic stuff. Back to my da. There was something . . . different about him during our Maldives trip. First of all, the trip was spontaneous. Father hates spontaneity. It makes him anxious."

"The Maldives." Cordy zones out. "A private jet. New Zealand. A hot dad. I'm so jealous."

"Jealousy's so middle-class."

"Anyway." Cordy Grey laughs.

"So Downton Abbey's Dowager Countess," we say in unison.

"Can I finish, Stephen King? I'd never seen it before, but there was a barcode tattooed on the inside of his bicep, just below his armpit."

"Sniffing pits again?" She laughs.

"Gross."

"Maybe he was for sale?" She shrugs.

"Totally sick."

"I'm being serious. Hello. Human trafficking."

"My da would murder anyone trying to sell him for sex. He pumps iron like a maniac. He's basically special-ops military; his shirts are starched enough to stand on their own. No one messes with my da and lives."

"I've got the picture." Cordy pins her lower lip between her teeth, holding back a wide grin. "Just the kind of man I'd like to grab hold of me and tell me what do."

"May I please find a friend who doesn't have the hots for my da?" I stare at the ceiling, waiting for an answer.

"She doesn't exist," Cordy says in a deep voice, breaking the silence. "Get used to it. Your dad is universally sexy. Zac Efron on steroids."

"Whatever. My da's shy. Modest. He never took off his shirt in front of me, not even when we swam in our family pool. He said that the only man's body I should be privy to is my husband's."

"Did you listen?"

"None of your business."

"Your mom did. She was a virgin when she married your dad after med school. She told me during our tell-all conversation over the phone."

"Cordy to Earth."

"Landed."

"It seemed like he was embarrassed about his body. I think that maybe the barcode was why."

"No, honey. Your dad's a tease. He understood mysterious equals not letting everything hang out. If only all the ten-month pregnant guys running around shirtless on the beach would follow his lead."

"For a second, could we stop talking about my da's body?"

"You brought up the barcode."

"You asked me a question—I answered." I rub my temples again. "I was just thinking that if there is a mystery in the letter, and I solve it on my own, Mother will be proud of me. Maybe I could even save her and Da."

"I get it. Not to mention that if we solve the mystery, I'll have enough material to write my best-selling young adult novel."

"YAs are annoying." I roll my eyes, cross my arms, and slump back into the sofa.

"Why?"

"No one listens to us seventeen-year-olds! Why do YA novelists act like people do?"

"Faith listens to you."

"She's my mother's dog."

"More technical fouls." Cordy Grey laughs, but I don't.

"I'll prove it. So, this super-cool chick featured in another YA novel storms into the local government's office and tells a room full of baffled adults facts they're somehow too stupid to figure out on their own. Then, said roomful of adults follows pimple-faced teenage girl like she's Joan of Arc? Yeah—right!"

"Dreaming isn't illegal, Addy Rose." Cordy rears back like a cobra ready to strike. "Try it. Dreams aren't just a figment of your mother's hallucinations. The rest of us dream too."

"That's a low blow." My eyes burn, but I won't give Cordy the satisfaction of knowing she hurt my feelings.

"Call me crazy, but I'm going to be daringly crazy like your mother."

"Mother wasn't crazy."

"She was—in a good way. Come along for the ride, help me solve the mystery, or stay home and coddle Gage. You choose. But one day, he may mistake you for a lioness."

Madder than hell because of her comment about my mother, I wait, remaining silent for a solid minute. "Sherlock was useless without Doctor Watson." I pause. "I can't let my studies slip. Straight A's are all Mother understands. I understand her standards, though. Exeter isn't cheap. How many kids in Africa or India could eat if I wasn't attending Exeter?"

"What about America? You live and breathe to depress me," Cordy whines. Then she fist bumps me. "Ride or die?"

"Those are my choices?" I shake my head. "What's the point of dying if you can't ride—just walk?"

Cordy Grey bursts out laughing.

"Fine. I'll ride. Beats dying."

"You're so bad and boujee." Cordy laughs.

"What?"

36—Orphan Dreamer

DANIELA ROSE CAVANAUGH, TAKE YOUR *nose out of that book!* Even while she slept, her grandmother's rebuke vexed her spirit; but there were no rules in the land of dreams—nor was there mercy. Anne of Green Gables wasn't real.

Beads of sweat christened Daniela's forehead. *Please don't say that.*

Twisting back and forth, she cut a trench into the straw mattress pressed against the wall in her grandmother's spare bedroom, soaking a set of periwinkle sheets that constricted her gangly frame like a hungry python.

She gasped for breath, struggling to lift her head.

Nutcase Danny Rose. Tie her up in a straitjacket. Her classmates' singsong taunts terrorized her even here. No place was safe. The idea of tight spaces—caves, closets, and hot-dog-shaped straitjackets—snaked a shiver down the middle of her soul. Daniela clawed at the bandages wrapped around her arm.

Please help me. The words floated within a green mist and emerged from a black hole carved into the boy's face that had been bruised and scarred. By a monster, perhaps? Still, his face had no eyes. Daniela jerked her head left and then right, hoping to shake the visual of oily boy.

It didn't work.

Lice the size of roaches crawled through his raven locks.

She scratched her scalp and then her arm with such ferocity that she ripped open the freshly scabbed wounds on her forearm.

Her skin burned, but a smile spread across her face because the pain meant she was emerging. Escaping.

Dinna leave me. The boy's voice trailed off into oblivion.

"Gotta go. I'm sorry." She had never spoken to him before, much less apologized. Why was she talking to a boy without eyes who appeared more dead than real?

The inquisitor couldn't know that she still saw oily boy. He would lock her up, forbid her parents from visiting, and throw away the key.

Period.

Daniela would settle the score with oily boy within her dreams. She'd get him to stop harassing her, once and for all.

And for the record, she was finished sucking up Claire's and Harry's harassment too.

"Leave me alone, oily boy! Stop picking, needling, and pushing me toward insanity."

She already knew Harry's and Claire's sins, and even if oily boy hadn't killed a thirteen-year-old boy by forcing him, like she had, to return and die from osteosarcoma, surely the ghost had committed at least one sin. She would find out what it was and shove it down his throat until he quieted. Time to fight back.

Her eyelids popped open. "The boy's not real," she whispered. "I need help."

Who could she trust?

Grandma Gertrude, Daniela's ride-or-die chick.

37—THE ORPHAN

ONE DAY AT THE ORPHANAGE turned into months, and months into almost a year. The routine was the same—breakfast, then chores, then school lessons. Everything happened like clockwork.

Cillian started to develop a halting alto voice, and his previously frail, boyish physique sprouted into a gangly stature.

He was becoming a man.

And men shed blood for freedom.

"Lights off," the orderly barked. When the shuffling, bearded man wasn't barking, he was a kind old man who reminded Cillian of Grandpa Barry.

Darkness blanketed the boy's dorm room, and Paul's anticipating smile pushed Cillian toward his destiny. Shoeless and sockless, Cillian crept out of his bed and snuck into the kitchen to claim his prize, a stolen piece of chocolate cake, for Paul's birthday. Miss Bailey had bragged about the cake—a gift from a benefactor of the orphanage—all during his English literature class. Finding the moist dessert, he wrapped a slice inside wax paper.

Down the hallway, shoes tapped across concrete. He crouched under a table, waiting for the footsteps to pass. Stealing would be punishable by a fierce beating, and according to legend, one kid hadn't survived.

All quiet.

Quickly, he scampered into the inky blackness toward their dorm room.

He entered the dorm, then counted cold metal bedframes until he stopped at number six. He pushed back Paul's woolen blanket and pulled the covers over both of them.

Click. A flashlight illuminated their blanketed hideout.

"What are you doing, Cil?"

"It's midnight, isna it?"

"I don't know."

"How old are you today?"

"Twelve."

"Yer wish, then?" Cillian whispered.

Paul shivered. "Heat during the winter. Dinner for longer than ten minutes." He sheepishly grinned.

"Aye. I-I-I cannae . . ." Cillian bit his lower lip and peeled the paper off Paul's gift. "Well, it isna what ye asked for, and sorry the cake's a wee bit lopsided, but happy birthday, Paul."

He gasped and then a big grin spilled across Paul's face. "Grey Thunder will beat you to death if she finds out—but thanks." Paul ate the moist treat, smudging chocolate fudge on his face. "Why did you steal it? She'll be thirsting to find out who did it."

"You chose to be my friend—my brother—when you didna ha' to, and one day, I'll be hopin' to be makin' ye proud."

"Let's hope we both make it to that day." Paul fell asleep, evidence of the missing cake slice plastered on his face.

★ ★ ★

"Paul, come on and take your bath before we get into trouble." Cillian tousled Paul's hair, waking him. Gray water awaited the boy; twenty orphans had bathed before him. He emerged from the bathroom with a towel wrapped around him.

"Why do you always want me to take my bath before you, Cil?"

"Are ye wantin' bugs to eat you alive?"

"No."

"Then stop being cheeky and get dressed."

Overnight, a hint of a halting baritone had teased Cillian's vocal cords. Neither his awkward demeanor nor his squeaky voice could decide if he was a boy or a man. Even so, he attempted to fill Paul's late parents' shoes the best he could. They had tragically died during the pre-Christmas Clapham Junction rail crash in London. Paul loved and usually obeyed his brother for the attempt.

After morning baths, Big Jake, the orderly, marched into the dormitory. "Cillian Finn."

"Aye, sir."

"The mistress wants to see you. Follow me." The orderly ambled back into the hallway.

Quickly, Cillian gave Paul instructions. "Get dressed. Dinna be late for classes." The cake thief ran to catch up with the big man.

"Are you going to get a prize?" Paul hollered as his brother disappeared down the hallway.

"Dunno!"

38—THE ORPHAN (PG 13)

SATURDAY, SEPTEMBER 17, 1994
WEEVIL, ENGLAND

CEILING BULBS SWUNG ON LONG black cords, bleeding streams of stale yellow light down concrete walls.

Cillian hadn't known that the care home possessed a basement until now.

"Did my chocolate cake please your palate?" Miss Grey materialized from the shadows of the cold, dank room. The orphan jumped and quickly answered. "I-I-I dinnae ken what yer talking about—"

"You're making this easy." She strolled into the light. A polyester, beige, mid-calf-length skirt showed her varicose-veined legs; no ankles, just long straight calves. "Honesty, boy. There's a security camera in my office."

Damn. Cillian hadn't known. He fiddled with the edge of his shirt. She couldn't know that Paul had eaten the stolen sweet. "Aye, ma'am. I enjoyed the cake."

"I'm delighted you enjoyed what wasn't yours."

"I-I-I'm sorry."

"After you've been caught, I dare say. That doesn't count. String him up."

Big Jake's shoes shuffled across the concrete floor, creating a sandpaper-rubbing sound. Head down, refusing to make eye contact with the orphan, he shackled Cillian's hands in manacles. What did the tyrant have on Big Jake? He didn't want to do this.

"Strip him and douse him."

The orderly stripped Cillian's clothes off, then cranked up a water hose and sprayed the shivering boy down.

"Willow switches dance best on drenched flesh." Miss Grey groaned as she cranked a metal lever attached to the wall clockwise, hoisting Cillian's cold, wet body into a tiptoed stance, his bound hands stretched above his head.

The mistress glared into a wall mirror in front of the boy, sneering at her victim. "Evil sleeps inside you, child." She ran callused hands down his bare back, buttocks, and thighs. "I'm not the first to administer a proper flogging, yet you've learned nothing?"

"Please dinna do this." Skin stretched taut, he gasped more than spoke.

"Nor will I be the last. Until you're dead and no longer a threat to humanity's existence."

"What're ye talkin' about, madam?"

"You're daft to who you are." She chose her instrument of punishment: a green rod, tapered at the end. "What is your name, boy?"

"Cillian Joseph Finn."

"Wrong." She slid her palm along the back of the stick, slicing open calluses without flinching. "You are Leviathan—Job's sea monster—the dreaded antichrist born to suffocate life from Earth."

"I-I-I dinnae ken who Leviathan or the antichrist are. I swear it." He parted his lips, thinking to beg for mercy, but as she ambled from the table, he noted the void in her eyes. *Like Joe Sanders's eyes.*

There would be no point in begging, so he waited as he had done before.

"We must all do our part to save Earth from your pandemic." She straightened her hair and then her skirt. "If I die while killing the devil, a martyr I shall be, for I shall drive the prince of evil from your dark soul, from our home—Earth." Her lips smirked, daring him to beg for mercy.

Tired of bullies, but helpless to do anything about them, he glared back. His ice-blue eyes hardened. His tongue stilled. Boys begged, but men shed blood for freedom.

"Cry out for mercy. I'll not think less of you." The mistress wrapped both hands around the stick and drove the switch across the middle of his back, meting out her exorcism.

His breath, hers, and the reed's *whoosh* mingled into a haunting melody.

"Cry out! Devils cried out to Jesus when He threatened to cast them from a sick boy into Hades. Christ showed mercy on those evil spirits, sending the demons into a pack of pigs, and they ran into the sea and drowned." She laughed, her mouth twisted. "You won't drown me, sea monster—Earth's sea devil, Leviathan."

A soft breath escaped his lips, barely a whimper, as he begged the quiet voice for peace as he died. Could anyone hear his cry? Pain vibrated through his body. Unable to hide his misery any longer, he screamed, and the room reverberated with his agony.

"I've unsettled the demons in you. Take courage. They'll soon flee." The mistress beat him until she had her fill. She wobbled back to the table and tossed the bloodied, splintered switch on top of the steel table, then reached for another rod.

"D'ye not think you've beaten me enough?" He gasped, fighting for breath—for life. "I-I-I'm not what you accuse me of being."

"Defiance hides within your voice."

"I'll be bakin' ye a thousand cakes, then."

"I'd not eat your poison." She stumbled, grabbed the table, and rested. Her pallid skin darkened to purple. Clenching her chest, she fell forward. *By the god's will, she's dead.* Cold sweat mingled with blood and dripped from Cillian's body.

Jake ran to the woman's side and felt her pulse.

Standing, Jake shook his head, then ran out of the room—to look for help, no doubt. Indeed, the mistress had secured her martyrdom, but who would find him before he joined her in hell? The door creaked upon its hinges. Muted footsteps slid along the concrete floor.

"I-I-I'm sorry, Cil." Paul's oscillating voice reached Cillian's ears. "I covered my ears, but I never left you." He embraced his brother's legs.

Cillian flinched. "Aye, lad, dinna cry for me."

"There were no onions in my breakfast soup. This is for real."

The older brother laughed softly. "She's not the first to believe me possessed wi' demons, nor will she be the last." His world dimmed, and his voice slurred. "If ye'd be so kind as to be helpin' me down, I can be gettin' my sleep and gainin' my strength before she wakes to finish me off."

"She's dead."

"No, Black Jack. Devils live forever. Didna your parents tell you?"

He was right.

At first, the front of the mistress's ivory chiffon blouse fluttered, then her chest heaved unevenly. A minute later, Cillian was down, and breath had filled the witch's lungs once more.

"Should we run away, Cil?"

"And how would I be feedin' you or schoolin' you?" Cillian leaned heavily on Paul, reached for his shirt and jacket, and dressed before pinching Paul's nose. "Chin up. Did ye turn in yer homework?"

"I did."

"Help me back to the dorms. I need a bath."

"How did you survive? I couldn't." Paul helped his brother to the door.

"I was thinkin' of you."

"Should I try to kill Grey Thunder?" Paul glanced over his shoulder. "I've never murdered anyone, but I don't want her to hurt you again."

"Didna ye parents never tell you, dinna be givin' up your innocence so fast?"

"Never."

"Because ye cannae be gettin' it back again."

"Cil?" They stumbled down the hallway and back up the stairs to the main level.

"Aye, lad."

"Are you really Leviathan, a sea monster?"

Cillian stopped leaning on Paul. Supporting his own weight, he wrapped his arm around his little brother's trembling frame. "Maybe I am."

"Cool. Let's go swimming."

"Aye, then. Into the safety of the sea."

39—Adelaide:
#Goodbye, Mom and Dad

I SHOULD BE SLEEPING.

I want to, but I can't.

Rain falls, thrumming down the windowpanes of my dorm, smearing a haze across the night sky. I tug my great-great-grand-mother's quilt up over my slight frame, blocking the night winds as they slap dead branches against the windows before seeping around rotting-wood casements and swirling around the room.

Cordy's asleep.

I'm jealous.

A ghoulish hand seems to slide through the night, clutching a sickle in its bloodless grasp. Its icy presence chills me to my bones.

Desperate to shake the creepy feeling I've had all day, I borrowed Gage's prayer candles. I light them. They flicker, casting shadows on bare walls but refusing to give me any comfort as they burn inside small red votives, leaving pools of wax in glass. Why do people burn candles in religious ceremonies anyway? Dancing shadows are spookier than just plain darkness. I tighten my grip around Mother's letter. *My Dearest Adelaide Rose . . .*

She adored the Seurat painting, and now it belongs to me.

Where would I hang it? The dorms? Priceless paintings combined with chipped, pressboard furniture? Definitely bad feng shui.

Where would I live after Mother died?

The day before Da disappeared, he'd called me at 5:00 a.m. EST and confessed why he was acting weird—spontaneous.

"Yer mother's dying, lass. I dinnae ken how else to say it to you."

"Can we help her?" I asked.

"I cannae save her. Her doctor says it's too late fer a lung transplant." My da's voice sounded as though it would break, not a frequent occurrence. His physical presence usually barked, "Think twice before acting stupid."

"What is she dying from?"

"Blood's floodin' her lungs, and she's drownin'. Fate's cruel. She's always hated water—lakes, oceans, pools—it didna matter. Never mastered swimmin'. Now her heart's broken, and I'm tellin' the good Lord, I didna break it. I'm a man of blood. I've never deserved yer mother, lass."

I'm a man of blood. I never deserved her.

My heart skips a beat, then pounds my ribs.

I tuck Mother's note inside my flannel pajamas, placing it close to my heart as I thought about Da's phone call. "Mummy, get better. Stay a while longer, please?" I breathe the plea into the darkness, but my voice won't travel the hundreds of miles from New Hampshire to the Blue Ridge Mountains of North Carolina where she lives alone with Beatha, her friend and, according to Father, her nurse.

It sucks to be a teenager.

Adults keep us in the dark and then wonder why we bump into things.

I need clarity. I've never done this before—closed my eyes, knelt, and prayed. "A month longer with Mummy. That's all I ask. Let her watch me graduate."

I open my eyes, already knowing that today is going to be a sucky, armpit kind of day. Since leaving the library and going to bed, I've been staring at the ceiling for six hours.

Red block numbers on the face of my digital clock tell me it is 3:49 in the morning.

Before the sun dares to rise, I slip on a pair of spandex leggings, a lavender hoodie, well-worn trainers, and my shoulder lamp, then stuff my mother's letter into the hoodie pocket. I need to be near her. The letter is all I have.

Tiptoeing from my dorm room, I'm careful to not wake Cordelia. I need to be alone.

Beneath an audience of stars, I jog across the slick, wet grounds of Exeter Academy. Cold sweat drips down my back. Endorphins flood my muscles, and I pump my arms and legs harder, charging past my lecture hall, a redbrick, four-story building hidden behind a cluster of maple trees. Fog hovers over the lawn, and crickets whistle a nightingale's song.

Out of nowhere, a wobbly form charges toward me.

My heart races, fueling my legs.

The creature's stride quickens, and as it comes closer, I recognize him. He's uglier in the dark, like a swamp monster on two legs.

"Hi, Addy Rose."

"Levi?" I slow my pace.

For some insane reason, he croons, "If I could be a minnow, I'd swim out to the deep-blue sea."

"What are you doing out here? Why are you singing?"

Glaring at me, his panther-blacks lighten to winter-blues. *Weird eyes.* I back away, just out of arm's reach.

"Addy-girl." His speech slurs, and hell's funk plays on his breath—stale beer and sulfur. "You know what I came for."

"What? I didn't know you'd be here." Without turning, I inch toward the dorms and slide my hand over my hipbone, protecting Mother's memory—the letter.

"Didn't you? Gage's prayer candles." As I try to evade him, he mirrors my movements. "Only one request?"

"How did you know—?"

"Walk with me." He flashes a leering smile. "I'll tell all."

"What is there to tell?"

"*Hode esta sophia*—here is the riddle. Determine the multitude of the beast; for it is a multitude of men, and this multitude is Chi Xi Stigma."

"Six-six-six." I think of Mother's journal, the letter, and the puzzle hidden within the mysterious Greek words, then gulp hard. *Maybe he can answer the riddles. Feel him out.* "What's a guy doing running outside while everyone else is sleeping?"

"I could ask you the same question." He winks, and gradually, his face appears less threatening. "A quick run? Peel off the night's cobwebs?"

"I need sleep before class."

"I'm not asking you to run a marathon."

"Just a five-minute walk, and that's it." I cross my arms. Giving him a sideways glare, I move slowly into the night with Levi. He sets the pace. I keep up.

"Missing your mother and father?"

"What do you know about my parents?" I attempt to bite my nails, but they are not long enough.

"The library." He chuckles, easing my fear. "When Cordy Grey screams, she believes she's whispering."

"Got that right." We laugh, and my neck muscles and shoulders relax.

"I miss mine."

"You're an orphan?" I ask, but Levi breaks into a sprint, then stops and turns around, running backward. "Actually, I'm lying. I don't miss my parents; I miss my sister."

"She must have been special. What's her name?"

"Natalia. Beautiful. Kind. A dancer and a violinist."

"Where is she?"

"Gone. Disappeared."

"Sorry to hear that." Something in his tone didn't ring true. The force of my breath comes lighter than a feather, and for the record, feathers are dead. I slip my asthma inhaler between my lips and inhale one puff. I should have inhaled two, but how could I know the future?

He smiles. "I didn't know you had asthma."

"Why should you? We don't talk."

"Maybe we can change that?"

"Why? We're graduating in three weeks. I'll never see you again."

"My sister disappeared. Your father disappeared. We have something in common. Besides, I know where your dad is."

"You know about my da?" I stop. Fear prickles the back of my neck, telling me to run, but my curiosity defies my common sense. "Why? I mean, how?"

He leans in, his foul breath dousing my face between each consonant and vowel. *Dude, buy some toothpaste; I'll pick up the tab.* "Let's just say that I know some powerful people."

"Then why haven't those powerful people helped you find your sister?"

"That's different."

"Why?"

"My sister isn't a murderer like your dad."

"Don't tell lies about my da. You'll be sorry."

"Don't threaten me, Addy Rose." Levi laughs. "Threats aren't ladylike."

"Who said I'm a lady?"

"But you are—one of the finest." He winks at me. I cringe.

"Whatever. My da isn't a murderer." But I wasn't sure. "Levi . . ." the tone and volume of my voice softens, ". . . if you can help me find my da, no matter what he's done—"

"I can. I will."

"But what?"

"You have something I need, something that can help me bring Natalia back."

"What?"

"A relic."

"I don't own anything old . . . well, except a Seurat painting."

"I've no use for art, but I'm desperate to get a hold of the Glass Tattoo. Give it to me, and I'll tell you how to find your beloved father."

"I don't know what you're talking about." Thoughts of the ancient stone, its rumored powers, and my mother's mysterious past silence my tongue.

"Don't believe you, Addy Rose." He buries his hands in his pockets. "You and your mom are like the Bobbsey twins. You know everything about each other. Besides, what kind of daughter leaves her father in danger when she possesses the power to rescue him? *Hode esta sophia.* Let's just say Chi Xi Stigma is alive even now, and your mother knows him—really knows him. 'I Will be Here' . . . Steven Curtis Chapman . . . Chi Xi Stigma's musical prelude before biblically *knowing* your mother."

"Chi Xi Stigma—six-six-six—the antichrist?"

"The big bad wolf himself. The son of perdition prophesied in your mother's precious Bible. She's protecting him—hiding him."

A star shoots across the sky. *What was that about?*

"You're accusing my da of being the antichrist?" I burst out laughing. "You're pathetic. But I'll tell you this: I've heard of the Glass Tattoo, but I've never seen it. For the record, my mother would never aid and abet a monster destined to annihilate humanity when she's the one charged to save us."

"Lucifer is the clever one. Checkmate, Yahweh. The Orphan Dreamer won't end her orphan's life. It's natural. Most women would do anything for the man they love. Kill. Turn a blind eye. Harm their children. Stupid females. Ask your grandma. Dad's side."

"You're reaching."

"Addy Rose, the Glass Tattoo—where is it?"

"I don't know anything else."

"Your dad would be so disappointed in you." Levi begins to walk away.

My breath catches. "Stop!" I grab his arm. "I'll help you find it."

Levi faces me. "Now, we're getting somewhere." His flesh is too hot for exposed arms on a cool New Hampshire morning. I release him.

"Sorry. I didn't mean to grab you. It's just that . . . if you know where my da is, tell me. Is he alive?"

"Assaulting your classmate. You don't fall too far from the paternal tree." He studies me and then grins. "Orphans like your dad are disposable. For now, he's alive—but not for long."

"My da's not an orphan. Or trash. So please don't hurt him. Mom will help us find the Glass Tattoo if you promise not to harm him."

"Who are his parents? Have you ever met them?"

I avoid Levi's piercing gaze. It's true; I have never met my da's biological parents. "No."

"Did a stork drop him on a garbage pile for your mother to find?" He chuckles. "Trust me: your dad's an *orphan*. But not the kind who doesn't have parents. The barcode? He's the devil's spawn."

"How did you know about the barcode?"

"Cordy's a loud talker." He brushes stray hairs out of my face.

Levi rakes his fingernails across his lips. Blood trickles down his chin. The bleeding stops. The cut closes. *What the heck?*

Storm—I'm out of here! I lunge, prepared to sprint back to the dorm. But I can't leave. Levi knows where my da is. My legs wobble like overcooked noodles. I square my shoulders and fire off a round of threats. "Listen." My voice is quiet but laced with poison.

"You know what I hate about your kind? You're boring, insignificant, and predictable. I'm dying for you and those like you to go back to where you came from—dirt or a primordial blob, whatever version you prefer."

"Go back? This is my home, and I don't know who you are or what your problem is, but you better not mess with my family." My hands curl into fists.

"Or what?" He waits.

I don't deliver.

Stupid.

Don't make a threat unless you can back it up. Fighting 101. My face flushes. *What now? He might know where my da is, and no matter what happens to me, I am not leaving until I squeeze every drop of information out of Levi. Even if I have to beat it out of him or take a beating myself. Father's worth the pain.*

"Did your mother tell you it's time to rewind history?"

"Why would she?" My voice sounds mouselike, as though rodents could talk. I take another puff from my inhaler.

A grin widens his cheeks. Levi winks and fakes a bad British accent. "Your father's no saint." A sneer distorts his face. "The relic won't protect your mother. Quite the opposite. It's why she's dying so young. Give it to me; I have permission to save your mother and find your father. Trust me, Adelaide Rose." He strokes my cheek with his left hand.

"Don't you dare touch me." I back up. Hot tears flood my eyes. I blink, trying to hide them, but they fall, and I hate myself for showing emotion. I wasn't supposed to know the relic existed.

I saw it once.

That's all.

"Look at you—crying." Disgust ices his words. "Mother knows best. Her daughter is too weak of mind, body, and spirit. I despise your feminine, pallid flesh." He pecks my forehead, and his lips are amazingly soft, but I slap him hard across the left cheek.

"Feisty." He darts his tongue in and out of his mouth as though he's a serpent.

Where's my da's Smith and Wesson when I need it?

"Looked in a mirror lately? Did it reflect a sun-kissed Greek god?" I wipe my face with the back of my hand.

"Funny girl. I'm about to change that." He glances over his shoulder while tapping his foot. "Last chance, wannabe superhero. Give me the relic. Give me the Glass Tattoo."

"I told you. I don't have it."

Frogs stop chirping.

Crickets cease humming. *Run!*

I shift into a runner's stance.

Too late.

Lunging, Levi grabs my neck between sweaty, desperate hands and forces me to the ground. I form a defensive pose, but even though I've studied martial arts, he's too quick and powerful for me, as though he's much more than just a teenage boy. Tousled mousy-brown hair shades his wild eyes. My pulse throbs beneath his icy grip.

If I survive, how will I face Mother?

Air plunges into my mouth, but asthmatic breaths restrict my large airways, staunching a scream. I lift my inhaler to my lips. He grabs it and tosses it into the grass.

"Whimper, and I'll shame you, then leave you to be discovered by our classmates." He clamps his hand over my lips. "Nephilim are a messy business." I taste dirt and something more fetid than curdled milk and gag. I bite his hand.

"Stupid girl." He flips me onto my stomach, knocking the wind from my lungs.

I gasp for air, my bravery wilting. "Please," a high-pitched wheeze whines past my lips. "I need my inhaler."

He squeezes tighter, muting my pleas. "Begging, are we?" He twists my face toward his, and his breath washes over me—ragged, foul. His buckteeth press into his lower lip. Grunting, his movements grow more erratic as he yanks my spandex pants down from my waist.

No. Don't do it.

I fight. My lungs clamp down tighter than Fort Knox, starving my muscles of oxygen. My strength quickly wanes. "I'll scream—a-a-and your life will be over," I say, breathless. "My da will make sure of it."

He grabs my ponytail and slams my face into the dewy ground. Mud clogs my mouth. "Missing fathers don't defend naughty girls." He breathes heavily, dousing my face with his stench. "Spotted you working those steel bags at the gym like a boxing champ, boss. Screaming isn't like you."

He's right.

Screaming guarantees an audience; gawkers add up to gossip.

Poor Addy Rose—her innocence pilfered.

No different than Mother, I hate playing the victim. The idea of pity makes my muscles tense and nose flare, but asthma still constricts my large airways, limiting the oxygen flow that would spur my muscles into action.

Stay calm.

Rest, then channel your adrenaline.

I suck in a ragged breath. Cold slime snakes down my throat, suffocating me. Levi lifts my head. I cough and suck in a meager breath. He wraps his hands around my trachea and squeezes lightly.

"I can't breathe—hurt—"

"This isn't hurt. This is a prelude." Levi grins. "Your father knows about preludes and hurt. Ask his victims."

I twist my torso, trying to gain some leverage, but he tightens his grip around my waist with his other hand. I should have been smarter. How could I have let myself become a statistic: young, single, white female runs alone in the dark like a gazelle straight out of the South African savannah? But I needed to sweep the cobwebs from my mind.

Mom's dying.

What would you do?

That's what I thought.

"More slippery than a greased eel, Addy-girl. Delicious when you fight." He makes a slurping sound with his mouth and releases my neck.

Gross. My gut heaves, threatening to hurl acid and bile. "I'm giving you a choice." I whisper. "Would you like your jujitsu served up with a side of pain or humiliation? Last guy I sparred with was out in six seconds."

"Stop with the empty threats." He sweeps his paper-thin lips across my earlobe, then pauses. "They called your mother the 'Orphan Dreamer'—but that's not who she really is. She's a ghetto rat."

Big mistake. My face flushes. Don't. Insult. My. Mother. "Screw you. Stop touching me!"

"Look at you, giving orders. Hardly in the position, I dare say?" He lays his full weight on me.

Wounded and starving for air, a grizzly's courage returns—eventually. Stop struggling. Let your muscles rest. I lay still, and he stops his search, finding what he's been looking for.

"A mother's letter tucked away inside her kid's pants." He laughs—low, eerie. "I should've explored earlier. The relic must be close by." He continues looking with his hands.

Kennedy Space Center's Mission Control doesn't launch a space shuttle until it throttles its three main engines to 100 percent. A few more seconds, that's all I need, but he may not give me a few more seconds. A knowing smile tucks into the corners of my lips. My da taught me everything he knew about fighting.

But my mom taught me the art of distraction. Changing tactics, I pin the biggest, cheesiest grin to my lips. Distract him. "I take it you've never walked through a ghetto or seen a rat."

"I hoped the sun would rise, then you smiled." Suddenly, his face darkens to a surfer's tan, and his buckteeth recede and bleach to a dazzling white.

"What's happening?"

"Change. 'Everyone thinks of changing the world, but no one thinks of changing himself.' Leo Tolstoy."

Seriously? Quoting Tolstoy?

I glare into my assailant's eyes while, methodically and quietly, my hand searches for my inhaler. Wet. Cold. Mud.

Scales inch across his hands and up his arms, armoring pale flesh with pearlescent-white and gold crocodile skin. "My father calls me Leviathan." His eyes were level with mine.

"Leviathan. What a lovely name." Keep smiling. Keep him distracted. Kiss him. I swallow my pride and peck him on the lips.

"I knew you'd come around." He goes for tongue. I lean away. He stops. "Stop thinking that every guy has a thing for you. I don't want you—never have."

Without thinking, I spit in its face.

His pupils narrow into crocodile slits. Balling his hand into a fist, he reaches back. "I'm going to be your worst nightmare."

I arch back while rotating my head to the side, but his jab lands square in in the middle of my left eye.

Pain. Liquid fire burns inside my face. My fingers keep searching for my lost inhaler. Plastic. Warm. A tube.

Quickly, I turn my head, inhaling two puffs of airway muscle relaxant. Albuterol mixed with epinephrine—the most potent bronchodilators—surges through my veins, relaxing my large airways. I inhale deeply. Oxygen floods my lung sacs through my newly dilated bronchi, releasing pent-up energy into my muscles.

Mission Control, ready to launch!

My leg and arm muscles ignite. "Don't freaks belong in a zoo?"

His manicured brows slant downward, forming a question. Engaging my abdominal muscles, I pivot forward and slam my forehead into his chin. *Crack.* Pain explodes through my skull. A pit of blackness threatens to consume me, but there's no turning back now. Ride or die.

Not planning on dying. I hit again.

A tooth cracks.

Blood gushes over his lip and drips onto my face. He reaches for my neck. Arching back, I ram my elbow into his chest—one, two, three.

He grabs his chest, rolls to the side, jumps to his feet, and balls his hands into fists.

I scrabble to my feet. He lunges. I dodge his grasp and with one hundred and twenty pounds of momentum throw a foot jab into his neck, cutting off a good part of the blood flow to his brain by compressing his carotid artery.

His eyes roll back into his head.

I inhale again, deeply, then grab his wrist, flipping him onto his back. Mud splatters. I yank the letter out of his hand. After tucking Mother's memory away, I slam my open palm into his face repeatedly. My shoulder throbs, a volcano of pain. Blood spatters onto his shirt, the grass, and my jacket.

"Circus fricking idiot!" Finally, a crack.

That would be his nose.

All done.

"You were right. I am a boss." Satisfied, I leave him moaning on the soggy morning lawn. "And my da isn't your six-six-six, moron."

At least, I pray he isn't.

40—Orphan Dreamer

"YOU'LL BE JUST FINE, ADELAIDE. I'm here." Daniela opened her eyes, then catalogued her surroundings, reorienting herself.

Shiplap-whitewashed walls.

Metal headboard attached to the straw bed beneath her drenched frame.

A patina brass–framed mirror anchored to the wall above the antique rosewood desk. Grandma Gertrude's farmhouse. Warmth hugged her, but one question flogged her mind—*was oily boy the antichrist?* The orphanage's mistress and Levi believed he was. And would she really become kindred spirits with oily boy, then marry him and, potentially, bear his children?

A cold shiver rattled Daniela's slight frame.

In the corner, a chair rocked. Had someone just gotten up? Daniela's breath caught, spurring on a litany of coughs. She bolted upright, swung her legs over the edge of the bed, and attempted to stand. Her legs softer than overcooked noodles, she collapsed, smacking her backside on the wood floor. *Fudge!*

Daniela gazed up at the rustic, wood-beam ceiling. *Relax. You're safe. Would it be so bad if oily boy was real?*

Could Adelaide exist without him?

Light streamed past the room's lone window.

Squinting, she shielded her eyes, and a memory of Ethan flooded her mind.

"Follow me," Yeshua said.

"Sure, dude. Where are we going?" Ethan got up and started walking.

Bright clouds hovered over the farmhouse; filtering out light. Still. Quiet. Promising a peaceful fall day—but even clouds could break a promise.

Strength returned to her legs. She ambled to the small writing desk.

She removed a sheet of scented paper from the desk drawer. Lavender wafted through the air. She sat on a backless chair and grabbed a pencil. From a magical place, the words flowed, her fingers struggling to keep up: *My Dearest Adelaide Rose . . . My life is a Georges-Pierre Seurat painting—and I'm mortified . . .*

She finished the odd letter. With trembling hands, she folded it, stuffed it into her journal, then sauntered into the hallway before entering the kitchen. "Grandma! Grandma!"

A potbellied stove radiated cozy heat into the tiny room.

On the dining room table, her grandmother had laid out fresh butter, biscuits, and a glass pitcher of iced lemonade.

Daniela whirled around, intending to face the front screen door, but the rickety table seemed to reach out and grab her shoelace, faceplanting her into the floor. Her newfound clumsiness was due to the sedatives that the doctor had prescribed.

"They can test your blood for that stuff," her father had said, afraid the shrink could commit their daughter for the minor infraction of refusing to drug their child.

"Blessed Jesus, that girl," Grandma hollered from the porch. "What's possessed you now, Danny Rose?"

"Nothing." She peeled her gangly frame and pride from the floor.

"You still in one piece, button?"

"So far."

"You plan on changing that?"

"No, ma'am." Dusting her pant legs off, she eyed the lemonade jar. Tart and sweet, but more dangerous than lost pirate's treasure to obtain. "Want some lemonade, Grandma?"

"Lordy Mercy, no! I'll get my own. I don't want to be picking glass out of your pretty face. Sit down, girl; pour you a glass, drink it, and when you finish, come out to the porch and help me peel these beans. We'll sweep those cobwebs out of your head, help you walk straight."

Attempting to pour a glass of lemonade, she found the jar heavy and missed the glass by an inch.

"Forget it." She wiped up the spill. "Coming, Grandma." Daniela burst past the screen door, skidding to a stop right before she tumbled over the edge of the shallow porch.

"Enjoy the lemonade?" Her grandmother glanced over her wire spectacles.

"Wasn't thirsty." Daniela rubbed her earlobe, a nervous tic.

"Um-hum." Her grandmother tapped the empty seat beside her on the porch swing. "Sit down, button, and help me shell these peas for dinner." Daniela sat.

"You give up too easily. If your ancestors and I threw in the towel because of a few scrapes and bruises, where would you be?"

"Sitting in the back of the bus." Her hands shaking, Daniela attempted to snap peas.

"Look at me, child." Grandma wiped her gnarled hands across her tattered paisley apron. "I never ever depended on another blessed mortal soul to do what I could learn how to do myself, and the good Lord never let me down. He gave me the wisdom to pay for this place."

Daniela gazed down the dirt driveway, across the road, at corn stalks waving beneath the sun.

"How many women 'round here own their own forty-acre farm?"

"Not many?"

"Button, if your old granny can't gift you anything else, I'll give you this—be your own woman, and depend on the Lord while making your own place in the world."

"Is God real? Sometimes, I don't feel Him."

"Look at the heavens. What do you see?"

"Cotton-ball clouds tacked to a blue sky. Look! A cardinal—red as a rose."

"You're smart—a genius. You don't believe all that came from some evolutionist's primordial blob or some ape? If the evolutionist's link existed, shouldn't a scientist have found it by now? I couldn't lose my keys for that long, even if I tried."

"No. I don't believe in fairy tales, Grandma . . . except for the possibility of kindred spirits, but shh." Daniela raised her finger to her lips as though Ms. Bender, her science teacher, stood in the room. "Don't tell Ms. Bender. She'd be disappointed in me." *Talking about missing, where had Prince Jonathan's arrowhead gone?*

"It'll be our secret."

"Grandma, what do you say about hell?"

"Bad place. Don't go." Her grandmother made life sound so simple. She gave Daniela a studious look. "One snowflake falls from heaven to quench hell's thirst. I believe you are that snowflake." Now, she was speaking in riddles, but Daniela knew that whatever her grandma meant in regard to snowflakes and hell, it must be good.

"Grandma, I love you." Daniela hugged Grandma Gertrude. Bones protruded beneath her tattered dress. Why was Grandma Gertrude so thin?

"Help me move this swing. It's hotter than a Florida swamp out here."

Daniela pumped her legs back and forth, and the swing picked up speed. They shucked a pan of purple-hull peas.

Her grandmother rested her hand on Daniela's face. "What were you goin' on about in there while you were sleeping?"

Heat flushed Daniela's cheeks, but her grandmother's tongue had been trained to keep secrets. The white ladies on the other side of the tracks had taught their *help* to keep their lips closed. "Is the sky friendly or mean?"

Grandma crinkled her brow, her coal-black eyes studying her granddaughter's face. She spoke, slow and clear, "The clouds. The rain. The sun. They're too busy to become one of your imaginary friends, nor do they possess an ounce of feeling, and when you visit that psychiatrist in three weeks, act as though spiders haven't eaten up all your common sense."

Daniela gulped hard, trying to swallow the words, but they refused to be buried. "I was dreaming about oily boy. Pale as a bottle full of milk. Doesn't have eyes. Face covered in bruises."

"What have you told your papa about him?"

"That he exists—but not how he looks."

"You'll grow up into a lady one day. If you want to make something of yourself, discipline your mind. Tell it where to go." She sighed heavily. "Your momma told me that you've been writing in a journal. Go get it. I want to read it."

"It's private."

"Not from your grandma." She stopped shucking. "Go get it."

Daniela returned with her journal—nothing fancy, just a spiral-bound notebook—and gave it to her ally. Her grandmother read, starting at the last page, then the second-to-the-last page, and so on. She pointed at a rusty stain. "Nosebleed?

"Yes, ma'am."

"When do you bleed the most?"

"When the kids at school exclude me or after I dream of him—oily boy."

"Um-hmm. Someone else shed His blood under great stress, even sweating drops of blood while he prayed all alone in the Garden of Gethsemane. You bleed when you are rejected, lonely, or under stress. Your shed blood serves a greater purpose. Do you know what empathy is? It's what you feel for the boy."

"I'm still scared of him."

"I was afraid of your grandpa when I met him." Her grandmother rubbed Daniela's slight shoulders until she massaged the cold dread from her granddaughter's soul.

"Really? Grandpa was the sweetest soul."

"I had to discover that."

"Oily boy is covered in bruises and sometimes smells like rotten eggs. He asks me to help, but I don't know how." She told her grandmother everything, but that was what grandmothers were for: sharing secrets.

"Button, he needs your empathy—to survive the pain, to share his burden. He won't survive without it."

The clouds shifted overhead, darkening to a menacing gray and blocking out the sun as though a war cry had echoed across the universe and armies assembled in the heavens. Chills ran across Daniela's skin faster than ants crawling over a dead bug on the porch. She clung to her grandmother's arm.

"Pray for him." Grandma sat tall.

"That's all?"

"It's everything."

"What if my prayers are frozen?"

"Spring follows winter, and ain't no prayer that can't freeze hell while thawing heaven's blessings like the prayer of the child who feels the pain of the one for whom she's praying. Your prayers can—and will—defeat the boy's tormentors. If you're persistent. That's the point of the rejection. The loneliness. The waiting. The good Lord wants you to feel his pain without having to live in his shoes. Take the ache from the head to the heart."

"Why?"

"Even Jesus' power came after he felt compassion. Read the book of Mark." She opened her Bible.

"It says 'He had compassion on the multitude' and then He did something—healed the sick, fed the hungry, and even raised the dead. Patience. Persistence. Even the sun fights to shine past dark clouds."

"It's going to rain."

"Rain quenches fire. You're a snowflake—frozen prayers—but one day, oily boy may thaw your delicate bones of ice and then you'll pour down a rain shower so fierce that it'll wash away all that's hopeless."

"Is that code for falling in love?"

"If you want it to be." Her grandmother's eyes twinkled.

"Yuck."

"Tell me something, button. Why did you scrub your arm raw with that Brillo pad?"

Daniela looked down at her arm. "My skin is brown. The preacher said we should be whiter than snow—sinless. I don't want to walk around with sin covering me. Besides, my classmates always tell me to go back to Africa. I thought that maybe Claire would accept me if I looked like her."

"Slow down, button. You're all over the place."

"But I need to tell you everything, and besides, I don't even say everything that comes to mind. What do you do when everything you love dies? It hurts, Grandma. A whole bunch."

"Take a breath, then another. Fight for life. Ignorant people say ignorant things. The Bible says sins are scarlet. That's red, not brown or black. What's next, cutting off your nose because somebody doesn't like the shape or size?"

"It's sort of big. Not a bad idea."

"You don't know your history, and that's your problem. Your skin. Your nose. They tell powerful stories, but you've allowed negative words to settle in and play house. Fight lies with truth."

"Tell me the truth, Grandma."

"Your ancestors helped build this country. We belong. This is *our* home, and we've been fighting from the beginning to protect the freedoms of all citizens of this great country. Pity the day if we stop fighting."

"Dad says the same thing."

"Believe us. We wouldn't lie to you."

"Claire refuses to let me join the Untouchables because I'm not white or blonde."

Her grandmother laughed. "In India, being called an untouchable isn't a compliment."

"Really?" Daniels slid to the edge of her seat. "Why?"

"Because they're born in a certain caste, they're considered less than others. Every culture can be stupid, and sometimes the ones making the rules hold others back because they don't have enough going for themselves to run the race fair and square. Shaming others for things they can't or shouldn't change is the oldest trick in the bag. Stop buying into the trick."

"Tell me the truth, Grandma. Am I beautiful even though my skin is brown?"

"You're breathtaking. It's no accomplishment to be born with a little less or a little more color in your skin. When Yahweh created you, His Son kissed you and kept kissing your cheeks until the sun tanned your skin a rich brown. Don't ever be ashamed of what the good Lord has done."

"What about oily boy?"

"Be honest. Tell your dad everything."

"That'll start Armageddon." Daniela sighed. "Maybe my dad is six-six-six."

"Your dad's not a racist or the antichrist. He's hurting. He's experienced some situations that would make the strongest man never forget, but if the boy—pale or midnight black—is to be someone special for you . . . Let's just say there's nothing Austin Cavanaugh wouldn't do for his little girl. Even dealing with his own demons."

"Talking to you makes me brave."

"Next time oily boy shows up in your dreams, whisper, 'Here I am, Lord,' and then lie still and wait. Then ask the good Lord how to pray for the boy."

"If I'm too afraid to hear what Yahweh has to say?"

"Then you join the ranks of every prayer warrior I know."

"Do you *really* think he's real, grandma?"

"You're not crazy. I know that, but it's best to keep oily boy from the doctor. Your redhead obsession provides enough adventure for one shrink." Her grandma spit out a mouthful of chuckles.

"Pinky swear." Daniela linked her pinky finger into her grandmother's. "I'm going to prove to everyone that I'm not crazy. Adelaide is real. Oily boy may be real."

"How?"

"Prince Jonathan's arrowhead, of course. I'll find it." Black clouds tumbled over each other, eager to spill their soggy guts.

"Who's Adelaide?"

"My daughter—a beautiful, smart redhead."

"I imagine the Almighty's supply of redheads is running low?" They both laughed, and her grandmother whistled up a breeze—as Southerners did when humid air refused to move and create a breeze on its own. The storm rolled in faster. "Might as well get it over with. You hungry for some fried chicken, purple-hull peas, cornbread, and molasses?"

"Hours ago." Daniela followed her grandmother inside, carrying the pan of peas.

"Give me those." Her grandmother took the pan as she hummed a spiritual. "Don't want our dinner on the floor. Those drugs wearing off?"

"The fog's clearing. I'm glad." Outside, rain poured, creating mud puddles in the dirt road.

Grandma Gertrude lit the stove, then placed a cast-iron skillet on the open fire. "A hero's beginning appears insignificant until she comes into her purpose. You've never been an ordinary child. That fact scares your momma."

"Don't blame her. It must suck to have an alien for a kid. Ethan understood me in spite of my weirdness—so do you."

"A sense of humor will be the lifeline that keeps you from swimming in that dark place, depression." Her grandma poured grease into the iron skillet. "The Christ-child was born in a stable full of animals, and as He grew up, the religious leaders believed Him to be crazy. Turned out, they were the crazy ones. It took time for the plan to unfold, no different than it takes time to cook a good meal." She coated chicken thighs, wings, and breasts in spiced egg-flour batter.

Daniela dipped her finger into a bowl of fresh butter on the table. The curdled cream spread smooth across her tongue, tasting of a grandmother's love.

"Be patient. Wait for the good stuff." Her grandma pinched her cheek. "You don't want to arrive at the cross until you can endure it. Everyone needs a bit of polishing before show-and-tell." A quiet stillness surrounded her grandmother. "Your momma shared something that concerned me."

"What's that?" Daniela stirred the beans.

"She said you believe you killed Ethan."

"I did." Daniela stopped stirring.

"How?"

"He didn't want to leave Gibeah."

"Prince Jonathan's country?" Daniela nodded. "How did you travel?" Her grandmother slowly wiped her hands on her apron, worry running lines into her aging face.

"Found a portal in the basement of the Smithsonian during our class trip to Washington DC." Daniela stared at the steam rising above the pot.

"Button," her grandmother rested her hands on her granddaughter's shoulders. "You never made that trip."

"But we did."

"You were sick, in the hospital."

"I had the arrowhead until someone stole it. I'm sure of it." Daniela stepped away from her grandmother. Maybe she really was delusional. Her reality contorted, and her hope hit a wall of cold doubt, evaporating with the steam rising from the pot.

"That's when the doctors first diagnosed you as a schizophrenic with depressive episodes. Do you understand what I'm telling you, button?"

Daniela sipped lemonade, and she saw her grandmother's hand wrapped around hers, but she couldn't feel the bony fingers. Numbness consumed her.

"Are you listening?"

"I'm crazy. A nutcase. My classmates are right." She thought of the letter. The words came so freely, naturally, as though they belonged in her world.

"No, darling. It means you're not responsible for Ethan's death. You did not kill him by forcing him to return from a faraway land.

The cancer finished him off—with or without you—and that means, my darling granddaughter, that you deserve another friend."

"You're right." *Just agree.* Daniela didn't want to talk about Ethan anymore. "But what about Prince Jonathan's arrowhead?"

"Where is it?"

"It was in my dresser drawer, near my underwear."

"I'm sure you won't find it there."

"Never?"

"It's time to move on from Ethan. Don't hesitate to open your heart wide to whatever kindred spirit the good Lord sends your way, even if he's oily boy. Your daddy may throw a fit, but your heavenly Father won't mind a bit."

"Grandma." Daniela's tears erupted like Yellowstone's famous geyser. "Thank you."

Outside, the rain clouds shifted, and light spilled into the tiny kitchen as a wide smile spread across Daniela's face.

"I like crunchy fried chicken. Watch that oil on the stove. Let me get some more flour." Her grandmother entered the pantry. Daniela stared at the pan of oil. The amber liquid bubbled and popped.

Cans fell.

A thud.

"Grandma!" Daniela ran inside the cramped pantry.

Laying on her back, her grandmother clutched a jar of blackberry preserve to her chest. Blood seeped from a gash across her forehead. Flour caked the frail woman. *A ghost. Lily pale, like oily boy.* But Daniela loved her grandmother. She didn't care what color she was. Love did that to a person—made them not care.

"The good Lord's calling me. I'm gonna keep on following Him, button."

"It's okay, Granny." She forced a smile across her face as sat down beside her grandmother. "I'll be okay. Ethan will show you around. So will Grandpa. You won't be alone." Daniela's body shook, but she swallowed her pain in the form of sobs as she stroked her grandmother's brow.

"Trust Him, Danny Rose. Dream again—for me," the ghost whispered.

"I promise."

Grandma Gertrude's paper-thin eyelids closed; her pulse faded beneath Daniela's fingers. She dialed 911, knowing it was too late. She would see her grandma again—in heaven.

When the ambulance arrived, they wheeled her grandmother outside, beneath a cloudless sky, then lifted her into the back of the ambulance.

41—Orphan Dreamer

IT'S TUESDAY.

Time to visit the shrink.

Her grandmother was right—Prince Jonathan's arrowhead hadn't appeared inside Daniela's dresser drawer.

How would she prove her sanity to the inquisitor?

The day after Grandma Gertrude's funeral, Aglaope, the Greek siren's incessant song of depression lured Daniela into the abyss.

A depressed person's thoughts refuse to recycle as fast as a non-depressed person's, allowing life's sewage to back up. It would take an act of God to flush out the negative thought pattern running through Daniela's mind.

School ended.

Standing at the curb in front of her school, Daniela held a handkerchief to her nose. A rose blossomed across the cloth, staining it the color of Claire's lipstick. *The bleeds serve a higher purpose—to share oily boy's pain.*

"You'll be okay, oily boy. Not such a good day for me either. You can do it, Danny Rose." she repeated the mantra out loud over and over, effectively stuffing cotton balls into her ears to block out the siren's sweet song. Daniela had hidden Adelaide's letter in the deepest compartment of her backpack.

Her mother parked her Ford LTD beside the curb as Daniela's classmates stood on the grass behind her, giggling and pointing. "Banana boat! Banana boat. Psycho-girl's riding in a banana boat!"

"Get a life!" Daniela screamed. More irritated than sad, her stale emotions rotted inside her stomach, shooting funk through her entire body. Shoulders slumped, she slid into the backseat.

"Another nosebleed?" Her mother glanced into the rearview mirror.

"Unfortunately."

"You'll grow out of them. I used to wet my bed," her mother said in a cheerful, unnatural voice.

"Pugh-wee." Daniela squeezed her nostrils tighter. Her mother had shared a bed-wetting secret. Should she share her secret— Adelaide? She clicked her seatbelt, then slid down the seat until only the crown of her head could be seen from the city-bus-sized car windows.

Her mother shifted the car into drive and allowed it to roll forward.

Claire crossed in front of their car. Jeanette applied the brake. The banana boat jerked, tossing Daniela's head forward, then back. The banana boat's V8 engine torqued three hundred pounds a foot and guzzled a gallon of gasoline every thirteen miles; its steel frame extended over ten feet long.

God help the poor soul that took it on.

As they exited the school's driveway, her nosebleed stopped. She remained quiet, but dark thoughts spoke loudest in the quiet. "Why did Dad ask Joe to paint your car ten shades too yellow?"

"Your dad's color-blind—and maybe that's the best way to be."

"Claire calls our car a banana boat . . . when they laugh, I want to disappear and visit with my friends inside my world."

Mother glanced into the rearview mirror, concern darkening her features. "Let's not tell that to the psychiatrist—okay?"

"Deal." But what about the letter?

Could it save her, make the inquisitor believe that Daniela Rose Cavanaugh wasn't crazy but would become someone—a mother?

If she didn't play her cards right, she would vanish . . . forever. The pit hardened inside her stomach. She gagged.

"You okay?"

"I'm scared." Daniela rested her hands across her bag, the letter protected inside. *Scared and angry all at once.*

Her mother gripped the steering wheel, her knuckles flushing fiery red. "Silence is our friend, especially when the person listening refuses to understand."

"Whatever you do, Mom," Daniela's voice broke into a million desperate pieces, "don't leave me at the hospital." Tears stung her eyes, but she dared not cry. "I don't belong—okay?"

"Try not to cry. This isn't a place to show our feelings. This isn't a safe place."

"Okay." Daniela swallowed her emotions, and they burned as they entered her private vault—the abyss.

After they returned home, Daniela ate a snack and bathed—insane people don't bathe—and got ready to leave.

Thirty minutes away from her house, the inquisitor waited for her. This was her punishment for murdering Ethan and harming herself.

Her parents took her in her favorite outfit: a faded-pink corduroy jumper over a white button-up shirt, and a pair of hot-pink jelly shoes, fresh off layaway from Pic 'N' Save.

Before she climbed into the backseat of her mom's banana boat, her rafiki hugged her and whispered, "A mother's love knows no limits. Remember this."

He hated lying—from his perspective, he wasn't. But Daniela didn't think he was right about a mother's love being available in endless supply. Nothing that hot-chocolate-chip-cookie-gooey-good could exist into infinity.

Or maybe it could? Daniela silently whispered *I hope so.*

While sitting in the back of her mother's car on the way to her newest version of hell on earth, she tried to understand his point of view.

Jeanette turned onto Main Street, her voice chipper and fake again. "Silly people with all those gobbly-goo diagnoses. Daggummit!" Her mother hit the steering wheel.

A shock reverberated through the body of the car, slamming Daniela into the back of the driver's seat. Dazed, she peered out the window. A bloodied deer sprawled across the vacant road. "Mom, we killed it!"

"Stay in the car." Her mother jumped out of the car and tiptoed toward the fallen creature. The fallen animal's legs thrashed. Daniela opened the door, climbed out, and stood in the middle of the road.

"It's dying, but it's not dead," her mother said. "God, have mercy. Don't make it suffer any longer." Jeanette waited. "Get back in the car, Danny Rose. It's dangerous."

"I want to help."

"Stay in the car."

"Yes, ma'am." She climbed back in and closed the door. Grandpa Cavanaugh. Mister Spider. Ernie the frog. Ethan. Grandma Gertrude. Now the deer.

Was she a black widow?

Would she murder her parents next?

"Let the deer die, Yahweh." Daniela prayed, hoping springtime had arrived, unfreezing the permafrost blocking her prayers. "Don't be angry with Mom. It's not her fault; it's mine. We wouldn't be driving if I wasn't seeing things and talking to people no one else can see."

Her mother rested her hands on the deer's head, her lips moving.

The creature's nostrils flared. Its chest heaved as blood seeped from a gash sliced through its chestnut-colored fur chest.

Minutes later, its nostrils relaxed, chest deflated, and body remained flat. Vultures would swarm soon, followed by maggots.

Daniela's mother grasped the deer's front hooves and dragged the dead animal to the shoulder of the road.

Had her mother prayed for the deer to die quickly? Daniela's heart thumped against her ribs, and her mouth cried. The deer killer opened the car door, sat down, and dabbed her glistening brow with a frilly handkerchief.

"Mom," she whispered. "Do you want me to be crazy?"

"Why on earth—" She stared at Daniela.

"You prayed for it to die quickly."

"The windows were up. How did you hear?"

"I'm a good listener."

"Hearing keener than a dog." A beautiful smile erased the hurt from her mother's face. "It won't always be this way—the pain. The loneliness. The nosebleeds. People calling you every name in the book except child of God. I see the disappointment in those big brown eyes."

"Mom, we shouldn't be late for the doctor." Daniela held her bag tight to her chest, protecting the letter, the last evidence of her sanity. In the letter, the inquisitor called Daniela crazy, but she would survive and mother a beautiful child.

"You're right." Her mother glanced at her watch and started driving. "I'd been married to your daddy for a few years before the Almighty answered our prayers for a baby. Your father knew you would be a girl. I wasn't particular—give me a baby, anything will do—but He gave me a special baby girl, you." She fidgeted with her hair as she spoke, hiding her face, twisted with her own painful memories. "No one will take you away from me."

"Promise?"

"Pinky swear."

With three minutes to spare, Daniela and her mother registered at the front desk, then sat in the waiting room. Not a kind eye met their gaze. An hour later, the doctor confirmed his diagnoses: childhood-onset schizoaffective disorder with severe depression—previously on the verge of a break.

Now, not fully stabilized, but somewhat stable.

She would take it.

Daniela had made progress. Hand in hand, they left the office and stepped outside into a balmy Florida summer. The humidity seeped into Daniela's skin, defrosting her muscles and then her bones, but not her dreams.

"Mom, do you believe me about the arrowhead?"

For a while, her mom didn't answer. "If you could remember where you left the arrowhead, then the doctor would believe you."

Daniela looked into her mother's eyes.

Disbelief.

But somehow the emotional impact of people's opinions—including her mother's—about her sanity had faded. No one had to believe her reality for it to be truth. "I was in Gibeah. One day, your eyes will be opened too." Daniela screamed, "I'm done telling my story. Adelaide will tell it." She released her mother's hand and raced ahead to the banana boat.

"Who's Adelaide?"

Daniela ignored her mother's question.

She stretched out her arms, wishing she could fly with apricot sulfurs all around her. Questions flitted around in her head, but Peace and Hope had taken up residence in her heart.

In time, Peace and Hope would tell Daniela His name.

42—The Orphan

A YEAR HAD PASSED. WHEN the boys awoke, mischief twinkled in Paul's eyes. Cillian noticed his brother's playful demeanor.
"Dinna do anything stupid."

"We've not even eaten breakfast, and you're already spoiling
my day." Curious green eyes peeked from beneath Paul's shaggy
blond hair. Cillian stared at his brother's face. In time, the athletic
boy would break a few hearts, but Cillian would teach his younger
brother to break them quickly and gently.

Would Cillian break any hearts?

I dinna think so.

With vampirish white skin, he could pass for Dracula's brother,
albeit blessed with a muscular frame, a strong jaw, and electric-blue
eyes, accented with a killer smile. That's what the cooks had said,
but what girl would give him the time of day unless she wanted her
blood sucked?

"Since the cellar, Miss Grey has been scared of you, Cil. We could get away with anything." Paul laughed. "You did cast a spell on her. Can you perform magic? Are you a warlock, Cil?"

"Are you?" Cillian's neck hair bristled.

"I'm not mean, Cil, just playing."

"Playing? Last time I took your whipping. You'll not be so lucky next time." Cillian bumped Paul on the shoulder.

"Ouch." Paul nursed his shoulder.

"We're leaving England, going to America. Try surviving until then."

"We should've run away after you returned from the hospital." Paul headed to the showers.

"How would I be feedin' a hungry twelve-year-old? D'ye think of that? A thrashin' isna reason enough to watch my little brother starve."

Paul turned on the bath water, waiting for it to warm. It never did. He climbed into the tub, his teeth chattering.

Cillian lathered his hair and washrag, then cleaned himself. "Aye, Paul. Ye'll be stayin' out of trouble, then?"

"Do my best." Paul playfully snaked his wet towel around his brother's legs.

"Stop playin'. Get dressed."

★ ★ ★

After their baths, Paul exited the breakfast hall and sauntered into his classroom. No one was watching, or so he thought. He swiped Miss Bailey's bell—a gift from her late mother—and hid it underneath his desk.

Minutes later, Miss Bailey, their teacher—prison warden—waddled into the classroom and dropped her bag full of books onto the desk. She perched her hands on her hips and scanned her desk. "Who took my bell?" She sounded slightly nasal, like a turkey. Must have had a cold.

Children covered their mouths, stifling giggles. Paul reclined in his seat and enjoyed the scene.

"I suspect foul play, and I'm going to get to the bottom of it this very minute." She plowed her way between the student's desks, peering over her thick spectacles. "Where is it?" she demanded.

No one answered.

She stopped at Paul's desk. Her blue-gray eyes studied his face. "You enjoy playing games, don't you?"

He didn't answer. "You took it, didn't you?" Miss Bailey aimed an accusing finger toward him. Guilt masked his face, but he said nothing, even as Miss Bailey's hand made contact with his cheek. "Answer me, class clown!"

"I-I-I'm sorry, Miss. Bailey." He cowered. "I was joking."

Her eyes squinted into a devilish determination, and Paul's heart sank as his tongue dried into a cotton ball. Miss Bailey rubbed her enormous belly in satisfaction. "Give it to me."

Paul retrieved the bell.

"Go to lunch, everyone. I've got an appetite for something else." She squeezed Paul's shoulder with her pudgy hand. "You, stay here with me."

He slid back into his seat. *Cil was right.*

43—THE ORPHAN

CILLIAN SWIRLED HIS SOUP WITH his spoon but couldn't eat. "We'll be finishing up in a few minutes. Did Paul lose his way?" he asked Tim.

"He stole Miss Bailey's bell." Tim ate the last of his soup.

"Paul, why?" Cillian sighed. It was his birthday, and he didn't want to make a fuss about it. Paul didn't even know.

Moments later, wails rang out. Cillian turned on the creaky lunch bench. *Why, lad?*

Miss Grey pulled Paul into the lunchroom by his ear. Paul cried in pain. "I was joking!" His eyes pleaded with his brother's.

I cannae be doin' anything about it.

Miss Bailey marched in behind them. "Since you want to make a fool of me in front of your classmates, I'll return the favor," she said between labored breaths. Cillian's heart sank. He covered his eyes. Black spots danced beneath his lids.

He's not bad, but these women are determined to humiliate him. He stared, helpless, gulping hard and praying that Paul could withstand the punishment.

"Lie across the bench." Miss Grey prodded Paul toward the bench in the front of the dining hall. The children shifted uneasily in their seats. Silence cloaked the room as fifty pairs of eyes stared at Paul's bare buttocks.

He took hold of the metal bench, tensing in anticipation of the first blow. He'd never been beaten before—Cillian had seen to that. Could he dash to the front and take the punishment?

No, the gesture would infuriate Miss Grey.

She demanded order.

Miss Grey's face darkened to a tomato-red as she seethed. "Let this be a lesson for you all." Then, she commenced with beating the child.

Maybe she'll die—again.

One minute and eleven seconds later, she was fatigued.

Her lips lay in a flat line instead of a scowl, and her shoulders relaxed from their ear-high position. Satisfied that Paul's buttocks were covered with red welts, she stopped. "That'll quench your mischievous spirit." She faced the children. "Dismissed. Go to recess."

Cillian stayed back as the other boys filtered out. "I'll be makin' it up to you, Paul," Cillian whispered to himself as Paul lay over the bench while the children passed by. "I tried keepin' your skin perfect."

Big Jake squeezed Cillian's shoulder. "The paddling was bound to happen sometime. You deserve a medal for keeping him from the beatin' for so long."

"I've enough scars for us both."

"He'll learn from it, son. Time to go." Big Jake nudged Cillian toward the lunchroom door. Instead of going outside, Cillian hid behind the boys' restroom door. He pressed his ear against the cold metal, listening for any sound of Paul.

Soon, he heard shuffling feet and the fast clomp of high heels.

Cillian opened the bathroom door partway and stared into Paul's sad eyes—eyes that willed his big brother to rescue him. Lost in casual conversation, Miss Grey and Miss Bailey guided Paul down a long hallway. Paul limped until he disappeared into the boys' dormitory.

Orphans were forbidden to enter the dormitory except for at sleep time, so Cillian could not console his brother.

The old woman with waterlogged legs trudged behind her younger counterpart, Miss Bailey, until Miss Grey's pace crawled to a stop. Turning, Grey Thunder locked eyes with Cillian. He looked away, watching her from the corner of his eyes.

Her veined hands clamped across her chest.

Eyes rolling back, she collapsed.

Miss Bailey screamed.

Big Jake knelt and felt the crook of the old woman's neck. "She's a goner."

Cillian's racing heart shot up into his throat, almost choking him to death. Had he murdered his tormentor? He trudged through the exit and shuffled down a hill.

Left to listen to his own demons, questions peppered his mind. *Am I possessed with devils? Did I throw curses? Am I Miss Grey's sea monster—Leviathan?* He collapsed, surrendering to the cold, cracked concrete. He wrapped his arms around his chest and rocked back and forth.

Devils dinnae deserve love.

The whistle sounded, and the boys lined up.

Cillian ran, tripping over an untied shoelace. He dusted the grit from his hands as he snaked his way between boys, making his way to the front of the line. Head down, he marched behind Tim.

As soon as the bell rang, Cillian bolted into the sleeping quarters and ran to Paul's bunk.

Was he dead too?

Sniffles escaped from under the wool blanket. Cillian gently uncovered Paul's boyish frame and swallowed hard. Blood splotches stained Paul's thin, white sheet. Cillian clenched his fists; his face darkened. "They'll not thrash ye like this again."

"Promise?"

"We're leaving."

"You said we shouldn't starve because of a thrashing."

"The rule didna apply to you."

"Where to, Captain Finnegan Prometheus?"

"I dinnae ken, but Grey Thunder's dead."

"Really. Did you kill her?"

"I dinnaa ken. Maybe there's something evil inside of me."

"You're not evil. You're the best—my hero."

"Or your curse." Cillian forced a smile, then tended to Paul's wounds, pressing a warm washcloth to Paul's bruised flesh.

"Ouch, Cil. You're hurting me."

"I'm being verra gentle. The blood's dried, and I dinna want ye to get an infection."

"Superman doesn't get infections." Paul turned his head away from his brother, but Cillian could hear the sniffles.

"Aye, ye didna look like Superman with yer arse exposed. Be still. My treatments will keep ye from scarring."

"I would've flown away, but I forgot my cape."

"Shh. We're already being watched because of the old woman's death." He cleaned the last open wound. "You do contrive some hare-brained ideas, but ye didna deserve such a severe beatin'."

"Have I disappointed you?"

"A wee bit. But I have enough scars for both of us. You dinna need any." Cillian handed Paul soft, clean pants and a shirt, then covered him with the bedsheet. "Dress, then keep the sheet over yer head."

Cillian hoped the orderlies who normally checked the rooms before lights-out would not pay any attention to Paul. If they did, they would be curious to know why he was dressed in street clothes. Cillian tucked his own warm street clothes under his covers. He would dress once the lights were off.

Time passed slower than usual.

He tossed and turned, fighting his sheets for the next three hours until he spun himself into a cocoon. Sleep evaded him. The bright red numbers on the wall clock finally rolled from 12:59 to 1:00 a.m.

Cillian shot up in bed, bile creeping up his chest and settling in his throat. He swallowed his fear, dressed, and climbed down from the upper bunk. "Paul, are ye awake?"

"I don't want another beating." Paul blinked, his eyes wide with fear.

"Trust me. Ye'll not be sufferin' another. Climb down." Cillian placed a small knapsack around Paul's shoulders. An apple and a rotten banana lay in the bottom of the bag, saved from lunch a while ago. "I willna let anyone hurt you."

The boys crept out of the dorm room in their socks, their shoes in hand. The only way out of the care home at this late hour was to go through the basement and exit into the alley by the trash receptacles.

The boys crept down the basement stairs. Dim light bulbs hummed and swung on gold chains from the ceiling.

Stale, damp air filled their lungs.

Cillian stopped and placed his finger to his lips. "Shh, I think I heard something." Paul hunched low. They crept ahead.

Scratch, scratch. The boys heard the sound again and froze.

"We'll be safe if we're quiet." Desperate to identify the source of the sound, Cillian scanned the long, dark hallway. A shadow shifted in the dimly lit room. Paul's fingers dug into Cillian's flank.

Cillian winced. They waited a few minutes and stood in the shadow of an old filing cabinet. Cillian buried his hand into his pocket and fondled the coin Grandpa Barry had given him. A red-neon exit sign glowed thirty feet away.

Freedom.

"Shh, the sound's closer." Cillian knelt, pulling his little brother underneath him. Back tense and rigid as a board, he prepared himself for punishment.

Scrape, thud, scrape, thud . . .

Cillian's eyes darted back and forth but didn't see any other intruders inside the dimly lit orphanage basement. He flipped the silver dollar nestled inside his pocket—heads to tails and back again—while he shielded Paul with his right arm.

His breath fragmented, his tongue parched.

More scratches—louder and louder.

Paul clung to his brother.

Dust invaded Cillian's nostrils. He pulled his hand from his pocket and pressed his nose and lips flat. A muted sneeze escaped between his fingers. Was the eerie sound of chalk scratching against a blackboard inside his head? He slapped his hands to his ears, but the sound grew louder.

Hairy and wet, it tickled.

Then, claws dug into the back of his right calf.

Cillian turned, ready to fight.

44—ORPHAN DREAMER

IN HONOR OF ETHAN'S MEMORY, Daniela had decided to go on an adventure to celebrate her fourteenth birthday. She ran into a nearby field, wet air clinging to her skin. Ducking to miss a low-hanging tree branch, she realized that the Glass Tattoo and oily boy had been the furthest things from her mind for the last several months.

Blades of grass tickled her legs.

A bouquet of earthy scents—lilacs, soil, and a skunk's sour spray—floated into her nose. Eyes to the sky, she inhaled deeply.

Then, spreading her arms wide, she ran faster. Stagnant air roused, blowing hot breath into her face. Birds cawed. Leaves rustled. Mosquitoes whined.

A doe galloped into view. Daniela stopped and held her breath. *Ravishing.*

At her feet, grass swished and leaves crunched. "Be careful of water moccasins!" had been her mother's final warning before

Daniela left the house with a backpack slung over her shoulders. It contained a book about butterflies, a magnifying glass, and her journal.

She scanned the ground.

Nothing.

Today she was searching for yellow butterflies with black stripes called tiger swallowtails. They were strong fliers with large wingspans, and on this early Tuesday morning, she launched a mission to find one at its beginning. Since receiving the Glass Tattoo as her birthday present, her dad seemed to speak to her in riddles versus plain old English. She had informed him a week ago that she had stopped praying for oily boy.

She needed a break.

As far as she could tell, nothing had happened. Her prayers hadn't made a difference.

The Glass Tattoo had seemingly sensed her hesitation and rejection of her calling, ejecting itself from her palm and returning to its snowflake diamond form. She had hidden the powerful relic inside its patinated box and stuffed the box beneath her underwear, where Prince Jonathan's arrowhead was supposed to be.

Secretly, she'd avoided pondering her dad's question about beginnings and endings. "If you knew your ending, how would you live your beginning?"

Too busy trying to navigate her present: nosebleeds, homework, and everything else that high school could offer a student who had enrolled a year early and was completing college credits at the same time.

When did she have time to think about the ghost locked inside her dreams?

45—THE ORPHAN

A RAT THE SIZE OF a small cat ran across Cillian's calf. The noise ceased once the rat found a hole in the wall. The orphan released a sigh.

"We're safe?" Paul said.

"No, lad; we're free."

Paul slid from underneath his brother. "Freedom feels . . . like nerves and static all bottled up?"

"It's called potential—energy in its rawest form." Cillian had completed trash duty multiple times, so he was familiar with this exit route, but he had never ventured past the alley.

"When we open the door, will an alarm sound?"

"Believe yer free. No time for questions." Cillian grasped the metal handle. Paul clamped his eyelids shut.

"I believe. I believe. I believe." The handle clicked. Paul opened his eyes and stopped breathing.

Cillian pushed. The door creaked on its hinges. No alarms rang, and no guards waited for them. "Breathe."

Paul sucked in a long breath. "I almost fainted."

"Dinna do it. Yer heavy." They stuffed their feet into their shoes, then escaped the grimy- gray orphanage.

"I wouldn't have believed that freedom smelled like the toilet after Rusty ate greens."

"She doesn't." Remembering Bibury, Cillian noted an unlidded garbage can—the source of the stench. "Would ye like to be our guide for this part of the wilderness journey?" *Distract Paul. That's why big brothers did.*

"You're my wingman." Paul grabbed Cillian's hand, and they ran down the alley and across the field.

Forty-five minutes later, out of breath, the boys stood at the edge of town. Cillian released Paul's hand and looked back. Behind them, lights flickered in fog so thick that the little town appeared to be covered by a woolen blanket. "I dinna remember the fog being so dense when we ran through it."

"It wasn't."

"Interesting." Cillian faced their future, the blackness as heavy as an ill-equipped brother's responsibility to his younger brother.

Paul inched closer to Cillian. "I'm scared."

"Me too, but fear's no crime." Miss Grey's death had awakened something protective—feral, raw. "No harm will be comin' to ye, then. I'd kill for ye, lad."

"I don't want you to."

"Then stay out of trouble."

"What about not giving up your innocence so fast?"

"It's gone." He tasted blood—smooth, rich, and sweet, like the stolen chocolate cake. Spine straight, the corner of his mouth upturned into a smirk, Cillian strolled into the night.

They walked for the rest of the day, looking for a safe town in which to settle.

Something otherworldly—a tingling sensation like static electricity—refused to let them go and seemed to guide them to a cluster of white houses on the horizon. The boys crept to the outskirts of the town. Red blossoms spotted the grassy knoll. Dogs barked. People chattered. What they had thought were houses were actually tents "Look normal." Cillian crept past the town's entrance—the only opening in a fence.

"We're orphans."

Cillian sighed. "Fake it."

"What if someone notices?"

"I cannae be thinkin' of our plans and solvin' our problems if yer asking me a string of questions."

"Sorry." Paul kicked a rock down the road. "What if they ask us where we're from?"

"We'll say our mother died of a fever, and we're looking fer work, a place to live, and food. Isna that what normal people want—food, clothes, and a home?"

"We don't look like brothers. Your hair's black, and mine's blond."

"I once knew a lad whose brother's hair had been bleached by the sun while his remained black."

"Did you read about that in one of your books?" Paul's lips hinted at a smile.

"Probably." Cillian squeezed his brother's hand.

"I don't want to make you nervous, but your hands are sweaty, and you're acting weird again, Cil." A lady dressed in a cotton shift walked toward them, pail in hand and a baby on her hip.

"Okay, um, new names." Cillian pulled Paul behind one of the main tents. "We're gonna need new names."

"I wanna be Arthur, like King Arthur!"

"Yer a Dane, dummy, not English."

"I'm not the one that sounds like a B-list American actor trying to sound English." Cillian administered his own punishment, squeezing Paul's hand so hard that his own ached.

"Ouch, Cil!" Paul tugged but couldn't free his hand. "Thought you were rescuing me, not chopping off my hands."

"Quiet. We dinna ha' to change our first names." Cillian allowed his native Scottish burr to dominate his speech.

"Okay, okay, got it."

"Ye'll be Paul Barry, and I'll be Cillian Barry, and we'll be brothers. Can ye remember that?"

"Can ye be rememberin' to speak like an Englishman, so we sound like brothers?" Paul mocked Cillian's burr.

"Yer impossible, and that's what I'll be knowin' for sure." Cillian tousled Paul's golden locks.

Of all the tents, one seemed to draw him in. He couldn't explain the feeling, but he knew that the tattered tent would be their home for a while. Inside the plain white tent sat two cots, a rusted metal table, and two cooking pots. After traveling all night, they lay on the cots, but Cillian couldn't sleep.

A man with rotten teeth and a smell to match charged into their tent.

Cillian jumped up.

"Calm down there, laddie. I'm Michael," the man said with a slight upward swing in the intonation of a Northern Irish accent. "Are you new to these parts? I haven't seen you around the village before."

"Aye, we're new."

"You're an Irish Traveller, like the rest of us?"

"I'm part Irish, and I travel, so I guess."

"I'd be beggin' you then, what's the other part of ya?"

"Scottish."

"Weel then, *madainn mhath.*"

"Guid morning to you as well," Cillian spoke, acknowledging his understanding of Gaelic but remembering Paul could not speak it.

"The old scab left her tent and said a new neighbor would be here in the morning. Didn't think it would be two snappers."

"The old scab?"

"Calls herself a fortune-teller."

"A witch?" Something cold seized Cillian. He shuddered.

"She'll be knowin' the future. Ah, don't be afraid, they never get it all right." He raised his hands and rapped his fingertips together. "Let's say a witch's source is—unreliable." The unkempt man looked around. "Looks decent in here. Cleaned it up yesterday morning after she demanded it." The man stretched, seeming to make himself comfortable. "Need anything?"

Cillian gazed at the man warily. "No, thanks."

"We help each other out here, no fuss about it." Michael nodded slowly. "What's your name, then?"

"Cillian."

"That's a good Irish name. No need to be ashamed of your heritage. The English don't like us Travellers."

Was it true? Could an Irish-Scot orphan boy be comfortable inside his own skin? Cillian grinned a child's grin—naive, vulnerable, and hopeful.

"Ah—and there's a smile to be dying for. The young lassies will be chasing you from here to the great shores of America. You're a handsome lad."

"Have ye been—to America, that is?"

"Never. I despise boats. Floatin' coffins is what I call them."

"Didna the Irish build the *Titanic*?" Cillian asked.

"Don't get smart with me, lad."

"What about planes? The English didn't build all of those."

"If the Mighty One would've wanted you to fly, he'd attached wings to yer rump. Turn around."

Cillian obeyed.

"Nope. No wings."

"Do ye ken—I mean know—of any work close by?" Cillian asked.

"There's a farm about two miles west and a construction site about three miles north. The construction pays better, but I'm guessin' you'll want a posh job if you're goin' to America."

"Which pays the most?"

"The posh job, of course." The man delayed for effect. "I heard of a chap named Bushcroft. He's taken some of our young fellows to a better life."

"A better life?"

"Yes. The scab sings his praises."

"Where does he live?"

"Don't know, but his office sits five miles east."

Cillian found a piece of paper. "Can ye give me directions?"

"Certainly." The man scribbled a map, then handed the paper to Cillian, sealing the orphan's fate. "Be careful. What's too good to be true, probably is."

"D'ye hear from Bushcroft's lads?"

"A letter or so. Then they stopped."

"Why?"

"Some say the boys are too busy kickin' up their heels."

"And what do the other people say?"

"Nothing."

Ignorance wasna always bliss. The man shared a pot of beans with Cillian, then followed him to the door of the tent. They watched Paul sleep—peaceful, not a care in the world. "I'll be needin' a better life for my wee brother."

"He don't look so little to me."

"Aye. He's still little on the inside."

"You mean innocent?"

"Aye."

"And you?"

Cillian shrugged. "No."

"You may be more innocent than you think." The man turned to leave. "Good luck."

"I'll be needin' it. Track record's a wee bit rocky."

While Paul slept, Cillian ran his fingers along the apple and banana tucked inside his bag, saving the fruit for a time when hunger showed little mercy to a hungry stomach. Cillian had known many such days.

★ ★ ★

For the next several months, the boys lived in the tent village.

Cillian walked Paul to the library each morning, and a corner room served as Paul's

schoolhouse during the day. At night, beneath candlelight inside the tent, Cillian studied chemistry, biology, and calculus. Education equaled better jobs, and better jobs provided more food.

Nothing in life was free, so during the day, Cillian labored in the fields of the nearby farm, his hands calloused from the grunt work. But he scraped together enough money to feed himself and Paul.

After a drought, the farm work dried up.

Cillian mixed the last of their food—corn and potato stew—over an open fire, then scooped the gruel onto a tin plate, walked inside the tent, and handed the plate to Paul. "Eat."

"What about you?"

"I already ate. Ye'll be cleanin' yer plate." Cillian turned away from the makeshift dinner table and sat on a tree stump outside. *If ye dinna look at the food while he eats, the hunger pains die faster.* His belly hadn't been filled with a hot meal in more than thirty-six hours. Glancing over his shoulder, he stole a peek at the plate of food and his mouth watered.

Failures cannae feed their families.

"I dinna deserve his love," Cillian said to the voice that hadn't spoken since he'd left the Barrys' home. "Why d'ye not talk with me anymore? Are ye cross with me, then?" Hunger gnawed at his willpower. He clenched his hands into fists to keep himself from snatching the stew. "I'm no murderer. I dinna kill Grey Thunder. I wanted to, but I didna do it."

A better life and meals for two.

He pulled the map from his pocket.

46—Orphan Dreamer

THE FLASH OF A YELLOW-WINGED butterfly launching from a tree branch caught Daniela's eye. She gasped, not expecting to find a specimen so quickly.

Clutching the sides of her homemade paisley dress, she strolled toward the brown pupa. It clung to a blade of grass. Her discovery rested much lower than a tree branch. Treasures are often found in low places.

Squatting, she studied her finding.

"Professor Rollings said you started as an egg, then transformed into a hungry green caterpillar, but now you're resting—not eating or drinking at all, and that's why you're drier than the Sahara Desert. I'm going to the Sahara when I turn seventeen. Haven't told my parents. When you hatch, I'll take you sometime. I'll wait. I'm patient." She rested her elbows on her knees.

"Knock, knock." She touched the pupa. "Can you hear me?"

The cocoon didn't answer. Daniela spread her blanket and sat in the grass. Hidden from prying eyes, for the first time she relished being invisible.

She chewed a blade of grass and thought to pray for the first time in over six months.

"I don't think I'm an impatient person, but if You could come through on Your promise about the friend. I mean . . . I can exist alone, but I don't like it. And pledging a sorority when I attend college isn't an option. Mom hates the idea of sororities. As for oily boy, I prayed for him—nothing happened."

She reached up toward the pupa and stroked it with her finger. "Brown isn't such a bad color. You'll be beautiful one day." She held her mahogany arm near the butterfly's cocoon. "We both will."

With no fanfare, the shell split down the middle, creating an escape route for the green bug that had transformed into something beautiful.

Daniela thought of the possibilities that would come with being born as a creature with wings. When Claire launched her insults or the small capillaries in her nose betrayed her heart and leaked blood, she could fly away.

Wet yellow-and-black wings struggled to push through the small slit.

"Don't help. Everyone must go through their own struggle. It makes them strong," her mother had warned after Daniela shared her plans to go exploring at last night's dinner table. She squeezed her hands, not wanting to disobey and cripple her winged friend for life, but a tear formed in her eyes as she watched its struggle.

Why was struggle necessary?

Nomed pushes himself into the unseen world, where he unsheathes his raven-tinged-with-iridescent- green wings and takes flight. "Die, Daniela!" Nomed screeches.

"Your understudy, Depression, failing?" Legna draws his winter-white wings to his side, propelling himself out of Nomed's reach.

"The Orphan Dreamer's hope is frail—like a butterfly's new wings—but swallowtails grow stronger during their struggle. Know this, Nomed: hope is hard to kill."

"Touching."

"Go back to the nursery, play with the fallen ones."

"I'd prefer to follow you around like a lovesick girl. You follow the Orphan Dreamer. I follow you."

"Trouble is, I'm already in love."

"With the girl? Angels aren't supposed to . . . procreate with humans. Nephilim's—remember Elohim's temper tantrum?"

"Don't worry about my future. You're the one destined to lose."

"Details?"

"One day, as general of Elohim's army, I'll send a junior warrior to Earth armed with a set of dainty chains and a little-bitty key. He'll kick your butt into your hellhole with your master and lock you away for a while."

"Who decrees this—you?" Nomed sneers.

"Elohim."

"When, and by what prophet?"

"The year 95 AD by John—Yeshua's beloved apostle."

"Where?"

"The Isles of Patmos, after Rome's Emperor—Domitian, your evil leader—exiled John. As he toiled in Rome's rock quarries, Elohim encouraged him, showing John a vision. John penned the contents of his vision in the Book of the Revelation—"

"I know what he wrote. I've read the entire Bible."

"But your version is twisted."

"Been misquoting scriptures to humans since Eve's deception in the Garden of Eden. I don't care what your criminal prophet wrote. I choose not to believe the prophecy."

"Choosing a lie. I'd expect nothing more."

"Chew on this. Earth will be our home. Lucifer promised."

Legna releases a belly laugh. "When has the old dragon accurately predicted the future? Never."

"You forget our viewing room."

"Lies cloaked in sorcery. Maybe you're targeting the wrong humans for elimination, missing the ones who will annihilate your feeble plans. Earth will never be yours again. Marinate on that."

"It will be."

"Delusional."

"It will . . . if I murder them all." Nomed sneers. "A global pandemic should do. We're already preparing—training. But I'll share your newest insults with my master."

"Tattle. Doesn't change reality."

"Oh, but it does." Nomed stops mid-retreat and clanks his long fingers together. "She longs for a friend . . . but refuses to pray for oily boy."

Legna narrows his gaze.

"All ears, are we?" Nomed flutters his wings, showing off the metal barbs attached to their edges. "We'll use her future kindred spirit to destroy her. By the time she values him and longs for his touch . . . he won't be worth spit. If he survives. Earth belongs to us."

"The Earth belongs to I AM, my master. He decides who manages His real estate. The Orphan Dreamer deserves a kindred spirit entrusted with impeccable character."

"He'll be dead or a drooling invalid when she comes for him." Nomed laughs—evil, guttural. "Count on it."

"I didn't say Yahweh destined oily boy to be her kindred spirit."

"Bibury, England? Ten thousand angels protecting a quaint village while the orphan recovers from his wounds? Common sense dictates an *orphan dreamer* requires an orphan to dream about."

"Sense is not that common. Torment the orphan for a season, but one day, he'll grow up into a man. He'll come looking for you."

"Not if I eliminate him first," Nomed says.

"Give it your best shot. You've already failed once, killing the care-home matron as she tried to do your bidding."

"I have an idea, Legna. The multibillionaire Asher Valerian Bushcroft. He owes me a favor. I was—I am—his houseguest. He'd kill to get his sister back."

Legna tucks his wings tight to his side and free falls toward North America. "Danny-girl, don't eat. Don't drink. So you can hear with clarity. Listen to Wisdom. Pray for oily boy. She will direct your prayers, so my army can fight and protect oily boy."

* * *

Eager to become an ordinary girl, Daniela applied for college and continued looking for butterflies in her free time.

The most beautiful thing we can experience is the mysterious. It is the source of all true art and science. He to whom this emotion is a stranger, who can no longer pause to wonder and stand rapt in awe, is as good as dead: his eyes are closed. This insight into the mystery of life, coupled though it be with fear, has also given rise to religion.

—Albert Einstein

47—I Am Wisdom

"YAHWEH CALLS ME WISDOM." SHE whispers—soft and unassuming, yet authoritative. "Come to the beginning with me, Daniela." Wisdom strolls through cold darkness, traveling through centuries passed.

"When there wasn't a sea or springs abounding with water, Yahweh created me. After I was formed, Earth's beginning started: 'In the beginning, God created the heaven and the earth. And the earth was without form, and void; and darkness was upon the face of the deep.'"

Amid the endless space of a cold, dark universe, a luminous sphere rotates in the distance—Earth.

Darkness hovers over the face of the deepest ocean.

Before humans are created, I see an angel blowing his trumpet and lightning falling from heaven, the third heaven. Lucifer plummets, clutching the key to Hades and Death—his weapon—close to his chest. During his descent, he sheds his radiant jeweled mask and crashes into a mound of rubble.

He stands.

Dark shadows clothe him as he stalks the quagmire of sulfuric gas, energized by rogue energy—Earth before Yahweh shapes it into beauty. Before Yahweh begins to shape Earth, He casts Lucifer into the second heaven.

Like a nomad, Lucifer roams the second heaven—a cold, dark, vast space.

Time lapses into pages of unchartered history, then "the spirit of God moves upon the face of the waters," and Yahweh says, "Let there be light."

Crackles of light charge from His being, for He is the Light of the World. Hydrogen vapor organizes into a bright fiery orb, pushing back centuries-old curtains of darkness, lighting up the kingdom . . . and then quietly, and with great care, invisible hands gather clumps of dust, forming flesh.

Slowly, the Creator breathes into the being's nostrils, and the creature stands erect on two legs. Man becomes a living soul.

Lucifer focuses on a warm light.

He slinks toward the source. *Why are they here? They are intruders. Intruders must die.*

Nomed, chief of his legions, and hordes of the fallen march through the darkness behind their master, mistakenly believing that their fates rest upon his actions.

An arm's length from the tangerine glow, Nomed hunches beside Lucifer and peers through a wall of impenetrable clear gelatin that separates Earth's skies from the second heaven—Lucifer's new reigning realm, making him the prince of the air. He studies the mysterious creatures who have moved into his previous home—Earth—and learns their names. Man. Woman. On the other side of the barrier, birds chirp and scaled creatures splash on the surface of a translucent sea. A newborn lamb rests upon the haunches of a full-grown male lion.

"Peace. Perfection." Nomed taps his daggered fingers on the wall. "The same presence is in Elohim's celestial home. I miss home."

"Waste no time looking to the past." Lucifer studies the mysterious place. "Earth is our new home—it will become our new heaven."

"Then why are *they* there?" Nomed points at the two-legged creatures. Lush trees shade two iridescent forms strolling between supple canopies of twisted branches draped with emerald leaves. A monkey clings to the taller and more muscular one's back.

"His latest pet project—formed in His image, Legna tells me." Lucifer snarls.

"Curious creatures." Nomed furrows his brow at the two odd forms. "What are they called?"

"Man. Woman." Lucifer pushes his finger into the gelatin, but it shocks him, throwing him back into the darkness. Fists clenched, he charges back to the front of his army.

"Elohim has forgotten us?" Nomed chews his nails. Green ooze drips from the tips of his fingers.

"Worse. We've been replaced. Next question: how do we exterminate the intruders?" Raging winds like those found in Jupiter's storms thrash the army.

"But—"

"Are you a leader or sniveler?"

"Th-th-the earth is the Lord's," Nomed challenges his master.

"Irrelevant detail." Lucifer shades his face from the wind's cat-o'-nine-tails and raises his sword. "It's time to fight," he shouts. "Destroy the intruders—Elohim's humans!"

"Teach us how," voices crescendo into squawks as the fallen work into a chanting frenzy, "and we will fight. Make our planet great again—eliminate man, eliminate woman!"

"Nomed," Lucifer says, "for questioning my judgment, you're demoted."

"But I didn't—"

"Be quiet." Lucifer plunges his finger into Nomed's chest. The injured angel dares not cry out, so he chews his lips, almost biting them off.

"Belial." Lucifer motions to the minion to his left, whose head crawls with hordes of flies.

"My lord?" The leader of the flies bows low. Flies tumble to the ground, then buzz and dart until they return to their resting place— Belial's head.

"Are you ready to lead the legions?"

"Yes, my lord."

"Advise me."

"Divide and conquer. It worked with us."

"I've not forgotten the last thousand years of misery," Lucifer sneers. "Finish."

"If the humans unify, my lord," Belial cowers, squirming in his own skin and his voice squeaking, "and we fail in our quest for Earth, may I suggest a Plan B?"

"We don't have another millennium to lose. Speak."

"Prepare Venus, the morning star, and prepare Wormwood." His right eyelid twitches, belying his confidence in his Plan B. "Venus will be ours, away from this pathetic creation, and Wormwood will be our Trojan horse for invading Earth."

Eager to score a few points to reclaim his position as leader of the legions, Nomed interjects. "Then we train, return, and eliminate man and woman."

"Exactly." Belial plucks a brown-winged bug the size of a scorpion from his beard of dangling, rotting flesh.

"You're a genius, Belial." Lucifer crosses his arms. "Two-thirds of my legions will remain on Earth to brainwash the humans. The legions will teach the humans to despise each other until humans willingly slaughter their neighbors."

"Effectively reducing their human army," Belial says.

"Less to fight in the final war—my Armageddon, the pandemic." Lucifer sneers at the protected humans.

"Genius, my lord."

"Belial," Lucifer says, "take the less experienced one-third of my legions to Venus. Train and strengthen them. The humans will never reach that planet to interfere with your training."

"As you wish, my lord."

"When will Belial return to Earth?" Nomed asks.

"After Elohim's promised time of peace but before we unleash hell on Earth."

"What a plan!" Nomed says.

"It's not mine. Didn't Elohim say 'Peace and safety, then sudden destruction comes'? Belial, from Venus, take the legions to Wormwood—our invisible planet."

"Our Trojan horse. They won't see Wormwood coming," Nomed says.

"Is there an echo? Stop repeating me." Lucifer's shoulder brushes the barrier. White-hot energy rips through his body and catapults him up into stagnant air. He lands with a thud.

"Master." Nomed reaches out to help.

"Leave me." The dark underlord slaps his minion's hand away, and Nomed stumbles around, as though he fell into a vat of fermented grapes and swallowed them all. Lucifer grins. "Before lightning invaded my body, I saw an additional solution. Walking upright, they are vain—naked, unashamed. Pride is the key into their souls."

"Your radiant beauty," Belial says. "They will feel small in your presence, not proud."

Lucifer flashes a jealous look at the mortal's perfect world.

"My lord, how will you get in?"

"I will transform myself into something smaller, spineless, and twisted."

"Your grace." The fly master bows. "Your plans are excellent and sure. Am I to lead the legions when we return from Wormwood?"

"You accepted defeat before the battle began."

"I was thinking of our safety and success."

"You're not ready to lead." A slight grin rotates the corners of Lucifer's lips upward. "Stay with Nomed, your groveling foolish friend, until you go to Venus. Learn from each other what *not* to do."

"Maybe the humans will refuse to believe we exist—or even Elohim's existence." Belial rubs his hands together.

"The fool says in his heart there is no God," Nomed defends his intellect. "I believe Elohim exists. I'm not that stupid."

"Talking back?" The dark underlord knows Nomed is ready to lead another mission but waits, making Nomed beg for power.

"If I could be a minnow, minnow, minnow," Nomed sings with a forlorn, soft tenor voice—something he did whenever regret for following Lucifer overwhelmed him. "If I could be a minnow, I'd swim out to the deep-blue sea."

"Singing your song again?" Lucifer asks in a gruff voice. "Being a fallen angel," the dark lord says, stroking Nomed's back, "isn't so bad."

"But it is."

"We possess the freedom to do as we please."

"I'd prefer to be a minnow because Elohim's not mad at them." Nomed smiles weakly.

"We are warriors." Lucifer slices Nomed's back, cutting scaled skin wide open with his razor-sharp fingertips. "Act like it. Don't show your weakness to Legna. He'll slice you to pieces."

Arching his back, Nomed cries out.

"You should have followed Legna. He still grovels at Elohim's feet, tucked away in celestial safety, refusing to use his full potential."

"Please, give me a mission," Nomed begs. "I'm not a bad demon."

"Somewhat of an oxymoron—a good demon." Lucifer smirks. "Today, I will seal man and woman's fate. They will fall out of favor with Elohim like we did. Then, they will become His enemies. Fight Him. And lose. Armageddon."

"Humans. Egomaniacs they will become," Nomed says, "and they will assume their weak ancestors inhabited Earth first. I guarantee you. But they will never belong—not ever—and they must leave."

"Belial."

"Yes, your grace."

"I have a third plan. Activate it. Possess the humans who reject Elohim. There will be a few at least. These rebellious humans will be our agents—our spies on Earth. Nomed, you will become Asher Valerian Bushcroft's houseguest. Follow me to the viewing room."

"Marvelous. What should we call these rebellious humans?"

Lucifer stops. "Call them the Sons of Venus—they're sons of the morning star—and I shall shine throughout eternity."

"How can we recruit more agents?"

"Give them money, sex, pleasure—whatever glitters. Call them God's blessings so the humans stay in the dark as to who we are."

"Yes!" Belial dances a jig.

"Can't wait to watch the humans suffer," Nomed's voice upticks, then lowers. "As for Aglaope—my dying wife—"

"Silence!"

Nomed bows, and Lucifer's minions follow him to Hades—the underworld, the abyss, a dimension off-limits to those who still draw breath. During his retreat, Lucifer hears a voice and stops.

"In the beginning was the Word," the powerful voice declares.

"Wisdom, is that you?"

"You know who speaks. I AM that I AM—the Word, Yahweh."

"Elohim? Is it not enough that you steal my home and give it to your pets on two legs?"

"Jealous. How you have fallen from heaven, O Lucifer—son of the dawn." The heavens rumble with laughter. "You are cut down even as you say, 'I will ascend to heavens and rule the angels. I will claim the highest throne and be like the Most High.'"

"You won't win." Lucifer trembles.

"Big threats from something I created." The voice pauses. "You will be brought down to the pit of hell, and everyone in the abyss will ask, 'Could this be the one who shook the earth and the kingdoms of the world? Could this be the one who destroyed the world and made it into a shamble, demolished its greatest cities and possessed no mercy toward its prisoners?'"

"Your humans invaded my home."

"Lucifer—son of the dawn, prince of the air, the one formed with my own hands—I will not forget your betrayal and your misleading part of my angelic warriors into your doomed deception. You may spread your deception among my newest creation—humans—for a season. I have set your appointed time . . . your kairos time, the day when I will annihilate you. Your end."

"Pray tell, when?"

"No one knows the date except for Me, not even my Son or the angels."

"That's convenient."

"There is one predestined to seek my truth—my reality. She will solve the mystery of time: after blood stains the moon, the clock ticks to your end."

"Not so fast." Lucifer dares a glance at the heavens—Yahweh's home. "I get it. You're bored, so You created weak stick figures and called them humans. Desperate for companionship, You told them how badly You want a relationship with them."

"Odd perspective, but then you've never gotten anything right after your rebellion."

Lucifer squeals as he dodges a geyser of hot gas erupting through cracked soil. "You may hurt me, but the humans will hurt you. I'll make sure of it. I will twist your plan for a relationship into religion; they will become their own gods in ritual and self-righteousness." He hisses the words. "Religion—with or without a deity—will destroy them."

"Relationship, not religion."

"What's the difference?"

"Oppression versus freedom. The humans who choose to enter into a relationship with Me by Yeshua, they are my chosen ones, the children of God. I don't force myself on anyone, but the path to me is narrow—albeit simple: 'Follow Me.'"

"Humans will yearn for independence. I can see the lust in their eyes. They will choose religion. Tweak it. Rename it. They will use your idea for their own purposes and finally for my ultimate purpose—to thin the herd before Armageddon, humanity's end—my victory."

"Humans must choose who they will follow: you or Me."

"Choice? One-third of Your angels chose to come with me."
Lucifer straightens his back and looks up.

"Love does not exist without free will."

"Love? What do humans know about that?"

"I'll teach them." Yahweh spreads His arms wide.

"I'll teach them my version—lust, greed, gluttony. We'll see
which version is more palatable to your humans—sacrificial compassion or self-indulgence and pleasure."

"I will remember you. Dismissed."

The fallen prince shudders, hating the idea of being remembered.
He bolts into the changing room inside the abyss and transforms
into something small, spineless, and twisted, then slithers beneath
the gelatinous wall.

Time to make a choice, humans.

Me or Elohim?

Wisdom raises her voice and cries, into the freezing bowels of
space, "Then I saw an angel come down from heaven with the key
to the bottomless pit and a heavy chain in his hand. He seized the
dragon—that old serpent, the devil, Satan—and bound him in chains
for a thousand years. The angel threw him into the bottomless pit,
which he then shut and locked so that Satan could not fool the
nations anymore until the thousand years were finished. Afterward
he would be released again for a little while . . ."

Time ticks forward.

Nomed transforms into the houseguest, then revisits the
Orphan's tormentor.

It remains a foolish exercise for humans to murder other humans, unaware of the real enemy who lurks in the shadows of the vast universe, awaiting judgment day while manipulating humans to execute his evil bidding. Who will be left to fight on the day of reckoning?

—J. Nell ʀ

48—THE ORPHAN

MONDAY, AUGUST 21, 1995
PARADISE, ENGLAND

SUNRAYS PEEKED PAST EVERGREENS, SPLASHING light against the east side of the boys' tent.

Crisp, clean scents of pine sap drenched the cool air.

Birds chirped.

An old woman from a nearby tent hummed an Irish tune. The scent of fried bacon wafted from her home.

Cillian sketched out a plan for a better life, intending to find the golden path that would lead him there. He walked to a manmade watering hole where he filled his bucket with water before returning home.

He started a fire in their fireplace—a metal trash can—then stepped outside to douse his body with water from the bucket. Cold water stabbed his skin like a million needles, waking him. Professional men needed to smell fresh. Once clean, he reentered the tent and huddled near his morning fire, dried his skin with a threadbare towel, then brushed his teeth.

"Paul, wake up. Time for school."

Cillian stirred the remnants of yesterday's stew in a pan over the open fire as Paul rolled out of bed and stumbled to the makeshift table inside. "I hate being cold."

"Stand by the fire."

After breakfast, Paul bathed, dressed, and walked behind his brother to the library—a small, redbrick building that smelled of dusty old books and stale air. The space was quiet.

"Pick you up at five o'clock," Cillian said.

"No earlier?"

"Study. One of us needs to be makin' a good living. We'll be goin' on an adventure walk if you've completed your homework."

"Deal." Paul disappeared into the library, and Cillian stood at the doorway. The entire floor, usually bustling with librarygoers, remained empty. The utter lack of movement unsettled Cillian, as though the apocalypse had come and they'd awakened to find everyone gone. He backed away slowly, a yearning for food erasing his concerns.

Once Cillian reached the small town of Paradise Village, cars honked and people scurried through the business district.

The apocalypse hadn't come.

He studied the map and then walked down a side street, dodging the crowd as he navigated through back alleys toward Mr. Bushcroft's office. Inside, behind a frosted glass door, a bubbly blonde wearing a soft-gray wool sweater jumped up and extended her hand. "Come in. The name's Marlow. What's yours?"

"Cillian."

"Here to see Mr. Bushcroft?"

Cillian smiled. "Aye. I mean, yes, I hear he might have interviews on Tuesdays for a bit of work."

"You've come quite in time." She tapped a pencil on a notepad. "He's leaving to check on one of his charity orphanages in India. Sit down. I'll call him."

Mr. Bushcroft helped orphans. *I'm an orphan. Maybe he'll help me.* The blonde wasn't looking, so he stuffed four scones and juice from a nearby table into his pack. In time, he'd pay Mr. Bushcroft back.

"Yes, sir, he's sitting in the waiting room," Marlow said into a black box on her desk.

Cillian faced the door on the other side of the room. A man—

whose hair hadn't quite decided to be black or gray—entered. A wee man when compared to the tall doorframe.

The man straightened a silk scarf beneath the collar of a posh navy suit before sauntering over. A scent entered the room—a much too floral of a scent for a man. Mr. Bushcroft lit a large cigar, the bitter, dry camphor eliminating the fragrance of roses. An oversized gold ring decorated his right forefinger. His face lost in a cloud of smoke, he spoke. "May I help you?"

"I-I-I'm looking for work," Cillian said in his most posh English accent. "Are you Mr. Bushcroft?"

"I am." As though he had just finished boot camp, Cillian stood at attention, his heart racing.

"At ease, son." The man held back a laugh. "Age?"

"Fourteen."

Bushcroft nodded. "Turn around and take off your shirt."

He helped orphans. He'd understand. Cillian lifted his shirt, revealing years of physical abuse.

"Barbed wire wouldn't let go, son?" He hadn't been called *son* in a long time.

Cillian smiled, liking the feeling of belonging to a father. "N-n-no, sir." He hoped Mr. Bushcroft wouldn't ask any more questions about the scars. He faced the man and slipped his shirt back over his thin, scarred torso.

A wry smile crept across Mr. Bushcroft's handsomely chiseled features, followed by a devilish grin. "You'll do. Button up your shirt."

Cillian fumbled with his shirt buttons, his eyes focused on the carpet. He hadn't known a physical was required for a job interview, but he had heard of the generosity of the man from the Irish Travellers.

Some Travellers said they received monthly letters from their children who had left—some wrote that they were safe, even prosperous. Other parents, like the woman in the next tent, had received only one letter from her child.

Why only one?

"Start date?" Bushcroft puffed a mouthful of smoke.

"Right away, sir." Cillian had read a book from the library, *How to Ace an Interview*. It had said that asking questions made the interviewee seem smart and interested. He swallowed. "May I be askin' a question, sir?"

"Sit down."

Cillian obeyed. The man reclined in a maroon chair.

"What is the starting pay?" Cillian fidgeted with his crumpled shirt. *Smile. Don't fidget.* He released his shirt and grinned wide. "I'm saving up for a trip."

"Well, well." A smug expression dimmed Bushcroft's eyes. "A homeless boy so posh he demands to know the starting salary."

"I'm not homeless." Warmth flushed across Cillian's face. "I have a home and a family."

"I was kidding, boy." No longer *son* but *boy*. "Do you want the job?"

"I do." Cillian glanced at the man, then looked away. They had said that he was friendly. Don't mess this up. Paul needed food.

"Tomorrow, come back to the office. Be ready to work hard and follow instructions." Bushcroft stood and straightened his tailored suit jacket.

"Sir, I-I-I have a little brother."

"Bring him. I provide lovely accommodations for my workers' families." Bushcroft puckered his lips. Whistling a peppy tune, he exited the room.

On the way out, Cillian stole the two remaining scones. Marlow peeked around the corner. "They're rich. Don't eat too many."

"Thanks for not telling." Cillian exited the office.

That evening, Cillian collected Paul from the library and handed him the scones. "Eat yer dinner."

Paul ate his fill. "You eat the last one."

"I'm not hungry."

"Okay." Paul gobbled up the scone.

"We'll be eatin' healthier soon. D'ye learn anything?"

"I learned about the Statue of Liberty."

"Will ye be tellin' me, or must I drag it out with the will of a thousand steeds?"

"She stands ninety-three meters tall. Seven rays jut from her crown, one for each continent. At her feet lie the broken shackles of oppression and tyranny."

"Freedom's image."

"America will give us a chance at a good life, Cil."

"One day at a time. Tomorrow's an adventure, so it's early to bed."

"What about our adventure tonight?"

"I've walked ten miles today."

"Just trying to cheer you up. The walk will give you time to clear your thoughts."

"I dinna need cheerin' up. I need a job. Let's make a quick stop at the store instead."

"You're the adult—by two years." Paul ducked, expecting a playful thump that never came. After a few minutes' walk, they stood outside Fred's Secondhand Store. Cillian opened the glass door and a bell tinkled. "Good afternoon, sir. May I speak to the manager?"

"I'm the manager. Fred Sutton, at your service."

"I dinna ha' any money, but I'd be willing to exchange my services for a new outfit for my brother and one for me."

"Got an old storage room that needs cleaning out. Interested?"

"Verra much so." Cillian turned. "Go outside and study. You may not have time to study tomorrow."

"It'll get cleaned faster if he helps."

"No. I'll do it. Go on." Cillian said, and Paul obeyed. He needed to be alone. Two hours later, the closet was neat and clean. Cillian rubbed his sore muscles while selecting a few clothes. "Thank you, Mr. Sutton."

"Godspeed, lad."

Cillian tossed the bag with slightly used clothing over his shoulder. They didn't compare to Mr. Bushcroft's fine suits, but a man had to start somewhere. "Learn anything while I was breakin' my back?"

"Each country has its own currency. The stock market facilitates trading currency."

"That book dinna tell you how to obtain a few more pounds, did it?" Cillian pulled his silver dollar from his pocket.

"No."

"If ye find an instruction book on that, ye should be tellin' me right away." He flipped the coin in the air as they walked back to the tent.

"Don't worry, Cil. I'll discover the secret to a rainbow's lost treasure."

"And I'll be thankin' ye for doin' yer part." Bicycles sped past, and strangers hurried by. Scents of fresh bread wafted from the bakery. Cillian's mouth watered.

"I'm happy you're my brother, Cil."

"I've not messed ye up, then?"

Paul shook his head, then migrated closer to his brother, brushing his side as they walked. Cillian rested his hand on Paul's shoulder. "We'll be alright. Dinna worry yourself a bit."

They arrived at the tent. "Remember, straight to bed," Cillian said, and moments later, he climbed underneath the blanket with Paul. The events of the day replayed in his brain as he tossed and turned. His pajamas, one of the new items from the secondhand store, clung to his sweat-drenched body. Sleep evaded him; peace avoided him.

Was he making a bad decision? How could he know? They had to eat to live and work to eat.

Morning broke through a bank of gray English clouds, but yielded little illumination to his questions. Cillian grasped a handheld mirror, another item from Fred's, and shaved. He dressed in his new outfit, then adjusted the tan dress shirt, trying to hide a small stain on the cuff. Respect—a working man's payment for wearing a suit.

He straightened his shoulders and smiled gingerly—a simple act he'd not done for a while.

49—THE ORPHAN (PG 13)

CILLIAN AND PAUL TREKKED TOWARD Paradise Village, their new shoes leaving muddy tracks in their wake. The familiar sight of grayish white tents, trash cans used as fire pits, and the murky man-made pool in the middle of the community faded until they were specks against a rising sun.

"Where are we going, Cil?"

"Paradise—bacon, eggs, and bread."

"We eat as soon as we arrive?"

"Aye, but patience."

"Can we walk faster? I'm starved."

"The book? Givin' up on finding our lost treasure, are you?"

"After breakfast, I'll finish reading the book."

Miles and miles of the dark unknown lay ahead, so Paul reached for his brother's hand. "I'll find our treasure. I won't disappoint you, Cil."

Cillian gripped the trembling, cold hand. "Ye couldna be disappointin' me if ye tried wi' all yer might." Cillian rubbed the silver dollar with his other hand, calming his nerves.

An hour passed, and they reached their destination. Cillian stood in front of the frosted glass door. He inhaled, then pushed air from his lungs as he turned the handle.

"Good morning!" The same blonde returned his gaze, her voice cheerful and chirpy like a bird's. "Bright and early."

"I dinna want to be late." Cillian released Paul's hand, and Paul wandered around the foyer, touching each piece of furniture.

"Is the bacon served in here?" Paul asked.

"Be patient. Dinna touch anything."

Paul obeyed and waited by his brother.

A door creaked.

Moments later, Mr. Bushcroft swaggered into the room with an unknown man. The man was tall, with a jagged scar coursing down his cheek. *Scarface.* He glared at the pair of boys, then grinned.

Bushcroft stood shorter than Paul, but his eyes glinted with wickedness. Cillian stepped backward, pinning his back against the entry door. He reached for the doorknob, turned, and jerked. The door was locked. *Why?* Cillian's heart pounded against his chest.

"Let's get on with it," Bushcroft bellowed.

Cillian faced Paul. "Stay close."

"What about breakfast?" Paul whispered.

"Soon." Cillian followed the men. *God, what ha' I done?*

Mr. Bushcroft led them outside where Cillian and Paul climbed into a military-style truck, already holding ten other young boys. Scarface jumped into the passenger side. "Are ye lookin' for steady work as well?" Cillian asked.

"Yep. Right truck." A tan-faced boy massaged his bare feet. *Would Bushcroft prove to be a good man?*

A redheaded, freckled boy offered a handshake to Cillian. "John's my name—Mom used to call me John-Boy, but that's before she jumped off a bridge and I escaped a mean mistress at the care home."

"Verra nice to meet you, John. Sorry about your mom, and I know a wee bit about angry mistresses. My name's Cillian. This is Paul, my brother."

Two more boys—Alex and Thomas—introduced themselves before the truck's engine rumbled to life, fiercely shaking the bed.

Cillian cradled his abdomen with his hands, attempting to quiet his stomach.

His efforts accomplished little.

On their journey, the driver found every bump in the road, jostling Cillian's insides into a pulp until a mouthful of green bile launched from his mouth and landed on John's trousers. A person didn't have to eat to make stomach acids. "I'm verra sorry. If ye like, I'll trade pants with you. Mine are clean."

"Keep 'em." John gazed past Cillian, then moments later met his eyes. "Be my friend—we'll call it even."

Cillian leaned forward and shook his new friend's hand. "For eternity."

John grinned wide.

A year seemed to pass before the driver sped past a chain-link fence, meandered past a cluster of cars, and parked—if that's what one calls driving up on the sidewalk, slamming on the brakes, and cutting the engine. Scarface banged on the truck's rusted bed door. "Everybody out!"

Cillian scooted to the edge of the bed and helped Paul and John down before jumping down himself.

"Cil, I'm terrified," John said as Paul read his book.

"I'm scared too."

"You look brave."

"I'm good at faking." Cillian grinned—crooked, guarded.

"Where are we?" Paul asked.

"Why do you care?" Scarface snarled and snatched Paul's book away.

"That's mine."

"Not anymore."

"Thought we'd have bacon, eggs, and toast by now."

"Who told you that, stupid boy? I ain't got one strip of bacon for you, but I've got a strap if you don't keep moving."

Paul glanced at Cillian. Cillian smiled weakly, one stubborn tear escaping from between his long black lashes. "I'm verra sorry."

"You tried your best." Paul followed the other boys as fast as his legs could take him.

"Cryin' already. Wait until I give you something to cry about." Scarface smacked Cillian on the back of the head, then strolled ahead, whistling. The boys followed Bushcroft's two mean-faced men onto a small airplane.

"I never flew on an airplane before." Paul inspected the small cabin, chose a seat by the window, and patted the one next to him, signaling Cillian to sit. "It's better than bacon, eggs, and toast. Thanks, Cil. You're the best."

Cillian avoided eye contact with his hopeful brother, but inside, he was glad Paul had spared his feelings. Failure had been a merciless mistress. "You couldna ha' gotten a plane ride on your own, now could you?"

"Maybe—but it wouldn't have been as much fun without you." Paul kicked his legs.

"Hey," Alex said, "stop kicking the back of my seat."

Cillian placed his hands over Paul's legs and held them still. "Fasten your seat belt."

"Ten-four. Over and out."

"You're a policeman now?"

"If you only knew the things I imagined and didn't tell you."

"Tell me. Let me dream." Cillian clicked his seatbelt. After Paul fastened his seat belt, he told stories of faraway lands, some even otherworldly. Smiling, Cillian closed his eyes and fell asleep. Sleep blocked out the fears of his new reality.

"Plane ride's over! Out!" Scarface's voice forced Cillian out of his dream, where a beautiful brown girl was telling him she loved him.

Paul muted a chuckle and whispered to Cillian. "Maybe if he'd stop screaming—"

Hot, stale breath brushed Cillian's cheek. He glanced up at Scarface; pale-blue eyes glared back. He diverted his gaze and clenched Paul's hand. "Let's go."

"Don't give me an excuse, boy. I promise. I'll hurt you bad." Scarface talked through a clenched jaw.

"Yes, sir." Cillian stood, but his stiff and wobbly legs protested, requiring him to grab the seat in front. Scarface and his friend herded the boys outside. They walked for at least ten minutes before climbing into the bed of another truck. During the ride, gusts of wind blew through Cillian's locks and became trapped somewhere between hair, dirt, and sweat. He inhaled. "The sea."

"The ocean!" Paul said. "Seriously, Cil. You're the best."

"Come here. Look!" Thomas waved the boys to his side of the truck. They all crawled to Thomas's side and peeked through a small slit between the tarp and the truck's bed.

"I see it," John said. "The sea's bigger than the pictures—and bluer." He stretched his arms as far as he could.

"You've never been to the ocean?" Cillian focused on the shoreline.

"No. Have you?" John said.

"Of course."

"Lucky devil."

"I grew up on the coast of Ireland." Cillian returned to his seat. "I'll take you there one day."

"I'd like that." John flicked his forefinger into the air—a nervous tic. "Did you see sea monsters—like Nessie?"

"Mister Finnegan: he looked like a monster with his scruffy beard. No. Nessie lives in Scotland."

"How do you know?" Thomas asked.

"I'm an Irish-Scotsman."

"Are you sure?" Thomas squinted and pushed his glasses up his nose.

Cillian frowned.

"Most of the time you sound English with a few odd words," Thomas said.

"Odd words?"

"Aye—thought you liked pirate books." Thomas shrugged. "That's all."

"I've never read a pirate book."

"I have," Paul said.

Cillian tousled his brother's hair. "Found out how to locate more gold coins, then?"

Paul shook his head.

"Dinna worry. I've not fed you your bacon, eggs, and toast."

"I don't want bacon anymore. Scarface will strap us if we ask."

"He won't touch you."

"Promise?"

"I'll be doin' my best for you." Cillian looked at John. "Do you have a preference?"

"For how you talk?"

Cillian nodded as heat pulsed through his cheeks.

"Talk like a Scotsman. You make me brave."

"Aye then?"

"Captain Blackbeard, the pirate." Thomas chuckled.

The boys showed off their own versions of a pirate accent until the truck lurched forward and stopped, ending their journey and their joviality.

"Ouch." Paul rubbed his forehead.

"The old guy drives worse than my grandma did." Thomas smirked. No one laughed. Fear creased deep lines into the foreheads of their youthful faces. The routine repeated itself, but this time, the youngsters boarded a bright red boat as it rolled and dipped upon a choppy sea. Cillian covered his nose with a rag; the smell of rotting fish assaulted his senses.

"I think I'll be sick." Paul clenched his abdomen. Seagulls called in the distance.

"Listen to their songs." Cillian watched the seagulls glide over the boat deck toward the ocean. A big white bird swooped low and Cillian lunged, hoping to grab its feathers and be lifted to heaven.

Avoiding his grasp, the bird ascended.

Defeated, he stood still. Quiet.

Was his feathered friend afraid of its journey or excited?

As if answering, the seagull stopped flapping its wings and allowed the wind to carry it along an invisible jet stream. If Cillian could fly, he would ascend and escape with Paul and John in tow, soaring out of reach of the mean men on deck and into cottony banks of clouds and freedom's endless blue sky.

He slipped his hands over his biceps. Alas, he possessed only bony shoulders and spindly arms, making flight impossible—at least for today. He grinned wide until he saw his brother's face. It had paled to green. "Are ye okay?"

"I want to go back to the tents—our home. Can we?"

"One day we'll fly, goin' where we like."

"I'm something awful sick."

"I cannae make the sick disappear. I dinnae ken how. But if I could, I would." Slowly, Cillian walked to the boat's edge and studied the water. The ocean answered, spraying her icy wet breath into his face. His face numbed. A dip would be cold, alright—most likely deadly. If he attempted a watery escape, he would die, just like John's mother. Cillian stepped away from the edge.

"Sit beside me." Paul gripped his stomach. Like any good big brother, Cillian sat with his little brother until he slept. Men's boots pummeling the metal deck woke Paul. Four of the men hoisted rusted anchors and tossed ropes thicker than Paul's forearms onto a dock. "Even if I'm not at my best, will you stay with me?" Paul clung weakly to Cillian.

"I dinna wish to leave you . . ." Cillian thought about the bacon, eggs, and toast, and remembered he'd considered jumping into the sea. "It isna right to make a promise and then break it, so I'll be doin' my best."

The boat drifted away from the dock, and salty winds lashed Cillian's face, burning his eyes with sprays of cool mist. The intrusion of saltwater gave him an excuse to tear up.

"Cil," John said. "Why did you go to Mr. Bushcroft's office?"

"Find work. Make a better life for us." He'd steadied his voice, but no longer believed his canned answer as the vessel meandered from the pier into the unknown. Men served the boys a bowl of slop.

"That's why I went too." John inhaled the chow.

"Stay with Paul and me." Cillian ate his food.

"I'd like that."

Time and tumultuous waves eroded the red, sandy shore. Had days or weeks passed since they'd departed Bushcroft's office? Odd— they hadn't seen the preening man since their departure.

At least four sunrises had passed.

Cillian rubbed sleep from his eyes before cupping his hands around them and looking out over the ocean. "I see land!" Like starved mice bolting toward a block of cheese, boys appeared from every nook and cranny, huddling at the ship's bow. Paul pulled himself to his feet and joined them.

"Where are we?" John asked.

"Somewhere safe—I hope." Cillian tugged Paul's shirt until he followed, and they returned to their resting place—a stack of the ship's old rags and rope. "We'll need our sleep and a plan."

"To escape?" Paul asked.

"Or survive," Cillian replied.

Out of the mist, a thin, smiling man whose angular face ended in a thick, graying beard appeared. "You hungry, lads?"

"I am," Paul said, loudest.

"Follow me, and I'll be leadin' ye to treasure." The man vanished into a curtain of mist. Cillian, John, and Paul entered the mist, then descended into the bowels of the ship behind the man as the others slept.

"Told you we'd find our pot of gold," Paul said. Their frayed shoes clopped down metal stairs. Footsteps sounded ahead.

The man halted, hunched low, turned, and laid a gnarly finger across his parched lips. "Shh."

The boys stood rigid, not daring to take a breath.

Finally, the man proceeded to a small room. A weird lamp encased in slats of metal hung in the middle of the room and cast a green-tinged light. A steaming black pot sat on a stove in the corner.

"Smells good." Cillian gingerly stepped forward while Paul and John remained in his shadow.

"Sit at the table." The man ladled red broth with beans into three bowls. "Eat yer fill." The stranger placed a bowl in front of each boy. "Say your grace."

"Before we eat?" Paul sighed. "I don't know how, and I'm starved."

"Grandma Barry and Mama Kelley showed me." Cillian held Paul's and John's hands. The man smiled wide, revealing a yellowed-picket-fence set of teeth, complete with spaces. "Paul, hold John's hand."

"Gross."

"You hold mine without a fuss."

"But you're my brother and that man . . ." Paul pointed at the stranger. "He'll think I'm a sissy."

The stranger held John's and Paul's hands, completing the circle. "Thanks." Cillian closed his eyes. "Quiet voice. I'm scared. Make us brave."

Warmth tingled deep inside his hand and then burned hot in his arms, finally exploding inside his chest. He opened his eyes. No burnt skin. He looked into the stranger's eyes. They darkened to violet. The stranger winked, then disappeared. Cillian jumped up, his chair legs scraping the metal floor. "Where did he go?"

"Don't know, but way cool. Look. Bacon." Paul's plate now contained bacon, eggs, and toast.

"I have some too—so do you, Cil." John slipped off his jacket. Cillian ate his eggs.

"Was he a ghost?" Paul chewed another slice of bacon.

"What else would disappear?" Cillian stared at the space where the scraggly man had been standing.

"Poof—like a dandelion." John closed his hands into fists and then opened them. "Like a wraith."

"What's a wraith?" Paul asked.

"A ghost," Cillian said.

"I feel brave." John shoveled a spoonful of eggs into his mouth.

"My eggs have cheese in them."

"I didn't even ask for cheese." Paul ran his forefinger across the plate and licked it. "I love cheese in my eggs. Thanks, Cil, you're the best. I knew you'd find bacon, eggs, and toast."

"It wasna me."

"But you found the man."

"No—he found us."

After eating, they retraced their steps and arrived on deck.

During their absence, the tangerine sun had ducked low, leaving stripes of orange, purple, and pomegranate. At the ship's bow, a man curled rope into a pile and then descended a set of what seemed to be invisible stairs.

"Let's get some sleep." Cillian strolled to their bedding, and John and Paul followed. They slept until morning.

A clanking bell sounded the alarm clock.

"Move-in day! Move-in day!" A man with a handlebar mustache, deep-brown eyes, and swarthy skin sang the words more than he spoke them.

Five men threw ropes toward the dock. Back and forth, the fishing boat slammed into the pier until the seamen had completed their task.

Finally, a stocky man lowered the gangway as he nursed a drink in a tall brown bottle. "Last port of call. All must disembark."

"What does *disembark* mean?" Paul yawned.

"We're out of gas—get the heck off," cheeky Thomas quipped. Boys scurried onto shore. In the early morning's light, Thomas's hair burned bright orange, like a freshly lit match. A splotch of freckles tanned his cheeks.

"The funny man's telling his jokes," John said.

"Practicing my stand-up routine. After I make my fortune here, I'm opening my own funny house."

"Isn't it called a comedy house?" Paul squinted, keeping the sun out of his eyes.

"In this house, you tell jokes, right?"

"Yep."

"Jokes are funny, right?"

Paul nodded.

"Then it's a funny house—got it?"

"Paul's just foolin' around." Cillian pulled Paul close.

"Why don't you let the baby grow up?" Thomas said.

"Leave him alone," John placed his hand above his brow and surveyed the dock.

"I hope they leave him alone. I hope they leave us all alone." Thomas focused on the welcoming party—seven men, each brandishing a leather belt.

"Paul, grab your bag." Cillian breathed his instructions, and his brother quickly obeyed, then wandered ahead. Cillian clutched his brother's shoulder and yanked. "Stay close."

They approached the first man. Cillian stared at the tips of his shoes. Paul smiled. "Mister, thanks for the breakfast."

"What are you talking about, boy?" The man eyed Paul and wrapped the leather strap tight around his open hand.

"Nothing." Cillian pulled Paul along. To their right, just past the dock, a group of about a hundred onlookers gathered, their curious brown faces staring at the pale-skinned boys.

"I'm guessing we're not in England anymore."

"Good guess," Thomas said.

"I'm glad," Paul said. "Didn't like the weather. Too rainy. The sun's already awake here. We won't be cold like we were in the orphanage."

"Sometimes I wonder if you left your head at Fred's Secondhand Shop."

"Aw, shucks. I hope not, or I won't be able to figure out where our pot of gold is hiding."

"No rain, no rainbows."

"Didn't think of that," Paul said.

"That's why I'm here; ye cannae think of everything." Cillian's legs felt more like rubber than muscles and bones—sea legs, no doubt. Dabbing sweat from his brow, he gripped Paul's hand tighter and led him to the edge of the group. "Wait."

"You've thought of a secret plan?" Paul rolled from his tiptoes to his heels and back, over and over again.

"Your brain's burstin' with blarney from those fancy books."

"You made me read them."

"A big brother's job." Cillian paused. "I'm daft for bringin' us here. It would've been bad enough for me, but I shouldna ha' dragged you with me."

"Funny—I don't remember the dragging part." Paul was determined to cheer him up, so Cillian forced a laugh, but the bravery he had faked this far started to crumble, and a paralyzing fear broke through his mental fortress. Hunched over, he emptied his guts again and again until nothing was left. Another lad bumped into him from behind. "Hurry up."

"Don't push," Paul said.

"I'd die for a handful of sea water." Before Cillian finished his sentence, Paul bolted.

"Come back!" Cillian's heart raced, but his little brother was fast. One muscled man charged after the escapee.

"Run, Paul. Dinna let him catch you." *What if he ran away?* Cillian would be alone.

Oblivious to the impending danger, Paul removed a ladle from a silver-colored barrel and dipped it into a water trough. With the same quickness, he turned and ran back to this brother's side. "Drink it."

Cillian lapped up the water. Big but slow, Muscles half-stumbled and half-jogged toward them. "Come." Cillian dodged into the middle of the boys and hunched low, pulling Paul with him. "Keep your head down." Cillian smiled. "Thanks for the water."

"Want a glass of milk?"

"Ye'll be stoppin' while yer head's attached to your body."

"If you insist." Grinning, Paul rubbed his hands across his neck.

The boys stumbled behind their overseers, through cardboard-house slums and mud huts.

Finally, they arrived at a cavernous metal warehouse. Nickel-colored ceilings touched heaven, but no smiling cherubs greeted them. Oversized men scrutinized each boy as he passed through the metal doors, and each snarl and glare weakened Cillian's knees. He rubbed his belly.

Not again, please not again.

His mental mantra worked, and it felt as though his stomach hardened into dried concrete. Showerheads lined the back of the metal warehouse.

"Strip and shower." A tall, gangly woman strutted down the middle of the room as she repeated her command. "Cleanliness is next to godliness."

"It'll be nice to clean up." Cillian quickened his pace toward the showers, still preferring Grandma Barry's hot baths. He undressed and turned the handle, expecting a cold shower. Instead, warm water massaged his body.

"Cil," John asked. "What happened to your back?"

"Nothing." He rubbed soap inside a washcloth, creating a lather, then polished his skin to a shine and cleaned the grime from his hair. Clean, he towel-dried and digested his surroundings.

"What job forces their employees to shower?" John asked.

"I was thinkin' the same." Once dry, each boy was given a linen tunic and khaki shorts. Cillian deposited the washed coin into his pocket, and a wet circle showed through the beige material.

The same gangly woman tossed a pair of sandals at each boy and hollered, "Put them on and stand outside!"

From high above, the sun baked the ground, cracking the tan soil. They walked past a little garden into an area of picnic tables, surrounded by a circle of concrete-block rooms.

"Say hello to your new home," Scarface said.

"If we say hello, will the houses talk back?" Thomas asked.

"Keep makin' yer smart remarks," Cillian warned, "and ye'll be makin' it harder for yerself and maybe all of us. Keep a lid on it."

"Yes, Papa."

Each boy was assigned a room, hardly more than a closet, with a tattered cloth hanging in each doorway. The fabric added splashes of color to the otherwise drab palette of gray, white, and soot. Cillian entered his new home. His head brushed the concrete, so he hunched over. In each little room, two concrete slabs were bolted and braced onto the wall, like bunk beds.

"Say something—anything," Paul whispered. "I'm terrified."

"Welcome home, Paul. It's a bit small." Cillian sat on the edge of the concrete bed as he flipped his silver coin. Not much of a better life.

"It's warmer than the tents." Paul reached up. "I can touch the ceiling."

"I'll be savin' money. We'll buy a house so big you couldna touch the ceiling if you stood on the clouds." Cillian removed a threadbare sheet from his knapsack. "Wrap it around you at night. It'll be cold."

"I don't like sleeping on concrete."

"I dinna much like it myself." Cillian shouldered Paul up onto the upper slab. "Sleep up there." *Gentle voice, hide Paul like you did Moses while he was a baby and You hid him from the Egyptian slave in the bulrushes by the Nile.*

He reached into the knapsack, giving Paul an apple he'd stolen from the ship's galley, then peeked around the cloth door and saw other curious boys peering around their tattered curtains.

Each boy's eyes asked the same question: Would their future be worse than their past?

From outside, a refined voice spoke into the wind, loud enough for the boys to hear. "They're caged animals in a zoo."

"We're not animals, are we?" Paul asked.

"Let's play a game. You're a fish, and I'm a shark. They dinna make noise, do they?"

"They do. I promise."

"Well, we dinna hear them with our ears, and that's all that matters."

Scarface marched from cell to cell, throwing back protective curtains and letting the boys know who was in charge. "Out! To the tables." He would arrive at Cillian and Paul's cell after three more visits.

Cillian retreated inside. "Hide. Dinna make a sound." He reappeared in front of the cloth makeshift door just in time, closing the curtain behind him.

"Eager to work." Scarface pinched Cillian's cheek. "I like that. I'll visit later. We'll become *great* friends." Scarface fondled Cillian's chest as he spoke.

What the fu—? The orphan steeled his expression as disgust flooded his body. Scarface's tone changed. "Go to the courtyard, boy—now!"

Cillian ran to a table and sat. He dared a glance over his shoulder. Paul had stayed put. He breathed a sigh of relief. *As long as he's safe, that's all I'm askin'.*

The boys sat around him. Cillian's knuckles blanched white as he gripped the concrete bench. Whimpering, Thomas sat beside Cillian.

"We'll stick together. Stay brave."

"It's not okay."

"Weel be makin' the best of it. Ye'll see." Cillian rotated his silver dollar in his pocket. Across the table, John rubbed his rosary, and Alex's stare never left the dirt beneath his feet.

"Mr. Bushcroft's here." John leaned toward Cillian. The small man, dressed in a navy-blue suit, yellow shirt, and pale-blue tie, strolled into the picnic area. Two of his goons flanked him. "A bit hot for fancy clothes."

"One day, I'll be buyin' clothes like his," Cillian replied.

Like a caged lion planning some unspeakable carnage, Mr. Bushcroft patrolled the dirt paths between the rooms and benches. Dust clung to his polished leather shoes. "Orphans, pay attention."

Scarface punched a boy in the face. Blood spurted from his nose. "Listen up."

Cillian covered his nose. *Keep quiet.*

"Privilege. Luck. Call it what you like. You groveled for a chance. I answered. Not your parents. You work for me." The tempo of his voice punched out his orders in a staccato rhythm. "Be thankful. Be obedient."

That's easy enough. Grandma Barry always said my manners were impeccable. Cillian sat up, confident he could please his new boss.

"Keep my customers happy."

Customers?

"Don't leave the compound unless we are escorting you to the hotel for work, or we'll make you sorry—very sorry." Bushcroft removed a pocket watch from his suit pocket.

"It's a bit like the orphanage," Cillian muttered to himself.

"Simple rules?" Bushcroft perused the boys' faces. Silence answered the boss. The little man continued. "In two weeks, some will stay here, and others will go to a palace. We follow a simple schedule: wake up, eat breakfast, and attend school. Dumb little boys don't service my customers."

"School?" Thomas said out loud. "I hate school." Scarface strode toward the boy, no doubt to punish him.

"Stop!" Bushcroft raised his right hand. A gold band glistened on his finger. "I like boys with spirit. They work better. What's your name?"

"Thomas, sir."

"What do you want to be when you grow up?"

"A funny man—I mean a comedian."

"How will you be able to negotiate contracts if you're illiterate and dumb? Don't you need to be able to have an intelligent conversation between the jokes? Nobody listens to a foul-smelling jokester. Shower each day. Practice impeccable hygiene." Was he talking about Thomas's comic routine or their future jobs in this desert?

"Yes, sir."

"My customers don't want to smell rotting flesh or dirty mouths." Bushcroft clapped his hands together. "I have a great lunch prepared for you. *Bon appétit.* After eating, you'll cycle through medical." Bushcroft rubbed his hands together. He studied the boys' faces, especially Cillian's. A smile etched his face. "Stay seated until it's your turn for medical."

Evil or kindness?

Cillian doubted it was the latter.

The boys finished their lunch of Swedish meatballs, pasta with a side of green beans, and chocolate brownies. After lunch, Scarface grabbed John by the shoulder. "Time for a visit with the good doctor."

"I don't like doctors or needles."

"What about nurses?" Scarface silenced John's protest with the back of his hand.

Cillian said, "He's afraid."

"What's that to you?" Scarface grabbed John by the scruff of his neck and pushed the boy forward until they both disappeared behind white concrete walls.

Screams erupted from the medical building—John's cries, the only evidence he still lived, a familiar sound, like Paul's cries the day Grey Thunder pounded his arse in front of the lunchroom crowd.

Get Paul and run! Cillian stood, his knees threatening to buckle.

Bushcroft sauntered toward Cillian, closing the gap faster than the little man should have been able to on his short legs. He leaned in, his nose inches from the orphan's chest. "Going somewhere, my son?" *My son? A scary proposition, indeed.*

"Catching a wee bit of air."

"Catch it a few feet lower. Sit." Cillian obeyed. John's screams ceased. Had they murdered him? Hot, dry air lay motionless, cocooning the boys in deadly quiet. Scarface trudged out of the white building.

Cillian's throat dried.

The scarred man lifted Thomas by his neck and dragged him into the building. In a few minutes, screams ripped the heavens open again. This time, the sky answered. A storm lanced its veins, spilling its blood—rain—as a chorus of fear and agony rose from the rest of the boys.

Rain drops pelted Cillian's shaking body. His stomach turned somersaults. *What were they doing to Thomas? Were they killing him for making jokes?*

A lightning bolt zig-zagged across the darkened sky.

Silence once again.

"Come with me!" From behind, massive hands dug into Cillian's shoulder.

"No! Leave me alone!" Cillian struggled. His tormenter slapped his face, and blood trickled into Cillian's mouth as daylight darkened to stars and then blackness. An antiseptic odor jolted his brain awake. They'd entered the white concrete building, and he squinted, trying to make the fuzzy scene clear.

When his vision cleared, he wished that his attempts had failed.

Three burly men with folded arms stood in front of him. They resembled ravenous wolves, thirsting for the pain and blood of their victims. In the orphanage, Cillian had watched a program on the telly about a pack of wolves going to work on a newborn fawn. The images had stolen at least a week's worth of sleep. How much sleep would these memories steal?

A whimper drew his attention away from the men. To his right, John and Thomas lay strapped to concrete slabs. Agony was etched on their pale green faces as their heads lolled.

"D'ye give them drugs?"

"You wish." Scarface's hands roamed over his arms, legs, and neck.

"Leave me alone!" Cillian tried to pull away. Massive hands pawed at his sweat-drenched body until he was strapped to his own concrete slab where he learned the reason for John's and Thomas's screams.

A hot iron pressed fire into his right arm and then on his foreskin, taking away his freedom and marking him as the property of another: Asher Bushcroft. Then, they rolled him onto his back and fire surged down his right shoulder blade. Blackness sucked at Cillian's mind, and he slipped into a cold, dark place.

50—The Orphan

SEARING WHITE PAIN YANKED CILLIAN back into consciousness as his backside slammed against a cold slab. His eyelids flew open.

Another slab of concrete seemed to descend toward him. He raised his arms so he wouldn't be crushed. Weak, his limbs fell back to his side. Cillian had returned to his concrete cell. His throat burned; hoarse whimpers escaped his mouth. Scarface's sneer blurred in and out above him. "I'm in pain. Help me."

"No one's here to help you. Not even God." Scarface exited.

The midday sun gave way to dusk. Paul disobeyed and climbed down to Cillian's concrete bed. "Cil . . . Cillian, wake up, wake up. Please wake up." Paul repeated the stifled cry over and over while shaking his semiconscious brother's shoulders.

Cillian moaned. "Paul."

"I'm here." Paul spread himself over Cillian's chest.

"It hurts so bad." Cillian's ragged breaths fought to suck in oxygen. He ebbed in and out of consciousness.

"Before you passed out," Paul's voice trembled, "you said they hurt you. Cil, what did they do to you? I'll fix it. Promise." He rolled back Cillian's sheet. Sobs shook his boyish physique.

An image of a bull's head with a belly spewing fire was branded on Cillian's foreskin, and a barcode was branded on the inside of his right arm. The devil's henchman had claimed his brother's body—the orphan's seed mingled with evil.

Outside, wails, whimpers, and unanswered prayers haunted the concrete hell.

51—Adelaide:
#TheOceanGlows-
TheColorofMyDasEyes

FOR HUNDREDS OF YEARS, IT'S been a tradition of more pomp than circumstance.

During commencement ceremonies at Phillips Exeter Academy, female seniors don a white dress instead of a cap and gown. While my girlfriends shopped for their virginal graduation threads, I flew to KeriKeri, New Zealand—red-rock bays, sailboats, and luscious green islands—with my da and purchased the swankiest Kauri wood casket my trust-fund allowance could afford.

Three weeks till graduation.

Is this the only white dress Mom will see me in?

Fluorescent lights hum overhead, and my classmates whisper around me. Book pages rustle as studious students turn endless pages filled with words and formulas. The brightly lit library closes in twenty minutes. Perspiration moistens my forehead. I've been sitting here for five hours and haven't studied a bit.

Finals are in a week.

Mother doesn't understand any grade point average lower than a 4.0, but I can't focus on this integral equation.

The morbid memory of purchasing a casket for my very much alive mother still depresses me and creeps me out. She's not been feeling well, but I'm sure she's not dying. I tap my mechanical pencil on the cover of my calculus text, allowing myself to remember New Zealand and the casket buying while trying to make sense of it all.

"Why are we purchasing a casket for Mother?"

"Addy Rose," Da had said, "dinna be afraid. We'll be makin' the selection together. Dinna worry about the reason for now. Ye'll do well to be livin' in the moment. The next minutes are not promised, lass."

When my father spoke, my friends typically noticed the musical rise and fall of his Irish-Scot lilt, but I remember the familiar voice of a gentle man trapped inside a low-carb, muscled-out, six-foot-three frame.

That day—the day we bought Mom's coffin—we strolled into the New Zealand luxury wood shop holding hands.

I was afraid.

Terrified.

Da and I were buying a casket for my mother, but she wasn't dead—and still isn't.

Normal people don't purchase caskets until after a person kicks the bucket, but there we were, writing a several-thousand-dollar check for swanky graveyard digs while my mother unsuspectingly brewed tea inside our North Carolina mountain chalet.

After our shopping trip, four men loaded the heavy, rare-wood box into the cargo hold of my da's private jet.

Destination: New Hampshire, then back to Exeter for me.

Engines hummed beneath us, lulling me to the brink of emotional exhaustion as I sank into my pillow-top seat. I lay my head on my da's shoulder, his unforgiving muscles digging into my ear as he chewed his last bite of roasted salmon, wiped his mouth with a cloth napkin, and then kissed me on the cheek, his breath smelling of Alaskan fish.

"Up for a surprise, lass?" His endless icy-blues twinkled with bashful handsomeness beneath a head full of manicured raven locks.

"Does it include tombstones or mausoleums?"

"No." He laughed. "Yer funny. A comedian. Ye remind me of a friend . . ."

"I'm glad."

"Sleep, and when you wake, I'll be showin' you something magical. Something innocent, but bruised."

My brain begged for a reboot, so I conceded and slept.

Sometime later, the jet wheels skidded to a stop, jolting me awake. Groggy, I peered past the plane's windows. An isolated tarmac was our only company. My heartbeat upticked several beats. "Father, are we in New Hampshire?"

"Live in the moment." We disembarked and climbed into the backseat of a waiting Range Rover, and I knew that this leg of the trip had been planned. Inside the plush leather cabin, Boyz II Men crooned "It's So Hard to Say Goodbye to Yesterday" through Bose speakers.

Creepy.

After a thirty-minute drive, the driver stopped the truck, cut the engine, and announced, "We've arrived, sir. Shall I wait in the car?"

"I'd be grateful. We'll return in a wee bit." Night surrounded us, promising nothing.

"*Mo chridhe*," he said, *my heart* in Gaelic, "close your eyes." I hesitated. "Dinna be afraid, especially of your da, Adelaide."

I obeyed.

He opened the door and cradled me in his arms. Father's embrace promised me the world: *In my arms, everything will be okay. I'll protect you. I'll always be at your side.* He didn't need to say the words; the power of his embrace whispered the deepest thoughts of his heart to me. The unspoken love of a quiet, shy man.

He walked.

I clung to him and waited.

Hot, humid air moved against my skin. The bounce of his gait jarred me, but his firm steps were slow, self-assured. Waves crashed in the distance, and minutes later, a tangy brine coated my tongue.

"D'ye trust me, Addy Rose?"

"Forever, Father."

"Aye then, open yer eyes and behold the majesty of it." I opened my eyes and gasped. Magic surrounded us—luminescent-blue wave caps glowed against the black sea. "Where are we?"

"Breathtaking isna it? They call it the Maldives. Dinnae forget to breathe, Adelaide. I'll not be losing you as well, lass."

I inhaled a deep breath. A rush of oxygen defogged my brain, and questions spilled into my mind.

Why did he bring me here?

Why was he afraid of losing me as well?

"Stop thinking. Enjoy yer surprise." Da read my mind. "A lass's last memory of her da should be special, no?"

"Last memory?" I reached for his hand. "Cordy Grey and I don't set sail until a week after graduation. I'll see you after finals. Promise." He said nothing and led me into the ocean.

"It's dark. I'm afraid, Father." I pulled back.

"I'm with you. Dinnae be afraid." His words reminded me of the biblical passage that my aunt read to me as a little girl: "Do not be afraid. I will never leave you or forsake you."

Fingers intertwined with mine, he guided me into the dark, cold sea.

Waves roared.

Were they laughing at us or cheering us on our journey?

Water sloshed against my ankles and waist, then crested over my shoulders. I reached for him, clawing at his flesh and finding purchase in the bare skin stretched over the taut muscles of his neck—stalwart, no different than a Kauri tree trunk.

"When the road darkens, ye'll do well to trust your other senses to find your way home." He spoke above the noise of the waves. He was right. The salty taste. The rhythmic drone of the ocean. All of it was familiar, and I relaxed.

"Why does the water glow blue?"

"Adelaide, now you're seein' what you couldna see during the day." He kissed me hard on the cheek—desperate, as though something lurked in the shadows waiting to rip him from my arms. "I'll be tellin' you a secret, *mo chridhe.*"

"Tell me."

"The sea's no different than life—turbulent, lonely, and ice cold. She's a hard taskmaster, pounding wee organisms in her surf and spillin' their guts and blood without remorse."

"We're not on one of your battlefields."

"I'm glad of it, but if I'm to go and fight, do your da a favor when he's gone—kiss yer mother every day for me. Tell her I love her."

"I will, but as I said, Da, I'll see you after finals. We'll be together—you, me, and Mother."

Still, he said nothing as he slung me piggyback style onto his shoulders before running into the shallows and emerging from the sea. Seawater plastered his T-shirt against ropes of muscles, and I clung to his back like an octopus.

I was safe.

Was he?

We reached the shore. Safe from the grasp of the black sea, he released me, allowing me to stand. As I stood on my own two feet, I noticed the single set of footsteps leading into the ocean. When I was terrified, Father carried me. The feeling of unconditionally belonging to someone rushed through my chest.

Could this moment last forever?

Like a little boy treated to his first time at the ocean, Father ran down the beach, the sea air combing through his wet hair.

I chased after him, learning to live in the moment as if it were our last. Laughing, he tumbled onto the sand, then lay on his back. Stretching his arms wide, he tilted his chin toward the heavens. "Smell the sea, Adelaide. Most importantly, make each day count."

"Why are you talking this way?" Something told me this was a sad moment—final, complete, refusing to be undone. A tear stung my right eye.

"Canna a father be talkin' to his daughter wi' honesty pourin' from his heart? Life isna all blissful selfies. It's real. Raw. Relentless."

"I can handle it." I lay on his chest, wanting to drink him in and never stop, but I stopped short of planting a kiss on his cheek, my breath hitching when I saw something I hadn't seen before.

Contrasted against his pale skin, illuminated beneath the full moon, a black mark marred the inside of his arm, directly beneath his right armpit.

A barcode?

Why would Da's flesh be stamped with a barcode? Only objects listed for sale were stamped with barcodes. My father's gaze tracked mine, and his face flushed deep red. He embraced me, hiding the mark.

For the first time, he lied to me—quietly, not saying a word.

I planned to embrace Father when I returned home after finals, kiss his cheek, and lie in his arms until we both fell asleep. The

Saturday after my da and I returned from our trip, he ate breakfast with Mother at the mountain chalet.

By lunchtime, he was gone.

No rhyme.

Definitely no reason.

Now I languish in a town of fourteen thousand, studying for final exams and wishing I was lying between Mother and Father on our favorite couch. Even after Da went missing, Mother insisted I remain at Exeter, score high marks on my senior exams, and graduate with my classmates, but I loathe white dresses—fake masks of innocence.

Emerald accents my complexion, not Dracula white. If my family wasn't falling apart, I could tolerate the white graduation dress, but we're not just falling part, we are disappearing. Picked off by something sinister.

Truth: no matter how uncool, I'd rather be with Mother looking for my da.

But I've never won a fight with Mother.

52—Orphan Dreamer

"YOU NEVER WILL, ADELAIDE." DANIELA smiled, but fate could be cruel, taking a mother from her child.

After class, the Orphan Dreamer must clear her name if Adelaide was to ever exist. Daniela was not crazy; the inquisitor must be convinced of this truth.

"I'm gifted." Daniela stood near the curb, waiting for her ride.

Claire passed by. "Good luck on the exam tomorrow."

"Ditto." She smiled, finally believing her grandma and parents' assessment of her value.

A new problem surfaced: Would a medical school admit a straight-A student into their school if said student had been labeled a depressive schizophrenic?

Not likely.

She slipped on her sweater, hiding the jagged albino scars freckled with brown pigment and zigzagged across her forearm—the evidence of her grief after Ethan's death. No need to remind the inquisitor.

Warming to the idea of embracing her destiny as the Orphan Dreamer, she stared at the midnight-blue snowflake that stained the middle of her right palm.

"The Glass Tattoo."

Wear it until you love it. A voice taunted her. During her doctor's appointment, she would hide her right hand in the sleeve of her sweater.

"Ready, Danny Rose?" her dad hollered from the banana boat. His leukemia had gone into remission again.

"Ready." She hopped in.

The office visit lasted for more than an hour as the inquisitor peppered Daniela with questions. "You stopped your medicines a year ago. No psychotic break."

"I wasn't crazy to begin with, Doctor. Just super stressed about Ethan's illness and subsequent death."

"Any friends?"

"Acquaintances."

"Voices?"

"Listening to God and His creation doesn't equal a mental illness. You're a Christian. It's in the Bible."

"You're convincing. I'll give you that."

"Doctor, please reverse the diagnosis." Daniela clasped her hands together. "I want—no—I need to attend medical school and heal people."

"What's that?" The doctor pointed to her right palm.

"A tattoo." She rolled her shoulders back and jutted her chin into the air.

"Mr. Cavanaugh, did you allow this?"

"I did. But she didn't get it in a tattoo parlor."

"Where then?"

"The hand of God."

"Excuse me?"

"The Almighty chose my Daniela Rose to become the Orphan Dreamer, and the Glass Tattoo is Yahweh's mark." Time to show off. In her subconscious, Daniela rejected her calling. The tattoo faded. The snowflake diamond resurfaced.

"What the heck?"

"If you reverse the diagnosis . . ." Daniela reaccepted her calling, and the snowflake diamond disappeared beneath her skin. Sapphire ink spilled across her hand, forming a blue snowflake tattoo. "I'll do you a favor."

"What's that?"

"Save your butt."

"It's what she was born to accomplish: save Earth from Lucifer's antichrist and his pandemic." Her dad crossed his arms. "What do you have to lose, Doc?"

The doctor stared at his patient and her father for a while, then shook his head. "I guess everything." Dr. Spotnick's Adam's apple rose and fell at an unnatural rate. "Your grades are impeccable. You've completed two years of college courses during the first two years of high school. Your IQ test—you're Einstein-level genius. I will reverse the diagnosis on one condition. Come in immediately if the dark thoughts return. I don't want to lose my favorite patient."

"I will."

"Go kick butt and take names, Daniela Rose Cavanaugh." Dr. Spotnick laughed. "Save all of our butts."

"Done." A grin burst across her face.

Daniela and her father returned home. Lunch was ready. They ate as a family.

"You earned the coveted spot fair and square. You should go, Danny Rose." Her father's voice yanked her out of her zone of excitement.

She was normal—not crazy, almost ordinary!

Daniela's father encouraged her to accept the US Department of Energy's undergraduate grant for a research semester at Los Alamos National Laboratory in New Mexico—the prestigious lab where Oppenheimer and his team created the atomic bomb. During this semester, Daniela would research methods to repair double-stranded DNA breaks caused by radiation exposure with eighteen other students.

"I want to go, but I hate to leave you and Mom. You're better, Dad. We should spend time together."

"Don't stop living at the ripe old age of sixteen."

"Who knows?" Her mother chewed a piece of jalapeño corn bread. "Maybe you'll meet your Anne-girl and take your nose out of that children's book."

"I need to confess." Her parents stopped eating. "I heard you,

Papa. On my thirteenth birthday, you were prepared to lie to me and keep the Glass Tattoo a secret."

"Eavesdropping again?" He dropped his fork onto his plate.

"Parents keep their kids in the dark, then wonder why we run into things."

"From a sixteen-year-old girl's perspective, you've figured out Parenting 101."

"Why, Dad?"

"I didn't think you were mature enough to balance the power of the Glass Tattoo with your unhappiness, due to Ethan's illness. You were unreliable. Imbalanced."

"We hate it when you sneak around, Daniela Rose." Her mother leveled a stare.

"I'm sorry. That's why I'm confessing." She twirled spaghetti noodles around her fork.

"Are you ready to experience the full power of the Glass Tattoo—entrance into the higher realm?" her dad asked.

"Don't know." She shrugged.

"I'm surprised the doctor was convinced, but you were fabulous—bold, charming. Most people can't process anything more complicated than the obvious—touch, sound, sight, smell, and taste. They're scared of people like you. So sometimes we must play their game." Her dad sipped his lemonade.

"'Great minds discuss ideas,'" her mom said, quoting the late Eleanor Roosevelt. "'Average minds discuss events. Small minds discuss people.'"

"Mom, you've been on my side all along?"

"From the beginning," her mom promised. "I—we—didn't know how to protect you from *the system*."

"When you scraped your skin off your arms—" Her dad shook his head. "I was in shock—frozen, helpless. Then I went into fight mode, fighting for the right to continue raising my beloved little girl."

Daniela's gut catapulted into her throat and shame flooded her cheeks.

"I'm your papa—your rafiki. You should have told me."

"I'm sorry."

"Tell us the truth. We're your allies."

Even about oily boy's race? Daniela snickered. "So you both played the doctor to keep me safe?"

"We would die for you. Sane parents are allowed to take care of crazy kids, but crazy parents are not allowed to raise crazy or sane kids. The system takes those kids away. Brave? Clever? No parent is. I'm just your father—a man trying his best to raise a beautiful and extraordinary daughter."

"Thanks, Dad." She blushed.

"A young lady. Look at you: so stylish, smart, and graceful."

"Dad, stop. You're embarrassing me."

"I love watching your humility glow. Don't lose it, gorgeous." Daniela had grown into an attractive teenager. "It's time for me to tell you . . . everything."

"Everything, Dad?" She held her breath.

"Take a deep breath and listen."

For the next hour, Austin told his daughter about his past. His mother's death at a young age. The humiliation of growing up as a black man in the South's Jim Crow system. His dishonorable discharge from the US Navy at sixteen. The drunken brawl that followed. Taking the life of the other man during that fight. His subsequent imprisonment, working on the chain gang, then attending seminary to become a pastor. She relished all she learned, but it was the last few lines that set her free, allowing her to fly away like an apricot sulfur.

"Ethan's parents told me something odd."

"What, Daddy?"

"The night Ethan passed, his parents returned from dinner to find you two holding hands while you were both lost in a deep sleep—they called it a coma."

"Sorry, Dad." She paused. "I know your rules about boys. Especially those boys."

"I'm not upset, Rosebud. That's when you traveled."

"I remember," she said, shifting in her seat, "reaching for Ethan's hand after the tattoo had already integrated into my right palm, and a strange gravitational pull tugging at me until . . . I don't remember anything else except for Prince Jonathan's Gibeah. The Feast of Trumpets. He gave me the arrowhead right before I dove into the pool and followed Ethan back to our world."

"At least we understand how the tattoo works." Her mom cleared the table and filled the sink with dishwater.

"That means . . ." Her dad wiped the table. "The arrowhead is somewhere between here and there."

"But I don't want to dive into the pool again to find it."

"You may not have to."

Deep water. She shivered. "Okay. I'll try." Daniela retrieved a manila envelope and removed a stack of papers. "Let's go over these dates again, making sure I've got them memorized. Each time a tetrad of blood moons falls on a sequence of Jewish holidays—Passover, Sukkot, the Feast of Tabernacles—something significant happened to the Jewish people."

Tetrads of Blood Moons and Their Effects on Jewish People

The Spanish Inquisition—1492

* Passover, April 2, 1493
* Sukkot, September 25, 1493
* Passover, March 22, 1494
* Sukkot, September 15, 1494

The War of Independence—1948

* Passover, April 13, 1949
* Sukkot, October 7, 1949
* Passover, April 2, 1950
* Sukkot, September 26, 1950

The Six-Day War—1967

* Passover, April 24, 1967
* Sukkot, October 18, 1967
* Passover, April 13, 1968
* Sukkot, October 6, 1968

* Passover, April 15, 2014
* Sukkot, October 8, 2014
* Passover, April 4, 2015
* Sukkot, September 28, 2015

"So based upon what I learned in Gibeah, I think the antichrist will start his rise to power after 2014 to 2015, twenty years from now," Daniela told her dad.

"Good job. I imagine something big will be happening in Jerusalem. The friend of Israel will turn out to be their worst nightmare. A wolf in sheep's clothing."

"We've got some time. It's only 1998."

"Pop quiz: What's a blood moon?"

"Blood moons are lunar eclipses that are significant when they occur in a tetrad and fall on a pattern of Jewish feasts: Sukkot and Passover. The moon appears red because the light from the sun is bent due to the earth's atmosphere, and a band of particles reflects the light. That's why sunsets in the evening appear red or orange."

"What does a blood moon represent?" Her dad studied a map.

"It's a clock, a countdown of some sort."

"Correct."

"But we're followers of Yeshua. We don't practice astrology, do we?"

"Astronomy isn't astrology." Her dad flipped through his black leather-bound Bible and read. "'And God said, Let there be lights in the firmament of the heaven to divide the day from the night; and let them be for signs, and for seasons, and for days, and years . . .'"

"The sun, stars, and moon tell their own mysteries. The answer to *when* Lucifer's pandemic will torment Earth has been written in the sky from the beginning of time."

"Good job." Her dad shifted his notes. "Next riddle: Chi, Xi, and Stigma—number of a man. Who is he?"

"I didn't discover *who*—Lucifer's human agent—during my travels, only *when*. After the blood moons of 2014-2015, near or on Rosh Hashanah."

"What if the blood moons are to sound an alarm for the Orphan Dreamer to warn humanity of Lucifer's impending attack and the arrival of his principal human agent to Earth, giving people time to prepare, repent, and be spared?"

"Then they'd have to sound before the antichrist slaughters humans at the behest of Lucifer. And yes, warning them might be a good call."

"Danny, figure out the identity of Chi, Xi, and Stigma before it's too late."

"That's a tall order, identifying Earth's dreaded antichrist." She scribbled *Chi=600 Xi=60 Stigma=6* on a sheet of paper then whispered, "Six-six-six." She chewed down the eraser end of her pencil in two seconds flat.

"Read Proverbs 8," her dad said.

Daniela flipped to the passage. "'The Lord possessed me in the beginning of his way, before his works of old. For whoso findeth me findeth life, and shall obtain favor of the Lord.'"

"Who's speaking?"

"Wisdom." She tapped her pencil on her notepad.

"Correct. Wisdom existed and walked with Yahweh before He created the heavens. She watched Yahweh write His riddles and answers in the sky. She knows the answer to any riddle put forth. She is the brain behind the Glass Tattoo. Yahweh is the raw power."

"Miss Know-it-all—literally." Daniela studied her hand. "Dad."

"Yes."

"You know that I'm not a natural fighter. How do I defeat this evil antichrist?"

"Spiritually—prayer. Physically—maybe your kindred spirit, the one who will succeed Ethan, will fight that battle."

"My Anne Shirley?"

"Or oily boy. Maybe he's the brute and you're the brains," her dad said.

Daniela thought only of oily boy's frail appearance—translucent lily-white skin, emaciated, with bugs crawling through his black hair. "He's no brute."

Should she tell her dad everything?

Not now. What would she say to him after he'd shared his treatment in a Jim Crow South at the hands of whites? She settled for "Good try, no cigar."

"Do you remember the Apostle Paul's promise to the Church of Ephesus in Ephesians chapter three, verse twenty?"

"I do. 'Now unto him that is able to do exceeding abundantly above all that we ask or think, according to the power that works in us . . .'"

"Bigger and better than what we can imagine. Don't underestimate God's ability to use the outcast. I was once an outcast."

"I know, Daddy." Daniela rested her hand on her dad's. "If Yahweh can use me—the girl with bushy hair, nosebleeds, and a dead crippled friend, He can use pretty much anyone. In my visions of oily boy, some believed him to be Chi Xi Stigma—six-six-six."

"Time will tell."

"But when will I be wise enough?"

"You are a humble young lady, gifted with great empathy, but you must be humbled further so your compassion grows."

"Haven't Claire and Harry humiliated me enough?"

"Only a compassionate person can be trusted with unfiltered access to wisdom's knowledge. Then you can fulfill your calling with ease."

"Stop evil. Humanity should be down with that. I won't have to scream warnings on a street corner."

"Let me tell you a story. Stalin sat at dinner with his generals. They questioned his tactics of torturing his own people, asking, 'How long will people follow you when you torment them?' Stalin picked up a live chicken and started to pluck its feathers."

"Sadistic!"

"Agreed. The chicken squirmed and squawked while struggling to free itself from its torturer."

"So much for lunch." She grabbed her abdomen.

"Stalin released the completely denuded chicken, picked up a piece of bread, and squatted beside the bird."

"Why?"

"To prove a point. The denuded chicken followed Stalin around the dining room, pecking at and devouring the stale bread while blood ran down its pale skin. 'They will follow me for food no matter how much I torture them,' he said. And he continued killing fifteen million of his own people. Another example of a godless dictator bending the will of his subjects. The antichrist will be no different."

"What about religion?"

"Some believe that faith and religion are linked by a confession of a supreme being, and if people don't believe in a supreme being, they don't practice religion."

"They're atheists, nonreligious."

"Wrong. Atheism is a religion: a theology that excludes the divine and places a human in the seat of God, as Stalin placed himself. Stalin's bible was his own flawed conscience, coupled with Charles Darwin's *Origin of Species*. That book seared his conscience, giving him confidence in his belief of natural selection and survival of the fittest."

"Mom said Darwinism seared the consciences of the English slave traders, allowing them to make money off what they believed to be an unevolved human form—the African."

"Brazil traded more slaves than the Brits ever did, and they practiced Catholicism. Whether void of the divine or inclusive of the divine, religion—when used to acquire power and money without regard to human dignity and preservation—is by definition blasphemy against the truest nature of Yahweh's wish for relationship with humanity. This is the religion of the antichrist and his false prophet."

"'And that no man might buy or sell, save he that had the mark, or the name of the beast, or the number of his name: Chi, Xi, Stigma.'" Daniela's mom quoted the Apostle John from Revelation, the thirteenth chapter and seventeenth verse.

"That's six-six-six," Daniela said. "Dad, you believe the antichrist will use Stalin's tactics of withholding food to force the masses to follow him?"

"I do."

"That's sick."

"Unfortunately, the masses are no different than Stalin's chickens. They will follow this madman, persecuting you for defying him. You are an eagle. Soar above the chaos."

"What about pastors, priest, and rabbis? Won't they warn the people about six-six-six?"

"Some will, but others are wolves in sheep's clothing, pawning off money-seeking schemes that are simply blasphemous ideologies, substituting Yeshua's teachings of redemption, hope, and compassion with the love of money and power. You must lead your friends and enemies to Yeshua."

"I'll try."

"Yeshua didn't not come to Earth to make bad people good or good people better. He came to make dead people live again."

Like Ethan.

"More doomsday preaching. You know I'm self-conscious. I don't even like public speaking."

"This is why your compassion must grow; then you'll think less of yourself and more of your neighbor. Then, your tongue will loosen."

"I'm a selfish jerk now?" Daniela rolled her eyes.

"Don't be silly. Share the truth. They will decide if they want to follow Yeshua, take up their weapons, and fight with you against Lucifer and his human agent—Chi Xi Stigma, six-six-six.

"My high school science teacher wasn't pleased when I repeated what you said about Yeshua being the only way to heaven."

"But it's true—He is."

"Why?"

"Because He is heaven."

"And that's why you're the Orphan Dreamer's dad. You're smart. Confident. Believable. Your voice booms with power."

"I've lived a little, so I know what's on the other side. Pure misery."

"Why don't you complete this mission, and I'll support you?"

"You were chosen. Wisdom will illuminate your journey."

"Then here's my gauntlet. If Yahweh really wants me to solve His sky puzzles and save the world, let me prove my sanity once and for all." She paused and looked up at the sky. "Help me find Prince Jonathan's arrowhead. Then I'm all in." She crossed her arms and leaned back into the chair.

"That's your prayer?"

"It is."

"Then dive deep, Danny Rose. Swim in the fiercest ocean, Orphan Dreamer. When it becomes the norm for humans to kill with no remorse, we will need a snowflake to quench hell's fire. Sleep. Dream. When you wake, we'll finish packing for Los Alamos. Even if it's midnight." Her dad grinned a knowing smile.

Daniela lay down, holding the Glass Tattoo in her right hand.

The edges of the diamond darkened into midnight blue.

Dark-blue ink spilled into the center. Warm energy burst into her hand, pulsing throughout her entire being. The jewel disappeared into her palm, leaving behind a beautiful snowflake tattoo. A feeling of warmed honey poured over her body, embracing her and pulling her into a long, dark tunnel.

A languid voice spoke, "Come up here."

53—Orphan Dreamer

THE TUNNEL'S DARK COCOON SPITS me out onto a razor-thin mountain ledge. Warm blood drips from my nose. I wipe my face with the back of my arm, smearing blood across both my forearm and my cheek as I run along a path that seems narrower with each stride.

Clusters of stars speckle a navy-blue sky, casting cold shadows across the horizon. A nighttime forest charges into the clouds, blackening the lower part of the sky.

Fog hazes my path.

I taste salt.

In the distance, the sea plunges into a cave. Below me, deep in a ravine, volcanic lava oozes out of rocky crags into the sinister moonlit valley. Behind me, the earth falls off into ink-black nothingness. I keep running, but a mountain looms in front of me and blocks my path. The Glass Tattoo has transported me to another world—an unknown place.

I crouch behind a dried shrub, breathing hard and clutching the Glass Tattoo. A steady mist clings to my face as I inhale unadulterated air, then exhale my contribution to pollution.

Moments pass, then I close my eyes, rest my cheek on my bent knee, and breathe. Sleep begs to settle within my brain. Sighing, I clasp my shins, lean up against a rock, and steady my head's bony pillow.

Time ticks on.

Something's changing.

My heart tells me before my senses do.

Mom calls it Yahweh's voice—or my knowing, whenever she's around those who can't understand that the Creator possesses a tongue and knows how to use it. My teachers call this ability a sixth sense, and a Cherokee spiritual leader calls it the wolf within.

Dread wraps its spindly fingers around my waist and pulls me into its treacherous embrace. I shudder. The fresh smell of evergreens shifts to the stench of rotten eggs. My heart begins to race.

Nothing.

But there must be something.

My senses haven't caught up with my heart yet.

Seconds later, the odor of rotting meat assaults my nostrils. My stomach churns as I jump to my feet and scan the desolate lands. I hold my breath, thinking that if I don't smell the beast, maybe it will disappear.

To my right, a shadow shifts.

I back away from the threat, carefully avoiding the edge of the precipice. Another rustle, and then I see. Fangs bared, blood dripping from its jowls, foam puddling in the creases of its lips. A gray wolf with a snow-white stripe on its back lunges toward me.

I'm dead!

My only path of escape is to my left, through a patch of brambles with sharp thorns. It's gonna hurt. I charge into the shrubs. Thorny spines slice through my skin, and trails of blood appear.

My right foot slips on a bed of pebbles, and I slide down the hill toward the volcanic lava. Fiery breath roasts my legs. Above me, the gray wolf howls, licks slobber from its lips, and quickens its stride. I dig my hands into the soil and slow to a stop. Pain rips into the tips of my fingers and blood moistens my skin. "Please, help."

A form with a sprinter's physique appears in front of me, the same form and height as the shadow in grandmother's mirror. My mind moves as frantically as my fingers—both fighting to keep me from falling into nothingness. I reach for the stranger, but all I touch is air.

Who is the runner?

I cannot see the person's face, just the back of the lithe form, dressed in dark-blue pants, white sneakers, and a red hoodie. I don't even know if the runner is male or female, but the strong muscular legs and wide shoulders suggest it may be a man.

"Help," I cry.

The sprinter halts, and without revealing his face, throws a ball of fire at the wolf. *Now, that's a gift.* My foe dodges left, stumbles, then careens over the edge of the plateau.

"Storm!"

"Let's go then." Face shadowed, the sprinter reaches into the ravine and grabs me by the arms, pulling me up. "You're halfway there."

"To where?" Pain shoots into my ankle, but I crawl back onto the ridge of the hill.

"The crossing between your world and mine."

"Am I dreaming?"

"Partially. Once you reach my world, your mind won't hold your spirit captive anymore. You'll be fully awake. Patience. You'll experience many setbacks before you can completely penetrate my world." In front of me, the runner darts into a cave that appears in the side of the mountain. The runner stops and reaches back with a gloved hand and beckons. "Follow me."

"Could I die?"

"Once you've awakened, all things are possible."

I hobble into the cave after him. Mistake number one, because after I enter, he's gone. I cross my exposed arms over my torso, trying to block the icy and somehow musty wind, but it seeps through my skin and chills my bones. I step forward.

A branch cracks.

Are there supposed to be trees in a cave? Why try to make sense of the inconsistencies of the journey?

I glance to my right. A hairy black spider, its center as wide as my five-foot-six body is tall, scurries toward the exit—my way out—and covers it, blocking the moon's cold-blue light.

I back away slowly, trip over something, and slam onto the cave's floor. "Face your fears," I whisper to myself. Pain shudders from my hip into my spine, making my head spin. Even in the fuzziness of my vision, the spider's form looms large across the cave entrance.

"Help me!" I scoot away from the enormous spider, going deeper and deeper into the cave's blackness. Something brushes my shoulder. Another spider? *Please, no.*

My mouth dries. Within a sliver of moonlight, a shadow dances across the wall behind me, moving closer. Hugging the cold wall, I run until an unnatural glow brightens into an apple-red hoodie.

He's back.

"That spider isn't friendly; you'll have to learn how to tell the difference." For the first time, I see the edges of the runner's face: coal black skin, a glistening white smile, and eyes that shift color from brighter than cobalt to violet to the ebony of a jaguar's coat. He reaches for my hand and helps me stand.

I raise my arm across my eyes, minimizing the blast of light from his eyes. "W-w-what's your name?" I ask, breathless.

He's silent.

I shrug. I'm used to rejection.

The runner slightly tilts his head.

"You're reading my thoughts." I look away and study the cave floor. Bat guano coats rocks and dirt. It looks like my romantic journey—one pile of crap.

"Rarely do human thoughts match what's spoken." His lips break into a wide smile. I blush. He doesn't care.

"I don't want to be here. Do you know that too?"

"Yes. You've a lot to learn, but you're honest. I like that." After invading my thoughts, he charges into the depths of the cave. "The wolf and the spider are different forms of the same foe—my enemy, your enemy, humanity's enemy."

"Lucifer's bunch?"

"Yes. He's slippery. Takes on different forms, so be careful around anyone new."

"I wish he never existed."

"Me too."

"What is this placed called?"

"Ellesmere—the transitioning."

"That's corny. Sounds like a name stolen from a fantasy novel." I glance over my shoulder. The spider's still there. It crawls toward me.

Closer, it changes into a hideously scaled, feathered creature. A trail of smoke follows it as it approaches. As if tethered by an invisible connection, my legs carry me after the sprinter, but he stays out of reach. I don't remember how we exit the cave and arrive at the ocean, but I charge into the churning, cold surf.

Mistake number two: I can't swim. My body stiffens as I try to remember the video I'd watched on how to tread water. The runner disappears beneath a wave.

The spider charges me.

I dive deep, then splash and kick, trying to keep my face above the water, but the ocean's power sucks me into its liquid tomb. Water fills my mouth, and I know suffocation is next. I've been flirting with death for a while now. Today, not finding a choice, I'm saying, "I do" to death.

How would death feel?

I tilt my head back and relax, allowing the ocean to pull me into its depths. I inhale once more, sucking cold brine into my mouth and nose.

Before I black out, an image fills my mind: my mother sitting on grandmother's rocking chair in our tiny living room, quietly rocking and praying for me until I return home. In my selfish defeat, I hadn't thought about Mom and Dad's heartache if I don't return.

I shouldn't die first, no matter how much I want to.

My eyelids fly open, and I fight death's icy grip.

The runner appears in front of me in the turbulent sea—his face visible, just inches away. No longer cobalt and ebony, his violet eyes bore past mine, reading my soul, and then he smiles, swims behind me, and pushes me deeper into the ocean.

I should be furious, but I'm not.

We enter another tunnel.

The walls are crawling with maggots, so I know our destination, like the cave, will be disturbing. After the tunnel ends, we roll on top of each other, landing in a garden of emerald grass, pink flowers, and a towering tree with branches that hang low, all marred with the fetid metallic stench of human sweat and blood.

I look around. I'll find what my knowing tells me is here.

Hunched in a corner, he's looking at me with eyes that are gutted black holes set in a moon-pale and otherwise blank face—no lips or ears, but raven hair crawling with lice hangs across what should be a forehead. His waiflike body shakes. "Oily boy."

Moving closer, I learn why.

Sitting, his back is exposed, displaying skin that has been bruised and bloodied by the frenzied lashes of a tormentor. His arm is raised above his head and resting against a burnt tree stump. Something impales his trembling, bloodied hand.

A rusty metal spike.

"Why?" I whisper. "What has he done?" I say, as though any young man could deserve such torture. "Are you real?" I whisper, hoping he'll answer no. If he's not, no need to fret.

Silence.

My heart sinks an inch closer to my trembling knees. I'm still on the hook. What if he answers? I'd be scared out of my mind. Besides, this thin boy who's haunted my dreams looks more like a ghost than a living person. As though he means to confirm my thoughts, a hole opens where a mouth should be, and green mist wafts from him. I slap my hand to my nose and gag.

He smells of death.

Watching me, the runner kneels down beside the abused waif, who doesn't move. The hooded, nameless boy reaches for my hand.

I'm not ready.

I take a deep breath and then reach out to touch the waif's back, but my hand goes through mottled skin. I yank it back, realizing that I'm nothing more than a ghost in my nightmarish travel. His inky eye sockets fill with opaque white jelly and form sclera, like fresh snow falling into pools of black oil.

I lean forward, studying his eyes.

Weird. There's something missing—pupils. "What is he?" I stumble backward, scooting away. "You're not real. I want to be normal. Stay out of my dreams." I hug myself.

The dejected form turns his face and crumples into a rounded slump, then rests his head on bruised and bloodied knees. I look at my arms, embracing my well-nourished build. He deserves this hug, not me. I step toward him, but I'm too afraid to touch him again.

"My name's Legna."

Why is the runner finally revealing his name? "I'm Daniela, but my mom calls me Danny Rose." I extend my hand, and Legna shakes it. His grip is more powerful than a teenage boy's should be.

"And your rafiki calls you the Orphan Dreamer." His words entice me to stay—not that I know a route of escape.

"Yes." I smile, then step back as a thought occurs to me. "How did you know?"

"It's not important." Legna shrugs. "What is important is that you learn to trust me."

Trust a strange boy. Nervous, I fill in the silence. "I don't know why he calls me that. I'm normal. Okay, maybe not normal, but definitely ordinary. And I'm not an orphan."

"I don't spit balls of fire to defend ordinary girls." He grins, and my cheeks flash hot. "Beautiful necklace." He points toward the Glass Tattoo dangling from a strip of leather around my neck. "Who gave it to you?"

"Someone who crashed my thirteenth birthday party."

"What did they look like?"

"Don't know. Didn't see them."

"Good." Legna's lips hide a smile.

"Why do you care? Who are you?"

"I told you. The name's Legna." He dips his hands into his pockets.

"L-E-G-N-A—angel spelled backward. Cool."

"You're a natural at solving puzzles." He points toward the forgotten boy, and Legna's gaze begs me to do something. "What about him?"

"Does he need my help?"

"He needs somebody's help."

"Fine." I sigh then do what my mom and dad would do. I kneel beside the boy and whisper a prayer to the Almighty. "Protect him wherever his journey takes him." As my hand moves toward his raw flesh, my fingers tremble. Finally, I touch him, believing he is real.

His skin is ice-cold and clammy, but he's no longer a ghost—at least not by touch. Have I entered his world and left my own?

The boy glances at me.

His eyes—I gasp. His blanched facial features are still fuzzy, but now through clouds of fog, pale-blue irises luminesce in the darkness and bore a hole into my soul. Compassion rips my heart wide open. I promise him, "I'll pray for you."

"Follow me." Legna stands to leave the open-air prison of the blue-eyed boy and strolls through a flower garden.

"Should we abandon him?"

"You haven't."

"He's back there." I point over my shoulder. "By default, we've abandoned him."

"Being present doesn't always equal connection. Believe me. You're connected now, linked by a vow."

"I'm destined for a zombie?"

"Your spirit was dead once, and Yeshua rescued you from eternal death." Legna fingers the jewel at my neck. "Do you like it?"

"It's okay." I shrug.

"Seeing the boy's eyes gave you a glimpse into his soul. His reality. His future. He's your ally. A kindred spirit, one who will love you as you are and fight beside you . . . if he survives."

"Oily boy against Lucifer isn't a fair fight. Will he always look like this—pale, emaciated, and crawling with lice? Like a wraith?"

"Of course not, but his skin color won't change."

"That's a problem."

"Talk to your dad. Stop making quick assumptions."

"If oily boy dies, whose fault will it be?"

"Yours."

"That sucks. For the record, the butterfly, Ethan and Grandma Gertrude didn't fair that well in my charge."

"It was there time." Legna interlinks his fingers with mine. A warm effervescence tingles within my hand. His stride long with a masculine bounce, he walks back toward the sea. "Stay close."

"No complaints here." She smirks. "Who is Chi Xi Stigma— six-six-six?"

"That's cheating, asking an angel to take your test."

"I'm only a teenager trying to save Earth." Sarcasm laces my words.

"If I knew, I'd tell you. I'll tell you what I know. Look for symbols."

"Why symbols?"

"Humans respond to them without thinking. Leaders have controlled the masses for centuries with symbols: from a crucifix to a crescent moon, to the Star of David, to hate symbols, to a country's flag. What do you think about when you see an American flag waving?"

"Freedom and justice for all."

"How do you feel?"

"Proud. Grateful."

"You prove my point."

"Glad I'm predictable."

"Symbols stimulate human emotions, and most humans never think about why. After you enter the portal, sometimes you'll observe a world of the past or the future from a distance—you'll only be dreaming. You've already done this with Adelaide, your daughter."

"She's only a dream? She's not real?" My heart pounds inside my chest.

"She'll be yours one day—if you don't bend time incorrectly and create a different stream of reality. Other times you'll travel all the way into another human world of the past or the future."

"Like Gibeah?"

"You've got it. You solved the riddle of *when*, by the way. Congrats."

"Thanks. So the bottom line—the beginning of Tishri denotes when Yeshua will come back for his followers. Christians call this the rapture?"

"Correct. And the significance of the 2014–2015 blood moons?" Legna quizzes me.

"Starts the countdown before Chi Xi Stigma—six-six-six—the antichrist is revealed, makes peace with Israel, then switches sides and become Israel's worst nightmare. The antichrist is the last major entity that will seek to annihilate Elohim's chosen people and steal Jerusalem for himself."

"He'll be a political and a religious monster—the antichrist and his false prophet. Hitler will appear tame compared to Chi Xi Stigma."

A shutter quakes beneath my skin. "Will Christians be able to easily identify the antichrist, Legna?"

"Are you kidding me? Most professing Christians have never read the Bible. He'll promise them money, racial and national superiority, even world dominance, appealing to their human lust while concealing his identity. Judge his character, not his promises."

"I'm a nerd. I like to understand. Explain the mechanism of how I visit other worlds?"

"The science is based upon action potentials. Movement from the dimension of kairos time into the dimension of chronos time creates massive amounts of energy, which bends your reality."

"Kairos time?"

"Elohim's appointed times, His predetermined time. Like how He knew you would be born July 8, 1981."

"And chronos time means minutes and hours?"

"Yes. To Elohim, chronological time resembles a movie reel: the whole film has already been created, from beginning to end, but you and other humans only see one image at a time, like a projector shining light through picture frames, one by one, to create a story—your fourth dimension, time."

"Making that moment my present reality."

"I AM knows the whole story, from the beginning to the end. He already knows when everything will happen, so He sees events as being predestined—appointed—versus chronological, humanity's interpretation of past, present, and future."

"Got it. What's the worst that can happen as I travel?"

"The world collapses, erasing that period of time from history or the future. Years vanish, deleting and inserting people and events into the wrong times and thwarting your purpose for existing."

"My parents would never meet?" My mouth dries.

"You'd return an orphan—alone, without a family."

"I'm not losing my parents, not for a friend, my enemies, or humanity—okay?" I press my finger into his chest. It's harder than steel. I shrink back. He smiles.

"Then stay focused." He stops near the ocean and releases my hand. "You may not always see me, but I'm there. Watching your back. Fighting mortals and immortals alongside Yahweh, the King of the Fight." He reaches into his pocket. "For you." He drops a polished obsidian arrowhead into my shirt pocket and zips it. "Don't want you to lose it again."

"You stole Prince Jonathan's arrowhead?"

"You needed to prove your sanity using your wit. School bullies and the inquisitor won't be the last to call you crazy."

"But I'm not."

"No, you're not." He strokes my cheek. Cold waves lap my torso, grabbing me and pushing me further from the shore. I flail my arms, fighting a riptide.

"Fighting doesn't equal control." He swims after me, lifts me above the surf, and cradles me.

My heart flutters. I breathe in and out, anticipating the dunk and hating that his embrace will end.

"Danny Rose." His lips brush my ear. *Will my heart explode, projecting fragments of muscles into the sea?* "I'd hoped this detail wouldn't apply to you, but it does."

Boy, can he ruin the moment. "Spit it out, Legna." Water splashes my face. He slings me onto his back.

"Traveling will weaken your body and empower your spirit. You will die young."

"Just like that." I pause.

"Yes."

"Well, if the majority of people are going to call me crazy because of my mission, and loneliness or a zombie ghost will be my only companion, maybe an early exit won't be so bad. Besides, I'm not sure if I want to live when six-six-six has a say, but for now . . . the Glass Tattoo officially sucks!"

Resting my hand against his chest, I gaze across the ocean's horizon. Dusk settles over slate-gray waves capped in white foam. A dolphin plays in the sea.

"When your body dies, your spirit will join Yahweh. You'll never be alone in my Master's home . . . Rosebud."

"Ethan?"

Legna flips me onto my back. His hand bears down on my neck. I inhale. He pushes me under. At first, I kick and thrash—but fighting doesn't equal control.

I surrender.

54—Orphan Dreamer

GET REAL! DANIELA TIPTOED TO her parents' closed bedroom door. *A bosom friend—that's all I really need, not a handsome, kick-butt boyfriend who will protect me.*

Dream, Danny Rose.

At sixteen, a cute boyfriend would be nice. Daniela's entire being pulsed with heat, settling in places she'd never felt before. Flushed, she fanned her face as she arrived at the door, took a deep breath, and peeked inside.

Her mouth dried as she watched her mother dutifully hold a small wastebasket to her dad's face, collecting yet another round of vomit. *Had her dad been lying about the status of his chronic lymphocytic leukemia? Why?*

"Danny," her father called, his voice raspy and quiet.

"Dad," she said, more plea than statement.

"Did you travel? Did you find the arrowhead?"

"Yes. I met Legna. He returned the arrowhead."

"You're committed now."

"Scared senseless, but I am—committed." She tiptoed into the room as though he was asleep. It smelled of bleach and Pine-Sol. Her mother insisted on cleanliness. Caring little of her destiny at that moment, she challenged her father. "I thought you were better."

"Ups and downs." He smiled, and she gingerly kissed his forehead. "What's wrong?" Chemotherapy had sandpapered his throat raw, leaving crackles and static. Grandma's old red-and-blue quilt shielded her father's thin frame—evidence of an ill-matched war between leukemia and the rest of the cells that dared to survive within his bone marrow.

"You lied to me."

"No—I'd never lie. It's the nature of the CLL, my cancer."

"I'm scared for you," she said so quietly that her parents didn't hear her.

"What did you say?" her mother asked.

"I'm scared."

"We're all frightened sometimes." Her mother tapped the foot of the bed. "Sit down." Slick beads of fever dotted her father's face as he clenched his jaw and attempted to hide the wave of pain still shining within his coal-black eyes.

The eyes never lie—even when the lie has been told to protect the listener.

The corners of Daniela's lips curved into a forced smile. Another lie. Her eyes belied the attempt at brave happiness as she watched her mother interlace her fingers with her husband's. Lack of sleep had plowed deep lines into her mahogany brow. What would Daniela do if her rafiki died too?

"Tell us about your travels," her father said.

"I saw his eyes," Daniela said, never taking her gaze from the floor.

"You've never seen his eyes before," her father said.

"Only milky gelatinous blobs."

"And?" her mother prodded.

"They spoke to me." Daniela rubbed her right earlobe between her thumb and forefinger, something she did when she was beyond nervous. A Cherokee leader once told Daniela that when a person looks into another person's eyes, their souls speak to each other, making an agreement to hate or love. If they choose to love, their souls are bound together forever even during life's roughest storms.

"What did they say to you?" Her dad smiled, holding on to every morsel of Daniela's story.

"Believe in me. Love me. Stay with me."

"That changes things." Mrs. Cavanaugh's smile vanished. "Your commitment to him must be unshakable. You must help him, Danny Rose."

"I want to . . . but what if I fail?"

"You won't. No more apathy," her dad said. "Be consistent in your prayers. The prayers of a righteous person accomplishes much." Her father's cheeks appeared less gaunt. Peace lingered where pain should've been. "Will you stay with him?"

"How could I? Wherever he exists, he doesn't live near me," Daniela whispered. "Dad . . . Mom . . . does it bother ya'll that I'm dreaming of a tormented dead boy while my classmates are day-dreaming of Tommy, our school football star?"

"Don't judge individual puzzle pieces. When the Almighty completes your picture, you'll know what's right with it."

"He works from eternity backward," her mother added. "Your dreams about oily boy will become clear—maybe even real."

"The deceiver creates nothing, but perverts everything." Her dad winked. "Stop judging yourself by others' standards. Every oyster hides within a shell—your jocks and cheerleaders—but not every oyster conceals a priceless pearl, the undiscovered ones like you."

"I've never seen an oyster or a pearl, and after last night, I'm so tired of the ocean. I don't want to be near water unless I'm drinking it." Her parents laughed. "Wasn't trying to make a joke."

"The ocean's not tired of you, comedy-girl," her dad said. "You're Yahweh's pearl, entrusted with a mission before your mom and I conceived you."

"Conception again! Gross." Daniela's face warmed at the thought of the necessary mechanics for conception. She'd never been kissed on the lips, much less been naked in front of a boy. Sure, she had pecked Ethan on the cheek before he died, but that wasn't the same. And she'd been fully dressed.

Would she be afraid when the time came? Would her nose start bleeding? Was the zombie the best she could do—her dream date?

More flight of ideas.

Exhausting.

She told her parents about Legna, his confirmation of the fact that the madman—the antichrist—would start his rise to power after the 2014–2015 blood moons, that Yeshua's followers would be raptured near or on the date of a future Feast of Trumpets, and that they would tabernacle with Yahweh during the Feast of Tabernacles—Sukkot—while Armageddon collided with Earth. She left out the gruesome parts: oily boy's appearance, the spike in his hand.

No need to freak them out.

Maybe his injured appearance was metaphorical and not real?

Daniela hoped so.

Shivering, she held her father's hand. His hands shook, and Daniela's cold, clammy fingers slipped. She gripped his hands with all her might as though her inability to maintain her grip bore a deep psychological meaning—that she was losing her grip on reality, and her dad was losing his grip on life. "Go to bed. You fly to New Mexico in the morning," her dad said.

"I've decided. I'm not going. You're sick again."

"And waste the scholarship money? How many other kids would've loved to earn your spot? You're going. That's final."

"Yes, sir." She stopped in the doorway. "Dad. Mom." She paused.

"Tell us."

"His eyes—they saw me."

"What?" Her mom asked.

"I get it." Her dad reached for her mom's hand. "Eyes that look are a dime a dozen, but eyes that see . . . they are priceless—rare. That's how your mom's eyes look at me." Jeanette kissed Austin on the lips.

"Thank you, Rafiki." A second later, a cold wave crashed over the warmth growing on the inside of her soul. She looked up at her dad, finally seeing him. Understanding his pain. The shame and wounds inflicted by Jim Crow—a.k.a America's terrorist of the South. "Daddy, I have a question."

"You sound serious."

"I am."

"Shoot."

"To kill?"

"You're not a muderess."

"You told me not to abandon oily boy . . . but what if he's all cream—no coffee?"

Her dad fell back into his bed as though Daniela had blown a hole into his gut with a shotgun. Seconds lapsed into a full minute.

Had she murdered her father, too? She rested her hand on his chest. Rhythmically, his chest lifted, then recoiled.

The lapse of time could devour a kid's last scraps of courage. She rained sweat. His Adam's apple rose and fell four times before he spoke. "Dr. King told us, 'I have a dream that my four little children will one day live in a nation where they will not be judged by the color of their skin but by the content of their character.' If oily boy's the one who will love you as you are—your kindred spirit—as Yahweh wills."

"That's it?"

"That's everything. Your mom and I won't live forever."

"Thank you." Daniela kissed him. Now . . . did she want to kiss oily boy or Legna?

Legna!

A nightlight cast a swath of yellow across her bed as Daniela wiped sleep from her eyes. Her grandmother's patchwork quilt lay on the floor atop a green shag carpet. Sitting up, she reached for her journal and opened it.

Dark liquid dripped from her nose and pooled across the fresh page. With the corner of her bedsheet, she staunched the nosebleed. Another load of laundry in the morning. Holding the cloth to her nose, she fanned through old journal entries and noted dried splotches of blood—reminders of oily boy's suffering and her humiliation.

We are not victims!

She stood straight, shifting any vested energy from pity to power—power for her mission, her education, and even her future loves. Then, she looked at her reflection within the dresser's mirror and whispered a promise, "Danny Rose, you won't die alone or a virgin. Promise." Even the Virgin Mary didn't die before knowing a man's love.

I think assassins are sexy. Claire's words as they faced off in front of Tommy four years ago ran through Daniela's mind. She thought of Legna throwing balls of fire. A warm, firm touch. Daniela grinned. "So do I, Claire. Let's see who can find one first." Not a guy who had actually killed a person. Just a guy who could kill—if he was forced to.

"Yahweh, make oily boy strong, so he can punish the bad guys." But in reality, her zombie was frail, hardly a punisher.

Another drop of blood stained her journal.

She flipped to a new page and wrote the details of her dream, ending her entry with these words: *This nightmarish adventure wasn't the first and won't be the last. But I must find oily boy. Meet him. Give him a chance—and hopefully, solve a lot of puzzles with that sexy angel.*

Legna's eyes were magical, almost otherworldly.

Cautiously, she looked up at the door, then crossed the word sexy out. What would her parents think—what would Legna think? Would he appreciate a girl like Daniela crushing on him? Her skin tingled with anticipation.

Dabbing her bloodied nose with a tissue, she bit her lower lip and scanned the room, making sure the mysterious runner hadn't crossed over into her world to notice the blush that surely blossomed on her cheeks.

Would Daniela give her first real kiss to . . . Legna? She grinned wide. Oily boy? Her smile evaporated.

It was a fact: she possessed a knack for kissing almost-dead boys.

She flipped to the front of her journal and traced the outlines of Ethan's photograph that was taped there. "Keep on running." She fingered the Glass Tattoo diamond and remembered his words—*live for me.* "For you, Ethan."

Daniela peeked at her clock—01:21 a.m.—and then slid under her covers, packed and ready to fly to New Mexico in the morning.

55—ORPHAN DREAMER

HEART RACING, DANIELA EXITED THE plane at Albuquerque, New Mexico's airport.

She strolled into the airport terminal.

Nondescript beige walls lined the never-ending walkway out of the airport. She slung her backpack onto her shoulder, then unfolded a crinkled piece of paper before searching for a phone booth.

At the phone booth, suits strolled past, pulling suitcases, while Daniela kept an eye out for Emmaline Georgiana Winterlyn Darbyshire, a girl with too many first names who had promised to wear an emerald green scarf and an ivory cowgirl hat. She had arrived yesterday from Boston and was picking up Daniela at the airport.

Daniela and Emmaline had spoken on the phone once; the words flowed easily. They talked for hours.

Emmaline intended to study weapons engineering at MIT part-time—and boys full-time. The boy-crazy dual-enrolled high-school senior and college sophomore had promised to pick Daniela up at the airport, then room with her in the dorms at Los Alamos National Laboratory (LANL), where they would conduct a semester-long research project.

They would both graduate two years early from high school, and in two years, Emmaline planned to graduate with her four-year degree and matriculate into a highly coveted graduate program at the Air Force Institute of Technology—a master's-level program that lasted for six academic quarters, teaching bright students nuclear, biological, and chemical weapons technology.

Hopefully, Daniela would be accepted into the University of Florida's College of Medicine's Junior Honors Program.

Studies aside, one question haunted Daniela: Was Emmaline the one, her Anne of Green Gables?

Daniela found a pay phone, dropped a coin into the coin slot, and dialed. The phone rang. "Dad?"

"You're safe."

"Can't talk long." She tapped her foot. "Emmaline's arriving soon." She looked up and spotted the cowgirl hat, then gasped. "Gosh, Dad. She's gorgeous!"

"And so are you."

"Not like this, Daddy."

"May I make a suggestion, Danny-girl?" Usually he just gave his opinions, but she was growing up and young ladies who behaved like grown-ups earned respect.

"Please do." She faced the phone, turning her back to the approaching girl.

"Be your own person. Don't be so excited to meet someone new that you lose yourself, compare yourself, and become a side story in your own book."

"I'll try, but I'd be happy to be the table of contents—necessary but unnoticeably boring."

"Have fun, Danny-girl. Don't make any decisions that will haunt you for a lifetime."

"Got it." Daniela jerked forward. *What was that?*

"Hi, Doc." Someone hugged Daniela from the back. "It's me, Emmaline. Thought you could use a hug."

Daniela turned. "Gotta go, Dad."

The redhead. "Finish up on the phone, I'll give you some privacy."

"Okay." Daniela gasped. "Dad!"

"What's wrong?"

"Nothing." Her voice broke. "Everything's so right. She has red hair!"

Daniela's heart fluttered, and her dad laughed. "So, Danny Rose. Dreams do come true."

"Life's going my way."

"Maybe you got out of the way of life, Danny-girl. I'll be near the phone. Your mother sends her love. Call me when you arrive in Los Alamos. Tell Emmaline hello."

"My dad says hello."

"Hi, Dad." Emmaline leaned toward the phone.

Daniela's excitement charged through her body. "I've got to pee!"

"Don't pee in the girl's car. Grab your luggage, empty your bladder, then have some fun. Love you."

"Love you more." Daniela hung up the phone and stared at Emmaline.

She inhaled and forgot to exhale. The bathroom would have to wait. Deep red hair—the same hue as the North Carolina autumn leaves splattered around her late grandmother's farm—bounced around Emmaline's bare, porcelain-white shoulders. She wore stone-washed flared jeans and a white tank top beneath her green scarf. Playfulness danced beyond her green eyes.

Daniela had rehearsed her introduction in her mind. During their previous phone conversation, Emmaline had talked and Daniela had listened.

Hi, my name's Daniela Rose Cavanaugh, but my friends call me Danny Rose. I like archery, libraries, archeology, art history, lemonade, and collard greens. Emmaline would reply, *So do I, and I've been looking for you from the moment I took my first breath. Can we be best friends forever?*

Daniela sighed.

Ugh.

Totally dumb.

Act normal.

Her hands slicked with sweat.

"Hello. We finally meet." Emmaline stood in front of the nervous, mute, dual-enrolled high school senior and college sophomore and smiled. Perfect straight white teeth sparkled behind her well-formed, rose-pink lips. "I'm Emmaline. My friends call me Limy." Emmaline's elegant persona echoed her proper English accent.

"I-I-I'm Daniela Rose. I-I-I mean Danny Rose. Actually, my friends—no, my friend, Ethan. The dead one—the one I killed. No. I didn't kill him, just thought I did." Her voiced dropped two octaves. "He called me Rosebud." Daniela sponged moisture from her hands onto her sweatpants and then extended her hand. The girls shook hands.

"Pleasure to meet you. Just call me Limy." She winked. "You hungry, Danny Rose?"

"No, I ate a sandwich on the plane. Where are you from?" She blurted out her question a little too eagerly, then slid the back of her pointer finger above her lip, making sure her nose hadn't started bleeding.

"Originally?" Emmaline asked.

"Before the dawn of time." Daniela removed her oversized teal suitcase from the conveyor belt.

"A primordial blob—I guess."

"You believe in . . . evolution."

"I guess."

"Oh."

"Guess you don't. I'm not hard-core either way. My mother's family hails from Scotland and my father's side is related to the English royals."

"Should I call you Your Majesty?" Daniela studied her subject. If she had to curtsy, how could they ever be friends?

Dumb question.

Act normal.

"Save that for the queen. Your Highness will do." Emmaline's face didn't show a hint of emotion. Daniela straightened, her dreams of finding a kindred spirit crumbling to bits. She wasn't royalty, unless being called ghetto princess by Harry and living on the wrong side of the tracks earned her a title as well.

"Just teasing." Emmaline wrapped her freckled forearm around Daniela's waist. "I don't doubt that we will get along as old chums."

"Promise?"

Emmaline extended her fifth finger, and Daniela hooked it with her own, making a finger vow as though Emmaline had performed the gesture a thousand times before. Emmaline grabbed Daniela's bag.

"I was afraid to ask before," Daniela reached for Emmaline's arm. "A West Point dropout?"

"That's me." Emmaline winked and kept walking. "Didn't like the uniforms—stormy gray, garnet, and wedding-dress white. Didn't look good on gingers." She grinned wide, yet crooked—mischief hidden just beyond the corners of her lips. Daniela cocked her head to the right.

"Just joking, Danny-girl." She jogged ahead. Stopped. Then faced Daniela. "It was HOCM."

"Hypertrophic cardiomyopathy." Daniela clasped the front of her shirt.

"Doctor Cavanaugh. And you haven't even attended med school."

"I read about it. The disease kills young athletes all the time." Daniela's smile faded. A run. An adventure. All could increase Emmaline's heart rate. Would Daniela's newest candidate for a kindred spirit suddenly drop dead?

"Don't worry. A Harvard cardiac surgeon fixed me." Emmaline yanked down the top of her T-shirt. A bright white line dipped down between her chest, seeming to travel for miles.

"Open heart surgery?" Daniela thought of her own scar.

"Off the bucket list." Emmaline shot me a grin. "So . . . what's your boyfriend's name?"

"I'm only sixteen!"

"So?"

"It's my dad's rule—I'm not allowed to date."

"So?"

"My parents care about my future, so I listen to them." After Daniela made a pit stop, they walked out of the airport into Albuquerque's chilly January weather. Not one goosebump sprouted up on Emmaline's bare arms.

"So medieval. Do you live in a stone castle beyond a moat?" Giggling, Emmaline pulled away and ran ahead. "I'm sixteen, and I'm dating my third boyfriend. Why can't you have a boyfriend?"

"Why does a girl ask another girl about their relationship status as soon as they meet? Do you have a communicable disease, hairy legs, or have periods?"

"Yes to all three." Emmaline's eyes twinkled, and Daniela stopped in the middle of the busy road.

"Really?" A car horn sounded.

"Get out of the street. Loosen up. I'm kidding. Girls are notoriously catty and nosy, but that's not why I'm asking." She jogged toward the parking lot. Daniela followed. "Life's short, Rosebud. Make each day count."

"That's so *90210*."

"Good comeback." Emmaline gave a thumbs-up. "More *Titanic* than *90210*. Have you seen the movie?"

"Yes—three times." Danny felt warmth flooding her cheeks. "It was the first movie I saw in a real movie theater."

"Did your parents force you into a cult: can't date, don't go to the movies?"

"No. That's weird."

"Leo's a dream." Emmaline flashed a Princess Di smile—eyes down, lips smiling. "Have you traveled before?"

"I won a scholarship to participate in an archeological dig in Israel next summer."

"What will you do there?"

Daniela laughed. "Schlep to the Middle East and work with a really cool instructor, Professor Jakob, my best friend's uncle."

"Will you sleep with him?"

"No! He's married. Besides, he has a big belly."

"I'd sleep with a married man—if he was hot and rich. Note to self: find a guy for Danny Rose, preferable one who's not ten months pregnant."

"Ugh. Why are you so boy crazy?"

"I'm normal, Danny, but suit yourself."

"Professor Jakob is raising money for another dig."

"What's he digging for—gold?" Emmaline asked, and Daniela burst out laughing.

"We'll be searching for a blueprint."

"Hire an architect. It's cheaper. Less dangerous."

"You're impossible." Daniela was keen on Emmaline, so she whispered a prayer. "Don't let her break my heart."

Emmaline found her vehicle and piled Daniela's bags into the back of the navy-blue Jeep Cherokee, alongside her own bag.

"That's a Louis Vuitton."

"It's the only way to travel. Who knows, I may cross paths with an oil tycoon, and what would he think if I carried generic luggage like yours?" She pointed at the cheap nylon suitcase and carry-on bag. "At least yours match. That's a start."

"He'll think you're high maintenance." Daniela giggled.

"I am."

"I love your honesty. FYI: The attendants throw the luggage on the carts. They're not exactly gentle with it."

"And that's why I fly private or drive. Water attracts water. Oil attracts oil. Rich attracts rich. Poor attracts poor."

"I'm not really rich; I can't fake my reality."

"Cinderella's story is fiction. I'm trying to boost your chances of attracting a man who can take care of you. Change of topic. How does a sixteen-year-old start med school next year?"

"They haven't accepted me yet. I'll find out this summer."

"Only seventeen when you start?"

"I skipped a grade in elementary school and then another grade in middle school, so when I entered high school, I was two years younger than my classmates."

"The rise of the nerds." Lauren keyed the ignition. "Glad to meet another one. And college?"

"Mom and Dad are poor—remember? So I dual-enrolled and completed my first two years of college during high school."

"You're efficient. I'll give you that."

"More like motivated. I don't have a trust-fund blanket to fall back on. If the Junior Honors program at the University of Florida's Medical School accepts my application this year, I'll attend the program in the fall and start my first year of medical school a year from now."

"Holy Holyrood smokes."

"Holyrood Palace—the official residence of the British monarch in Scotland!" Sounding more like an encyclopedia than a sixteen-year-old girl, Daniela wrapped her fingers around Emmaline's arm as though she were a starving bald eagle and Emmaline's arm was an unfortunate mouse. "Have you been?"

"Oh of course—my father's family summers there." She flicked her long red locks over her shoulder and shrugged. "It's nothing special." Emmaline flashed another Princess Di smile and twirled her hair. "There *is* an ancient mystery, though."

"Really?" Daniela squeezed harder.

"The ghost of dead twin boys is rumored to roam the hallways at night."

"Ugh." She released the highbred girl's arm, leaving red marks. "I possess my own ghost—oily boy."

"Weird name."

"You're telling me. Anyway, I have enough ghosts of my own."

She thought of her lack of prayers. Why was apathy so much easier than purposeful awareness? Because prayer required inertia, hope, sacrifice, and commitment.

Focus on being normal.

Her Anne with an *e* was sitting in front of her. She'd pray for the boy tonight.

"If you change your mind, we're leaving the first week of July."

"Awesome! Thanks." Daniela hugged Emmaline.

Serious and silly girlish conversations peppered their drive. Emmaline sped without stopping. Brakes screeched as she parked crooked in front of old army barracks that had been converted into student apartments.

With numb fingers and blanched nail beds, Daniela released her grip from the door handle. She fought to swallow, but all moisture had left her mouth when Emmaline careened around the first switchback winding up the Jemez Mountains.

Be polite.

"Thanks for driving."

"I love driving." Emmaline reapplied her lipstick. "Wanted to be a racecar driver."

"What stopped you—the brakes?" They laughed.

After checking in with the apartment manager, Daniela inserted her key in the lock. Down the hallway, a shadow shifted and keys rattled. "Spooky." She shoulder-bumped the stubborn door open.

"This lock needs oil." Emmaline followed, escaping whatever was lurking down the hallway. Daniela locked the door, slung her large suitcase on the couch, and unzipped it. This would be her new home, lodging with an open and honest posh girl.

Daniela was ready for the adventure.

56—The Orphan (PG 13)

Monday, March 16, 1998
India

IF WEBSTER'S DICTIONARY DEFINED *RIGHT* as moral integrity, Cillian's customers had taught him that the customer was not always right and hadn't been for the last two years.

The sixteen-year-old's last customer, a corpulent man whose flesh soured of stale beef and beer, departed ten minutes late. A vase of yellow roses had been a substitute for a tip, but the fat man would not leave the palace without paying Bushcroft.

Try stiffing him; hell hath no fury.

Money mattered little. Cillian wasn't allowed to keep the payments—at least the flowers reminded him of Mama Kelley's garden. He would water them until the petals dried up and died like the others.

He nestled his nose between soft yellow velvet, then inhaled.

But the stench of stale ale and beef lingered on his smooth, shaven face, assaulting his nose once more.

Dressed in a black silk robe, he limped to the washbasin. Larry—as the man called himself—had, as usual, roughed the lad up as though he were a male bear in heat and Cillian was his sow. Feeling hot and clammy, Cillian doused his face with tepid water, then rinsed his mouth, hoping to remove the taste of the pervert.

Beneath a hot shower, Cillian massaged his shoulders, kneading muscles the married man's calloused hands had bruised.

Cillian wrapped a towel around his six-foot-three, lanky frame, glancing at a bronze clock that ticked forward to his next humiliation. Lunch, then back to work. He rubbed his tired feet across plush sandstone carpets as he returned to his "office chair"—a creaky bed draped in cobalt silk sheets—and lay down.

Food could wait.

Pistachio-and-beige paisley wallpaper clung to the room's walls and ceiling, making it seem more claustrophobic. Cold air blew from an air conditioner mounted high on the wall, drying his drenched, bone-straight locks.

He closed his eyes and imagined that he lay on carpets of soft grass beneath a high-noon sun. Pallid cheeks made sallow by a lack of sun exposure reminded him that he needed sun. He returned to the window, as he had five times in the last seven hours.

Had his view changed?

He pushed garnet velvet drapes back and stared at the redbrick wall that substituted as his window.

Light refused to penetrate the abyss.

How could it? Hell coveted darkness, and Hades's master, Asher Bushcroft, had proven to be a man of his word. The first day of business, the first, second, and third customers—businessmen and laborers of all nationalities—came and went to the compound where the boys lived.

A week later, the demands for the pale boy with raven black hair and luminescent blue eyes had soared, so Bushcroft's men took Cillian to the brothel rooms with velvet curtains and silk sheets for high-paying customers.

These days, he found himself at the brothel rather often, and his popularity bought him two personal guards.

Bushcroft's one-year anniversary gift, an ornate mirror—purposefully broken, then put back together to create a mosaic pattern—leaned against a corner wall. But for over a year, the orphan had refused to view his own reflection.

Would his evil deeds show in his eyes?

Cillian watched his hands tremble, followed by his arms and shoulders, until a cold sweat reached his toes.

Face yourself.

Inhaling deeply, he stood up. *Do it.* One foot in front of the other, he forced himself toward the mirror.

Head down, he waited.

His body, mind, and spirit had broken two years ago, when the customers had crushed his heart to satisfy their perverted sensual whims. Only a boy, he cried the first and second times. But soon his tears hardened to anger. Anger to numbness. Numbness to hopelessness. No life remained within his spirit.

His heart had hardened to a block of ice, and icy hearts allowed a man do anything, even murder.

One miracle transpired, though: Paul had never experienced Cillian's shame or seen him in the act of it. Never included in the initial work roster, Paul hadn't existed.

Eight weeks after the whole ordeal had begun and his body mended from the brandings, Cillian learned of a kindly woman who served as Bushcroft's seamstress. She believed in the same God Mama Kelley and Grandma and Grandpa Barry had believed in—Yeshua. Surely, God didn't dirty His perfect feet to walk in places like Cillian's home, the brothel, but outside, Cillian hoped He would keep Paul safe. Like a shepherd tended to his sheep.

Cillian had met the kindly lady at the brothel when she fitted him for his fancy clothing—a tuxedo with a white tie.

The next day, he returned to the camp.

Before the sun rose, she hid at the edge of camp, and Cillian snuck Paul outside to her.

The orphan hadn't known if he would see his brother again, so he had wrung the last drops of humanity from his bleeding heart that early morning by telling Paul the only two stories Cillian knew. "Tell me the one about Daniel and the lions' den," Paul had asked while leaning on Cillian's shoulder.

While looking into pools of apple-green purity, Cillian recited the story. "Grandma Barry said that Daniel chose virtue and feared Yahweh . . ."

"Cillian, why can't I stay with you? I hate the idea of going away."

"I gave you bread and fruit to eat while ye wait for me. Why am

I workin' my hands raw if I canna send you away to a good, safe place?" He tousled his little brother's hair.

"I just combed my hair."

"Comb it again."

"I'd rather be with you than spend your money. Why can't we leave, like we did from the orphanage?"

"Aye, I canna be escapin' again. This old pirate is a wee bit tired."

"I'll make the plans."

"Not this time." Cillian stared at his brother's face, committing every detail to memory. Inside a cell that no dog should live in, his final solution evolved in his desperate mind. "You're better off without me."

"No. I'm not." Paul's lower lip trembled, and liquid pooled onto his blond lashes. Cillian's joy had been remembering his brother's innocent eyes. Maintaining Paul's innocence had been his accomplishment—his legacy.

"I'll miss you."

"Please come. You promised you would never abandon me."

"I've tried to be keepin' my promise." Cillian hugged Paul as he protested, "I cannae come wi' ye now."

"When?"

"I dinnaa ken." He squeezed tighter.

"Cil, I can't breathe."

With that, he released his brother and gave him the only escape he could afford—an old woman's home in the slums of a foreign land. "It isna a fine boardin' school, but she'll take care of you. Listen. Complete your studies." Mrs. Moorjani's lean-to was no palace, but compared to the concrete prison, Paul's situation would improve.

As he looked up to see his reflection for the first time in two years, he painted happy images in his mind about his duties at the brothel—a private air-conditioned room, good food.

He opened the silk robe and glared at his reflection. Saying nothing, emotion lodged in his throat. Liquid pooled on his black lashes. His reflection, cut up by shattered glass, resembled the body of a monster.

Virtue had been stripped from his eyes.

Accept it.

He forced himself to look for a while longer.

A sneer curled his upper lip. He tightened his jaw and looked away, then dressed in a black tuxedo and polished shoes before leaving the room and looking for Mrs. Moorjani, as he always did before lunch. The slight Indian woman walked straight toward him with an armful of cloth.

"Mrs. Moorjani, how's Paul?" His voice was a desperate whisper.

"He's well, turned fourteen. Tall. Handsome. A fine young man."

Cillian's gaze locked with hers as he absorbed each letter, word, and sentence. "Is he mindin' ye, then?"

"He's charming. Obedient." She smiled. "And as smart as an elephant."

"I love him. Will ye be tellin' him that?"

"I will."

Cillian reached inside a paper bag. "Give him this apple for a birthday present. Tell him to eat it slowly and remember me."

"He'll ask me what you're eating." She stuffed the fruit into her pocket.

"Bacon, eggs, and toast every morning." His lips raised in a half smile. "Keep him safe, and if I ever make enough money from tips here, ye'll be sendin' him to America for me. D'ye understand?"

"He won't leave you here." She looked over her shoulder.

"He'll leave . . . if I'm dead." Cillian shared his plan with the gentle lady. When he finished speaking, a look of shock contorted her already wrinkled face, and she backed away.

Her eyes watered, pleading with Cillian. "Please don't." A guard walked over to eavesdrop. Not wanting to cause trouble for the old woman, Cillian walked back to his room, closed the door, and waited.

His appetite had vanished into a pit of despair.

Instead of another customer, Scarface slammed open the door.

Cillian jumped to his feet. Memories of his mother's boyfriend pushing the door back and pounding on his childish body flooded his mind. His breath raced, and he stuffed his hands in his pants pockets, rubbing the coin Grandpa Barry gave him.

"You're going back to camp."

"Why?"

"The boss thinks you're getting too familiar with the luxury; you keep talking to the old woman instead of focusing on your work."

"I was eatin' a bit of lunch, and I try to be kind to everyone."

"Rules are rules."

"I've done no wrong."

"Don't you know, boy?"

"Know what?"

"You were born, Cillian, and you should curse your mother for pushing you from between her wretched legs. She should've left you to die on the rocks. That would have been mercy."

Cillian stepped backward. The past and the present collided, yanking at the last bit of his sanity. Dizzy, he swayed as Scarface's poisoned words pierced his heart.

"Since you're here, you'll service me once more today." Scarface loosened his belt. The sound of metal clanking told Cillian everything he needed to know—he was a slave, and slaves had masters.

Scarface was one of those.

"Face the mirror." He pushed the slave over a chair that happened to be right in front of the mosaic mirror.

Jaw taut, Cillian glared at his reflection and the reflection of his master—despising them both while ignoring the pain. *Whoever hates his brother is a murderer, and you know that no murderer has eternal life abiding in him.* Mama Kelley's words haunted him. Cillian didn't want to live, much less live for eternity. If she was right, hell's hungry jaws waited at the end of Cillian's journey, but Scarface and Cillian were not brothers, so he allowed the hatred to set his blood boiling.

Scarface finished, then left.

The edges of Cillian's soft mouth had hardened into a sneer. He didn't need a mirror to see the disgust and pure hatred hidden in the corners of his lips. "If death refuses to embrace me, and I live . . . you're dead, Scarface. So is your boss." His words came out as whispers—he didn't know if he could keep his promises of retribution.

You will never understand the damage you did to someone until the same thing is done to you.

—Karma

#IamCillian—Karma in the Flesh

57—THE ORPHAN

IN THE QUIETNESS OF CILLIAN'S room, Scarface tied the sex slave's hands with ropes before dragging him outside and securing him in the bed of a military truck.

"I'm not tryin' to escape."

"Not taking any chances." Scarface added knots to the ropes and glanced up at his captive. "You look different."

"Do I, then?" Cillian dared to look the man straight in the face.

"Calm. Angry. Doesn't matter. Nothing's changing for you." Scarface yanked the fifth knot tight. "My father was a seafaring man, taught me all types of knots. I'd hate to think I forgot one."

"I dinnae ken my father." Cillian made conversation, attempting to hide the hatred brewing behind his eyes.

"You're the lucky one. Mine was a mean one with the strap, take the skin clear off your hide. No reason."

"That's yer excuse?" Cillian smiled, lathering on another layer of fake kindness.

"Do I need one?" He stopped mid-knot.

"Indeed, ye dinna."

"Smart boy." The evil man left his charge in the back of the truck and jumped into the passenger seat. The vehicle bumped along back roads until they arrived at the camp. On the way to the cells, Scarface walked in front. Sweltering heat intensified the pungent smells of urine, sweat, and blood. Cillian's legs almost buckled from the fetid stench.

"Get in." Scarface forced the orphan into a hut. Cillian ducked, then sat on his concrete slab.

"I'll be back after dinner," Scarface barked. "Wash the scent off from the others. You stink." Cillian looked away from his rapist. "Answer me, boy. I ain't like my dad, I don't wanna whip you, and you ain't as good when you're hurtin'."

"I've been hurtin' for as long as I can remember."

"Don't go psychological on me." Scarface exited the cell. "Your world's gonna change, and you'll not thank me. For starters, no more posh hotel. Time to sweat, boy." Death would be a welcome change. Liquid pooled on Cillian's eyelashes. "Don't you cry. Take your punishment like a man. You ain't a boy anymore."

"Then, ye'll kindly stop calling me *boy*." Scarface stormed back into the cell and punched Cillian in the face.

Dazed, with blood running from his lip, Cillian glared at the hard, gray sky beyond the door to his hut as Scarface left. He recalled living with Mama Kelley, longing to become a man so he could care for them both.

As a boy, he had no idea the hell manhood could breathe down on the shoulders of a sixteen-year-old boy.

Mama Kelley had said, "Pain was for hammering out the flaws, turning a boy into a man—a man fit to handle his snowflake—a kind, wise young lady—with care."

He had dreamed of a girl with skin as brown as Mama Kelley's. Was that girl in the dream his intended snowflake? If so, where was she? Cillian could use a kind girl, willing to protect his heart, refusing to let it bleed anymore.

Maybe an orphan's heart was meant to bleed.

"If you're there . . ." He glanced at the ceiling. "I cannae wake up to this life even one more day. Kill me or rescue me."

Cramps from dehydration gripped his body, shaking him violently. He had chosen not to drink water for two full days.

Death would be painful, but certain.

He rubbed his fingers across the barcode branded inside his right arm, beneath his armpit—then he lay down, resigned to surrender to the dark void sucking at his soul, hoping his end would arrive before the brute returned for another round.

If Cillian had known his ending, how would he have lived his beginning?

He would've refused to gasp for his first breath. Masters were allowed to make mistakes and be forgiven, but not slaves. He begged to sleep, but he didn't want to dream—ever. His life was already a nightmare. Closing his eyes, he prayed for death.

Was there a wee drop of water left in the world that could be quenchin' an orphan's hellish thirst?

58—ORPHAN DREAMER

WITH EMMALINE CLOSE ON HER heels, Daniela stepped inside the studio apartment and held her breath, her brain processing a litany of questions and answers: *Why haven't you prayed for oily boy?* The process of praying for a person Daniela had never met was exhausting, fantastical—a fairy tale. *Don't you think you're being selfish?* Not really. Daniela prayed for Emmaline every night. *What about the Glass Tattoo?*

What about it?

The relic could take care of itself.

Just inside the door, she soaked in the view beyond a large bank of windows—the Jemez Mountains. The mountains' raw beauty purged any remaining guilt. "That's a mountain to explore, Limy."

"An easy place to fall in love—hunks, cowboy hats, and torrid romances."

"We're not in a western, Emmaline."

"You may be a sexless, I'm-not-allowed-to-date double-X chromosome, but I'm a hot-blooded British-American girl. Giddyap." She tossed her cowgirl hat to Daniela. Emmaline climbed on the top bunk bed. "I'm exhausted. My research mentor was brutal today. 'Fix these specimens. Pour another hydrogel. Run this assay. Review those slides with the electron microscope.'"

"That's why we're here, to conduct research. Besides, only nerds refer to a girl as a double-X chromosome." Daniela set the hat on the deep windowsill.

Emmaline lay on her stomach, facing the foot of the bunk bed. "Only nerds know what I mean by it." Her voice changed into a contemplative tone. "My name is Emmaline Georgiana Winterlyn Darbyshire, and I am a hopeless nerd."

"With three first names, I'd agree. But that's why makes you deliciously marvelous."

"Did you skip lunch?"

"Didn't have time."

"Don't eat me. Let's order pizza."

The two girls talked through the night, taking a break to order pizza and eat dinner, then later ate cold pizza for a midnight snack. Daniela shared her dreams about oily boy and the letter had written to Adelaide. Emmaline told Daniela about her dying brother. They both cried and laughed until their sides ached. Emmaline climbed down from her upper bunk and lay on the lower bunk beside Daniela, cuddling up beside her.

Emmaline was the friendly one.

But Daniela's bones ached to receive love from someone other than her parents—a stranger who chose to love and accept her nosebleeds, big hair, and all. Maybe she would meet another Ethan in this rugged place, and this time she would kiss him on the lips.

"How does it feel to French kiss a boy?" Daniela blurted out, then slapped her hand to her mouth.

Slack-jawed, Emmaline pried the naïve girl's hand from her face. "You mean you've really never done it?"

Daniela shook her head, then, uncharacteristic of her personality, she made herself vulnerable and shared her feelings with a stranger. "I . . . pecked my dying friend's cheek before he croaked."

"Morbid." Emmaline cocked her head to the side. "But Jack-and-Rose-I'll-never-let-go romantic."

"*Titanic*'s fiction." Daniela averted her gaze. "My reality's . . . complicated. I have nosebleeds." She glanced at Emmaline. "I-I-I'm not contagious, but they're inconvenient. Embarrassing. What if I start bleeding while I'm kissing a hot guy—not that any hot guy would kiss me?" Slowly, she looked into Emmaline's eyes. "Do you think I'm gross?"

"Have tissue, will travel." Emmaline reached for Danny Rose's hand.

"That's it?"

"That's all, partner." Had a dozen fireworks exploded inside Daniela's chest? Was she falling in platonic love with her long-lost kindred spirit?

"So, how does a French kiss feel?"

A smile full of wonder played across Emmaline's dainty, aristocratic English features. "Kissing feels like sticking your tongue inside a rose at the beginning of dawn—mysteriously soft, cool and warm, sweet and wet all at the same time." Emmaline flipped onto her back. "You feel tingly all over . . . in places you never knew you could feel."

"The same as when your foot falls asleep?"

"No." She laughed, her apple-green eyes promising a good time. "Let's find a boy you can practice on."

"Your Highness," Daniela faced Emmaline. "My parents wouldn't approve, nor would the boy."

"Mr. and Mrs. Cavanaugh?" Emmaline called as she scanned the room. "I don't see your parents. Do you?"

"I couldn't face them if I did. I'd feel—indecent."

"One day you may have to." Emmaline winked. "Feel indecent."

"But what if a bee stings your tongue while it's darting between soggy rose petals?"

"Never thought of that." Emmaline shrugged. "Maybe the pain feels good—like a release."

"You're sadistic."

"I've been called a few names, but not sadistic." Emmaline laughed. "Wait here. I bought you a gift." She rolled off the bed and retrieved something from her suitcase, then ducked beneath the upper bunk and tapped a nail into the wall above Daniela's bed. With the nail anchored into drywall, Emmaline hung an eight-by-ten-framed picture.

"What are you hanging?"

"Don't look." Emmaline finished and then faced Daniela and knelt, blocking Daniela's view of the image. "Just now, you told me about oily boy and why you hate dreaming about him."

"Don't lecture me, please." Daniela crossed her arms.

"I'm not lecturing, only coaching. You want to be normal. You want to be loved—cherished, really. What if oily boy is real? You saw him in your nightmare. What if he's your morning rose—your Jack Dawson?"

"More like a titan arum—a corpse flower. It smells like rotting flesh. Attracts flies. Stinks to high heaven."

"I'm an agnostic. I don't even pray."

"You're preaching—again." Daniela rolled her eyes.

"Just listen." Emmaline laid the hammer on the bed. "I agree with your dad. At least whisper a prayer for oily boy. It won't kill you!"

"But hoping for love may make my heart hemorrhage. Then, I'll die an agonizing and lonely death."

"Don't be dramatic. Pray! If you won't, I will."

"And who'll be listening?" Daniela tilted her head. "Since you believe God probably doesn't exist."

"But maybe someone's home." Emmaline glanced at the ceiling. "Wouldn't He want to hear my desperate plea on behalf of a tormented boy?" Speechless, Daniela stared at Emmaline. "Fine. I'm doing it." Emmaline folded her hands and sat up. She'd prayed before. Without moving her head, she stared at the underside of the bottom bunk. "Hello," she said, her voice manicured and proper. "We don't talk much, especially since William was diagnosed with cancer." Her brother's struggle with cancer explained why she teared up anytime she tried to talk about him.

Daniela reached for her friend's thigh and rested her hand on it.

"If possible, give Danny Rose a dream that doesn't feel like a nightmare—a daydream—making her beg to pray for oily boy. The kind that makes her feel in places she didn't know she could feel." Emmaline looked down. "Show her oily boy's heart, not just his eyes. That's all for now. So be it." She fidgeted, and Daniela thought she could lose herself in Limy's apple-greens.

"So be it?"

"Amen." She shrugged. "Same difference."

"Thank you, Limy. It was beautifully warm—rays of sunlight melting an icy tundra, thawing my selfish heart."

"That's what kindred spirits are for." A timid smile pushed dimples into Emmaline's bone-china-white cheeks until she broke into a big laugh. "My specialty . . . defrosting prudes. Then living to tell the icy tale."

"Success."

"William once told me that an evil force separated kindred spirits at birth, splitting their hearts in two, leaving the bloody parts to find their other half. Didn't anyone ever tell you?"

"Gosh, no! That's horrid."

"What's your theory?"

"My favorite teacher, Ms. Bender, said my dreams were a map, leading me to my long-lost kindred spirit."

"Let's believe it. I love treasure hunts." She moved to one side and revealed the picture.

Daniela almost choked on her tongue when she read the words aloud, "Here sleeps a girl with a head full of magical dreams, a heart full of wonder, and hands that will shape the world." She whispered, "Kindred spirits are real after all."

Emmaline stood up, her posture more refined than the Queen of England's. "Hot cinnamon tea?"

"You bet."

"Danny Rose." Emmaline served a cup of their favorite Harney & Sons brew. "It's time to dream again."

"What about the pandemic, the Glass Tattoo, the riddles?"

"If the rest of us are to survive, the apocalypse will wait until you wake. But if it doesn't, aren't you the lucky one—trapped for eternity in an amorous dreamworld with oily boy and your beautiful Adelaide Rose?"

"I am the lucky one." Daniela slipped beneath her covers, and Emmaline tucked her in. *Trapped. Eternity.* "Wait for me, Limy."

"Sleep, and when you wake up—no matter what—I'll be here. Waiting. Now, just you mind that." Emmaline flashed a delicious grin.

Daniela palmed the Glass Tattoo, closed her eyes and fell into timeless love. And for the first time, she wasn't afraid.

59—Adelaide:
#FacingTheMusic

AFTER LEVI'S ATTACK, I RETURN to the dorms, throw away my clothes, and shower until the water runs cold.

Cordy hates cold showers, but she despises a moody dormmate even more, and my muscles beg for a massage that only a long, lava-hot shower can deliver.

I step out of the shower and grab my towel. My red hair clings to my cheeks, shoulders, and back. I wrap the towel around my bruised body, tiptoe to my dresser, and dip into my stash of peppermint patties, leaving three on the bathroom sink as a consolation prize for Cordy's cold shower.

"Cordy Grey, time to wake up." I gently rock her shoulders.

"Can't it be summer vacation already?" Minutes later and groggy, she gets up, enters the bathroom, turns on the shower, then shrieks,

"Addy Rose, how dare you!" After the fastest shower ever, my friend storms into our bedroom, shivering in her towel. "For the love of all things loveless, I cannot imagine why you would be so selfish and force your roommate—your best friend—to be doused by an arctic firehose!"

"So dramatic, Cordy. Puh-lease, write your novel."

"I will if I survive the shock of being dumped into an icy sea for my morning alarm. Besides, you've not delivered the content—your parents' story." Standing in front of our space heater, she rubs her hands together. "You so owe me."

"How can I make it up to you?"

"For starters, make me breakfast. Then hand over the content." She rubs her shoulders, kneading out the chill.

"You read the letter. Your guess is as good as mine." I open our mini refrigerator and remove two strawberry yogurts. "Breakfast."

"If I didn't know any better, I'd say you are trying to murder me."

I roll my eyes. "You should study theatre."

"I'm not being dramatic. I know you. You don't want me to publish my novel. How blazing long did you shower? And what in God's green earth happened to your eye?"

"Fell off the bed and hit the dresser?" I shrug while snapping together the last button of my flannel shirt. I shudder. The lie I just told my best friend came easy, too easy.

"You don't even know, and you wonder why I insist a professional captain navigates your dad's sailboat during our trip?"

"You sail the boat. I don't care." Trust me. *The Rose of the Ocean*, my da's sailboat lives up to her namesake—sleek and breathtakeninly gorgeous.

"I can barely steer a car, much less a sailboat, and you're not an epileptic, Addy Rose." She props her hands on her hips and narrows her eyes. "There's no dresser by your bed." Cordy removes the towel from around her head. Wet, black curls spill down over plump, white shoulders. "I don't believe you." She pops a peppermint patty into her mouth. "If I've not said it but a million times before, a friendship can survive secrets, but not lies. Fess up."

"The philosopher, poet, priest, and judge." I bounce a smile in her direction, hoping it will stick onto her scowling but beautiful face.

She sits almost naked on her bed, crosses her legs, and taps her foot. "Come clean."

I glance in the mirror—not exactly a dresser wound—then glance at my friend. "Levi."

"The mute creep in calculus who was spying on us at the library?"

"Turns out he knows how to talk. He calls himself Leviathan." I thread a candy-apple scarf around my neck. Mother gave me the scarf last Christmas. I pull my shoulders toward my neck—a non-Pilates move, but I can feel her essence, and my breath slows.

"The same name as Job's sea monster in the Hebrew Scriptures, right?" She cocks her head to one side.

"I'm not the priest."

"Don't act stupid. You mean a rabbi, Carrots."

"Okay, so I don't read Hebrew. Big deal." I zip up my ankle-high boots and fold my mauve wool socks over the top—a gift from my da last Christmas. Mauve and red aren't exactly complementary colors. Too bad. I'm wearing my parents' gifts!

Cordy Grey stuffs her curvy hips into her one-size-too-small, dark-blue jeans. "If that mute Levi assaulted you, I'm calling the police."

"Take a bullhorn and announce it to the whole school, why don't you?" My breath catches in my throat, and I cough. "Don't tell anyone, not even the police." Cordy Grey glares at me. I fidget with my scarf and shift my weight. "I think you're assaulting that zipper. Should we call the coppers to spare those jeans?"

"Hands up—don't shoot." Cordy Grey raises her hands. "It's just a hoodie."

"Not funny."

"Then don't be cheeky. It's not cute on you. Besides," Cordy Grey rotates left, then right, observing her curvy frame. "I'm on a diet, but I'll eat any perv for breakfast and lunch if he messes with my bestie." Her gesture of protection relaxes me, but I don't feel like being sappy, so I force myself to laugh, and thankfully, Cordy joins in.

After our moment of gaiety, I reach for her arm. I imagine emotion contorts my face into something hideous and desperate. Hideous I can tolerate, but I hate desperate. A polyester tangerine blouse would look less dreadful on me.

"D-d-did he r-r-r . . ." She can't say the word, so she spells it out, "R-A-P-E you?"

"No." I shrug the suggestion off. *Appear in control.* "He doesn't seem to like girls, and for the record . . ." I step toward her. "No one finds out about the shiner—especially not my mother."

"It's obvious, Addy Rose. Hello. Your left eye is the color of a chimney, and your face is paler than cotton."

"Then help me hide it."

"You so owe me. Again." She bats her eyelashes faster than a hummingbird's wings.

"What do you want now—my inheritance?" I flip my hair over my shoulders.

"Not a bad idea." She smirks. "But you couldn't survive poverty." Cordy finishes blowing her locks dry, then brushes her hair up into a ponytail, before slipping into a golden corduroy jacket that makes her white T-shirt pop. "For the record, I think your decision is cowardly. Too many women don't report. He did assault you even if he didn't want—well, you know."

"It's my choice."

"Look, I'm on your side, but people won't believe you when you decide to give a tell-all in ten years. They'll hardly believe you right after it happened. My mother didn't." She rests her hand across her abdomen.

"Cordelia." My voice lowers to a hushed whisper in respect for whatever dead memories my best friend is choosing to conjure up and share. "Whatever happened . . . I'm sorry."

"Thanks for saying that." She wraps her ponytail tightly around her forefinger and then releases it. "Sometimes you want to know people will still love you even after you tell. And finally stand up for yourself." Her voice drops to a whisper. "My dignity. Heck, even my humanity." She lifts my chin up with her finger and looks into my eyes. "Always and forever friends, whether you tell or not."

"Ride or die?" I force my cheekiest grin and look into my best friend's eyes, wanting to jump into those pools of chocolate, but she bursts out laughing, ruining the moment. "Cordy . . . I don't want to sound ungrateful, but I could really use a friend, not a shrink. Okay?"

"I'm cool with that. I hate being an unpaid professional wastebasket anyways. Most of my past girlfriends had no use for me unless I was listening to their problems and counseling them."

"*Past* is the qualifying word." She slips her feet into a pair of fire-engine red quilted boots. Red is the new orange. "Those look amazing on you." She smiles.

"True." She gives me a sideways glance. "Good sense and tenacity are the traits I adore about you." Cordy studies my face, and I shrink beneath her microscopic interrogation. "Don't crumble faster than a tart fresh out of the oven, especially not under Levi's pressure. He's nothing."

"You've got it all wrong, Cordelia. I'm not that tenacious or courageous. You are."

"It's a show." She shrugs. "Survival. No one asks about me, so why act like I care about me?"

"Sorry for not asking more often."

"Forgiven." Cordy grins. "But these help." She rotates her shoulders back, and Mount Everest after a fresh dusting of powdery white snow ascends toward the sky. As she tucks her lower lip between a set of dazzling pearly whites—one slightly crooked incisor adds character—she buttons up her corduroy jacket, accenting her lethal weapons. "Perfect."

"And those—" I say, pointing at the twin peaks, then back away from Cordy until my back rests against our dorm room door, "should be illegal, punishable by a lifetime of baggy sweatshirts." I reach for the door handle. "It's bad enough our calculus prof can't keep his eyes off you, stuttering while he tries to spit out differential equations. No wonder half the class is failing."

"Hello, world." She struts an abbreviated catwalk, retrieves a violet wool scarf, and stuffs it into her leather satchel. "It isn't my fault if our classmates fail."

While eating our breakfast of yogurt, we exit Wheelwright Hall and walk across the grassy knoll where the attack occurred.

The morning air hangs heavy with bouquets of rose blooms and freshly mowed grass, and all around us, our classmates eat breakfast while trudging to class.

"Cordy."

"What's up?" She slurps down more milk and tosses her yogurt cup into a trash receptacle.

"When I first met you—"

"You believed me to be the most amazing human being walking the face of the planet?"

"No, I thought you were the most obnoxious person on Earth, but I'm glad we're friends. More like sisters."

"To sisters who like each other." She taps her milk carton to mine. "Nothing as intoxicating as choosing to love someone even after you know the real person." A gust of wind tosses silken strands around her face. "Dying in the spring should be illegal . . ." I wait. She's not finished blowing a shotgun-sized hole in my chest right before class.

Cock the hammer.

Pull the trigger.

Boom!

"I'm sorry about your mom." She drops a nuke of words, and the fallout of radioactive emotion vaporizes my voice.

As if my mother could sense her daughter's distress from so many miles away, an apricot sulfur—Mother's favorite butterfly—decreases its altitude and nestles between the petals of a cluster of purple lilacs.

"Look!" My best friend points at the bright yellow insect and smiles. She's on my side, and I clench her arm as though I'm sliding down a ravine's edge and she's my climber's dynamic rope, absorbing the energy of my fall.

"I'm scared for you." She locks eyes with mine.

"Why?"

"Unlike me," Cordy rests her hand on top of mine, "you adore your parents, and they love you back. It's rather odd for a teenager to sign up for Parental Lovefest 101, but at the same time, it's touching," she sniffles. "I don't miss my parents."

"Gosh, Cordy." I tug against her grip, but she squeezes tighter.

"It's true. Your becoming an orphan will be more devastating than my becoming one, but don't become the resident Eeyore. I need to believe in love. Even hope." She stops walking again, so I stop too. *Will we ever arrive at class?*

Again, she looks deep into my eyes. "Let me believe in love through you and your parents' story." She blinks back tears. All around us, our classmates dash from the dorms to their classrooms. They'll see us blubbering like orcas.

"Fine," I say.

"Keep your chin up." She laughs. "Even if you have to mount it on a toothpick." I grin, imagining my big head held up by a hamburger pin.

"As long as you're the toothpick."

"Touching." She sighs, kisses me on the cheek, and we resume strolling to class. "Your mother's a fighter. She'll last through the school year. You'll see."

"And then what?" I release her arm. We've almost arrived at the science building, and Gage had already accused us of being lesbos. We're so not, but I don't want to hear it.

"Your dad's sailboat, our very own *Robinson Crusoe* adventure."

I swallow hard, then drop my own bomb. "Gage wants to come."

"After South Africa? I don't think so." Her knuckles blanch as she clutches the handles of her bag. "He probably wants to slaughter baby orcas next, and we *must* save the killer whales."

As far as Cordy is concerned, Gage Alexander Barrington isn't winning the boyfriend-of-the-year award.

"We're so different." I attempt to soften the impact of my suggestion. "He's Mister Capitalist. Crush the poor buggers who can't survive in his world, and I'm a micro-capitalist with a conscience, all for employees owning the companies they work for, like Publix grocery store."

"You know I'm a socialist."

"Doesn't all of Phillips Exeter know your opinions? Socialism doesn't work, Cordy Grey. Maybe the theory stands a chance in utopia where everyone possesses the same work ethic and values. The reality of socialism—everyone's equal, but some are more equal than others."

"According to you and Professor Ryland. Write your paper. I'm sure he'll give you an *A*."

"Stalin's Russia. Chairman Mao's China. Is that what you want in America? Why disassociate hard work from reward?"

"Enough."

"Then enough about Gage." *Gotcha!* I look at Cordelia from the corner of my eye.

"That's not fair."

"It is—checkmate."

"Okay! I understand dating a guy because he's hot." She shifts her bag to her other shoulder. "Gage fits that bill, but don't wrap your life into his. He's bad luck with a capital *B*."

"We're not married."

"I understand you may require a distraction from your bad news. Don't you think our solving the clues in your mother's letter during our trip the safest distraction? Don't allow Simba's assassin to mess it up—just sayin'."

"So dramatic." I change tactics. "You're going soft. I thought you loved to battle it out with Gage on politics, economics, and race relations—any time and any place. You said yourself, 'life isn't all puppies and butterflies.' We're Exeter students—think like one."

She stops short of entering the science building. "Trust me. I know life can suck, but a girl's got to have principles. Don't be Hitler's Eva Braun."

The comment made sense, and I loved her for her honesty. Cordelia's grandmother survived Auschwitz.

I don't know how to respond. "Uhh . . . umm . . ."

Our classmates scramble past us. "What happened to your eye?" Bethany, some senator's daughter, butts into *our* moment.

"Nothing." I stop. "Cordy, I'm sorry about your grandmother, but Gage isn't Hitler."

"Okay, so I'm being dramatic, but you didn't take an ice-cold shower this morning." She pauses. "So you really think your parents are perfect?"

"Really, Cordy." I laugh.

"Because usually teenagers don't believe their parents are normal, much less perfect, and that's why I know you're hiding something from me." Cordy faces me. "It's just . . . none of it adds up."

"What doesn't?" I cross my arms. "Can't we just agree to disagree about Gage? I'll tell him he can't come. He doesn't like you anyways."

"Forget Gage." She shifted to block my entrance into the science building. "Do you remember the secret chamber behind the fireplace in your parents' home in Austria?" She levels her midnight-blacks full of determination directly at me, and I shiver beneath her x-ray vision.

"Who said it was a secret?"

"The Nazi memorabilia. The high-powered weapons. The dried blood? I hope you didn't know about it before you invited me!"

"My da's not a Nazi," I whisper. "He didn't gas your grandma."

"I didn't say he did, but when I saw the swastikas plastered on memorabilia in that chamber, I'll admit, I planned to end our friendship the moment we returned to Exeter and I was safe."

"You're safe! I'm safe!" My voice registers high, shrill. Conscious that my classmates are lining up behind me, staring and waiting to enter the building, I lower my voice. My entire body is shaking. "I'm glad you didn't. Whatever that stuff means, I'm not my da, and if we find out that's what floats his boat, my relationship with him is as good as over." I reach around Cordy and open the door, allowing my classmates to enter ahead of us. "Please, everyone, enjoy the education our parents are paying through the nose for."

Warmth floods my face. I refuse to look into their judgmental eyes.

"Don't you want to know the truth about them?" Miraculously, at the age of seventeen, Cordelia Grey Anderson finally learns how to whisper. "Even if it's dark?" She continues her interrogation as she follows me into the chilly hallway.

"Not really." I bury my hands in my coat pockets.

"Maybe your father's still alive, and we can find him, Addy Rose."

Heat rises across the back of my neck and prickles my skin. *Don't bait me. I'm not a fish.* "Why would a half-Jewish girl want to find a man she believes is a Nazi?"

"He's your dad. Aren't you curious?"

"Not really. Growing a set of scales as well?"

As if I planned it, Levi shuffles by, wearing his usual, easy buck-toothed smile, tousled mousy hair, and stonewashed jeans. "Hey, Addy Rose."

What?

He's speaking to me!

He passes by as though nothing happened. The dude is permanently stuck in the eighties, where nothing good happened in fashion. But I'm relieved he's passing by, if for no other reason than to distract Cordelia, and so he does.

"He looks normal." Cordelia gives him a death stare. "Are you sure . . ."

"You're my best friend, and you don't even believe he assaulted me. Wonder why I don't want to tell anyone about the assault."

"I do believe you. I just said he looks normal. That's all. I'm not Levi."

"His sister, then?"

"Your friend. His enemy. Period." Cordy slams her fist into her hand for emphasis. She winces, and I giggle.

"It's over. Done. I'm moving on." But it's not over. Once a woman has been violated, it can never be *over*—unless she dies and is reborn, which according to Mother, is possible.

"Answer one question, then I'll stop bugging you about your parents."

"You're going to ask anyways, so ask." I linger a few feet away from the doorway to my physics class, hoping my classmates can't hear our conversation.

"Last night before we went to bed, you shared a poem. I wrote it down."

"Creepy." I roll my eyes and cross my arms.

Ignoring my annoyance, she retrieves the paper and reads the words out loud, "'They taught Mother to save lives, but they forced Da to take them. Da's scars tell an eerie labyrinth of intrigue. Mother's silence accomplishes the same, but her scars remain hidden—etched on the inside of her soul. Assassin and doctor, but I love their love—even still.'"

"So what?"

"Lyrical, yet so mysterious."

"Only to you, cursed with a fiction writer's mind."

"My imagination's how I survived my mother's house, and I'm asking you to love me—even indulge me—in spite of it." She waits. I don't answer, so she continues, "I want to write their story. No. I *need* to write their story—a story about a love so powerful it overcomes all the wrongs in the world, all the Hitlers and the Stalins."

I tap my foot and stare at her.

"Okay, so maybe Gage isn't so bad."

Finally, she's giving up ground.

"My da's missing. You believe he's a Nazi—which doesn't really work out since he's married to my mother."

She furrows her brow, not understanding, and I don't explain. Why should I? Cordelia Grey doesn't need to know everything.

A year ago, she started at Exeter, and she's never met Mother, only Father.

I fight a knowing smile, denying her the truth—the weapon that obliterates what I know she thinks of Father. "And my mom—the most amazing, compassionate person in the world—is drowning in her own blood, dying from a broken heart." I finish counting off my grievances on my fingers, and my voice cracks. I clear my throat. "I was being sentimental, nothing more."

"And her legacy—should it die with her? That's not fair," Cordy says.

Gage saunters toward me, smiling, then dives toward my lips for a kiss. His golden-wheat locks brush my face, and his lips feel like sunshine on a winter day. "I called you yesterday."

"I'm sorry. I was studying." I twirl a clump of hair around my forefinger.

"Can't you see we're busy?" Cordelia lashes out.

"I'm not talking to you."

"But I am talking to you." Cordy stacks her hands on her hips.

"Let up, Cordy!" I stick up for my on-again, off-again boyfriend. He's still a human being.

"Have it your way." She crosses her arms and gives me her plaintive look, eyelashes batting a thousand times a minute and lips pursed. "No matter what they do, the girl always chooses the guy."

"After the morning I've had, you accuse me of betraying you? When have I had time to plot such a thing?"

"Come on, girls. Lighten up," Gage says in his surfer-boy, South African drawl.

"Show me your loyalty and steal your mother's journals," Cordy demands. "The world deserves to know their story: a medical doctor and an assassin. Let's discover it together."

"What's up, girlies? Stealing? Assassins?"

"Mind your own business, Gage," Cordy snaps.

"Addy Rose *is* my business."

"How romantic." Cordy rolls her eyes. "Bored murdering innocent wildlife?"

"I'm a hunter."

"No." Cordy buries her finger into Gage's chest. "You're a bloody coward."

I enter the classroom, planning to leave both annoying creatures in the hallway, but then I turn and face my accuser and my generally stupid—but cute and mostly kind—boyfriend. "Cordy, I'm a lot of things, but I'm not a thief."

Cordelia Grey grabs my arm and pulls me toward her. "What about the Glass Tattoo?" Her cheeks deepen to a hot pink.

I whip around, my eyes narrowing into slits. "I never told you about that."

"What the heck is going on?" Gage butts in again. This time, he'll have to save his own neck.

"Cordy, how do you know about that?" I say in my angriest whisper. She doesn't reply. That's not like her. "If you're planning to betray me, do it already."

"I'm here, Adelaide." Gage traces the angle of my jaw with his partially amputated finger. The stump reminds me of why he's balancing on the tightwire of my last nerve. One of the cubs took a bite after he killed their mother. Serves him right. Kill for food, not for sport.

"Go somewhere."

"Where?" He retracts his stumpy finger.

Disgust mangles my face. "Anywhere but here."

"Fine." My boyfriend saunters away, vanishing into the sea of Exeter students.

Jenny stands nearby to pick up the pieces of his ego. "Hi, Gage." She flips her curly brown hair over her shoulder.

How many more outbursts will he tolerate?

Stupid.

When will I find another guy like him?

I attempt to salvage my relationship with Cordy, removing her scarf from her satchel and draping it around her neck. "Orphans need friends." I smile as I drape the scarf around her neck, allowing the cloth to hide her breasts. "So the rest of us can learn something."

"Addy Rose," her voice quivers. "Don't ever accuse me of not being on your side." She interlinks my pinky finger with hers. "Promise me."

"I swear."

"When the time comes, and your mother's gone, I'll be there—listening."

"As a spy or as a friend?" I laugh off my accusation, wishing to God that I found her promise of listening comforting. But we all need friends, or else life becomes solitary confinement.

"Not as a friend but as a kindred spirit, knowing and understanding you." She hugs me, and in spite of my uncertainties of her motives, I wish the embrace would last for days.

I want to say, "No matter what happened to you. No matter who tried to steal your dignity. You are human. Dignified. One classy chica." But I don't say anything, choosing rather to take, nursing my wounds in the balm of her comforting words, choosing to not share my own words of strength. There will be another day.

At least, I hope so.

She whispers, so my classmates won't hear. "And if your dad is still alive—even if he is a Nazi—we'll find him together. No one except us has to know that he's gone until the book is released."

"You assume I want to find him."

"And the plot thickens." Cordy Grey pulls back from our embrace.

"It's always been thicker than molasses." Still sore from Levi, I hobble into physics class.

It is 12:15 p.m., and Friday continues to suck. Beatha, my mom's nurse, texts me. *The news from the doctor isna good. Come home.* I eat lunch with Cordelia, finish up classes, board my da's jet at 7:00 p.m., and fly to North Carolina, not knowing if this will be my last weekend to cuddle with my mom, to tell her I love her.

More lost than found, I stand in front of the plane's lavatory's mirror as the pilot, Jacobs, engages the engines.

The thrust slams me into the wall.

Jet exhaust soils the air, tasting of tang and liquefied fossils. I pull myself to my feet. Gripping the washbasin with one hand and washing my face with the other, I attempt to remove Levi's touch.

Damp auburn hair clings to my face, and Mother's words echo in my mind. *Don't let the excitement of your youth cause you to forget your Creator. Honor Him before you grow old and say "Life isn't pleasant anymore."* Her version of being reborn—saved from eternal death, separation from the Creator. Her sayings and her past harbor greater mysteries than Levi's chameleon face.

"Mom." My face contorts. "I need to be close to you." *Dinna cry, lass.* My da's words replay in my mind. *Ye'll be roundin' the mountain in the morn. Give yer mother a wee bit more time. You've made her proud. Know that.*

I bite down on my thumb, transferring the pain until I stop crying.

I wipe my eyes and remove the evidence of my emotional meltdown. My right eye shades blacker than Levi's soul, so I dab flesh-colored foundation on the bruise and blend it. Before class, Cordy gave me her makeup kit and a quick lesson because I don't like to wear the stuff.

I sit, the hum of engines my sole companion. Cordelia Grey Anderson was correct. I am curious. She was right about one other thing.

I am a thief.

After retrieving my leather satchel, I remove Mother's journal, the one I stole during my last visit to our Blue Ridge Mountain chalet. I read the last ten pages, then trace patches of dried, rust-colored stains that splatter each page.

Is it blood?

Did my da—the assassin—cause the bloodletting that stains my mother's journal?

Did he torture Mother?

Is he the reason I'm to become an orphan?

No—it can't be true. Beatha had said, "Come home. The news from the doctor isna good." After pouring a cup of Hot Cinnamon Sunset tea, I inhale the rich scent of spice and then click on the cabin's overhead light. I reread the last paragraph of the first page. Once again, Mother's serene, alto voice seems to replace mine.

> Some say knowledge of one's joyful ending can make the present misery tolerable. But who knows if one's last act will be full of joy or sorrow? Maybe we all know our final act and don't realize it, or maybe we deny the facts of our final curtain call. Inspired by the One whose beginning and ending defies time—the Alpha and Omega—an ancient prophet wrote, "And as it is appointed unto men once to die, but after this the judgment." I am no prophet; I am a woman and a mother, but I am sure this saying applies to me as well.

> If I had known my ending, how would I have lived my beginning?

> —Daniela Rose Cavanaugh

Her voice trails off, and my opinion of her character remains the same. *You would have lived as you have—amazingly well, Mom—my kindred spirit.* I have to decide: Could Cordy Grey's novel create a Simmie Knox portrait out of Mother's legacy?

Maybe.

I glance at my reflection in the mirror on the inside of Cordy's foundation case. Trails of emotion have eaten away at the veil of cream, so I reapply the stuff. Then it dawns on me: I look like Dracula's wife—pasty white. I need sun. A trip on the sea—just the two of us—discovering Mother's and Father's secrets will be good for Cordelia and me.

I dab more foundation around my black eye.

Mom can't know what happened.

Not ever.

A mother's death plays in slow motion, and she should not be forced to worry about her daughter.

60—Orphan Dreamer

My Darling Rosebud,

I need your help.

The approaching four blood moons and Jewish holidays are related. The four lunar eclipses coincide with Passover and Sukkot in 5775—the Gentile dates of March 2014–March 2015.

The year 5775 will be big; it is the start of the final countdown.

Your interest in and perspective of my traditions and culture make sense to me now. You possess a mission given by YHVH. To ensure your success, Ezekiel's blueprint of the final temple as well as the contents of the Ark of the Covenant will be useful as you fulfill your mission. The rebuilding of the third and final Jewish Temple is a clock in its own right. Has its rebuilding not been prophesied at the end of all ends? Follow your Mongolian ancestors' footsteps to the lost tomb of Genghis Khan. There you will find your treasure—the blueprint, the Ark, and the treasure of the copper scroll.

I intend to skip the rest of the letter, but at the bottom of the page, three sentences stand out:

Your heart-song possesses espionage ties and swims in a sea of liquid gold. Blood stains his hands and cries from the ground. The statue is the key that solves the mystery of *who*?

B'shalom,
Professor Jakob
Director of Israel Antiquities Authority

I toss the letter onto my coffee table. Solving the mystery will have to wait.

The Blue Ridge Mountains kiss the ink-black sky.

Stars twinkle above the sprawling cabin. Quiet settles over the valley and on the mountains and my thoughts. Steven Curtis Chapman's "I Will be Here" plays softly throughout the chalet, and I know that upstairs, he has awakened.

I take a deep breath. Chapman's ballad ends and Karen Gibson and the Kingdom Choir's rendition of "Stand by Me" follows.

Written by Ben E. King, the song's lyrics are based on a psalm written by King David, the youngest of eight boys, a shepherd and a harpist who grew up into a warrior and a king then kept his promise of kindred friendship to Prince Jonathan—the prince who never became king—by protecting Prince Jonathan's crippled son.

The mysterious ways of the world, shifting shepherds, princes and kings around on the chess board of life.

As I listen to "Stand by Me," I whisper David's psalm: "'Therefore we will not fear, though the earth give way and the mountains fall into the heart of the sea, though its waters roar and foam and the mountains quake with their surging.' Psalms forty-six, verses two and three."

"Stand by Me"

When the night has come and the land is dark
And the moon is the only light we'll see
No I won't be afraid, no I won't be afraid
Just as long as you stand, stand by me

So darlin', darlin', stand by me, oh stand by me
Oh stand by me, stand by me

If the sky that we look upon should tumble and fall
Or the mountains should crumble to the sea

I won't cry, I won't cry, no I won't shed a tear
Just as long as you stand, stand by me

The ominous, almost apocalyptic, yet compassionate words of the song stop me in my tracks. Swallowing hard, I look up the stairs to a partially opened door, and my chest tightens. A glow of red seeps into the hallway like freshly spilled blood.

Is the glow a figment of my imagination?

It all feels too real to be a dream. I walk up the stairs, gripping the banister as "Stand by Me" continues to play. My pink silk nightgown dances behind me like a bridal veil. I climb the last step and cross a floor embedded with knots of deep brown.

A rugged pine door is the only obstacle blocking me from him and the mysterious light.

How did I get here?

That answer will have to wait until morning.

I open the bedroom door. A blood moon casts scarlet light into our bedroom, washing the beige blanket strewn across the foot of our bed in crimson shadows.

There he is.

I breathe deeply, the thoughts of Professor Jakob's letter blown from my mind.

I smile, cross the bedroom, and climb underneath starched cotton sheet—the lamb lying down beside the lion. He slides closer to his side of the bed, leaving a warm patch for me. He's more thoughtful and beautiful than I imagined any man could ever be. A swoosh of warmth dances through my body.

I wrap my French-manicured fingers between those rugged fingers of my kindred spirit. His hands look milky-white in comparison to the deep mahogany tone of my skin, bequeathed to me by my African, Mongolian, and Cherokee ancestors. He lifts my hand to his lips while flames from the hearth splash a warm glow in his eyes.

Eyes that could at once comfort me and warn me.

He first kisses my palm, then each finger.

I inhale deeply, drinking in the sweet musk of his cologne. I close my eyes but open them again. I couldn't lose a moment of these final hours. "If we would have known our ending, could we have hoped and believed a little more during the challenges of our beginning?" My eyes search his Black Irish features—a gift from Spanish blood, long ago. Black Irish. What an oxymoron—an Irishman with the palest Caucasian skin, raven-black hair, and sky-blue eyes.

A voice—quiet and very Irish with a hint of a Scottish burr, replies, "Maybe . . ." He is a man of few words, letting his eyes do the talking, adding to the mystery of his persona. Mischief dances in his eyes as his face flushes red.

My skin prickles with electric desire.

The deep baritone in his voice sounds a warning. I will not sleep until he quenches his marital desire—nor do I want to. I playfully pull my hand, and he tugs back. I tug again; my fingers free.

I swallow hard and with trembling hands trace the starfish-shaped scar over his left hand with my fingertip. Evidence of the rusty spike.

Last week I'd raced past him—there was so much planning to do—but I now feel the need to memorize every moment and recall every curve of him. My finger slides from his hand to his masculine biceps, shoulders, chest, and back. As I trace a line, each muscle tenses, then releases under my touch.

Inside, my spirit anticipates what is to come—a heavenly reunion—while my body and soul ache, knowing that soon we will no longer be in this time, this place, Earth's realm.

His body has been a refuge for me, a place of acceptance. His arms protected me. His mouth comforted me. His touch calmed and awakened me. My fingers lift slightly as I rub a patchwork of tangled keloids, blanched scars, and divots of carved-out flesh across his back. I wipe a solitary tear from the corner of my eye.

"Dinna cry, *mo nighean donn*—my brown-haired lass. The good Lord allowed me to survive." Desire stifles his vocal cords.

"The thought of losing you. The thought of the pain—"

"Dinna think about it again, *chuisle mo chroí*—pulse of my heart. Hold my heart. Dinna let it bleed anymore."

"I will. Promise."

Pulling me close, he whispers, "Ye've been a dear mother to our children, and one day, they'll be makin' us both proud. I dinnae deserve ye, lass. Not ever. I know that I've caused ye anguish, and I'm sorry for it. But I've been beggin' the good Lord that I've gifted you a wee bit of joy and pleasure as well." He pauses. One tear slips down his right cheek. "I've been the ruthless one, pushing back the darkness so ye could be kind. Earth is balanced, rotating on its axis because of your compassion. Love me once more, Daniela, *a rún mo chroí*—secret of my heart." His lips seal mine, quieting my mental exercise as only he could.

He nestles deep into his wife's softness.

Until the sun rises, we weave mahogany and ivory webs together in the moonlight. For the last time, I finish, then he finishes.

A silver fleck sparkles between his fingers—a coin.

He always keeps it under his pillow. I loosen his grip. He moans in sleepy protest. I smile and hold the coin up in the air. The reddish glow filling the room illuminates a 1994 silver dollar. I press the coin to my lips, my breath warming the metal as the memories it evokes warms my soul. In spite of me—or of my apathy toward prayer—he survived. "Thank You, Yahweh."

Embers too stubborn to die flicker in the stone hearth. "Yahweh, if this is a dream, don't wake me." I gaze at him and whisper. "Chi. Xi. Stigma. Six-six-six."

I exhale.

He exhales.

Quiet settles over the cabin.

"Mom." A gentle voice urges me to come where I do not want to go. "Mom, wake up. You'll freeze to death."

I open my eyes, ripping the iced lace from my eyelids.

The Glass Tattoo stains my right palm midnight blue. A freckled-face framed with auburn locks materializes into someone breathtaking—Adelaide Rose. Magic surrounds me in the form of two additional redheads—Limy and Beatha. "You waited, Limy."

"Of course. I'm here." Emmaline wipes a frozen tear from her cheek. Adelaide brushes a bunch of curls from her face; they spill down her back.

"You're here, Limy." I squeeze my kindred spirit's hand.

"You should be wearing a hat, Adelaide. You'll catch a cold."

"I'm okay, Mom." She slips her earbuds into my ears and plays our song, "Feels Like Home." With a gravelly alto voice, Chantal Kreviazuk sings to me, telling me how my daughter feels about sitting beside her mother, outside our mountain chalet in the heart of a spring blizzard.

Depressive schizophrenic or not, I *am* home to my breathtakingly beautiful, brave, and very sane daughter, Adelaide Rose.

And that's all that matters to me. "Welcome home, my darling." I attempt to smile, but icy snow restricts my skin, twisting my mouth.

Adelaide reaches for my hand. "Mom . . ." Fear darkens her bright eyes, full of youthful sunshine. "We'll be findin' my da—we'll not be leavin' him out there all alone." When Adelaide speaks of her father, her voice dips into the lilt of an Irish girl.

"We'll find him." I reach up and hold her hand. "We girls are a tough lot. Capable of anything."

"Well, ye'll be needin' your rest, and we'll be takin' you inside to do so," Beatha, my nurse, says.

My three redheads—Adelaide, Limy, and Beatha—lay me on a cloth stretcher and carry me up the final steps of the hiking trail, up the mountainside and back to the chalet. After weaving through the forest's snow-white canopy of evergreens, a cascade of butterscotch sunlight seeps through the forest's canopy, bathing my face in its warmth.

I lift my chin.

My spirit soars.

Mother was right—the Son was and still is shining on me—but the realization of His presence required patience. I endured life's storms.

Storm clouds part.

Sunlight blasts though the forest.

I dig into my right jacket pocket and remove Prince Jonathan's arrowhead. "Take this, Adelaide."

"What is it?"

"A prince's dying gift to me."

"Who are ye talkin' about, miss?" Beatha asks. "The Master?"

"No, someone who wasn't quite a prince; but then, not all princes are as brave as the Master of this house." My father's words come back to me. *Empathy is your gift, but you must be humbled further.*

* * *

"Danny Rose, wake up." The Demi Moore–esque voice was familiar: Limy's. The room was also familiar: a bunk bed, a plaid couch, and a picture window that faced the Jemez Mountains. Mouth dry and eyes gritty with sleep, I sit up.

"You were talking in your sleep."

"What did I say?"

You called my name, as well as Adelaide's and Beatha's. Then, you whispered three Greek letters: Chi. Xi. Stigma. And six-six-six. Who is six-six-six—the man in your dreams?"

"I spoke of a man?"

"Details in a sec. Who is six-six-six?"

"I don't remember."

"But you called someone six-six-six. Can't you travel into the future and find out?"

"No. I don't decide when or where I time travel. Yahweh does." Biblical words filled Daniela's mouth. "The twelfth chapter of Daniel says, 'But you, Daniel, keep this prophecy a secret; seal up the book until the time of the end, when many will rush here and there, and knowledge will increase.'"

"In the Bible?"

"Yes."

"Didn't know it held such secrets."

"It does, but it seems as though Wisdom isn't ready to tell me the identity of six-six-six . . . or maybe she is."

"Well, don't keep me in suspense."

"I think the antichrist—six-six-six—was born on a blood moon, a lunar eclipse, and that maybe he will be revealed after a tetrad of blood moons as the antichrist."

"When is the next tetrad of blood moons?"

"From 2014 to 2015. The Hebrew calendar year of 5775. At least it's a clue, a start. I remember something about a letter . . . and a statue made of different types of metal."

"That's odd."

"I've seen that statue before . . ." Daniela scratched her brow.

"Back to the dream." A sheepish grin spread across Emmaline's face. "You spoke about a man—Black Irish: black hair, pale skin, and sky-blue eyes." Daniela's face flushed hot. "I think . . ." Emmaline nervously giggled. "I think you were making love to him."

"What?" Daniela shot up in bed. "No—never. I couldn't . . . I wouldn't." She buried her face in her hands. "Don't tell my parents. I'm supposed to stay a virgin until I marry."

"Don't be embarrassed." Emmaline peeled Daniela's hands from her face. "I'm sure your hymen is still intact. Just a wet dream." Emmaline winked. "Besides, you deserve oily boy, a man who's the reason love songs are written."

As if on cue, Emmaline's CD player cranked out Etta James's "At Last."

"Dance with me." Emmaline smiled.

Daniela obliged. Was all of this real? She hoped so yet felt guilty at the same time. "Limy."

"At your service, Mrs. Oily Boy."

"Stop it." She pushed away from the dance. "I don't even remember that part of the dream." Daniela fingered the arrowhead. "Do me a huge favor."

"I'm your girl."

"It sounds crazy but . . . but help me save Earth from Lucifer. He wants to wipe us out and reclaim our home. I like Earth—love it, actually; so many kindred spirits to meet. Will you help?"

"Have gun, will travel."

"Thanks, Limy." Daniela rested her hand on her friend's shoulder. "One day, we'll be able to lay down our swords, but from this moment on, this house prepares for war."

"A dastardly plan. I'm dying to kick butt."

"So am I." Daniela grinned—wide, free, and hopeful.

"Go take a bath, Danny Rose." Emmaline kissed Daniela on the cheek. "You smell like sex."

Daniela blushed and disappeared into the bathroom, where she found a hot bath already drawn. She slipped off her drenched pink nightgown, stepped into the water, and hid her lithe frame beneath the surface. Like a submarine's periscope, only her head stayed above the surface. She made waves with her hand.

One day, she would conquer the water, learning how to swim.

But not tonight. She tried to remember her dream, but the details hid behind a mental fog. She clenched her jaw. This was the dream she wanted—no, needed—to remember!

She inhaled deeply. Better than she could imagine.

That had been Yahweh's promise.

Would His promise prove true?

Could oily boy be an even greater kindred spirit than Ethan? Butterflies fluttered inside her belly. An apricot sulfur! She rested her hand on her abdomen and whispered a prayer. "Thank you for my defenders who protected me when I couldn't fight the sand dragon. My parents, grandparents, and the ginger who stands beside me— my kindred spirit, my Anne with an *e*, my Limy."

It would soon be Daniela's turn to protect her family and friend from whatever evil lurked in their future.

Hope possessed a name. Yeshua. Refusing to surrender to death, He conquered it instead, embodying hope. "O death, where is your victory? O death, where is your sting?" The sting of death is sin, and the power of sin—by which it brings death—is the law; but thanks be to God, who gives us the victory—as conquerors—through our Lord Jesus Christ."

She would follow in Yeshua's footsteps and conquer her enemy.

Reflecting the Son's light, the Orphan Dreamer's future shined brighter than the stars, and Earth's occupants could hope.

"Because one day, 'Before they call, I will answer; and while they are still speaking, I will hear. The wolf and the lamb will graze together, and the lion will eat straw like the ox (there will no longer be predator and prey), and dust will be the serpent's food. They will do no evil or harm in all My holy mountain (Zion), says the Lord,'" Daniela whispered, repeating the words of the Hebrew prophet Isaiah.

The day when war ceases. When peace reigns. *Blessed are the peacemakers, they will inherit the Kingdom of God.* Heaven—her forever home. Until that day, the Orphan Dreamer would dream, bending time and pushing back the darkness to give a voice to the voiceless and fight for the faceless—her orphan, her oily boy—until they could fight for themselves.

Because without an orphan to dream about and fight for, Daniela Rose Cavanaugh could hardly call herself the Orphan Dreamer.

The hot water massaged her aching muscles. She relaxed. Bravely, she slipped down into the tub. The water covered her face. Warmth embraced her.

A question torpedoed into her mind: was oily boy the antichrist—666? The orphanage's mistress and Levi had believed that he was.

Daniela propelled herself above the surface of the water like a submarine blowing its ballast. Water sloshed over the lip of the tub and flooded the tiny bathroom floor. Her chest heaved as she fought for air. The reality of the answer to her question struck her heart. If oily boy was indeed the antichrist, she had made love to a mass murderer—666!

"God, if this is true, don't let me live."

"You okay in there?" Emmaline knocked on the door.

"I'm fine." But depression hammered at her mental resolve.

Don't cry. Her chest ached. *Calm down.* Daniela took a deep breath and swallowed the ache, but it exploded into a throb. She grabbed her chest, refusing to lose her heart; it's where she would remember oily boy—the good version, God's choice for her.

But every human possessed free will, including oily boy. Maybe he would seek revenge, doling out retribution to the person who gave him his scars?

She steadied her breathing. Her heart rate slowed. "Is it true, Yahweh?"

A gentle voice seemed to answer: *Was oily boy born on a blood moon?*

"I don't know."

Better than you could imagine. That was My promise. I cannot lie. Others may see you as a clinically depressed schizophrenic, but I see you as a child—My child—one who hears My voice without a filter. Would I marry off My Orphan Dreamer to a monster, an Adolf Hitler?

No.

Never, my darling Rosebud.

Know this about oily boy: I take my greatest leaders on a journey to hell, so they know the way in and the way out. But Lucifer seeks to entrap them— keeping them as hostages within his spidery web of revenge. Oily boy must choose to forgive or exact revenge.

Pray that he chooses forgiveness; love will follow—love for you and for his enemies. You will never lose My love because I AM love. Love is my essence. My reality. Honeyed warmth seemed to surround Daniela. Yahweh's embrace. She released a long, fretful sigh. Her muscles relaxed.

"Okay."

One snowflake falls from heaven to quench hell's thirst—the miserable reality of oily boy, an orphan who lived somewhere, lost inside Daniela's complex web of time—her reality, her essence. Ethan's Rosebud closed her eyes. She sank back down beneath the surface of the water, palmed the Glass Tattoo, and titled her chin heavenward.

"Take me to the stars, oily boy . . ."

—THE END—

"The Word" by Isaac Wimberley

If there are words for Him, then I don't have them . . .
So it's not just words that I proclaim
For my words point to the WORD
And the WORD has a name
Hope has a name
Joy has a name
Peace has a name
Love has a name
And that name is Jesus Christ
Praise His name FOREVER!

Enjoy "The Word" by Isaac Wimberley
https://youtu.be/MHQPuok_LnY

Frederick Douglass once said, "Believe in yourself. Take advantage of every opportunity. Use the power of spoken and written language to effect positive change for yourself and society." And so I have written *Orphan Dreamer*. I pray Daniela and Cillian speak Hope into restless hearts—because in truth, I have known no greater love than His, the Friend who sticks closer than a brother or sister. Writing for the One, for when I couldn't walk He carried me. To every orphaned spirit, dream! #IAmDaniela.

—J. Nell Brown

Acknowledgments

Yeshua, thank you for inspiring this book through my imagination at a time when I needed it most. You've always been faithful to me.

Special thanks to my late father, Chaplain Austin Brown; my mother, Mrs. Jeanette Brown; and my sisters and friends.

To my editors, Ann Castro and Emily Dings at AnnCastro Studio, Faralee Pozo at Upwork.com, and Courtney Rae Andersson at Elevation Editorial—thank you all for your eagle-eye talents.

To my readers, thank you for loving this story. These characters exist for you.

Dear Reader,

Thoughtful Amazon reviews about an author's work are like a pay raise or a tip to employees in traditional jobs. If you enjoyed this novel, Orphan Dreamer and the Glass Tattoo, please take a moment to place a review on Amazon.com, sharing with other readers what you've learned. Your feedback is invaluable.

The A21 Campaign, a nonprofit organization to abolish the human trafficking of children, is my charity of choice. When you purchase a novelette or novel in the Orphan Dreamer saga, ten percent of the profits will be donated to A21 Campaign or to organizations with a similar mission.

I look forward to saying hello to you on Facebook. Please like my page so you can keep up with the writing journey. Also, please sign up for my semiannual newsletter, and I will notify you about future releases, sales, and special events.

With gratitude,
J. Nell Brown

Dear Reader,

Quite a few publishers would consider *Orphan Dreamer and the Glass Tattoo* the backstory for the main characters Daniela Rose Cavanaugh and Cillian Joseph Finn. However, I have written this first book to build a foundation for the series' overarching question, "If you knew your ending, how would you have lived your beginning?"

At times, contemporary cultures discount those whose beginning years are tumultuous and insignificant. However, I believe that Yahweh loves His entire creation and possesses great plans for us all, but He does not force His will upon humanity. He invites. We ask and seek, then we receive and find. Prayer is the mechanism of asking. Faith is the mechanism of seeking. I am not ashamed of my faith, nor will I allow anyone to shame me for my beliefs.

As a medical doctor and lover of science and mathematics, I agree with Albert Einstein:

> The most beautiful thing we can experience is the mysterious. It is the source of all true art and science. He to whom this emotion is a stranger, who can no longer pause to wonder and stand rapt in awe, is as good as dead: his eyes are closed. This insight into the mystery of life, coupled though it be with fear, has also given rise to religion.

> —Albert Einstein

To me, the mystery of life is Love, and this same unconditional Love gifted from above broke the physical chains from my ancestors' wrists and feet as well as the mental fetters that oppressed my mind for so many years, flinging every chain of depression and oppression into hell's depths—deeper than the Marina Trench—setting my spirit free. Today, my spirit eternally soars higher than an apricot sulfur. Freedom. Amazing grace, how sweet the sound. "Free at last, Free at last, Thank God almighty I'm free at last."

The God factor is this unconditional Love, a person who bears a name, Yeshua.

My faith is my story. It is my essence. My life raft. Despise it, but don't deny its power to set free and heal broken hearts, including mine. "I'm no longer a child of fear. I am a child of God."

To ask an American of Cherokee, African, Mongolian, Irish, and English descent—this is me, J. Nell Brown—to separate her faith from her story would be as sacrilegious as asking a WWII Jewish veteran to fly a Nazi flag in his front yard.

The original title of *Orphan Dreamer and the Glass Tattoo* was *Frozen Prayers*. Many times in my life, I have whispered "frozen prayers"—fervent prayers uttered in the winter season of my life that seem to go unanswered. But during the waiting room of unanswered prayers, Yahweh's love prevails when humankind's love fails.

All characters are fictional. The proper names of God and Jesus are used in this book: Yahweh (YHVH), Adonai, and Elohim for God; Yeshua for Jesus. The Sons of Venus in later books represent a conglomerate of religious, financial, and political secret societies and bear no resemblance to one in particular.

It is true. David and Prince Jonathan vowed to each other an unshakeable friendship, promising to protect the other's family if one of them should die. Prince Jonathan never became king. He was killed in battle with his father, King Saul. Prince Jonathan's dying in the desert in a young girl's arms is fiction.

It is true. Blood moons, known as lunar eclipses that occur in sync with Jewish holidays, warn of a significant event concerning the Jewish people. Acts 2:20 and Joel 2:31 speak of these blood moons. A study on this subject may be found in my eBook, *Blood Moon— God's Warning*.

Compassion drives my motive to paint a story of the lives of disenfranchised children. I keep to the grim facts but leave much to the imagination.

The characters' stories are loosely based upon the deportation of English orphans to Australia from 1940 to 1960. This book transports this story into the 1980s and 1990s. Nottinghamshire social worker Margaret Humphreys established the Child Migrant's Trust, a charity designed to help reunite these children with their families. Fortunately, many more safeguards are now in place to protect orphans after the atrocities of the 1940s and 1970s.

By purchasing, reading, and telling your friends about the Orphan Dreamer Saga, you are helping kids like the ones featured in my book series because a percentage of the proceeds from this saga will benefit the real-life Cillian Finn, Paul Hansen, Daniela Cavanaugh, and even Emmaline Georgiana Winterlyn Darbyshire, a girl with too many first names. The A21 Campaign and similar organizations will be the predominant recipients of those funds.

If we want more love, we need more of God, because God is love; he who abides in love abides in God and God in him. For me, this is love in action: "For God so loved the world that he gave his only begotten Son, that whosoever believeth in him should not perish, but have everlasting life" (John 3:16).

Giving is loving.

Loving is giving.

Let's be generous!

With gratitude,
J. Nell Brown

Author Biography

J. Nell Brown, the daughter of a chaplain and a teacher, is a Florida native.

Her relationship with Yeshua (Jesus) is fused with experiences in life, travel, extensive Bible study, and people's stories, and she combines all of this to create characters, plots, and settings for her novels and short stories. An involuntary insomniac, Brown practices medicine and writes in her free time.

She is a self-proclaimed nerd and loves all things scientific. Her love of science is demonstrated by her research at Los Alamos National Laboratory, the site for the development of the atomic bomb. She graduated with honors from the University of Florida (U of F) College of Agriculture and received her medical doctorate from the same. After completing an anesthesia residency at The University of Chicago Hospitals, she began practicing in Florida.

Her heart overflows with compassion for people who are hurting, particularly children. A portion of the proceeds from this book will go to the A21 Campaign, a rescue charity for human-trafficked children, and Eastside Baptist School in Gainesville, Florida, a school of love, values, and solid educational curriculum for children whose parents would not otherwise be able to afford an alternative school education.

Her first nonfiction book, *Shhh, My Father Is Speaking, and I Am Listening,* is about her prayer journey. The Bible is her favorite literary masterpiece. You may follow J. Nell Brown on her author website, JNellBrown.com.

www.ingramcontent.com/pod-product-compliance
Lightning Source LLC
Chambersburg PA
CBHW030355200726

48286CB00014B/1420